ROBERT ALLEN STOWE

THE FIRES OF RUBICON

Black Rose Writing | Texas

The author grants the final approval for this literary material.

First printing

ISBN: 978-1-68513-302-3
PUBLISHED BY BLACK ROSE WRITING
www.blackrosewriting.com

Printed in the United States of America
Suggested Retail Price (SRP) $21.95

The Fires of Rubicon is printed in Book Antiqua

*As a planet-friendly publisher, Black Rose Writing does its best to eliminate unnecessary waste to reduce paper usage and energy costs, while never compromising the reading experience. As a result, the final word count vs. page count may not meet common expectations.

Acknowledgement

Writers need criticism and editing of their work, even though they grimace when receiving the requested feedback. Despite some reluctance, the writer grudgingly takes the honest recommendations to heart, although he or she is never willing to admit that the criticism is correct. That is why acknowledgements exist — to pay written tribute to those who help the writer make the work as good as possible without forcing the author to physically bow with reverence to the reviewers. Instead, we prefer to treat them to high-priced dinners and a bottle of fine wine.

Nevertheless, it is with great appreciation that I thank Christina Jenkins, Kathleen Hinkelman and fellow-author David Allen Edmonds for their detailed and well-considered suggestions that actually made this work both printable and readable. You have made an interesting story so much the better.

And I also thank my lovely wife, Kathleen Stowe, for her pre-read assessment, even though she fibs and says that everything about the book is "perfect". Your constant encouragement urges me to attempt the perfection you deserve.

THE FIRES OF RUBICON

Monday, November 1, 1971

Cleveland Police Headquarters, Interrogation Room #3
"I don't know why he did it. I'll probably never know for sure. Anton, he's strange sometimes. There could have been a lot of reasons, I suppose. A lot of different reasons. Or maybe just one. Or maybe no reason at all. Reasons, reasoning, rationalizations — as if there were some sort of logical thought. I don't think he used very much logical thought. None of what he did seemed to make much sense, at least to me. It made sense to him I suppose. There have been a lot of theories. Mostly my own…in my imagination…not that I shared my thoughts with anyone else. I seldom discuss any of what happened with anyone else. It's none of their business, anyhow, know what I mean? Why would I bother someone with something that's none of their business? No one else seems to care anyway. Just me mostly, in my own head. I have theories. Concepts. Ideas. Okay, possibly lies. Maybe. If my theories are just a bunch of lies, who am I lying to? Does it really become a lie if you only tell it to yourself? Sort of like that tree-falls-in-a-forest philosophy problem. Does it make a sound? But, you know, if what I believe to be the truth is really just a lie to myself, why does it seem to make a sound in my head? I don't like the sound. I tried to talk him out of it. Really, I did. But he wouldn't listen. He couldn't see the logic. I'm always very logical. I showed him both sides — both side of the equation, see? Loads of wisdom, that's what I gave him. I'm known for being logical and

smart, wise in a way. Lots of people think so, don't they? And that's what I gave him, you know, a taste of my wisdom, whether he wanted it or not. He was really confused, I think. That's why he needed to see both sides of the issue. We all knew he needed it, at least I think so.

"Anyway, I think it was a good idea to share my thoughts with him, my wisdom. Someone needed to set him straight, to put a different spin on things, to make him think twice about what he was about to do. He didn't appreciate it, I guess. Apparently. Or maybe he chose not to listen to all of it. Maybe he followed some of my suggestions, my recommendations, my guidance. Someone once said, 'Others may hear you, but they may choose not to listen.' I always confuse hearing with listening. Which is the most important? One of them means the simple act of hearing a sound--the tree falling in the forest, you know. The other is the act of understanding. Which is which? Hearing or listening? Neither one sounds right, neither sounds more important. Two sides of the same coin, I guess you could say. I think, as a friend, it was my job to try and talk some sense into him. Well, not really a job in the way that it is a task you have to do but don't really like or want to do it. It was more like a responsibility, don't you think? That's what friends are expected to do. Be responsible enough to talk your buddy out of jumping off a bridge with a too long bungie cord or something. Of course, you secretly want to see him do it. You don't want him to get hurt or anything. That would be hard to explain to the authorities or to your other friends, I suppose. And you'd never make the jump yourself, but if that's what he wants to do, well...no, you still try to make your friend see the danger, the stupidity, of some of the things he wants to do."

The two detectives puzzled at the gaunt young man seated before them. Neither was quite sure what he was saying — or, for most part, mumbling. The Lieutenant said, "All we want you to do is answer the question about your work partner. And, please speak distinctly. We're having a hard time following what you are talking about." The young man did not acknowledge that he was hearing or understanding the order given by the Lieutenant.

"That's what I was doing. Talking. Making sense. Being wise. Show him my wisdom. Let him see another path, a different approach, a novel way of examining the problem. But it's not like we were close friends or anything. More like acquaintances, really. We just happened to be assigned to the same work area at the same time, and we had some similar interests and backgrounds. It's not like we grew up together as best friends or anything. Not like my buddy, Jerry. I wonder whatever happened to him? Jerry and I went to grade school together. We hung out in the summer. We played a lot of baseball or rode our bikes around.

"Jerry was better at most sports than I was. He could run faster. Better hand-eye coordination, too, I guess. At the time, I was bigger and slower. Of course, he'd get hurt a lot easier running into things so fast. Maybe it's just that I was smarter. We made a good team that way. We had more time together during the summer, baseball season, a sport where Jerry excelled. We'd go to this one park--well, it was more of an abandoned field, actually. Used to be a small factory that burned to the ground. The city demolished what was left and leveled the dirt over what used to be some sort of chemical plant. The empty lot was the perfect size for us to use as a ball field. Even had a tall chain link fence for a home run wall. Twelve feet high, it was. Whoever hit it over had to go get it. I certainly wouldn't go over it. Dangerous, you know? Twelve feet up. That's too high to climb over without falling down the other side. None of us could hit it that far anyway.

"The part of the field that edged close to the street was fairly level and a weedy grass covered most of it. The deeper into the lot you went, the more uneven the land, and the less grass grew. It was easy to stumble and fall in the outfield, where I usually played. Way in the back on the other side of the home run fence there were two other factories still standing, not burned down, and a rusty screechy railroad track. The three formed a kind of corner in dead center field. No one hit one that far. Hard-packed dirt and a few nastier thorny weeds edged up to the chain-link. The hard-packed dirt with no grass resembled a pre-planned infield, but we never used it that way. There was something about that dead hard-pack that seemed to warn kids to stay away. Plus, there was a lot of broken glass and bits of sharp metal sticking out of the hard-pack. Whoever the city hired to clear the land from the burned out factory rightly figured that no inspector would walk all the way back there to check their work, so they left all kinds of junk close to the surface.

"And then there were the rumors, mostly spread by the older kids to scare us. They told us lies about stuff being buried behind the factory before it burned down, stuff the factory-owners figured would never be found: drums full of chemicals which is why nothing grows there; poisonous wastes which would kill any little kid dumb enough to touch it; and even a few dead bodies who would attach their soul to yours. Just trying to scare us, I bet. Anyway, we played ball there because it was a big empty field in the middle of the city in the middle of where we lived. Our neighborhood. It was made up of houses and small stores and mini-factories built side by side without even the room for a driveway between each.

"The city saw what we were doing, playing ball on what was left of a factory lot. They sent out some do-gooder park people to check us out one day. They ended up building a small shelter house next to what we had made into our ballpark. No backstop, mind you, just a hut. They planted a few heavy wooden picnic tables chained and anchored into a cement foundation under the roof. We'd gather around the tables until we had enough players to field a game. Sometimes we'd end up with about two dozen guys, so our games were pretty player-heavy. Home plate would be within several yards of the shelter house, which became sort of our impromptu dugout. And that's where Darla and Denise hung out. I'm sure there were other girls there, too, but no one could miss Darla and Denise. They were older than Jerry and me. They wore short-shorts and halter tops. They experimented with make-up and nail polish. They were there so they could see the older boys, but we were all drawn to them like hungry bears toward honey. We knew our place, though. Jerry and I could glance at them in lust, but we knew better than to stare. The older boys could sit next to them and talk if they wanted, but we younger kids didn't want to risk the humiliation of being the butt of the older kids jokes, so we would keep our distance. The *girls attracted the guys, several dozen at a time. The other guys our age mostly wanted to play ball. When enough guys were attracted, we would choose up teams. What you might call a mutual attraction system and it all worked.*

"Sometimes we'd play a triple-header. One game in the morning, two in the afternoon. Each a pick-up game where two captains would choose players from among anyone who was there with a glove. Everyone had a chance to play. Amazingly democratic, you know? No one was ever told to sit down or go away. Even with an odd-number or mix of younger and older kids, everyone played. Throw the bat for the first pick. You quickly learned whether anyone thought you were a good player or not, and how the other guys evaluated your ability. That democratic selection of teams always began with the best players chosen first and ended with the worst players picked last. You knew pretty quickly if you were considered a good ball player or not. Humbling, you know?

"Yeah, Jerry and I were great friends. We hung out together all the time. I'm not sure either of us offered the other advice, but we both sort of knew we could and would if the need ever came up. Of course, we were much younger back then, and there wasn't a lot of heavy stuff to deal with. Not like now. It's funny, but as close as we were, I don't think I ever knew much about Jerry's home life. He had an older brother I remember, but I don't recall much more than that. I wonder whatever became of Jerry? I wonder how we drifted apart? That was what--ten, twelve years ago? Maybe more."

The Lieutenant asked, "Did Jerry work with you and Anton? Is that why you bring him up?"

"I haven't seen Jerry in so long — no, he didn't work with us. I don't know where he works — if he works — if he's still…. You can see how we were close friends making it very different from this other situation. This one is much more serious, I guess. At least, some people seem to think so. I'm not so sure. Heavy implications, though. I tried to talk to

him, to offer advice. He heard, but didn't listen. Or is it that he listened, but didn't hear. I can't never keep that straight. Here's what I think was the problem: fires were burning. Everywhere there were fires burning. Sometimes you could see actual flames, some were in your mind, some in your heart. Maybe even some in your soul.

"Yeah, fires were everywhere--are everywhere--you know what I mean? For instance, in Pennsylvania, in some small out-of-the-way burg, they decided to set fire to their garbage dump as a way to get rid of their smelly eyesore of a garbage pit situated too close to the center of town. A nice controlled fire, monitored by the village volunteer fire department, that would eliminate the smells and chase away the wild animals that gathered around the open pit dump. Raccoons, forest rats, even some black bears were attracted to the garbage and added to the dangers for the town residents. It had to be taken care of. The dump was a deep hole, dug by who knows who back in who knows when. 'Pour on the kerosene, let's burn it all up,' they said. Seemed like a good idea at the time. Except the fire got very hot, so hot that it burned very deep, all the way down through the pile of decades-old garbage to a shaft of coal from an old abandoned mine that ran way far under the town. The coal shaft caught fire. There was enough coal still down there to make a real good fire. Buried some 60, 70, 80-feet down, the water poured onto the garbage pit, then later into the shaft by the volunteer fire brigade turned to steam before it reached the fire. None of the locals had any idea what to do, how to deal with the situation they had created. State officials were called in. Experts, they thought. That's what we need, they said to themselves. The experts, they tried to reopen the main mine shaft, but there was so much intense heat and smoke it drove them away. Tried everything they could think of. The estimate is there's enough coal left down there in the various shafts to burn for the next hundred years. Vents started to form in the middle of the buckling streets of the town, releasing toxic fumes. Sink holes claimed some houses as the ground under them liquified. Everyone with any sense packed it up and left. Others who thought the situation might improve stuck around, but now anyone who hasn't already moved soon will

move far away from what is already a virtual ghost town. Like I said, fires burned everywhere.

"Like in Vietnam, the city of Hue smoldered between open fires and hot bullets, as attack and counter-attack left dead bodies everywhere. The Tet Offensive lasted over a month targeting cities, towns and military bases throughout South Vietnam. The worst was in Hue. Some of the bodies would only be found weeks after they fell. Some fell dead instantly or were slowly dying with no one around to offer aid. The battle-scarred and burning buildings were like impromptu morgues and crematoriums, although there was no one to tag toes, whether they were American or Cong or unlucky citizens. If the body wasn't that of a soldier wearing dog tags, they were probably unidentifiable. If it was a soldier who didn't have his tags on, well, MIA--Missing In Action. That's what their families were told. Yeah, sure, missing. Maybe never really lost but never really found, either. Never actually identified. Maybe never really there. Who knows? Yeah, fires burned everywhere.

"Young men my age, we're considered soldiers-in-waiting. A lot of my friends got handed a rifle right out of school not so long ago. Some still get that treatment today. Guys my age, between the age of 18 and about 26--and let me tell you, there are a ton of us — after all, we are Baby Boomers, we are a ready-made army. If you are that age, a few years ago you could be drafted — maybe that will happen again real soon. We saw all the images broadcast on the news detailing the Tet Offensive. We tried not to look too close at the dead or wounded they were showing on the nightly news. Some of the bodies might be guys we knew, or someone we might have known, or someone we played ball with. Don't want to see that.

"We sneered at the TV. 'Well, that ain't gonna happen to me! I'll make sure of that, one way or the other.' We all gulped down beers and told ourselves stuff like that. But we knew there were damn few ways of getting out of it, if we did get drafted. None of us had a wealthy father or uncle or politician who could make the "Greetings" letter go away. None of us had the guts to shoot our own toes off. We had to depend on our own wits, and the smoldering images of the city of Hue matched

the smoldering acidity in our stomachs mixed with all that cheap beer. We didn't have much inner confidence that our wits could match our outward bravado. Your stomach could be full of gas but that alone wouldn't keep you out of the Army, not out of Vietnam, not out of a burning building in Hue. And the putrid beer churned like gas fires in the pits of our stomachs.

"Ugly fires, you know? There are ramifications to fires, aren't there? I had a teacher once who said we always need to understand the ramifications. Well, they burned down the ROTC building at Kent State last year. What were the ramifications? Soldiers shooting down kids on campus. That shouldn't happen in America, should it? But fire leaves ashes. Fire leaves ramifications—dead kids missing their next college class.

"Fires are everywhere. Why, not long ago they tried to burn down the ghetto. Fires everywhere, houses, businesses, even cars. Fire Department couldn't get through to put them out for all the rioters, some even carrying guns, shooting at firemen. Not that there was much value to what was burning. Those poor people lived in real bad stuff, you know? Lousy plumbing, bare electric wires, rats, stuff like that. No wonder they burned it down. You wouldn't live there, I bet. You wouldn't even step foot in one of the places they had to call home. Ahh, I'm not even sure they started all of the fires themselves. That was a riot, after all. People came there from all over, not just those folks that lived there. Who knows? A little old lady needed a glass of water. Bar owner wouldn't give her one unless she buys something. Later her nephew comes down to complain. Words are spoken--shouted. Pushing. A fight. Now some groups gather and sides are drawn--all for a lousy glass of water. The bar's nothing but ashes now. Fires burning everywhere.

"It's kinda funny, but the only difference between my neighborhood and that area we call a ghetto? Lawn mowers. Not those nice gas jobs you folks have in the suburbs--I'm talking about the push-from-behind-you-provide-the-power lawn mowers. We've got them, they don't. Why? Because we own the property while they rent. Those places are--

or were--the same age as my place. Built somewhere between the late 1890s and early 1900s. Running water added later, somehow a bathroom wedged in where one never existed, coal furnace that eventually might become a gas furnace someday, if they're lucky. Odd add-on structures that don't quite fit connected to the house making the whole neighborhood look like a drawing by Escher. I heard about him in school.

"We cut what little lawns we have just to keep things sort of neat and so the neighbors don't bitch too much. But in the ghetto, their landlords don't mow. So, the whole place looks un-cared-for, which is sort of true. The landlords don't care if their running water is brown, or if the heat works or if the hallway lights are burned out. The whole place looks like no one gives a shit. You live in that and you tend to pretend you don't care either. If no one cares, why not burn it down. It just doesn't matter. If only they could own their own place, someplace to care about, I bet things like the riots wouldn't happen--at least not the fires. Of course, I don't own my house. My uncle--but that's another story all together.

"Hell, even the Cuyahoga River caught fire a while back. What was that all about? Almost burned down a bridge. It did that once before, didn't it? Burn down a bridge, I mean. With all the junk that gets poured into that river I'm surprised it doesn't just keep smoldering, like the River Styx in Hades--heard about that in poetry class or something. I've seen couch cushions floating down river toward the lake. Bags full of garbage, too. I guess it was garbage. The bags are sealed and bloated. Could be anything inside. Or anyone, I suppose. If a body was dismembered and stuffed into a garbage bag, would it get bloated and float? You guys probably know stuff like that. You've probably seen a lot of awful stuff.

"Given all of that, why did he do what he did? He saw what we all saw, only he didn't really see anything at all, did he? He was in his own world, living his own dream. He knew the truth, or should have. He had to know what was happening, right? I mean, he wasn't stupid about it or anything. Did I tell you I tried to talk him out of it? No, he *wasn't stupid. There were some of us who were just plain stupid, igno-rant even. But not him. No, sir, he wasn't stupid. But why did he do it? I don't know that I could say. I don't even know what you think he did. I don't think I've got anything else to say."*

The two Cleveland Police Detectives left him in the interrogation room alone.

"Whad'ya think, Wheezie," said Detective Sergeant Benjamin Friedman, rubbing his bald spot in the center of a head of thinning black hair.

Barrel-chested and buzz-cut gray, a few months short of his retirement goal, Lieutenant Alex Wesner took this case because he thought it would be easy. So far, it was anything but. "This guy knows something more than what he's saying, Benny. Sometimes he talks in full sentences, then he mumbles a while or mouths words with no sound coming out. Did you notice? I think half the time he's talking to himself. Let's hold onto him for a while. We'll probably end up cutting him loose, but for now I want him to sweat a bit."

His partner nodded, "Okay. If you think we should put him up for the full three days, I'll drum up a charge. Otherwise, we've got him for maybe ten more hours."

"I'll talk to him again later today, then surprise him with his release. Sometimes you just have to be able to read the room, Benny. Know what I mean? Just read the room. Before you leave this afternoon, give the uniforms his address so they can run by his place and keep an eye on him." As an after-thought, he turned to his partner, "Hey, Ben, don't forget your wife's present in your desk drawer."

Benny Friedman had recently been promoted to Detective Sergeant, and was celebrating by giving his wife a diamond bracelet. It took years to save up the money, but now, with a bump in salary, he felt good about the gift. Proud, that's it. He felt proud. "Thanks. No, I won't forget the gift! You sure you don't need me tonight?"

"Go home. You been planning this for a long time. Say, have you moved into your new place yet? I hope you got a reasonable mortgage, you big spender, you. Go celebrate with your lovely wife. This guy's not dangerous. Just, I don't know, not all there, you know what I mean?"

Benny cocked his head, "Yeah. He's a bit strange, I'll give you that. I'll stop by the uniforms on my way out to request some closer looks at his residence. And to answer your question, yes, we moved in over last weekend. Marie is after me to finish painting all the rooms so she can show the place off to her girlfriends. She's got to stop being so demanding. My paycheck only goes so far." Benny gave an exasperated sigh as he headed to the elevator.

Lt. Wesner's old vinyl covered chair squeaked and groaned as he tilted and twisted reviewing his interview notes. He counted the hash-marks--the number of times the suspect mentioned fire. Ten. At least. Wesner missed some early on, before he knew the thought would be repeated so often. Fires burning everywhere. That's what the guy kept saying. The Lieutenant didn't think he was an arsonist. The reference to fire was more metaphorical, a symbol of what was going on inside him. A fire was burning in his soul.

He opened the front page of the file to look again. Just who is this guy? Seazy Lutz. What the hell kind of name is that. Booking desk checked for a sheet on him. Nothing there, at least not under that name. Probably not the name on his birth certificate. Prints are being run. We'll see what pops up then. So far, no reason to hold him. Just brought in for questioning. Seemed to know the missing person, the vic--if there even is a vic. That's not clear either. But Seazy says he doesn't know why he did it. Why he did what? And who's the 'he'? Is he referring to the missing man? Or is Seazy saying he doesn't know why Seazy did it himself? Talking in the third person about himself. Lt. Wesner had seen it before with half-crazy perps. Or is there someone else entirely who we don't know about?

Wesner reached toward the only personal item on his desk—a delicate, amber-colored glass horse, an ornament really. Likely an ancient Christmas ornament, it was handed down from his grandmother's grandmother, brought to America from a forgotten old village in a forgotten old district of somewhere in Eastern Europe. It hung on a thin gold stand, the stand a gift from a lost past love. Touching the fragile figurine horse caused it to swing or gallop on the stand, a movement that somehow allowed Wesner to focus on his case.

Everyone told him the horse was too delicate to be kept in a police station. It was sure to get shattered by some crazy accident. Thin blown glass perfectly shaped into the design of a running horse, the color ran from dark amber to light gold, depending upon the amount of light it received or Wesner's mood when he looked at or touched it. Wesner considered it his lucky charm. Simply touching it, making it rock on its small gold stand, made the Lieutenant certain he could solve whatever case he was working on.

But this case seemed different. "Stupid," he said to himself. "Why did I agree to grab this crazy case? 'Sure, Captain,' I said, 'I'll be glad to take this one. Should be fairly simple,' I said. Someone dope-slap me the next time I say something like that. I'll be lucky to get anything close to clarity out of this guy. Fires burning everywhere, huh? I need to check out the story about that Pennsylvania town. Just goofy enough to be real. But if he made that up, what else did he make up? A coal fire melting the streets? Got to be pure bullshit."

Almost an hour later, the fingerprint report came in and the Lieutenant returned to the interrogation room. "You said your name is Seazy Lutz?"

"Who says?"

"When you came in. You told the front desk that was your name when you volunteered to be finger-printed, remember? That is what this file says, and that's what your signature reads. Ring a bell?"

Seazy smiled. "Yeah. Sure. Seazy, not Sleazy," he laughed.

The Lieutenant gave him a weird look, "Did anyone here call you Sleazy?"

"Not here, no."

"Anywhere? Who called you Sleazy?"

He turned away and waved his arms, "Aw, you know how it is. Guys take your name and twist it until they find a way to make fun. Humiliate you, you know? No big deal. They do it to me, I do it to them. Just guys being…you know." He looked back at the Lieutenant, "Like you. I heard the other guy call you Wheezer, or something, but your name badge says you're Lieu-tenant Wesner. Same thing, right?"

"Sure. But it turns out your name isn't really Seazy Lutz, is it? Not Sleazy, and not Seazy. What is your name?"

Seazy looked around the sparse interrogation room, at the camera in the corner, at the large mirror dominating the wall he faced, "What is my name? What is any name? Does it really mat-ter? Does anyone really care what your name is? Does anyone know what their name means? Did you know that everyone's name has a special meaning--like what they do, what they're good at, stuff like that. You know, like in the Bible, Peter is a Rock. Don't know whether that means he's hard-headed, or su-per-strong, or whatever. But everyone's name means something. A guy named Miller was once a mill operator or something. See what I mean?"

Lt. Wesner let him ramble on. After he paused for several seconds, he repeated, "You're not Seazy Lutz. What is your name? And…try not to lie, because I probably know more than you think I do. Lying to the police is never a good idea."

He squirmed sideways in the chair, then centered himself, folded his hands on the table, dropped his head. "What do you think my name is?"

"Okay, I'll play it your way. Your prints came back showing that your fingers belong to someone called Cezary Ludzinski, who once got into a minor scrape that ended with you being arrested and finger-printed. Sound familiar?"

Cezary looked up, "I think I've heard of him. He's a real dork, know what I mean? No one likes him very much. He's goofy. Thinks he's smart, but he's not really. A real klutz, no coordination. Girls run when they see him. Well, some find him sorta quirky and cute, I guess. One girl thought he was sweet and lovable and kind and safe and…but most stay away like he's infected."

Wesner probed, "But Jerry liked Cezary, right? I think they were best friends ten years ago."

"Jerry's the one started calling him Seazy. He thought the name Cezary sounded too pompous, because it sounds like Caesar, Roman Emperor, you know? Jerry said I'd end up in lots of fights if I kept using the name Cezary. So, he renamed me Seazy. Even had a special christening with a water balloon. It was either that or taking a head-first dive into Shit Creek."

"Shit Creek? You mean that waste water run-off in the valley behind Washington Park? That orange crap spews straight out of the steel mills."

Cezary nodded, "Yeah, that's it. That's why I took the water balloon to the head. You could get polio just wading in Shit Creek. That's what everyone said."

Wesner said, "I can believe that. Polio or worse. But how did Ludzinski become Lutz? Was that Jerry's doing, too?"

Cezary shrugged, "It was just easier to write. Shorter. Less Polish-sounding. My family doesn't know, though. They'd think I was embarrassed of it or something. Don't want them getting all up in my face."

"You got a lot of family in town?"

"Nah. Not many left. Used to have big family gatherings on the holidays. Whoa, buddy, we'd all get together for big meals, card games, football in the streets with the cousins. The old guys, the uncles, they would be in the basement drinking beer and smoking and telling lies. The moms and aunts would be fixing dinner and chattering upstairs, playing cards. We were caught in between, didn't belong in either place. Go outside if the weather was decent. Make yourself scarce, but don't start no fires. Don't come in until dinner is ready. I was always seated at the kid's card table, never made the big dining room table. No, never made it. By the time I was old enough, mature enough like an adult, the family was mostly gone. Some died. Some moved away. Those that were still around just didn't care, I suppose. I didn't neither. The heck with it all. It was more fun hanging out with the guys."

"What guys do you mean," questioned Wesner casually. His method had been honed over decades of excellent detective work. Let the interviewee lead the direction of the conversation. It took more time but eventually you got to the heart of the matter with more clarity than direct confrontation.

Cezary shrugged. "You know, the guys I hung with. Neighborhood guys. Work buddies. That's what I remember of days like Thanksgiving. We'd all bring some beer or booze. Bags of chips. Maybe hit an afternoon movie or head to the bars after dark. No one had any invites for family dinners. No one had a family that wanted them around. No turkey for us. We scare people, I guess. We make people feel uneasy, you know? Seazy the uneasy. Hah! They don't feel comfortable with us around. Hah! We aren't criminals or anything. Other than a few traffic tickets, none of us are on the FBI's list of Most Wanted Criminals, or anything.

"The closest to a bad guy was Richie, although it wasn't really his fault. Really not his fault at all. He just got messed up by the system. You see, we were all trying to get through college without flunking out. Trying not to get drafted and sent to the war and killed in Vietnam, you know what I mean? You stay in college with passing grades, they won't draft you, see? But the colleges were jammed with guys just like us and the College Brass were using their freshman classes to flunk out a bunch so as to keep their enrollment numbers in line and the army barracks full. Could be the Draft Board encouraged them, maybe like, 'we'll send federal money to you, you know, if you send us your flunkies'. Anyway, Richie wasn't good in school. Tried a few months, 1st Quarter of his freshman year, then decided to quit before they flunked him out. Figured enlisting was safer than being drafted. You enlist, and word was you could get a pretty cushy detail: mess hall manager, desk clerk, distribution and logistics, that kind of stuff. But you get drafted? Son, this here's a rifle, learn to shoot straight and duck your head, and hope you like mosquitos. So, Richie, he dropped out of school and before they could report him to the Draft Board, he runs down to enlist. This was just a month or two after the Tet Offensive. Really nasty stuff during Tet. No one was telling us the truth about casualties.

"Now, Richie knew he could join the Navy, but he said he couldn't swim and they'd insist on a four-year hitch. He could have gone Air Force, but Richie wore glasses, couldn't fly, was afraid of heights. So, if he went Air Force, he figured he would be assigned to the dangerous job of loading weapons and fuel at the air bases in Nam. Those bases always got attacked with rockets and mortars. And the Air Force would want him for four years, too. Richie wasn't no hero-type. He'd go serve, but for as short a time as possible, then he wanted out. So, he went Army.

Two-year hitch, that's what he figured, and hoped for a cushy job like all the other enlistees. The day they called him to report, there must've been 80-100 guys, all doing the same thing. They lined them all up against a wall and told them to count off 1, 2, 3, 4.

"You gotta remember, this was just a few months after the Tet Offensive, like I told you. What the generals weren't saying publicly about that month-long attack was that the hardest push of the Viet Cong attack was against the Marines posted in Hue. The losses were huge--killed, wounded, missing. The Marines were in bad shape, down, I don't know, maybe 25%. So, here we are in the draft board with the volunteers. These guys count off 1, 2, 3, 4. The Sergeant says 'All #1s, take two steps forward.' Richie, he's a #1. He's thinking they're dividing platoons, or something, so he takes his two steps forward. The Sarge says, 'Congratulations, men! You are now Marines!' Restocking fresh meat for Vietnam.

"All the #1s, they grab their gear and board a bus. They're headed straight to Parris Island. Richie wasn't no hero. He wasn't gung-ho about anything except cigarettes and beer. He lasted about six, seven weeks of Marine basic training, although he had two short stays in the brig for dereliction of something. Then, after his last stay in the brig, he grabbed what few items he owned and made a break for it. Went AWOL. They caught him at the Greyhound Bus station in Winston-Salem where the bus stopped for a passenger change. Threw him in chains. I mean, right there, in front of everyone. MPs with silver helmets, carrying loaded rifles, black boots, tied him up in big heavy silver chains, wrists and ankles. Loaded him onto a military truck. Back he went to Parris Island.

"Now he's officially a deserter, that's what the Marines tell him. He's in the brig doing hard time. Starts in solitary for two weeks. Hot. No air conditioning in the brig. No breezes. Shower once every three days. Then they take him outside for a few weeks where he's doing hard labor--digging ditches, breaking up rocks, refiling the holes he'd just dug. Feet still in ankle chains, had to shuffle around, couldn't just walk around. Blistering heat. After eight weeks, they ask if he's learned his lesson. Yessir, he says. Will you ever go AWOL again? Probably, he says. He gets a DD, Dishonorable Discharge. Thinks it was all worth it. Came home, tried to get a job where I worked. They needed workers, always losing someone when you've got several thousand dangerous jobs and the military scraping off young workers. But they wouldn't touch him. The DD hung on him like a felony conviction. Couldn't get a job anywhere. He left town. Doesn't call me or anyone, I guess. Don't know where he went. His Ma calls me asking where he is. I don't know. Like I said, he's the closest we've got to a bad dude from the guys I hung with."

Wesner crossed his legs and took a casual position in the uncomfortable metal chair, "Where were you working that said they wouldn't hire Richie?"

"Same place as now. The Mill. Best place to work. Good pay. Best job I ever had. Night tricks are no fun, but they give you time and a half. Not that I've had a lot of jobs that I stuck with. A couple here and there. Warehouse work, mostly. Sometimes I worked loadin' trucks. God, that was tough work. Paid by the number of boxes you load. Had a quota! You believe that? A quota on the number of boxes you load in an hour. That ain't right, you know what I mean? Not fair if my boxes are heavier than the other guys, or he's got a bunch of smaller boxes so his quota gets met but yours doesn't so he gets full pay and you get dinged. That ain't right.

"No, I hated loading trucks. Driver was on a quota, too, a timetable. He's screamin' at you to finish filling the truck so he can get on the road and you're there sweating in the heat and the fumes from the other trucks and the stink from the boxes--boxes can really stink, you know? And your gloves get slippery so you lose your grip and boxes fall and you can hear stuff breaking but if you slow down to check everyone gets mad so you forget about it and they shout 'keep moving as fast as you can and fill the damn truck, fill the damn truck, don't slow down or I won't get my quota and I gotta get to Chicago by eight o'clock, shithead, so hurry it up already' and the boxes stink and the other trucks are starting up engines filling the dock with diesel fumes and you wanna puke but you won't fill your quota....

"No, sir. That ain't a job for me. I like the Mill. Best job going, I think. Dangerous stuff all around you, and scary as hell sometimes, but better than loading boxes in a truck, by God. But sometimes, it can be like a horror movie in the mill, let me tell ya'. There's this one time--you know there's always lots of loud noises in the mill with overhead cranes screaming their sirens as they fly some three or four stories over your head carrying tons of whatever, you got your sheet mills roaring--all sorts of noise. This one time we were working on something and we heard what sounded like a railroad train hitting a truck, but the sound lasted for a full three, four minutes. Like the train crash just kept happening. Louder than all the rest of the noises in the mill. Everyone just stopped dead in their tracks. No one moved. Old rule of thumb in the Mill: if you hear something that sounds dangerous, it probably is; and if it's not coming toward you, don't go running toward it. So, everyone just stood stock still until the sound stopped.

"The old hands, they knew exactly what it was. Until you experience it, no one can possibly explain it. You know those big rolls of steel you see on flatbed semis on the freeway? They're usually headed to an automobile assembly plant to make into cars bodies. Ever wonder why a big long semi only hauls one roll at a time? It's because that one roll weighs over ten tons, 25,000 pounds, the steel for probably dozens and dozens of cars. But it had to get all rolled up somehow, see? To get it all rolled up like that at the Mill, they take the sheet steel straight out of the big flattening rollers where it gets mashed down to a quarter-inch thick or even thinner and feed it onto a coiler machine--that's what they really call it. On the coiler, they start winding the sheet steel slowly into the spool like you see on the trucks. But if they continue slow spooling all that steel, that can take almost a half-day to spool one roll all the way up. So, once it starts moving properly, they speed up the coiler until its going about 60 miles an hour. It works just like a giant fishing reel, you with me? Okay, so, once in a while--not often but sometimes--the coiler mechanism jams and stops spinning. Now, you got twelve and a half tons of sheet steel moving at 60 miles an hour toward the coiler and there's no braking system on it. It just keeps coming toward the coiler that has stopped coiling in that it's jammed, you know? Nowadays there's a huge, heavy-duty cage at the rear of the coiler, a backstop kinda, that's there to catch all that sheet steel rushing forward if the coiler seizes up. The cage wasn't always there in the old days. Another scary story for some other day.

"Anyways, that train wreck we heard, well, that was all of that sheet steel crashing into itself and into the backstop. Twelve and a half tons! What a mess. Everybody nearby the coiler scattered fast in case pieces broke free flying around like giant scythes. After it all stopped, we went over to see the mess. Holy crap! That much sheet steel in a crumpled mess piled maybe forty feet up and maybe fifty feet wide. The backstop cage was torn to shreds, but it did its job. All that steel moaning and hissing and sweating off steam, some of it moving like an animated snake, slow like, slithering. Now a team of guys with blowtorches starts to cut it up into manageable pieces so the overhead magnet crane can carefully lift segments of the cuttings and take them to dump trucks for trashing. Had to be done careful like, so any sections coiled under stress didn't suddenly spring free and slice a few guys up. Took almost two weeks of triple shifts to clear it all so they could repair the coiler. A mess. And dangerous, know what I mean? Even after it had come to a stop, all that shiny knife-like trash just sitting there like a beast made of sharp blades looking for the guy stupid enough to get too close. Every time it slid or shifted it groaned again like a wounded animal with sharp, broken claws and vicious teeth. That still gives me nightmares.

Lt. Wesner sat forward so suddenly that Cezary snapped back in his seat. "OK, you say the Mill wouldn't hire Richie, huh? What about Anton Wojcik?"

A pause, a small, frightened shake of his head, "What about him?"

"He was in your work crew? You were friends?"

"I guess so. Yeah. We're friends. We worked together."

"Past tense?"

"Huh?"

"You said you worked together — as in the past — not that you are working together now. What happened to Anton Wojcik?"

"I dunno. Did something happen to him? He's my work partner. I have a right to know."

"Anton is who we've been talking about, remember? You gave him your wisdom, remember? When is the last time you saw him?"

"Couple days, maybe two or three. I thought he'd called off sick or something. Isn't that so?"

"You know where Anton lives? Got his phone number?"

"Yeah. Sure."

"You didn't check on him, call him? If he really was sick, shouldn't you have given him a call? That's what friends do."

Cezary shrugged and wiggled in his chair, looking around for an escape. "I...I...maybe he had a girl or something. You don't interrupt a guy who got lucky, you know?"

"Where's Anton now, Cezary?"

"Call me Seazy."

"Where's Anton now, Seazy?"

"I don't know. You'll have to ask him. I don't know where he is or how he got there. Maybe…maybe…I don't know."

"Is Anton Wojcik dead, Seazy?"

"What a terrible thing to say! No, he's not dead. I'm sure he's not. No. He's my friend and…."

"And what?"

Seazy shook his head, "I don't know nothing. Why can't you just leave me alone?"

"At the beginning you said, 'I don't know why he did it'. Remember? What did he do that you don't know about?"

Seazy looked up, over the top of the Lieutenant's head, "I'm so confused. I'm not even sure if he did anything. I don't know where he is, or why he's not around. He should have taken the deal a long time ago and we wouldn't be here. It's his own damn fault. I told him she wouldn't…but he couldn't be reasoned with. No rational thought. I gave him my best logic." He lowered his head and looked down at his hands, now stuck between his legs. Seazy started to cry.

Lt. Wesner was confounded. He didn't believe Cezary Ludzinski, Seazy Lutz, had done anything illegal. The emotion was of someone who had somehow lost a friend and wasn't sure what to do to re-find him.

"Who is the 'she' you mentioned, Seazy?"

He sniffled and looked up, shaking his head with resolve, "She's nobody's business but Anton's. She's fine. He wouldn't hurt her. I wouldn't hurt her. Not for nothing. Leave her out of this."

"You brought her up, I didn't."

"Forget I said anything. Anton needs to forget her, too. Maybe that's what he's doing right now. Forgetting."

The Lieutenant summarized, "So you say Anton Wojcik is still alive."

"Of course, he is."

"And nothing happened to him as far as you know. And the girl, if there is a girl, has nothing to do with his disappearance."

"Right."

Wesner pressed forward. "But you agree that he's disappeared, right?"

"I never said that!"

"So why did the Mill call in the police?"

"The Mill called you? Why?"

"That's what I'm asking you. They say he clocked in a few nights ago, Thursday night, to work the third trick in the blast furnace plant, but he never clocked out on Friday morning. They've searched for him and only found an orange hard hat—maybe his, maybe not. And you were assigned to the same work detail that night. That's why you're here. What happened that night?"

"Geez. I didn't know he didn't clock out. Why would he do that? Screws up their payroll something fierce and your check gets delayed for weeks. I know, I did it by accident once–okay maybe on purpose just to see if they'd pay me for a double or something—so I know it screws everything up. He'll be hitting me up for some cash until his check gets squared around."

"That's what you take from this, that his check will be delayed? Aren't you worried something happened to him?"

"No. He's okay. I told you. He's fine. Well, maybe a bit screwy in the head right now, but fine."

"Where is he?"

"I dunno."

"Then how do you know he's fine?"

"I just do, that's all, I just do."

Lt. Wesner sighed and ran his fingers through the thinning hair of his crew cut. He wasn't sure why, but he believed Seazy was telling the truth. At least for the most part. No doubt, he was holding something back, and the slip about the girl was new information to be pursued in the morning. But for now, there was no reason to hold him any longer.

"Centralia, Pennsylvania," said the Lieutenant.

"What?"

"That's the name of the town with the coal fire under it."

"Oh. Okay, yeah. That sounds right."

"Seazy, I don't quite know what to make of you. Are you just plain dumb, or are you smart like a fox? Which is it?"

"That's not much of a choice, Lieutenant Wesner. That's like asking someone if he robbed the bank or just drove the getaway car. Neither sounds very good."

"Alright, Cezary Ludzinski, also known as Seazy Lutz, I'm letting you go. Do not attempt to leave town without my permission. If you hear from Anton Wojcik, I want you to call me at once at the number on this business card. Understood? Okay, get out of here."

Lt. Wesner watched Seazy slouch to the elevators. Then, watching out the windows from the 4th floor, he saw him cross the street and head toward the central bus terminal. All the city bus routes heading into and out of the downtown area converged on the central terminal, so it would be impossible to see which bus Cezary got on. Wesner turned away from the window slowly, a pensive scowl on his face, and went straight into the Captain Theodore Mitchell's office.

"Crap, did I ever catch a mess, Theo," he said assuming a seat across from the Captain.

"Don't be so formal, Wheezie, just come on in and grab a seat, make yourself comfortable, and pull out my Bourbon why don't ya'?"

"Sounds good! Pour us both one."

Anyone else and Captain Mitchell would have verbally torn him to shreds and physically ejected him from the office. But Capt. Theodore Mitchell and Lt. Alex Wesner had a long and rich history, beginning together at the academy, then as partners in a patrol car, and along the way each saving the other's life at different times. Both promoted during the same year, and only a singular stain on Wesner's record separating them at the time of Mitchell's promotion to Captain. No one was happier at the announcement than Wesner, who had an unnatural fear of being stuck behind a desk all day. Now it was his old friend, Theo Mitchell, who had Captain's bars and a permanent desk job.

Since most of the other daytime detectives had already departed, the Captain did indeed pull out the bottle of Bourbon and filled two small glasses half-way. "I thought you took this case because it looked like an easy one. Now, you're whining because it turned into some sort of shit-storm? Give me a break!"

Wesner accepted the glass and drained it quickly, tapping it down hard on the Captain's desk. "That's just it, Theo. I'm not sure there's a case at all. And if there is a case, what it's all about."

"Give me the Cliff Notes version," said the Captain, refilling both glasses.

"We get a call from a guy at Rubicon Steel Human Resources. He says their private police force can't find one of their employees who didn't clock out from his night shift--fella named Anton Wojcik. The guy worked at the blast furnace where the hot steel gets poured into cauldrons. His job was to go around the catwalk on the rim of the cauldron and kick any hot splatter from the pour back into the bucket using a heavy, ten-foot-long iron hook. The cauldron is some thirty feet across. The walkway has a guard rail, and there's always a two-man crew.

"Human Resources says they go to great pains to make sure the two-man crews are friendly, so one doesn't get mad at the other. They've had some unfortunate--let's call them--accidental trips in the past where a few men have been lost."

"How do you mean, lost? You mean the guy fell or was pushed into the cauldron? Not much chance of survival if that happens. They didn't find a body?" asked the Captain, draining his bourbon.

"Theo, that molten steel is over 2000 degrees. Someone falls in, there ain't nothing left to recover. They can test a sample from that pour and detect a slight imperfection in the blend, if you get my meaning. That's about it. They ask the next of kin how much the guy weighed, then cut a piece out of the block of steel weighing about the same as the deceased so the family has something to bury."

The Captain stared at Lt. Wesner. "Holy fuck, that is grim," he said as he poured another shot. "So, are they cutting out a block for your missing guy?"

Wesner shook his head. "Not yet. First, no one's sure where the guy is, or if he fell in, or if he just walked away, or whatever. Second, no family has come looking for him. Since we just got this case, we haven't had time to look for family--although so far no one thinks he had any--and we haven't yet canvassed all his friends or other mill workers. The guy we had in here, his work mate on the day he disappeared, mentioned a girl might be in the picture, so we need to find her, too."

"Well, hell, Wheezie! You haven't done anything yet, and you're already belly-aching and drinking my bourbon. Go get busy!"

Lt. Wesner drained his glass and said, "Thanks for the encouraging pep-talk. It'll go a long way toward motivating me." He waived good night to the Captain as he left the office. Retrieving his coat and hat from the locker he mumbled his way down the stairs toward the parking lot. He often mumbled, simply recounting a list of the known evidence of a case, which helped him organize his thoughts. Sometimes he was able to reshuffle them into fairly accurate solutions. But not this time.

He started the car and just sat for a few moments, mumbling. Time card. Why not punch out? You forgot? You just don't want to, challenge the system, see what might happen, like Seazy? But he'd have told you how it would mess up your pay check, wouldn't he? He just can't stop talking, that Seazy, huh? You didn't punch out because it doesn't matter anymore? You're too dead tired to think about it? You're just too dead? You don't matter anymore?

Wesner put the car in gear and slowly left the parking lot. You didn't clock out because you're absent minded? Did something similar ever happen before? Gotta research his file. Were you distracted? By what? The girl, maybe? Who is she? What part does she play in this? The Lieutenant turned toward the valley where the steel mills belched orange and yellow and red smoke. "Fires burning everywhere. Fires burning in your soul."

■ ■ ■

Seazy pulled the cord to ring the bell, notifying the bus driver he wanted to exit at the next stop. He need not have made the effort. The driver always stopped at every major intersection where a passenger generally wanted off or someone always seemed to want on. Nonetheless, Seazy was never sure people actually saw him or believed he was a real human being, so pulling the cord made him feel somehow alive and worth being noticed. He desperately wanted someone to acknowledge that he was present in the world, hoping he was worth the effort for the driver to apply the brakes and open the rear door.

Shuffling along the sidewalk past the shoemaker's shop, Seazy was whacked by the stench forcing its way out the open shop door, a mixture of rancid oil, old leather, and even older shoe polish leaching out to the sidewalk. It was the same awful stink he had tried to avoid since first smelling it in his youth. He hated the smell now because it made him see himself as a weak young boy, always afraid, holding his breath as he double-stepped past the shoemaker shop, eager to be far away from both the shop and its owner. Frightful stuff in that shop: odd machine noises whooshing and ripping, accented by vicious pounding hammer blows, ancient-language curses from the shoemaker. The sounds and the smells gave the weak young boy chills down his spine. The old man inside spoke only broken English, and usually growled at the kids who made faces at him through the shop's windows. His heavy leather apron, white at some time in the distant past, was white no more. Now, it was stained by brown and black and other odd colors of shoe polish, rubs of leather oil, even some of the shoemaker's own blood. Seazy, no longer young, was the still weak boy who quickened his pace as he passed.

The bakery next door was already closed. Fresh donut aromas would return tomorrow, no longer today. Seazy looked up at the clock on the bank cupola. Way past closing time for most businesses. Dusk was already staining the routine gray sky an odd color of purple. A few low clouds exposed their bellies to orange reflections from one of the hot mills. Three steel mills in the valley just a half-mile away, one or the other or all three would belch smoke and fire throughout the day and night—as expected.

Well into autumn, but it was still warm enough for the corner bar door to be open. The odor of stale beer oozed out on clouds of cigarette smoke. The doorway angled at the corner of the intersection, diagonally opposite the neighborhood church. The bar entrance incongruously facing the statue of the Blessed Virgin tucked into a corner alcove. No one ever claimed to be cured of alcoholism by facing the Virgin upon their exit. Seazy wanted one of each: a beer, a cigarette, and a blessed cure. Peering over his shoulder, he slipped into the open bar door. Not even sure who or what he was looking for, he could not imagine why any on-looker would care about him going in. No matter, he still felt dirty, unworthy, slithering over the greasy stoop into the bar. He made himself small by grabbing the first stool he came to, putting his back to the door. But his back to the door made him quiver with chills, so he quickly moved to the opposite end of the bar next to the noisy juke box where he could face the entrance. "Uneasy Seazy," he mumbled to himself.

The balding bartender was drying highball glasses and talking to an older patron who was facially scarred and creased and bent. Probably an old steel worker, thought Seazy, the battle scars of a lifer. He turned on the stool and saw the cigarette machine. Great invention, Seazy thought. Put in the right number of coins and you get the smokes. No need to make eye contact or small talk with anyone. He bought a pack and searched for matches. They were behind the bar. If he could ever get the bartender's attention, he could get a cold beer and some hot matches. He waited patiently, only partially convinced that he was actually seen by anyone, either the bartender or the old patron.

Seazy would not be considered a regular, although he'd been in the bar three or four times over the past half-year, and he'd seen the same bartender each time. They had even shared a joke once at the barbershop across the street. Nevertheless, the deadpanned question, "What can I do for you, bud," seemed like the benign recognition of Seazy's anonymity.

Two beers and four cigarettes later, Seazy walked out, nodded to the Blessed Virgin statue as if to say, "I see you, even if you can't see me," and headed toward his house, the same one he grew up in. It was not really his house anymore, but sort of no one else's either. His uncle had paid off the remaining small mortgage after both of Seazy's parents disappeared. His uncle told Seazy he could live there if he paid a monthly rent and kept the place clean. Seazy could defray some of the monthly costs if he could find roommates. His uncle promised to sell the place someday, but it was unclear, and unlikely, whether Seazy would get any of the profits from the sale of what once had been his growing-up home.

Big Ed was the first of the roommates to be signed up. He always parked in the small one-car driveway, whether Seazy's car was there or not, sometimes blocking up the driveway, his car laying across the sidewalk, bumper dragging in the street. Big Ed was casually irresponsible and careless. He never worried about being offensive, preferring to ignore everyone else's needs as long as he was satisfied with his own situation in life. Big Ed was a big guy, heavy set bordering on obese. Everywhere he walked, the floors creaked. Seazy was pretty certain that one of the floors of the old house would give way one day under Ed's feet. An informal acquaintance, sort of a friend from some time back that neither could quite recall, Ed had a job so he could be counted on to help with the rent money. He made himself comfortable showing no desire to move out even though several other additional roommates had come and gone during the past few years. Seazy always breathed a sigh of relief when a roommate moved out without drama, and he was looking forward to the day Big Ed would leave, even if it meant finding a new well-healed roomie. He didn't care if there might be drama. He was just tired of Big Ed's…bigness.

Once, a different housemate just disappeared, all his clothes and personal items gone. No notice given, no excuse made, just one day gone. Left his stereo behind. Seazy pawned it for the rent owed. The guy came back four months later after another renter had moved in. He was pissed off about not getting his stereo back, but he wasn't planning on paying the back rent anyway. Drama.

Seazy saw Big Ed's car there, hanging half out of the driveway, dangling into the street. Parked on the opposite curb, a black-and-white city police car, motor turned off, windows open, two cops chatting and eyeballing the house. Seazy was sure they were thinking of towing Big Ed's car. If they would just wait a minute, Seazy would bring them the keys with a smile. Despite that pleasant thought, he chose not to make eye contact with the cops, preferring to pretend they weren't really there. Big Ed was watching TV with the volume set on the upper decibels, just in case someone down the street needed to hear it. He was sprawled across the entire couch, sublimely oblivious of the rest of the world, three mostly empty beer bottles dripping a new stain on the old carpet.

"Hey, Ed!" shouted Seazy. "Can you hear it OK? Think the cops are enjoying it?"

"Seazy! Where you been? The cops are looking for you."

Seazy turned toward the street to see the police car with the two cops slowly pull away from the curb and drive away. "Were they here because of your car?"

Ed lowered the volume approaching a whisper. "They came knocking at the door wondering if you lived here. I told them yes, but you weren't home. Didn't want to lie to the cops. Hope that was alright."

"Yeah. Sure. Thought they were here to get you for your car." He walked into another room, mumbling, "Me and the cops are good buddies by now, I guess."

"What's that? Didn't hear you, man. Gotta speak up, ya' know?" Ed had no idea that Seazy had spent the better part of the last four or five hours talking to Lt. Wesner and Sgt. Friedman. "What do these cops want with you? Speeding again?" Ed shouted from the couch.

Seazy opened the refrigerator finding only two beers left from the six-pack he bought last night. Returning with one to the living room, he said, "I'm working the late shift tonight. I need you to move your car so I can get out."

"OK. I'm heading out to the bars later, so I'll be out of the way. But you shouldn't be driving with a speeding ticket hanging over your head," said Big Ed.

"And you shouldn't be driving after drinking all of my beer."

"Were those your beers? I wondered where they came from. I guess I owe you. Where you been all afternoon, chasing that skirt again? Don't you get it? She's moved on, man, you are in her rear-view mirror. You should come out with me some night. I'll fix you up. You can keep one of my cast-offs! Hah!"

Seazy turned toward the stairs. "I'm gonna catch some zzz's before heading to work. Try to keep the volume down, OK?"

. . .

Darkness, well past sundown, but still a while before his shift would start. Seazy circled behind his old blue car, intent on his own special mission. In the tepid light from the street lamp, he bristled at the fresh dent in his rear bumper from Big Ed's muscled effort to squeeze into the driveway. His old blue car was nothing if not dented almost everywhere, a fact of life from the parking lot of the Mill, but it was galling to suffer another blow toward the machine's ultimate decay in your own driveway delivered by someone you knew.

Seazy drove off toward the southeast, even though the Mill was due west. He checked frequently but there was no black & white in his rear-view mirror. In fact, there were no cars heading in his same direction for more than a few blocks. Ten maybe fifteen minutes later, he pulled off into the small city park facing a row of multi-story, early century houses, designed to impersonate Victorian-style structures. Headlights off, he coasted as close as the parking area would allow, permitting him a clear view of one of the houses in the middle. A large home with what was likely a third-floor attic, it was clearly big enough for two families, one up, one down. The one up was where an aged aunt and uncle lived, he somehow knew. Lights were on in the downstairs living room which fronted the street. Thin gauze curtains, mostly closed, limited what could be seen beyond shadows and lamp glows. Still, the soft incandescence in the bay window made his heart leap with a desire to belong, then just as quickly sink, knowing he was forever forbidden. Off to the side, a blush from the kitchen windows painted two rectangles on the darkened driveway. Occasionally a shadow added life and movement, and each time it happened his heart leaped with an emotion he was troubled to describe. Was that a tremor of fear? Fear of what, of whom? Was that a jolt of passion? To what end? Did he not fervently wish to be discovered watching from afar in secret, yet welcomed, adored, embraced; or was it a fear of the possible label of stalker — one to be hated, spat-upon, discarded? He frowned in the rear-view mirror. How despicable are you, sleazy Seazy?

His whole body shook as he turned the car around and left the park, slowly moving toward another night shift at the Mill. His hands gripped the wheel as if to melt it, crush it, turn it into ash. He breathed deeply in half-sobs. He knew he had to stop what had become a devastating and self-destructive habit—an obsession--visiting the park, watching the house, imagining himself a welcome visitor, a future member, someone who could melt into the intimacy of those inside, gain entry into what had become his own personal holy-of-holies. But how? Not how could he enter, but how could he stop his nighttime visits. He could not give up what had become his most severe and searing dream without it becoming a nightmare.

He blinked the tears from his eyes and pointed the car toward the orange glow now igniting the black-purple sky and exposing billows of grey exhaust. The Mill had no time for frivolous emotions. There was steel to be made.

■　■　■

After leaving Police Headquarters, Lt. Wesner had circled around the industrial valley known locally as "The Flats", overrun with steel mills, oil refineries, assorted supporting factories and a stench that seemed indigenous to the snakelike Cuyahoga River in the center. He maneuvered along roads or pavement that followed no logical plan other than they were once determined to be the quickest path to bring raw materials or finished products to some place where they were needed. Criss-crossing the uneven and usually unmarked roads were rail lines connecting one section of the industrial complex to another. No warning flashers or crossing gates at the tracks, only signs saying, "Travel at your own risk. Train engines will not stop." He finally found the parking lot where Seazy's car would likely sit all night.

"You the guard here?" he asked the obese man slouching on a chair in a booth at the entrance gate.

"Who wants to know," the guard replied without moving.

Wesner flashed his badge, saying, "Let's try this again. What hours are you on duty?"

"Oh, shit! Why'd'nt you say you was a cop? Yeah, I'm the guard here. Second shift only. What's up? Somebody's car broke into?" He jumped up and scanned the yard to see if anything looked amiss.

"You keep track of cars left overnight?"

The guard turned his attention to Lt. Wesner. "Naw, I'm here to make sure kids don't sneak in from over the hill. Had a few break-ins, stolen stuff, broken windows. But nothin' beyond that while I been here." The guard straightened his soft shoulders to emphasize his self-proclaimed effectiveness.

"Is there a way of tracking license plates, to see who's driving what car? Or if any have been left here for an extended period of time?"

"Mister, this here's the parking lot for the workers in Hot Mill Number One and Cold Mill Number Four. Some of these cars might not belong to the guy what drove it, if you catch my drift. Guys sometimes work a double shift and sleep in those trailers back there," pointing at the distant fence line, "and they might not move their car for close to a week. Us guards, we're not here to do anything fancy, just to keep vandals away. Hell, they won't even give me a weapon to use if there's trouble."

The Lieutenant stifled a grin, "That's probably for the best. You don't want to be hauled in on a bogus murder charge, mistaken identity, stuff like that."

The guard held up his hands, "Aw, hell no. Anything goes sideways out here, they tell me to dial the Security Department on this line, here."

"Internal calls only?" asked Wesner.

"Yeah. Tried calling my girl first day out here. Ended up reaching the President's secretary's extension. Couldn't hang up quick enough. No way to make an outside call."

"Ever need to call the Security Department?"

"Couple times. Those kids I mentioned, came sliding down that grass slope and snuck under a gap in the fence, roaming through, looking for unlocked cars or something valuable they could see. Called Security. They got here in a hot minute, Jeeps with flashing red lights and big spotlights on their roof. Half-a-dozen security guards with silver riot helmets and shotguns strapped to their backs. Those kids shit their pants when one of the shotguns was fired at the sky."

"So, did they turn the kids over to us, city police?"

The guard grinned, "I don't think they ever did. Cuffed them and hauled them away in the Jeeps. They got a little lean-to building attached to Mill #3 where they take people for questioning, should anything come up. Took the kids there, is my guess. I had a beer at the nearby bar with a security guy once. He said they make it so the kids fear the guards more than they fear God or the Devil. Said they won't be back here again."

"Where's this tavern?"

The guard pointed West. "Up the hill, near the top. Place is called Steal Inn. Get it? Kinda a play on words."

Wesner looked up the hill where an old, outdated, two-lane bridge pointed a road to the western crest. He could almost read the neon sign. "Got it. Can I get to that Security hut you mentioned from here?"

"Nuh-unh. To get through that entrance you gotta show your employee pass to that real guard down there. And no civilian cars permitted past the gate without authorization. Way too dangerous in there."

"So I've been told." He took a final look around. "Thanks for the info. Helps a lot."

"Say," the guard finally brightened up, "what is it that you're investigating? You never did say."

"Oh. Sorry. Must've slipped my mind," said Wesner as he closed the door of the car and started the engine. "Time for a beer, I think."

The Steal Inn lived up to its name. It looked like it once was a multi-story residence, given way to an ersatz tavern. The former front door was boarded up with an arrow pointing to the rear. The entrance doorway was hidden in the back of the building, close to the main parking area. Patrons could quite literally steal into the bar without being seen from the street. If a worker wanted a couple shots before his shift, or a few beers after, neither his boss nor his wife would be the wiser. The interior was a filthy pewter color: sheet steel bar counter top, slate grey walls, brownish smoke-stained ceiling. Wesner had loosened his tie before entering, but he still caused conversations to descend to a muffled murmur as he took a barstool discreetly separated from the three and four-man grumbling groups scattered about.

A suspicious white-haired barmaid poured his beer from the tap as Wesner casually surveyed the clientele. He spotted one man sitting alone at a table. The man was powerfully built, and wore a dark khaki green shirt with matching pants and the steel-toed boots required for all Mill employees. His security badge was still pinned on his shirt—probably why he sat alone with no friendly companions. Wesner ordered a second beer and took it to the security man's table.

"Mind if I join you?" said Wesner as he sat down.

"I was enjoying being alone," the man said.

"I brought you a beer since I'm determined to bother you."

The man eye-balled the beer and looked around at the other men in the bar, all of whom were watching what they thought might be a dramatic confrontation. He looked directly at Wesner and said, "You got a brass pair thinking I'd let you just sit down at my table, beer or no beer."

Wesner tilted his head and grimaced. "I got something else brass in my pocket says you'll welcome me. And a half-dozen lead-heads in case you don't."

The man half-smiled and reached for the beer Wesner brought. "Cold beer is better than cold steel any day. My name's Thorpe. What can I do for you, officer?"

"I'm Alex Wesner, Lieutenant with CPD. I caught a case involving an employee of Rubicon Steel. Stopped by the employee parking lot, spoke to the guard, who said he'd run into some security guys here. I stop in, and — poof — like magic here you are."

Thorpe shook his head. "Parking lot guard, huh? That's the nicest thing he's ever been called. If it's the one I'm thinking of, he's about as worthless as…so what employee case brings you out?"

"Someone disappeared. Clocked in, never clocked out. Maybe left his hard hat by accident. Maybe had an accident. No one's quite sure. Head Office says you guys haven't figured it out."

Thorpe stiffened and sat back. "I know the case. Anton Wojcik. Worked the Hot Mill on the cauldron. Strange situation. Foreman reports the problem. But his boss wants it hushed up. We no sooner start investigating for about 24 hours and we get told to stand down. Human Resources gets wind of it, all hell breaks loose. Cops get called in. You. Homicide, right?"

"Well, I do investigate homicides, plus other odd stuff. Right now, I'm thinking this is odd stuff. That is, unless you've got other thoughts." Wesner waited, not wanting to give out any other information. Thorpe seemed like a good guy. Tough, but given his workplace, fair. Nonetheless, Wesner believed first impressions seldom lived up to second expectations.

Thorpe looked at the other workers in the bar, now all returned to their own conversations since no blows had been struck by either of the two men at the table. "Other thoughts. That cauldron is not someplace I'd choose to work. Even though the guys who work it get double pay, the life expectancy is way too short. I've been at Rubicon Steel for six years. Before that, four at U.S. Steel. Before that a double hitch in the Marines. I've seen danger. Still, you'd never get me to step on that catwalk."

"Really that dangerous, huh?"

"They're supposed to wear asbestos suits and gas masks. Says so right on the placard by the steps going up. These guys—like some sort of badge of courage—just regular work clothes, no safety gear. They come out with pants scorched, burn holes everywhere, skin baked, almost asphyxiated. We had to put a permanent first aid station manned 24/7 right nearby."

Wesner wanted to slow walk this conversation. "Yikes! Sounds like someone started a stupid people club. A person could get killed in that environment."

Thorpe nodded and swallowed half the glass of beer. "There's been some. I came in for a morning shift once and found the entire line shut down. Overnight a guy tripped and went in head first. Instantly incinerated. Flash of fire, then whoosh!"

"Isn't there a guard rail or something?"

"Yeah. Great. The edge of the railing is just above your knee. That'll stop you, right? We interrogated his workmate for hours. Story never changed. He said he looked away for one second and when he looked back, he saw his buddy taking a header from the opposite side of the cauldron."

"You sound skeptical."

"Maybe. Since the dead guy's wife cashed a big life insurance check and the work buddy quits The Mill and marries her three months later. Yeah, I guess I'm skeptical."

"Sounds a little like the case I pulled. You think this Anton Wojcik fell in? Maybe was pushed in?"

Thorpe shook his head slowly. "We only had the case a short time. There were lots of questions I didn't get to ask, but there was something off about it. Similar to some of the others. Not sure I can put my finger on what or why."

Wesner said, "I'll tell you what. My partner and I just had a conversation with Anton's work mate, Seazy Lutz. You know him?"

"Can't say as I do."

"Well, talk about something being off, this Seazy character is straight out of the Twilight Zone. You think maybe you can nose around some and get his back story for me? I'd appreciate an inside point of view."

Thorpe spit toward some broken floor tiles to his left. "We're not supposed to be looking at this case anymore. May not be the easiest ask to agree to. I'll see what I can do, but I gotta protect myself at the same time. So, no promises."

"Fair enough. I'll take info on Anton, too, if that shows up. Call me at this number if you need to talk," as he slipped a business card under his half-empty beer. Wesner rose, lifted and slammed the chair down, yelling, "Well, you've been absolutely no fucking help at all, you shit head!" He stormed out of the bar as the workers all started laughing at the obviously frustrated local cop. Wesner had just provided the perfect cover for Thorpe in case anyone was too interested. Only one person seemed to take note of what had just transpired, and she pretended to busy herself washing highball glasses.

Tuesday, November 2

Full output. That is what the foreman always told me. Even though I said I wasn't interested in learning about steel production, he taught me despite my indifference. The foreman told me each mill ran three shifts--known in the industry as a 'trick'--every day. Three eight-hour tricks filled a 24-hour work day while employing thousands of men, mostly men. Very few women even wanted to have the kind of equality that would put them to work in the pits of hell alongside us male steel-workers. I saw a few women in tough, physical jobs, but not many.

Three tricks with thousands of men could produce a hell of a lot of steel: steel pipe, steel girders, sheet steel for cars or appliances. Chunks sent to fabricators to fashion into other items everyone liked to buy: refrigerators, stoves, who knows what else could be made from bent steel. We provide a semi-controlled extreme fire, a hot enough blaze to melt ore and, with a bow toward some strange alchemy, the tools of industrial growth are formed.

If you think about it, the steel we make gives rise to the development of sturdier frames, gives rise to buildings of previously unimaginable heights, permits the replacement of old models, old structures, old architectural designs — no matter how beautiful or seemingly irreplaceable — and initiates the concept of planned obsolescence. Get rid of the old, the less modern. Don't fix or repair, throw it away and buy new. Turn your car in every three years. If it's got 75,000 miles on it, it's about to break down anyway. If I survive 20 years working in the mills, I'll break down, too.

How did the foreman put it? Was he joking, or serious? He said full output means all workers bent forward at full speed to provide product for the purchasers, the builders, the industry of the land. What did he leave out? He didn't mention the real stuff: precise measurements for precise needs, cut no corners but deliver on time, on a quicker time, on an even quicker time. There will be danger. There will be mistakes. Try for zero injuries and succeed for two or three days in a row. Then, someone loses a finger, maybe two. Someone will have to wear a glass eye the rest of his life. Flowers will be sent to another family. I've seen it all first-hand — the walking wounded, the sheet-covered gurney wheeled off the factory floor. But all in all, steel will roll, profits will be made, and we workers will earn more money in a single week than our grandparents earned in a year.

The lure of such wages…that's what makes the danger worth the risk. After all, the Mill is not a coal mine where an entire shift could be killed in a cave-in. This is not a shooting war where entire platoons or squadrons or ships full of men could perish simultaneously. This is a place where only one man at a time goes down, and only if he is careless or terribly unlucky. I always try to be careful. It seems like I have lived in fear of…well, just about everything for most of my life. This is no different.

Steel production is a business, and if you are smart enough to keep your nose clean and your boots planted safely, you can earn a lot of money. Maybe not to be wealthy as in really rich, but by comparison to my grandfather — whoever he was — I can be considered successful, just like the old guys I see shuffling along at the Mill. Even if their clothes are nothing but sweat and grease-stained filthy rags; even if the black soot under their fingernails is somehow permanent; even if parts of their body are missing, or no longer work; even if they won't live long enough to see the second year of their retirement. Their family will still say they are, or were, a success. They were lucky to have such a wonderful job, complete with union protection. They took care of their family by working hard and making money and not drinking too much of it away.

That is how I see it. Me, Seazy Lutz--me, Cezary Ludzinski. No, that is how I <u>must</u> see it. To believe anything otherwise would drive me crazy. But then, I think that Cezary sees a lot of things through a different prism than the rest of the world does, and different than how Seazy sees things through the same prism. No, that's not right. It's not a prism for Seazy. It's a kaleidoscope made up of fragile yet richly hued tiny pieces of glass. There are so many variables to every act or word, every thought I have. What would happen if…if I did one thing versus another. How would people respond or react? Differently, I suspect. One person responds to each act or word or thought in their own way, unique from the next person, whether they are strangers, friends, loved ones…. What are loved ones? No one I know. Even so, I must measure every word, every act, determine how I should talk or think or even hold my head. It changes based on who is in front of me--based on how I imagine that person might respond. Just like the view through a kaleidoscope. Maddening!

Seazy put his head in his hands. The kaleidoscope that was his view of the world was not simply a view through a single crystal prism. His world was a spinning crash of broken pieces of brilliantly colored glass all tumbling and changing his perspective simultaneously, sometimes as vivid as a stained-glass window, then as horrible as a shattered box of 64 crayons impossible to reassemble without melting the pieces back together in a blazing hot flame. In his mind he knew the absence of all color was black, but in his heart, he feared that the molten assembly of all the colors in the crayon box will not end up white. Rather, the resulting hot mess will be the awful, horrid, disgusting color of his simmering and scalding soul.

■ ■ ■

Lieutenant Wesner anxiously awaited his partner's arrival and grinned as he saw him stepping off the elevator. "Benny! How'd it go with the bracelet last night?"

The Sergeant giggled, unable to contain his happiness, "Oh, man, Wheezie! She loved it! Hopped around the house for an hour. Called her mom, her sisters, her girlfriends. Had to order in a pizza. There was no way she was spending any time in the kitchen, and you know I can't cook a lick."

"Very cool, Ben. I'm happy for you. I know it meant a lot to be able to do that for her."

Benny smiled and looked at his hands. "Yeah, she's been the best thing to ever happen to me. I get pumped when I can make her happy. New house, now the bracelet. Hope she's satisfied for a while. She doesn't understand what it takes to keep her happy, how much I have to do…." He sat down at his desk and pulled the file from Lt. Wesner's hand. "How about our case? What's up with Seazy? Anything new?" Wesner hummed a deep tone and wrinkled his face. Benny knew when Wesner was humming, something big was on his mind. "Woah! That much, huh? You gonna share?"

"You know what…something is starting to smell about this, and it's not the sulfur from the mills. Our boy Seazy may or may not be guilty of something. Don't know yet. Don't even know if there is a crime that someone can be guilty of. The smelly part is why Rubicon Steel called us in the first place."

"I thought their own internal investigation came up empty, so we're next in line. Right?"

"I made contact with one of their internal security guys. He says they only had the case of the missing worker for one full day before it was pulled. Someone didn't want them looking into it. Rubicon gave it to us because we can't go inside the Mill without an escort."

"You think this security guy's straight up?"

Wesner sat back in the squeaky chair. "He's ex-Marine, been in security for 10 years, two places. I hate to judge on a first date but he seems legit. And he knows more than he could say in public. Let it slip that there may have been other incidents."

"Other incidents? More missing people?"

"Hell if I know. He was a bit circumspect," said Wesner, shaking his head.

Benny pulled out his pad and pen. "How about I call the Human Resources guy at Rubicon--what was his name?"

"Tripp. Jonas Tripp."

Benny nodded, "Yeah. I'll call him early today before his second cup of coffee and ask again for the file he promised us on Anton Wojcik. I'll also see if he has anything on our boy, Seazy. Plus, I'll show him I'm interested in any other incidents recently that they'd suddenly like to report. That may shake something loose."

"Great! But leave any mention of our security guy contact out of the discussion. I get the distinct impression he might not be so safe after talking to us." The Lieutenant leaned in, "Oh, by the way. According to his finger prints, our boy Seazy Lutz is actually named Cezary Ludzinski. He may be on file at Rubicon Steel under that name." In reply to Benny's questioning look, he said, "Long story. Not pertinent right now. I'll give you the gory details later. Spelling of his name is in the file."

Benny said, "Looking forward to hearing what that's all about. What else should we be doing?"

"I'm going to contact the local colleges to see if Seazy or Cezary has any past presence at any of them. He made a few references to school or college. I want to see if either he or Anton were registered, either alone or at the same time. Then a call to the draft board is in order. Maybe one or both served in the military. Vietnam seems to bother our guy. Let's try to finish up our calls early this morning. I can think of several places I'd like to visit, including Anton's residence."

■ ■ ■

The calls took less than an hour. The detective team settled into their unmarked cruiser, each with a cardboard cup of half-stale coffee. "Ugh! I don't know why I brought this. It's cold and it tasted lousy even when it was freshly brewed," said Benny from behind the steering wheel.

"I got a trash can right here," said Lt. Wesner. "Gimme that. I'll dump them both. We should know better than to even try drinking the ink from the police station."

"Where we headed first? I vote Anton's place."

"Sgt. Friedman, I believe you are correct. That sounds like the right place to start. After that, I'd like to swing by the Rubicon Steel office and pick up the information they promised, then, if we have time, eye-ball Seazy's address. Whadya think?"

Benny nodded. "Makes sense to me. We can trade what we learned from our phone calls along the way."

The biggest piece of news the team discovered was that both Seazy Lutz and Anton Wojcik were enrolled at the same time for about three quarters at the local state university. Anton was an excellent student, carrying a 3.75 GPA. Why he had not re-enrolled for another quarter was an open question. At the same time, Seazy was struggling to carry a 2.25 GPA and did re-enroll after Anton left school. According to their transcripts, they shared only one class together, a freshman level English class. That was one of the courses most feared by freshman boys as a gauntlet course used to separate wheat from chaff, dividing true college students from future army privates, the difference-maker between a college cafeteria bowl of soup and a mouth full of blood in an Asian rice paddy. Both boys passed. And, as might be expected given the times, the Draft Board informed Lieutenant Wesner that, because of their grades, neither received a "greetings" letter calling them into military duty.

Sgt. Friedman's phone call to the Rubicon Steel Mill Human Resources office had the desired effect. They promised to have a copy of the personnel files on both Cezary Ludzinski and Anton Wojcik available within the hour. Apparently, Seazy was forced to provide his correct legal name so he could receive and ultimately cash a paycheck. They even verified Anton's address, the apartment building toward which Sgt. Friedman now pointed the unmarked police cruiser. Anton had selected a residence very close to the mills — both cheap and dirty.

Taking a right-angle turn off the primary east-west road, two parallel dead-end streets ran roughly even with the north-south ridge edging the industrial valley below. As if to prevent the valley from ever rising, three enormous anchors in the shape of huge powerful steel mills squatted along the river at the bottom of the valley. The three behemoths produced a chorus of roars and crashes symbolic of industrial progress while belching the corresponding smoke and steam — which now provided a coarse cover for nearby rooftops, including the three-story apartment building where Anton lived. Several of the houses on the street were occupied residences, by evidence of the TV antennas creatively attached, some lightly swaying in the breeze. Other structures were in various stages of dilapidation. The clapboard siding of several appeared unpainted since first nailed in place many decades ago.

Parking next to the apartment building, the officers scanned the neighborhood. Here and there an attic window was open or missing entirely. A few of the houses and the entire apartment building were sided with asphalt shingles, unsuccessfully veneered to look like something other than asphalt shingles. Years of neglect and exposure to the acidic mill effluence laid bare the remains of their inadequacy: torn shingle edges, dented to follow the bends of the buckling walls, mismatched shingles casually re-tacked at odd angles, discolored sections--soot stained on all sides.

"Lovely neighborhood," the Sergeant deadpanned.

"We're being watched," said the Lieutenant. "A few curtains closed as we pulled up, some windows were quickly shut. None of the doors are opening to welcome us."

"They made us as cops, I guess."

"Or even worse, bill collectors. No one here has a car as new or shiny as our cruiser. Only bill collectors or cops would bother coming down this dead-end street on purpose. Yeah, I'd say we were made. Which place is Anton's?"

Friedman leaned to the right, pointing to the forlorn apartment building. "This once-lovely mustard-colored multi-family dwelling is the home of our beloved Anton Wojcik, whether he is alive or dead. Apartment 2D. Let's see if there's anything in there to give us a clue."

As the two investigators approached the front door, an overweight and over-hairy man appeared as a blocker in the entryway, torn and filthy tee-shirt worn as his uniform. He leaned against the door jamb. "What you fellas want here?" Beyond him from the apartment on his right came a high-pitched wail of woe, as might be expected from an old cat whose tail was caught in a vice. The blocker shouted over his shoulder. "Shuttup you! I told you I'd be right back!" Turning to the two, he said, "My sister. She ain't right in the head. Had scarlet fever twenty years ago when she was eight. It did bad things to her mind. Pretty much a basket case now. I'm the super of this here building. Whadya want here?"

Wesner pulled and flashed his badge, and asked, "You need us to take a look at her? She sounds like she's in distress."

"Nah, she just wants another bowl of cereal. She's fine. What brings you two out here today?"

Wesner made a mental note to have Social Services pay this guy a visit while the Sergeant asked, "You have a tenant named Anton Wojcik? Lives in 2D?"

"Anton? Sure! He ain't done nothing wrong, has he? I like my people to keep their noses clean, know what I mean?"

"When's the last time you saw him?"

"Uhh, I guess a few days back. Maybe it was a week ago. Not sure. He works late hours. Down at the Mill. I think he likes the late shift, working in the dark. He's pretty quiet. Don't think I ever hear his radio or nothin'. What's he done?"

"We need to examine his apartment. Get your pass-key."

"Aw, Jeez. I dunno. Ought to get his permission to let you in, you know what I mean. Ain't right just lettin' two strangers digging through his belongings."

Wesner said, "You know what? That actually may be legally correct. But we didn't want to go get a judge's warrant, because that would have to be a warrant for the whole building to be searched--get a full crew of investigators out here, dump things out of everyone's drawers, your stuff, too, by the way. That can be a real mess. Take you a few days to put everything back together. Of course, if we discover anything illegal, well…that'd pretty much shut this place behind yellow police tape for at least a month. But you're right. We'll come back later with a warrant." He turned to walk away.

"Wait, wait, wait, wait! Okay, I guess it can't hurt anything really. He doesn't have that much in there anyway. I'll go get the key." He disappeared into the door marked 1A, shouting at his sister, "Here! Here's the damn Cheerios! Eat yourself silly!" Fumbling with a ring of keys, he said, "Right this way. Up the stairs back here."

The search of Anton's rooms lasted only a few minutes. As the landlord predicted, there were very few items in Anton's personal effects--no notes or documents indicating he was concerned over pending violence, and nothing to suggest a suicidal tendency. There were a few books on engineering and chemistry, even a few literary novels by Steinbeck, but no travel brochures implying flight. Most of his clothes were still in the closet or the bureau drawers.

Returning to the cruiser, Sgt. Friedman said, "A warrant for the whole building? Where'd that come from?"

"Had to put some legit fear into his stomach. He was right, of course. We did need a warrant. Something tells me he's been down that road before. Just needed to shake him up."

"Ha! Like a soda can. He almost barfed last night's six pack. Anyway, that was uneventful. Didn't know what to expect, but I don't think we learned much."

Lt. Wesner said, "Not from what was in there, but from what was not. Did you see a suitcase? Anything that could carry clothes?"

"No. Come to think of it, there was no way to carry anything out of there. No boxes, bags, cartons…. With what was in there, he'd be hard pressed to be traveling and taking his stuff. No suitcase."

"I checked the medicine cabinet. No razor, no toothbrush. Did you see a bank book, check book, anything that Anton would need to deal with his finances?"

The Sergeant stared over the steering wheel at a mangy feral-looking cat cautiously skulking its way across the street. "You're right. There's nothing in there like that. It's not what is in there but what isn't in there that raises the questions, like you always say. You thinking he's on some sort of planned trip? Whatever suitcase or satchel he might own is with him."

Looking back at the now closed main doorway on the apartment building no longer blocked by the landlord, Wesner said, "Could be. Let's go pay a visit to your new Human Resources buddy at Rubicon's Offices. See if he can help us unravel Anton a bit." He pulled out his notepad and wrote down the address of the apartment building, followed by "1A", followed by "Social Services", underlined twice.

Rubicon Steel's main office was a sprawling muscular, three-story, dark-red brick building perched on a difficult-to-get-to bluff. To the rear of the building, a cliff fell precipitously some sixty or seventy feet down to railroad tracks leading to Mill #1. To the front, a new freeway made a deep cut through what once was an old neighborhood of dilapidated and boarded up lean-to houses. The old structures were bulldozed or burned, the earth beneath them chewed by dinosauric machines, all to be replaced by a modern highway on which trucks and cars now sped by some 30-feet below the top of the bluff. The resulting effect was the positioning of the Rubicon Steel office building standing as an imposing fortress of strength rising above the creation of raw steel on one side and the finished steel products driving by on the other.

When originally constructed, the once bright red bricks of the building reflected sunlight with the promising glow one could expect from something as freshly-minted as a college engineering school. Now, some 50-years later, it was best described as foreboding. Tarnished by coal soot and stained from foul emissions, the bricks and unwashed windows resembled what many imagined to be the black-red color of Satan's Lair. The entire building now gave the impression that it had risen on its own out of the depths of hell to occupy the solitary, bald-domed bluff of the devil.

Friedman stopped the car in the circle by the front door rather than heading to the visitor's lot at the far edge of the building. "Put the flasher bar on the front dash, Wheezie. They won't tow a police car."

Lt. Wesner gave him a surprised look. "Why, Sgt. Friedman! That's a very bold move. I'm impressed."

"Yeah, well, I'm thinking these people haven't quite figured out that we're not a bunch of bumbling fools coming here simply to follow their orders."

"That phone call with them set you off, huh?"

Friedman nodded, saying, "Mr. Tripp transferred me to some underling. Got a bit of attitude from this Timmy guy when I politely requested the personnel files. So, it ended with me demanding the files or Timmy might find himself wearing my special cuff links on his way downtown. Let's see what kind of reception we get now." They exited the cruiser and headed to the main door. Two men held the doors open for them to enter.

"Sgt. Friedman, I presume?" said the older man. "I am Jonas Tripp, Head of Personnel Administration. This young man is Timothy Ratterman, with whom you also spoke. Mr. Ratterman wishes to apologize for his rather rude behavior earlier. Isn't that correct, Timothy?"

"Yeah, sure. Sorry. I was rude," said the young man unconvincingly. "Here are the files."

Friedman said, "Okay. We'll return these as soon as the case is concluded. Lieutenant Wesner and I have some questions for you, Mr. Tripp. Is there somewhere private where we can meet?"

Jonas Tripp was taken aback. "Well, I suppose we could go to one of the rooms behind my office...."

Timmy interrupted, "We can throw everyone out of the conference room around the corner."

Tripp's back stiffened. "We won't be throwing anyone out of any meeting they are in. There are suitable places elsewhere."

Lt. Wesner said, "We only need room for three, Timmy. Please excuse us. We won't be needing you for the discussion, at least not at this time."

Timmy blinked once, then blinked again. "Oh. I see. Okay. Have fun." He slowly turned and walked away, but made sure to give Mr. Tripp a long, cold gaze.

Once he was out of earshot, Tripp commented, "He's the grandson of one of the Board of Directors. Wanted a job in the Mill, but not one where he might get dirty. They stuck me with him. As if I don't have enough to deal with...." He led the officers down a long hallway to a small interview room behind his own desk. "Have a seat. What can I help you with?"

Lt. Wesner started the discussion, trying to make it sound more like a collaborative idea swap and less like the official inquiry it was. "Regarding your missing worker, Anton Wojcik: at the present time, we can only proceed as if we are following up on a missing person report. That is, unless you have more information." Tripp shook his head. "For instance," continued Wesner, "did your own security department find anything we should know about? And how long did they continue investigating before we were called in?"

Tripp's lips started to form different words, but none came out. Finally, he said, "Our security team hit some dead ends early on, so they did not spend a great deal of time investigating before bringing you in."

Sgt. Friedman said, "All we got was a brief two-page report from your office. It wasn't even signed by your Chief of Security. Do you have anything in writing from him? I think we should speak directly to him for his view of the facts."

"I agree, Sergeant, and the foreman of the missing man, too," added Lt. Wesner. "Further, we think it would be helpful to examine the scene where Anton Wojcik was last seen alive, don't you, Mr. Tripp?"

Tripp's head was swimming. "Well, I…surely you can understand…not all the people you want to interview work the same shift…dangerous area…can't just shut it down…most irregular…."

Sgt. Friedman said, "I think you're just the guy to cut through any red tape and get us in there." Wesner nodded his agreement. "How many other missing person reports have you had in the last year, Mr. Tripp?"

Jonas Tripp was squirming mightily on the slippery silver steel chair. "Red tape…yes…no, no other people missing, I don't think."

"How many people died in the mill over the past 12 months?" questioned Wesner.

"Ah…well…we had…you see we have over 4000 employees, Lieutenant. Some die at work of natural causes, not related to their job."

"Yeah, I get it. People die all the time. How many died here in the last 12 months?"

"I'd have to check the files...."

"Give me an estimate," the Lieutenant pressed, recognizing the reluctance to answer. "I won't hold you to a number as a witness. Whadya think, five? Ten? Twenty? More?"

Tripp was alternately sinking into his chair and jumping with each guess Wesner made. "No! No, certainly not that number. Purely a guess, mind you, but I think it may have been six or seven men, in the past year or so. We prefer not to keep an accurate rolling number over a twelve-month time frame. That sounds rather macabre. So, yes, six or seven sounds right. But as I said, not all were factory related incidents." Tripp regained some composure. "For instance, a few months ago a man working the 3rd trick died of a heart attack. Unfortunately, as the heart attack was occurring, he fell into the acid bath which greatly disfigured the corpse and made a legitimate autopsy all but impossible."

"Holy shit!" said Sgt. Friedman. "Yeah, I guess that made identifying anything fairly difficult."

Wesner asked, "You said he was working the third trick. I've heard that term before. What defines a trick?"

Tripp said, "We run three shifts, the mills are constantly working, 24 hours a day. The first shift, what we call a 'trick', is 7:00 a.m. to 3:00 p.m., making it an eight-hour work day. The second trick runs from 3:00 p.m. to 11:00 p.m., and the third trick is 11:00 p.m. to 7:00 a.m. Everyone gets 30 minutes for lunch in the middle of their trick. There are constantly workers in motion in the mill, constant production."

"Do you ever ask anyone to work overtime," questioned Sgt. Friedman.

Tripp nodded. "Yes, there are times when the work load piles up, or we have a manpower shortage for whatever reason--"

"--Like a swim in the acid," interrupted Wesner.

Tripp shot him a look. "Or if someone calls in sick. Then a worker may be asked to work a second trick. It's called working a double."

"A double," said the Sergeant, "even if he's only needed for a couple hours?"

Tripp straightened up, regaining the position of the person with the expertise. "A Steel Mill is a dangerous place, as we've already been discussing. We cannot have individuals begin a shift then, two or three hours later, be dismissed for the day. We would lose track of where anyone might be at a given time, casually wandering in and out of the plant in an unauthorized or unsupervised manner. No, that would not do. Far too dangerous. If you start a trick, you must remain until the end of the trick—resulting in a full 16-hour work day for someone on a 'double'."

Lt. Wesner smirked, saying, "I'm sure the Steelworker's Union also prefers that any overtime be for an entire eight-hour trick. Don't you pay time-and-a-half for overtime?"

"In any event," Tripp said, trying to regain control of the conversation, "despite the dangers inherent in the work, we have relatively few fatalities related to the operation of the mill. Frankly, there are very few injuries."

"Is there an infirmary, a doctor on premise, to handle those few injuries?" asked Sgt. Friedman, who was irritating Mr. Tripp by making written notes of all his responses.

"There is a Licensed Practical Nurse on duty most hours. There's a small office in the Security shed where most injured workers can receive treatment for minor wounds. If more assistance is required, a squad is called and escorted to the injured party by Security."

The Lieutenant said, "We'll need to meet with that nurse when we interview the Head of Security. Let's plan on everyone meeting in the Security Shed. That way they can escort us to the cauldron where the disappearance took place. Let us know when you've arranged that, okay? Make it in the next 48 hours. Sergeant, look over those files quickly and see if there's anything else you need from Mr. Tripp."

.   .   .

Returning to the car, Sgt. Friedman commented, "I think that poor guy's head is turning to mush. Someone wants this thing brushed under a rug, but poor Jonas Tripp got us cops involved too quickly, and now we won't go away."

"You give a guy a promotion and suddenly he becomes like Sherlock Holmes. You're right on the money with that analysis, Benny—excuse me—Sergeant Friedman. Our Mr. Tripp is caught between his boss, or his boss' boss, and the Police Officers who he properly called but did so before he was then told to squash the whole investigation. Now he's trying to keep both sides happy but neither is satisfied. Ten bucks says if he's got a bottle of Scotch in his drawer, he just pulled it out."

Benny said, "OK, try this on for size. I think Mr. Timothy Ratterman may know more about what bad shit happens in the mill than does Jonas Tripp. Timmy smells dirty to me. And given his connection to the Board, I'd guess someone up there may know about whatever has happened. Or, at the very least, that someone is aware of whatever it is that we're dancing around."

Wesner pointed toward a seldom-used road. "Turn right, down the hill. I want to show you something. I'll tell you when we get there. So, you suspect Timmy, huh? You sure you're not just pissed at him for his attitude on the phone call? I pegged him as a rich punk who didn't understand his place in the pecking order of life. But you may be right about him. Let's check his record when we get back to the station."

Benny said, "Where am I supposed to go? There are things that look like they may be roads leading in all sorts of directions."

"Ain't that the truth. I got lost down here yesterday. Take that paved area second on the left. It will make a few hairpins around chain link fences, but try not to leave what looks like the main drag. And watch out for trains." Five minutes later after several twists and turns and one brief close encounter with a too-fast moving Rubicon Transit train engine, they arrived at the parking lot Wesner had visited yesterday.

"I hope you don't expect me to remember how I got here," said the Sergeant. "And whose train was that? The engineer wasn't about to slow down when I couldn't get out of his way. Where are we?"

"This is where I met a semi-informative parking lot guard who did very little work. He was in that small guard house over there, which now sits empty."

"Is there supposed to be someone in it?"

"I'm not sure, Ben. The guard said he worked strictly second trick, after 3:00 p.m., so I'm not surprised he's not at his post yet. I'm guessing whatever trouble they experience may begin after dark, making a guard unnecessary until then. Let's head to the station and hash this out. I get the feeling we may need to talk to Seazy again."

They started up the road leading out of the parking area toward a main city street when a dark khaki green Jeep with spotlights on the roof came careening around the corner and zooming past the cruiser. "Pull over here, Benny. I want to see something."

The Jeep pulled through the rows of parked cars, screeching to a halt in front of the biggest of the three trailers parked end-to-end at the back end of the lot against the fence. Three people got out, covered by unnecessary hooded raincoats from head to toe. They quickly entered the trailer. Someone slammed the entrance door behind them. The Jeep sped away, entering the Mill property through a security gate which seemed to raise automatically as the vehicle approached.

"What the hell was that?" asked Benny.

Wesner wrinkled his nose, "Yeah, what the hell, indeed." He looked back at the guard house. "I wonder if the watchman was called away so he wouldn't see that."

On the way out of the valley, Wesner pointed out the Steal Inn, explaining its significance, and noting there might be a need for a return visit there as well. They agreed to pass by Seazy's house at a later time.

■ ■ ■

Too much sun pouring in the window. Burns my eyes just sitting here at the kitchen table. Too much effort to move. Unusually bright sun today. Milky white sky. And hot, too. What is this, October? No. November, I think. Is there such a thing as Indian Summer? If so, I don't like it. Maybe not too hot for early November, but definitely too hot for my mood. The clinking of my spoon spinning in the coffee cup is noisy, not gentle. Gets on my nerves. Woke up late. What time is it? Oh, shit! Almost dinner time. Yesterday was a long day. First the cops, then the third trick. In between, what did I do? Oh, yeah. Stopped at the corner tavern, Big Ed and the patrol car, drove to the park opposite the house at night and…wished.

What will today bring? I'm not working for a couple days after tonight. Maybe I'll go somewhere, anywhere, far away from here. Escape. Run away from everything. Sounds good. What did that Lieutenant say? I should not leave town without permission. Why do I need his permission to do whatever I want, damn it? What does he mean? What constitutes a 'town' in his mind? Vague. Didn't give me a map with borders outlined in red. Hell, just driving down the street means leaving one city limit and entering another city or a different suburb, or crossing a county line without even knowing it. Does that violate his order?

Did he mean leaving physically, or mentally, or emotionally? Could someone be physically in one place but emotionally--even mentally--somewhere else? What was it they talked about in that

Philosophy class…a metaphysical presence. Yeah, that was it. Like in Hinduism, existing in the essence of the present--or something like that. Mentally somewhere else. So, I could be physically somewhere else, but mentally and emotionally still right here. Maybe the cop is a Buddhist. I don't understand the Philosophy of Buddhism, so I can't follow his hidden meaning. That can be my story, my excuse, my alibi if I decide to leave, to run away.

But where could I go? Everywhere I go I always seem to search for something. Search for someplace that looks comforting. Search for someone who looks friendly. Search for love. Never seem to succeed. People say I need to go do something different to take my mind off my troubles. They don't know what troubles I have, or even if I have any troubles, but they tell me to do something else with my time. Take up a hobby. Maybe go fishing. Find a lake, get a boat, catch something to eat. Calming. Gentle breezes.

Can't go anywhere now. Already late in the day, might be evening before I get there wherever 'there' is — somewhere--anywhere. Just have to turn around and head back. I hate fileting fish anyway. Messy. Not very good at it. Not as good as Uncle Raymond. He tried to teach me when we went on the fishing trip. He said I was lousy with a knife. If I did go fishing, then I'd have to cook it somehow, buy the necessary stuff for a fish fry, the go-withs. Maybe it's better to throw what you catch back in the water. Then again, what's the point of fishing if you don't catch something you can keep? Some say the point is just to be. To be in the boat, to be one with nature. Just…I don't know, to be. Hell, I ain't no writer like Shakespeare--'To be'! And I'm no Thoreau on Walden Pond. Ha! I do like my literature, though. Just like Anton.

Maybe I can find a book to read. What kind? A classic novel? A love story? Oh, hell, no. Something about history? A biography? I hate biographies. They lead to comparisons. When I was younger, they always said I should read a biography, read about someone famous, someone to try to emulate. They said I should be someone else, like the person who was famous enough to have a book written about them. I never measured up to those standards, their standards. Be like someone else. Be somebody who was worthwhile for a change, not yourself. I never could be someone else. I can only be me, as weak and pitiful as everyone thinks I am. I'll never have a biography written about me.

Now, Anton--he's someone who could be the subject of a book. Smart. Sensitive. Cares about people. People care about him. He could be somebody someday, if he survives long enough. If he doesn't blow it. If he can stop the obsession. I wonder if he can. I wonder if I can. Maybe I'm the one with the obsession, not Anton. Or maybe mine is stronger than his. Doesn't really matter, though. Neither of us will succeed, not without some miracle, some act of God. Why would God act for either of us? Maybe for Anton, but certainly not for me.

I don't think God acts that way, anyhow. If there even is a God. He clicked his fingers and lit a spark in the sky and everything just went into motion. Bang! From there on, everything happened as a big acci-dent. God rested. He had a beer. Went and played pool with the planets--eight-ball, side pocket. Some planets have life, some don't. Some life has achieved a level of reason, brainpower. Some life hasn't. Hell, that's true of mankind on this planet. Plenty of people exist with only half a brain, no sign of intelligence, with the inability to reason things out on their own. That's proof enough to show that God doesn't really care, doesn't take an interest in what happens here. If he was watching, if he cared, he would limit stupidity. He would make it so that people weren't so dumb. He should make it so life didn't hurt so much. Not just physically, but in the heart. In the soul. The burning hurts so much.

I need to get out of here. I wonder if the cops are still out front. That's OK. They can follow me if they want. I'll take them through the forest where the parkway fords a small creek. That's a nice place. They'll enjoy the ride.

■ ■ ■

"As I see it, Captain, we may have one case, or no case, or two cases or three cases. We can't seem to get our hands around what we've got," explained Lt. Wesner to Capt. Theo Mitchell.

The Captain shook his head and grimaced, pointing to Wes-ner's partner. "What's your take, Sgt. Friedman?" Benny

Friedman was just entering the room after making a personal phone call at the pay phone outside the building. The Captain insisted that each officer keep his own counsel on cases until definitive proof is established. And he insisted on getting each detective's opinion until that proof is known. Neither officer could influence the other, for fear of Capt. Mitchell's well-known punishments. He had no use for a detective who couldn't think on his own, or worse, for one who wouldn't let his partner share his thoughts openly. His latest twist was assigning an offending detective--one who was trying to force his assistant to agree with everything he said--to spend the next month walking the night rounds at the City Prison Workhouse situated down-wind from the swine rendering plant.

Sgt. Friedman scratched his head, saying, "I wish I had something to add to Wheezie's assessment. Whether we got a steel corpse or not is still an open question. Whether that mill has something they're hiding beyond the missing worker--maybe. And then there are these strange trailers and the mysterious drop off of three small guys in raincoats. I know we've had this case for less than two full days, but every time we take another step forward, we get shit all over our shoes."

"Well, when you two Sherlocks figure something out, please keep me informed. If we get more than one case out of this, I'll divvy up the work to some other detectives under you, if need be. But until you give me something beyond crap on your shoes, you're on your own. Now, please move with some alacrity. Understand?"

Sgt. Friedman looked at Wesner as they stood up. "I think he means to speed it up."

"Why, thank you, Benjamin. If not for you, I'd be reaching for my Webster's Dictionary."

Back at their desks facing each other, each grabbed one of the personnel files provided by Rubicon's H.R. Department. "Any next of kin listed in Anton's file?" asked Wesner.

"Nope. Totally blank. But I gotta believe it was left blank on purpose. It's too empty, if you know what I mean. I'm going to look up any other Wojcik's in the city alpha file."

"Good luck sorting them out. I'll betting there's at least 30 or 40 in this town. Maybe you should begin by picking about a half dozen likely candidates. We can call to see if any of them are related to Anton. Concentrate on those who live within 3 or 4 miles of the mills."

"Got it, Wheezie. Good idea. Although I suppose, in one way or another, every Wojcik I come across will be related somewhere in their ancestral tree. By the way, the clerk should be bringing up a file on Timothy Ratterman. It seems little Timmy has had some brushes during college."

"Aww, Benny. And he seemed like such a nice boy, polite and all. Hmm, there's a contact person mention in Seazy's file," said Wesner as he flipped through the few pages included. "Female. Doesn't look like she's a blood relative. I wonder...." Wesner touched the belly of the amber-colored glass horse and watched it leap away from his finger.

The Sergeant looked up from the papers in front of him. "You've got that look about you. What wheels are spinning in your head?"

"There was a point during the interview last night where Seazy got jumpy, irritated a bit. He mentioned that Anton had a girlfriend. It was almost a slip, because he tried taking it all back as soon as he mentioned it. He said neither Anton nor he would do anything to harm the girl, and we should forget he mentioned her. It was almost like Seazy was trying to protect her, too."

"You think there's a connection to the female listed in Seazy's file? You think it's the same girl?"

Lt. Wesner sat back as his chair screamed a request for oil. "Why does someone list a contact in their employment file? It's for someone to notify if there's an accident, right? In a steel mill, accidents are frequently fatal. Too many places where a misstep can turn lethal. Therefore, you make your contact person your next of kin or a close friend so they can plan your funeral, right? But this person who Seazy has listed does not appear to be his next of kin, and may not be the kind of person to arrange anything. That being the case, why would you list her?"

Benny was listening while reading through Anton's file papers. "Beats me. Maybe you want someone to weep for you?"

The Lieutenant smacked his desk with both hands with such ferocity that Benny jumped up out of his chair and the rest of the detectives in the squad room stopped dead in their tracks. "Yes! That's it, you wonderful little bald man!" The glass horse kept bouncing on its hook stand.

"Jesus Christ, Wheezie! You took ten years off my life, there. How about a little warning before you decide to erupt next time?"

Wesner looked around at all the startled detectives. "Sorry, everybody. You too, Benny. One of those Eureka Moments. We need to find Anton's girlfriend or the girl listed as Seazy's contact. May be one and the same and she may just be the key to all of this."

"All of what? I'm not sure I even know what *this* is," said Benny, reseating himself. "And just how do you suggest we find this girl, who is mentioned in Seazy's file but not in Anton's file."

Wesner pointed at his file. "I believe Seazy has listed Anton's main squeeze as his primary contact. Her phone number is here, too."

Benny looked at Wesner sideways, saying, "You think the girl listed as Seazy's contact is actually Anton's girlfriend? That's kind of weird, don't you think?"

"I recorded the rest of the interview after you left last night. You should listen to it later. He mentioned the girl and quickly tried to change the subject. There's something there. I tell you--."

Just then the lieutenant's phone rang. "Yeah, this is Lt. Wesner.... Oh, yeah. Hi, Thorpe. Good to hear from you.... Sure, you name the time and place for...huh. You hiding from someone.... OK, OK, just seems a bit cloak and dagger, you know.... Well, I'll bring Sgt. Friedman since we're working the case together.... Yeah, I know the spot. It'll be kinda dark.... Two blinks of the flashlight, got it.... 11:30 p.m., got it.... Later."

Benny's eyes were wide open. "Sounds like we got a hot date tonight."

Wesner nodded. "Security Guard I told you I met at that bar yesterday, Peter Thorpe. I asked him to get some inside dope on our two friends, Seazy and Anton. He wants to meet us tonight after his shift to share what he's learned."

"Someplace special, I take it."

"You know out on Whiskey Island, the old Coast Guard Lighthouse where the Cuyahoga empties into the lake. There's an old noisy railroad bridge crossing the bend in the river. He wants to meet under there."

Benny chuckled, saying, "That was the favorite spot for the mob gangs of the 1930s to deposit their recently deceased snitches. Can't say I'm having happy thoughts about an exclusive invite to a soiree there."

"Aw, now, Ben. I'll be there to protect you," Wesner replied sarcastically. "Although, I strongly suggest we wear our bullet-proof vests and strap on back-up ankle holsters. I think this guy is legit, but something has got him skittish. And the meeting location doesn't smell too good, does it?" Benny grabbed his city map to look for the best routes around Whiskey Island. Wesner sighed with satisfaction, and said, "In the meantime, I'll try to contact the mystery girl mentioned as Seazy's contact person. Here it is--Mary Stone."

"Sounds familiar. I've heard that name before," offered Benny. "Better check her for priors."

. . .

They knew they were in for a late night's work. The detectives
spent the late afternoon and early evening hours tending to personal or family matters, agreeing to return to the precinct a few
hours after dinner. Lt. Wesner picked up his dry cleaning. Sgt.
Friedman made another personal call before heading home to
finish painting the kids' bedrooms. Both detectives changed into
casual clothes and bomber jackets against the cold. In the event
anyone was watching Thorpe's movements, it would be safer if
he was seen meeting with ordinary looking guys instead of obvious cops in suits. Plus, it is easier to hide a bullet-proof vest
under a leather jacket than under a suitcoat.

On his way back to the precinct that evening, Wesner once
again stopped by the Steal Inn just to check out the clientele. The
same white-haired bar maid handled the dozen or so customers
all by herself. It looked like she relished her role, appearing fully
capable of breaking up any disagreements without any additional assistance. From his stool by the side of the bar, Wesner
recognized the handle of a short, wooden baseball bat within her
easy reach. Further down and more hidden was the butt end of
what was likely a sawed-off shotgun. A casual glance upwards
revealed two or three replaced ceiling tiles which were not as
smoke-stained as those next to them, those stained ones still
showing a few remaining pellet holes after a recent blast from
the shotgun fired from behind the bar. Yes, she was capable of
handling things all by herself.

Wesner nursed his beer quietly, trying to look like someone
who didn't care about his surroundings or the people in them.
Whether the barmaid recognized him from the previous day or
not, she kept scanning left and right far enough to keep an eye
on him. Wesner was practiced enough to look down at the bub-
bles in his beer while actually examining just about anything

else. His old football coach used to marvel at his peripheral vision, allowing him to see potential tacklers almost coming from behind. Today, he focused on the Budweiser advertising globe, where miniature Clydesdales pulled a red wagon round and round a golden light shaped like a beer glass. But what he actually concentrated on was the barmaid moving to the other end of the bar and pick up the phone, punch one number, and begin talking while she watched him suspiciously. As she hung up, two toughs came out of an office door on a landing half-way up the far wall. They were still wearing their steel-toed boots and dark khaki green trousers.

Wesner drained his beer, slapped a dollar tip on the bar and headed for the door. Two visits in two days were too much. She did recognize him and she remembered that he was a cop. This was not the time to get into something with a couple security guards, especially since they might have more friends behind the office door. He quickly headed for the Police Headquarters to call the number listed for Mary Stone.

■ ■ ■

Benny Friedman arrived on the 4th floor of Police Headquarters around 8:30 p.m. to find Alex Wesner sitting at his desk with an angry glum face sunk over his folded arms, and a paper dunce's cap on his head, courtesy of the second shift detectives chuckling around the edges of the room. Benny didn't say a word, just took his seat at the opposite desk.

Finally, after shuffling papers for several minutes and keeping his head down, Benny said, "I take it you figured out who she was. I mentioned her name to my wife, and she knew immediately. Apparently, you and I didn't watch enough TV back in the day. My wife said it's been off the air about four or five years."

Lt. Wesner was taking the ribbing in stride. He knew it would play better for the other detectives if he pretended to be angry. "Who the hell watched The Donna Reed Show? And what kind of jerk lists her daughter as their emergency contact?"

Benny stifled a grin as best he could. "Maybe he's got a thing for Shelley Fabares."

"Fuck you," Wesner whispered, "and fuck you all," he shouted to the room, tossing the dunce cap aside. The room erupted in laughter. "Maybe you assholes ought to stop watching so much TV and learn how to follow decent leads on your cases." The men groaned and guffawed. Turning to Benny he said, "Well, if Mary Stone isn't her name, what is it, and how do we find out? Some old guy hung up the phone when I called the number Seazy listed. We'll have to ask Seazy who it was when we drag him in again."

Benny said, "The guys in the black-and-white said Seazy's got a male roommate. We should stop by and see what he might know. He might even have a handle on Anton."

"And there's our plan for tomorrow. Did you remember your ankle holster for tonight?"

"Yeah, I got it on already. Our vests are in the cruiser's trunk. You sound like you're expecting trouble. I thought this guy was OK."

Wesner screwed up his face. "Peter Thorpe is ex-military-- with the Marines for a couple of tours. I got a decent vibe from him. But some of what he said led me to believe he's seen something of the dark side of this thing, whatever it is we're chasing. And that bar, the Steal Inn--that's where I met him. I stopped in again on my way here. It's not a safe place for cops or non-steel workers. I don't know. Maybe it's just me, but I got the feeling that they're dealing in more than buck-and-a-half beers. They seem willing to chase off anyone who asks too many questions."

"Huh," said Benny. "You wanna pay them a visit on our way to meet Thorpe?"

Wesner shook his head as he reached for his jacket. "Maybe another time. I'd hate to get into something that would cause us to miss our rendezvous on Whiskey Island. But I do think on our way there, we should check in with the parking lot guard again. He likes to talk, and we need to interview more people who like to talk to us. Let's take a run by Seazy's place first."

Dusk settled over the city like a purple shroud floating down from the hands of unseen pall bearers. Smoke and steam billowed from the bruised valley, struggling upward, seeking an escape from the stench and the heat and the flames of their birth. Benny drove the unmarked cruiser along the route they had selected, atop the cliff rim, nearly parallel to the valley below. Occasionally they saw a flash of some fiery action below which illuminated the bottom of the clouds, followed seconds later by one of the great roars of industry, only partially muffled by the valley walls. But living and working in this city conditioned the senses to block out the furious sights and sounds and smells. To the regular city-dwellers, the tortured night no longer registered any alarm.

A series of turns and the cruiser departed the major avenues and secondary roads. It now turned down a small, short, numbered street, barely wider than an alley, one of the hundreds of numbered passageways in a city which seemed to prefer anonymous numbers to memorable names. Benny slowed, struggling to pick out addresses in the descending gloom. Few houses lit their porches, and a third of the street lights were burned out or broken. Even at a crawling speed, the cruiser made a distinctive rumble like fingers drumming on a hollow table, the tires plopping over the uneven red brick roadway. A cobblestone road adds a certain purposeful charm to a neighborhood, but a red brick road as uneven as a homeless man's teeth simply admits the city has forgotten you.

"Even house numbers on my side, Ben. Must be toward your side."

"I picked out a number a few houses back. Should be coming up soon," said Sgt. Friedman.

The Lieutenant snapped his finger pointing at a small dark grey two-story to the left front of the cruiser. Benny slowed even more, now only inching forward as they passed by Seazy's residence. "Doesn't look like anyone's home. No car in the drive, no lights on, door closed tight," said Wesner doing a quick inventory.

"Should we take a look out back?" questioned Benny.

"Not yet. We really don't have a reason to search, and without a warrant anything we discover might get thrown out. Let's just circle the block and take another slow drive by."

On the second pass, Benny actually stopped the car, retrieved a camera from the trunk, and quickly snapped off a half-dozen shots trying to capture the essence of the place on 35mm film. As they moved on, the detectives recalled their impressions: needed paint; screen hinges looked slightly off kilter; looked to be an old place, easily over 70 years old and with sections obviously added-on in the distant past; second-floor window had curtains, could be bedroom; driveway had two cement tire ramps, grass between; not a great lawn, but recently cut; no broken windows; no obvious signs of roof or gutter disrepair. All in all, the place looked to be decently cared for. Seazy was not living in a dump.

"Remember that parking lot hut down at the mills? Let's go see if that guard is there. We're still in the second trick window," suggested Lt. Wesner, "and we've got just over an hour before we meet with Thorpe."

You got questions for that parking lot guard?"

"I'm kinda hoping he'll beat his gums some about what he's doing there," said the Lieutenant. "This may have nothing at all to do with our missing Anton and even less about what Thorpe will tell us, but there's something fishy about those trailers we saw."

"I was hoping we'd get back to them. Why'd a Security Jeep drop off three guys there during the day, and then take off? That was very odd. I'd like to get inside those trailers to see what's up."

"Benny, Benny, Benny. You want to go jumping in everywhere even if you haven't been invited. If we ever get in to those trailers, it will only be because we have a warrant in our hands. And we'll only get a warrant with probable cause. Which is why we want to talk to our parking attendant--excuse me--guard to get more information. Remind me to get his name and address before we leave him tonight."

"Ooh! Can I ask him that right off the bat? Doing that first makes guys like him shit their pants and confess to stuff they maybe never did. Should loosen his tongue."

Wesner chuckled. "Okay, Ben, but please don't frisk him unless he puts up a fight. I'd like him to think he's on our side by cooperating, not have him clam up like a suspect."

Benny turned the cruiser down the mill driveway, a 40 or 50 foot well-maintained slightly curved two-lane ramp, wide enough for a couple semis to pass each other in opposite directions. At the bottom of the ramp, the parking lot sprawled to the right, a guard house at its entrance. The overweight and disinterested guard paged through a girly magazine while sitting on a chair which leaned heavily against the door of the little hut.

The guard looked up and waved them off. "You can't park here! Move on." As the officers exited the cruiser, the guard said, "Oh, crap. It's you, detective. Didn't recognize you. What now?"

"I see you're still employed," began the Lieutenant, immediately striking a fearful gong in the guard's mind. "This is Sgt. Friedman. He has some questions for you."

As the Sergeant took down the guard's personal information including his employee number, all which made the guard's stomach churn, Lt. Wesner wandered a few feet away, scanning the lot and focusing on the trailers lined up against the far fence.

They were very long, almost double-length, certainly not the kind of trailer people took on vacation. These were more like residential trailers, butted up tightly against one another. The windows had been blacked out by coverings on the inside. Stepping further aside to get a clearer look, the Lieutenant thought he spotted do-it-yourself passageways connecting the three trailers, the passageways partly obscured by weedy bushes placed to block the view.

Once he had the guard's personal data, Sgt. Friedman asked, "Does your supervisor--you said his name is Lucas Rowden--does he know you just read dirty magazines all day?"

The guard, now known to be Buddy Ward, cried. "You're not gonna tell him about that, are ya'? I was just takin' a short break. I regularly walk around the lot, makin' sure there ain't nothin' bad goin' on."

Lt. Wesner said, "Why don't we take that walk with you? We can talk some more as we walk. Let's go."

"Wait! Uh, you can't go in there, see? Private property, see? Only employees allowed."

Friedman said, "But we're the police. We can go wherever we want. Isn't that right, Lieutenant? Unless, of course, there's something Buddy here doesn't want us to see."

Before Wesner could respond, Buddy Ward pleaded, "You can't! You just can't! Rowdie will have my ass if I let you in!"

"Half the lot is empty. Why is that?" asked Lt. Wesner.

"The lot's big enough for workers from both tricks. Guys comin' in for third trick can park while guys from second shift are just gettin' ready to leave. Room for both sets of cars."

"What's with the trailers back there?" asked Friedman.

"Some guys sleep in them. They pull a double--16 hours straight on the job. Rather than going home for eight hours and coming right back here, they sleep in the trailer, then they're ready for their next shift."

"So, what's in the trailers? Just cots and stuff?"

"I…I don't know. Never been in one. Just what I been told, that's all I know."

"You said 'Rowdie' wouldn't like us inside the lot," said Wesner. "Is that your boss?"

"Yeah, Lucas Rowden. I don't wanna mess with him. He's the Head of Security here and he don't take nothin' from nobody and what he says is the law around here."

Friedman said, "Jeez, sounds like he's pretty tough. Ever get physical with anyone?"

"Shit, yeah! One time…." Realizing he was saying too much, Buddy changed his tune. "I mean, no, nothin' I ever saw. He's just…he's just real demanding, you know? Runs a tight ship."

"How can I get in touch with this Rowdie fella," asked Lt. Wesner. "Leave word with you, maybe?"

"No! I don't want him to know I even talked to you guys. You gotta leave. He may make his rounds any minute. You wanna talk to him, call the main office."

"Sounds like we're getting the brush-off, Benny. Let's head out. Okay, Mr. Ward. We might stop by to see you again some time, but for your safety, let's neither of us mention to anyone that we had this little conversation. I'd hate for 'Rowdie' to get angry with you. Call me at the number on this card if you want to talk."

Back in the cruiser, Benny asked, "What do you make of those trailers?"

"I don't know. Could just be bunk houses for the guys pulling double tricks. Or they could be something else entirely. Those trailers are not that old, but even so somebody spent some serious money to buy them and put them there, and then join them together. Did you notice the connectors from one to the other?"

"I did. Kind of awkwardly built, but effective, nonetheless. Someone could go from the front of number one to the rear of number three without ever stepping outside--without ever being seen."

Wesner said, "Yes, sir. Just what I was thinking. Well, we've got about 30 minutes to kill before our meeting. Find a blind turn so we can put our bullet-proof vests on without being watched. Then, if you think you can, find your way toward our meeting spot in the dark around these back roads down here without getting lost. They snake around between the mills and the oil refineries. Not sure what's a road and what's not. I just think the more we become acquainted with the area, the more we'll be able to understand what's going on."

Benny replied, "It'll be a bit tougher than it was this morning since there are no street lights or road signs, but I think I can dead-reckon us north toward Whiskey Island without falling into the river."

After a brief stop to get outfitted with their vests, Wesner said, "Take your time. Let's eyeball everything as we go. And watch out for trains. The engineers don't expect to see cars down here this late…and they don't seem to slow down even if they do see them."

"Yeah, I found that out earlier when it was daylight. The mills run mostly switcher engines, don't they? Quick little diesels for moving just a small line of cars to switch from one track to another." Benny mused, "I called some of the guys at the local precinct house. They said the engines with RT on the side are from Rubicon Transport, specific to Rubicon Steel. The inside joke is that the RT stands for Rip and Tear, because they have a tendency to crash into anything in their way, or even run off the rails."

"Wow. You just made me question this nighttime back-road trip and your ability to manipulate around in the dark while avoiding renegade train engineers."

"Not to worry," deadpanned Benny. "My driver's license is probably not expired or anything. I've got your well-being uppermost in my mind. Besides, they'll pour some hot steel shortly and the glow will light up everything."

"Yeah," mumbled Wesner, "like fires burning in your soul."

As predicted, a yellow-orange explosion soon illuminated the valley, followed by a muffled roar sounding like a wounded dragon. Bathed in the acrimonious color and frightened by the approaching cruiser, the last vestiges of valley wildlife scurried about seeking cover from possible predators, hiding from their own fears. Rats as large as house cats slipped into any hole they could find; emaciated raccoons sought cover in the sparse underbrush; almost fearless coyotes stood stock still, evaluating whether there might be an actual threat and which direction might provide safety. Even though the mills were operating, there was no sign of human life. It was almost as if the factory was running by itself, automatically melting ore into molten steel, pouring the lava into train cars, turning the bars into rolls of steel for production, not actually requiring any human hands.

The glow from the pouring steel painted everything in sight a dirty rusty orange-brown. Mill structures, smokestacks, abandoned train cars, broken pavement, empty dirt-covered fields-- all appearing as an odd still life in a dark bronze relief--an imaginative artist's cast of what might remain after all existence on earth ceases, only to be discovered by some future evolutionary society who would puzzle over the stupidity of their ancestors. An afterglow flickered orange throughout the valley, not only from the mill, but now from the methane burn-off stacks from the nearby oil refinery, a symbiotic cousin feeding off the success of the production of steel. The ugly valley was the obscene offspring of the incestuous relationship between the two industries. Neither had a reason to exist without the other.

Scrub-brush shrubs and tenuous trees clung to the bottom edges and ledges of the cliffside, a testament to the irrelevance of any attempts at landscaping or manicuring, yet proof that even the scrawniest living thing somehow clings to a margin of life, no matter how feeble or unlikely its longevity. The distorted branches provided skeletal margins to the bronze relief captured by the flashes from pouring steel.

"Can we get out of here? This valley is spooky," said Benny.

"Hell, yes. What's the best way to Whiskey Island?"

"Truth be told, we need to stay on this path and cross bridges over the river a few times. The Cuyahoga winds like a snake through here, but we're almost out of the heaviest steel mill areas. We need to get past the Hulett Unloaders. I think if I turn left here, we start to get clear."

"Do it. This place makes my skin crawl. You know there are thousands of people working in those buildings, but out here there is no sign of human life, only the sound of machines operating on their own initiative, and nasty diseased critters fighting over whatever is left to scavenge. I'm not sure it's any different in the daylight, but even the bums don't come down here at night. Spooky is the correct term."

It took Sgt. Friedman another 15 minutes to zigzag through the angled and stunted alleys, remnant half-roads or broken paths leading to the aging small factories and suspicious warehouses built chock-a-block along the edges of the dark river. Eventually, he turned onto Whiskey Island Parkway, which in no way resembled any other parkway known to the Western World. Dark and foreboding, barely paved and barely two-laned, bordered by side piles of slag left by unknown parties for unknown reasons. The parkway was poorly lit, with only two or three distantly related street lamps giving off faintly yellowish glows.

Lt. Wesner peered through the gloom. "There's the old railroad bridge on the right. Thorpe said he'd meet us under the bridge."

"Pretty damn dark under there. You got our flashlights?" asked Benny.

"Yup. And make sure your weapon is within reach. The one on your ankle, too."

Just as the cruiser turned off its lights and pulled onto gravel some 50 feet away from the rendezvous spot, another vehicle sprinted from under the bridge, headlights off, spewing cinders and slag in its wake, fishtailing up the parkway at high speed.

"Sonofabitch!" screamed Benny as Wesner jumped out of the passenger side, gun aimed at the fleeing car.

"You get a make on that?"

"Hell, I'm not even sure what that was. No lights, no license plate visible, couldn't even give you a make, model or color," said the Sergeant, still half shaken. "Give me one of the flashlights. Let's see if your guy is still here."

The Lieutenant flashed twice into the gloom as per the instructions. No response. "Got a bad feeling about this." Both men turned their flashlights on full beam while pulling their handguns, safeties off. Halfway under the bridge and off to the right on the edge of a pile of discarded tires lay the apparently lifeless figure of Peter Thorpe.

"Over here," said the Lieutenant. "Make sure there's no one in the shadows on the other side." Wesner checked for a pulse. "He's still alive! Call for an ambulance!"

"I can't get a radio signal under this bridge," said Friedman, discarding his walkie-talkie while rushing back to the cruiser.

The Lieutenant did a quick check for wounds and found blood oozing from Thorpe's side. "Looks like a knife wound, and his head's been bashed in pretty good."

Friedman repositioned the cruiser so that the headlights illuminated the area under the bridge, and he turned on the police flashers so they could be spotted. "Got a squad on the way. Here's a blanket from the trunk."

They made the unconscious Thorpe as comfortable as possible under the circumstances and waved the arriving EMTs to the spot. Turning over the medical treatment to the professionals, the detectives started looking for any clues left behind by one or more assailants.

"There must be over a hundred old tires down here," said the Lieutenant.

"I'm not eager to see what ugliness might be under them," added the Sergeant. "Wait! Did you see that?" He pointed his flashlight at the tires toward the far end, deeper in the shadows, that started to roll slightly off the pile. Once again pulling his weapon he shouted, "Come out of there! Show your hands!"

Slowly and awkwardly, a thin wretch of a man, skin the color of the tires, emerged from under the pile, trying unsuccessfully to keep his hands in the air as he stumbled to keep his balance. "Don't shoot. I'm trying to come out." He wrenched his shirt around and pulled up the rope-belt on his pants. His clothes were either two sizes too big or he was two sizes too small.

"What the hell are you doing under those tires?" asked Lt. Wesner.

"Well, the plan was to find a semi-comfortable, semi-warm place to spend the night. Didn't much expect a floor show."

"Are you drunk?"

"Not yet. Got a nice pint in my pocket, here. Kinda thought it'd be a fine nightcap, expecting I could have this place all to myself. Then guests started arriving. I wasn't in a sharing mood, so I hunkered down waiting for some peace and quiet. Then, you two went to lighting everything up with your headlights and flashers, which definitely ruined the ambiance. I'll just mosey on down here a piece…." He turned away from the detectives, aiming his nose toward the darker shadows beyond the bridge.

"Hold on there, buddy. You stay put. Did you see what happened here tonight?"

"Well, you got here and tried to help that guy. Then come that ambulance. Then you found me."

Sgt. Friedman took over the questioning. "Before we got here. What did you see then?"

"It was pretty dark until you lit up the place."

"But you could still see what was happening, right?"

"Expect so."

"I can keep you standing here all night long, and I can take your pint away and drink it myself. Or you can start cooperating better than you have. Now, what did you see?"

"Don't take my pint! Please? Okay. The dead guy there on the ground, he gets here first. Just walked in with a small flashlight. Then waited. There was a distant car horn beep that seemed to get his attention. A few seconds later, this Jeep pulls up."

The Lieutenant jumped. "Jeep? Are you sure?"

"Well, it didn't have its lights on, but it was like what I used to drive while in basic training. These two guys jump out and start arguing with the dead guy. Told him to keep his mouth shut. Things got a bit tense, a bit physical. You know, punches start flying and stuff. Then one of the two guys pulls a knife. Big one, you know? Looked almost like a bayonet. Saw a flash on the blade. The dead guy lets out a cry. He goes down and the other guy crushes his head with one of them big rocks over there. They get back in the Jeep just as your car pulls up and they floor it. You know the rest."

"You get a look at the two from the Jeep?"

"You mean could I identify them in a lineup? No way. Too dark."

The Sergeant asked, "License on the Jeep? Any words or names from the argument?"

"Couldn't see a license if I wanted to, and I didn't want to. I don't especially want to see you guys either. As far as what was said, the two from the Jeep wanted the dead guy to keep his mouth shut, like I said. Someone's name was something like Thorpe--you know like old Jim Thorpe, the athlete. That's what I recalled at the time. And someone said 'Don't be so rowdy', or something like that. I wasn't trying to eavesdrop, you know. I was trying to be real still and quiet. Then you two come along and ruin a perfectly fine evening."

One of the EMTs ran over and said, "He's hanging on by a thread. We're taking him to Metro right now."

The Lieutenant responded, "Make a note if he says anything. We'll follow shortly."

"He'll be lucky to keep breathing, let alone talking," said the EMT rushing to the ambulance.

In the meantime, two black and whites pulled up, light flashing, along with another detective cruiser driven by the Captain. He jumped out and said, "We monitored your call for the ambulance and figured we ought to come and see what you got yourselves into this time. Who's this fellow?"

The Lieutenant said, "He's just about to tell us his name and address."

"Aw, crap," said the bum. "I suppose I'd lose my pint if I don't cooperate, huh? Okay. My name's Cyril Herman. Everybody calls me Butch."

The Sergeant asked, "What's your address, Butch?"

Butch looked around, "This bridge got a name or number? Closest thing I got to a home."

The Lieutenant asked, "You were in the Army, right? I'm going to ask these uniformed officers to take you to a special place with a warm bed and a hot meal that caters to vets. The officers will be busy for a little while taping up the scene, so you can put some of that pint to good use. Can't drink it in the place where you're going."

The uniform officers came forward. The Lieutenant asked them to tape off the area and search for a possible weapon, likely a knife, or any other pieces of evidence, before they escorted Butch Herman to more comfortable quarters.

Captain Mitchell stepped aside, motioning Wesner and Friedman to join him. "I assume you didn't get a chance to question your guy."

Lt. Wesner said, "It looks like Thorpe went down just as we arrived, no chance to learn what he wanted to talk about. If the knife didn't do him in, then the rock probably did. Looked like he got hit with a ten-pounder. But we'll head over to Metro General to see if he makes it."

"Did you eyeball anyone besides this guy, Butch? Should we haul him in as a suspect?"

"He was more a witness than a perpetrator. Hiding under the tires when the attack took place. We did see a vehicle pull away fast, no lights, just as we pulled up. Butch says he thinks it was a Jeep. We think our bad guys were in that vehicle."

"More than one?" asked the Captain.

"Butch said two guys roughed up Thorpe and left him for dead. That's all we have to go on. Butch is a veteran. We'll send him to the Veteran's Rescue Mission over on West 25th. We can keep tabs on him there."

The Captain scanned the area. "I'll get another team to check out the forensics, see if there are any cameras anywhere near this god-forsaken place. This is now officially a second possible crime--the guy in the vat of hot steel, and now an attempted murder." He peered over the murky river's edge. "Jeez, it is really creepy dark down here. And the river smells like crap and death." He turned back, saying, "You two will have the lead on this, but I'll put Angel and Georgie on this as your back-up. Got it?" As with most of Captain Mitchell's decisions, there was no room for dissent, not that Wesner or Friedman had any objections. They recognized that this case was growing bigger by the hour.

■ ■ ■

The detectives arrived at the hospital emergency room just as the EMT team was getting back into their truck. Sgt. Friedman asked, "How bad is it?"

The ambulance driver lifted a fresh oxygen tank into the ambulance. "That's one strong dude. They've got him stabilized and stopped the immediate bleeding. He's up in surgery now to repair any internal damage. They'll check out his skull as soon as the knife wound has been mitigated. And, no, he did not regain consciousness or say anything. I knew you'd ask."

The officers proceeded to the nurse's desk in the emergency room to gather Thorpe's personal effects: his wallet, identification and keys. The Lieutenant tossed the keys in his hand a few times. "Hey, Benny. You see another car down there under the bridge?"

"You mean where we found Thorpe? No. Can't say I saw any other vehicles. Why?"

"Got a Chevy key on Thorpe's key ring. If he didn't drive himself, how'd he get there?"

The Sergeant looked Wesner straight in the face. "I doubt he walked. I don't believe there are any bus routes that go down there. A cabby would have turned down the ride to a dark location like that, figuring it would end up in a robbery. If he didn't drive himself, someone else drove him. And not being certain we'd even show, that someone would have waited close by just in case a return ride was necessary. Someone else was there!"

The nurse at the check-in desk was just finalizing the personal information paperwork on Thorpe. "Make me a copy of that, will you," said Wesner.

The over-worked and over-stressed nurse never looked up, but said, "Honey, you can just go sit down over there until I'm ready to hear what you think you need or deserve. Until then, I'm not listening," pausing as the Lieutenant flashed his badge, "and you can just put that thing away before I grab it and stick it pin side first into your hand!"

The Lieutenant backed away and turned to find Benny already seated, reading a magazine upside down. "Sometimes you need to be able to read the room, Wheezie," he said chuckling.

Eventually, Lt. Wesner had a copy of Thorpe's personal information, although destiny had already decided that the night nurse from the Emergency Room would never be his close friend. No one at the hospital had the time to reach out to an emergency contact, so Wesner and Friedman volunteered to do so instead. "At least it's not Mary Stone again," joked Benny.

Ignoring the jab, Wesner said, "It's 2:00 a.m., getting awfully late. I hate waking someone with a phone call announcing bad news. Let's go pay a personal visit to Ms. Rosie Dwyer, the lady listed as Peter Thorpe's emergency contact."

Sgt. Friedman unlocked the cruiser doors and said, "So his name is Pete, huh? Where do you think we can we find Ms. Dwyer?"

"No address for her is listed on Thorpe's documents, but let's make a guess that she can be found at his place. Something tells me she'll be awake, worried about the man she dropped off under the railroad bridge earlier this evening. If anyone else knows about her, she may be in some sort of danger, so our personal visit has a double purpose. Head south down West 25th to Broadview. According to his listed address, Thorpe's place is on a side street near there."

Ten minutes later, they pulled up in front of a shabby shingled bungalow, indistinguishable from the dozens of other shabby shingled bungalows lining the street, each separated from the next by a single car driveway leading to an unattached garage in the backyard. Homeowner individuality was expressed by different colored awnings or awkwardly tended flower gardens or unimaginative lawn art. Thorpe's house had none of the kitschy displays prevalent in the neighborhood, but it was well manicured, thereby preventing any clucking or gossiping among the neighbors.

Wesner said, "There's a light on upstairs. Probably a bedroom, don't you think? That means Miss Rosie is awake, I suspect. Let's go see."

The heavy rap on the door followed by a series of rings of the doorbell generally send shivers down the spine of occupants, exactly the response the detectives hoped to deliver. Home visits are seldom social calls. At 2:30 a.m., the normal response from occupants borders on panic.

"Who…who's there?" came the frightened almost cry from within.

"Lt. Wesner and Sgt. Friedman, Cleveland Police."

A pause, then, "Put your badge up to the peep-hole. And if I don't see it soon, I start shooting."

Wesner motioned Friedman off the one-step porch and said, "Please do not shoot. I'm putting my badge up to the hole. Let me know if you want to see my face. But I'm not getting that close unless you put down your weapon."

As a precaution, Friedman pulled his weapon and took aim at the door from an angle not visible through the peep-hole. Wesner put his badge up, a few inches from the hole. "Satisfied?"

"What do you want?" the still distressed woman said.

"We're looking for Rosie Dwyer. She's listed as Peter Thorpe's emergency contact. We need to talk to her."

The door opened two inches, as much as the chain lock would permit. "Where's Petey? Is he alright?"

The lieutenant raised both hands and said, "He's in the hospital. It's pretty bad. We can take you there if you want, but we have some questions first."

She paused, then said, "Just a second." Closing the door to remove the chain then opening the door to permit entry, she was startled to see Sgt. Friedman on one knee, gun pointed directly at her. Before she could react, Wesner grabbed both of her wrists and yanked them above her head.

"Where is your weapon?"

Her eyes began to tear up as she cried, "It's in my hip pocket."

The Sergeant entered rapidly and pulled the gun from the rear pocket of her jeans. Wesner let go of her wrists and closed the front door. "Never put a loaded gun in the back pocket of your jeans. Jeans are generally a tight fit. Accidental firings do occur sometimes, injuring the owner. Let's sit down, shall we?"

"Why are you here? Why didn't someone call me? Where is Petey?"

Sgt. Friedman spotted a suitcase at the foot of the stairs leading up. "You planning on leaving town?"

The woman spun her head toward the suitcase, then back toward Lt. Wesner, causing the heavy black curls circling her head to swing. "I want to see Petey!"

Lt. Wesner's face took on what his fellow detectives called his "Pastor Smile", a calming, benevolent, almost prayerful expression that caused many a recalcitrant evil-doer to gradually confess to everything, including if they cheated on a 3rd grade spelling test. "We will tell you everything you need to know if you are actually a friend of Pete. But we don't know your name, so we can't really begin, can we?"

The logic and the Pastor Smile were too much. "I'm Rosie Dwyer. I'm Pete's fiancée, okay, maybe just girlfriend, but I love him and I'm worried about him." She began to cry in earnest. Sgt. Friedman spotted a box of tissues and put them in front of her as he verified her identification from the purse on the table.

"Alright, Rosie Dwyer. Pete's been hurt. It's pretty bad. He was both stabbed and smashed in the head. He's in Metro General Hospital. They took him to surgery where they stitched up the knife wounds best as they could. They're working on his head injuries now. The EMTs think it's pretty bad. We'll know more in a few hours." Throughout Wesner's description, Rosie's hands covered her mouth and muffled her whimpering. "Sgt. Friedman and I were supposed to meet Pete at a secluded spot. We arrived just as another vehicle sped away. There were some men in that vehicle that attacked Mr. Thorpe. We called for an ambulance."

Rosie said, "Can I go see him now?"

The Pastor Smile returned, "Soon. You see, Rosie, everything I told you about what happened this evening, I think you already knew. Isn't that so?" She looked into Wesner's face with a mixture of shock and alarm. "Rosie, Pete didn't just walk down there tonight, did he? You drove him there, and you waited up the road in a parking lot in case he needed a ride back. When a car came by you beeped a warning to him. But that wasn't us, it was his attackers. When a second car came by--that was us--you panicked. When the first car came speeding by, you tried to follow them, but couldn't keep up. When you eventually returned, you saw flashing lights and an ambulance. That's when you headed here. Tell me where I'm wrong." The Pastor Smile was long gone, replaced by a cold stare.

Rosie broke down. "Petey said it was an important meeting. He said he would be safe. That's why he chose such a place. I'm sorry. I didn't know what else to do!" She was now a sobbing mess.

Sgt. Friedman asked, "What about the suitcase? Were you just planning on leaving town and wiping your hands of Thorpe completely?"

"No!" She flashed an indignant stare at him. "We made a pact that if things went wrong, we'd both get out separately, heading for his cabin in the woods and meet up there. I was going to leave at daybreak if I didn't hear from him." She looked back at Lt. Wesner. "When I saw the ambulance, I knew something was terribly wrong, which is why I kept the gun handy."

"Alright, Rosie Dwyer. Let's get you down to the hospital. And bring your suitcase. I'm thinking getting you away someplace safe is a good idea, and that cabin may be just the place."

The news at the hospital wasn't great, but there was hope. Peter Thorpe was in a coma, thanks to the heavy bashing with a large rock. Luckily, his skull was intact, the rock likely striking at an angle rather than straight on. If he survived the night, his chances for recovery would improve.

Dawn broke just after 6:00 a.m. The second detective team arrived at the hospital to be briefed by Wesner and Friedman. Angel Lopez was a 15-year veteran of the force, promoted to detective two years earlier. Conscientious and a fast learner, Angel maintained his finely tuned physique daily, to the envy of everyone in the squad room. Almost six-feet tall and rock solid, his slicked-back black hair never mussed up. He exuded confidence and not a little bit of danger. Detective Lopez was one of the only Cleveland detectives fluent in Spanish, a fact which made him increasingly valuable to the force. Further, he had the innate ability to sense danger when it approached, and could separate truth from fiction instantaneously.

His partner was a newly hired detective named Georgina Chouteau. Det. Chouteau recently settled in Cleveland after a 10-year stint with the New Orleans Police Department. An attractive 35-year-old with jet black hair almost always tied tightly to the back of her head, she had a stunning complexion of undetermined ethnicity. As one of the only female detectives in Cleveland, she wanted to be judged only on her detective skills. She tried, as best as possible, to not appear too attractive, but nature refused to be masked. Unproven stories followed her from New Orleans: the unusually gruesome and ritualistic deaths of two known rapists occurred shortly after a whispered rumor that the detective, herself, had been assaulted; and no one in the NOLA Police Department could confirm or deny that the detective practiced the dark arts of Voodoo. Lt. Wesner hoped to find out if any of the stories about her Creole-voodoo past were true. He did not intend to explore the other more personal rumors.

The teaming of Lopez and Chouteau was one of the brilliant initiatives of Captain Mitchell, known for arranging his teams in unique ways which, to the surprise of his superiors, generated quick and accurate results. The Captain was interested in seeing what his old friend, Lieutenant Alex Wesner, would do with the now disparate members of his team.

Before heading home for some much-needed sleep, Wesner drove Rosie Dwyer to Thorpe's cabin, tucked far away in the wooded hills quite a distance east of the city proper. A rickety, rusted gate blocked a twin-rut dirt driveway which led off the old farm highway. A hand carved sign labelled the property as 'Tall Timbers'. The name was appropriate, as the cabin was tucked into a thick and deep forest of 50 to 70-foot pines and towering oaks. Wesner fought the urge to keep Rosie's pistol. Leaving the weapon with Rosie would make return check-up visits dangerous. But removing the weapon would take away any chance of calm comfort while lodged deep in the woods alone. Whether or not she was in any physical danger from Thorpe's attackers, the weapon would bring her some semblance of security which was better for her mental well-being. Without transportation, at least she would stay put until they could complete her background check and assure her safety. It was a more practical solution than putting her in a safe-house in the city, especially given her familiarity with the cabin and the woods.

The cabin cupboard and refrigerator were stocked with enough food for more than a week, and the phone was hooked up, although the number was unlisted. Either Thorpe planned ahead for his retreat or he spent a lot of time at the cabin. Maybe both were true. Meanwhile back at Police Headquarters, Detective Friedman turned over the files to Detectives Angel Lopez and Georgina Chouteau, giving them a quick update on what little was known. He then made a private call from a pay phone and headed home for something to eat and a couple quick hours of sleep.

WEDNESDAY, NOVEMBER 3

"My internal clock is all messed up," Seazy mumbled to himself. "It's from all those days--I guess I should say nights--working the third trick. Anton told me about it once. What'd he say it was? Circum-something? No, more like the bug, whatchacallit, the cicada. Yeah, that's more like it. The Cicadian Rhythm--no, that's not quite right. There's an 'R' in there somewhere. Cicadaranian Rhythm? Maybe that's it. My Cicadaranian Rhythm is all messed up. Can't sleep at night, hard to sleep in the day. Wonder if I should try to get off third trick? But the extra money for working at night is good. Hate to lose that. They'd rather not change my shift anyhow. They'd sooner fire me than shift my trick. But I gotta figure out how to sleep.

"Booze doesn't work all the time. Drugs…well, hell. Don't want to get into something like that. I think that's why Richie stays away. He was getting hooked last I saw of him. Scary to watch someone disinte-grate before your eyes. Huh. Funny. Hadn't thought of him for a year until that cop interview couple days ago. And now here I am thinking of Richie again. Spooky. I hope he's not a ghost coming to haunt me. No, he's not dead. Don't think bad things about people. If they are dead, they might hear you telepathetically and haunt you. That's what that one skinny girl said. Where did I meet her? Did we ever go on a date? Pshaw! No one dates me! At least, not twice. Where did I meet her? At

that carnival, maybe. Did we kiss? Did she let me make love to her? Or did I just imagine all of that. Yeah, probably.

"Let's see, today is Wednesday. Don't have to be at work until night. I should plan to go away somewhere after my work week is done. Where would be good? Stick a finger in a map. Somewhere within an easy one-day drive. How about Niagara Falls? Cross over into Canada. Maybe then just disappear into the Canadian wilderness way north of the Falls. Find a lake to live on. Deep in the woods. All alone. That's all I deserve. Be alone. Shoot. Should have thought of that in the Spring. Getting ready to snow up there now. Cop said don't leave town without permission. Think he'd say 'OK' to Canada? Maybe I should just give myself permission. 'I grant you approval to go into Canada! Have a nice life!' There. That's all the approval I need. All on my own say so.

"Would my car survive such a trip? Maybe, if I took it easy. Take surface roads, not the freeway. That'd be fun. See the sights! Route 20, along the lake shore. But what if Anton needs me? Hell, where is Anton? He never even left me a message. Although, I suppose I shouldn't have to wait for him to reappear before I decide to go do something. It's not like I'm his brother or slave or anything. Maybe he doesn't even think about me at all. Selfish bastard. Hate how he's always so 'Mr. Perfect', you know? Anton the Great! Anton the Wonderful! Anton the Brilliant! Makes me look like a real jerk. But let's face it, we're just not that close. Even though the cops seem to think we're some sort of buddies. I mean, sure, we hang out, we drink beer together. Go to some ball games, some bars. Trade off being wing men and fail to get any girls at all. Selfish bastard just ran away.

"I should go knock on her door and ask if she's seen him. No. Oh, no. Unh-uh. I can't do that. I'd screw it up and say stuff I shouldn't say. Just seeing her....Nope. That would really foul up everything, wouldn't it? Won't you have to do it someday? Won't there be a time? No. I don't think so. I can't. Too painful. It was too painful that one time. It'll be too painful again. I can't take it anymore. Where is that selfish bastard, Anton?

■ ■ ■

The four detectives now assigned to the case gathered in an interview room converted into a conference room to compare what they knew, what they suspected, and how the case was splattered in different directions. Lt. Wesner continued the briefing. "This afternoon, we've got the uniforms bringing in Cezary Ludzinski, who goes by the name Seazy Lutz. He's headed for Interview Room #1. We talked to him a few days ago, but that was before this latest twist with Peter Thorpe getting attacked, just as Peter was about to give us information about the missing steel worker and Seazy's partner, Anton Wojcik. The uniforms are also pulling in Seazy's roommate, guy by the name of Edward Rumplik--likes to be called Big Ed--heading into Interview Room #3. Don't know if he knows much, but it can't hurt to find out. To start, I'll take Ed. Benny, you take Seazy. See if you get a different story than what we heard on Monday.

"Angel, Georgie: you two choose which interview to join or just watch through the mirrors. Take notes. Try to take in a bit of both interviews to get a feel for these two. While we had Seazy in two days ago, this is a first for Big Ed. I don't think either of these two know much of anything about the murder attempt on Thorpe. They're more like witnesses on the missing guy, Anton Wojcik. But we'll see if there's more. I'd like your point of view. And, Benny, if you think it might be a way to shake Seazy, feel free to invite Georgie in to take a crack at him. I'm willing to bet women scare him."

Angel said, "Yeah. Georgie scares the hell out of me, so I'll wager Seazy crawls under the table."

Det. Chouteau growled in her deep-toned voice spiced by a slight accent. "You should be frightened, Mr. Muscles. No man is safe against the curses which can be conjured." Separating toward their assignments, the three men chuckled nervously.

None doubted her ability to strike fear in a suspect, and they were secretly concerned that her threat to conjure a curse was not simply false bravado.

Lt. Wesner didn't bring his Pastor Smile to the interview with Big Ed. He had a sense that Ed didn't much care for Pastors. Ed did not even have the decency to look Wesner in the face. Not a good first impression.

"My name is Lieutenant Alex Wesner, Cleveland Police. You were brought here as a potential witness. Do you understand?"

Sloppily spread across the chair and looking at the door to his left, Big Ed replied, "Yup."

You are Edward Rumplik," started the Lieutenant quietly, not a question but a statement.

"Yup." He still looked at the door.

"I bet guys call you Rumpy, don't they?"

Big Ed simply snorted derisively.

"The paperwork you filled out says you live at the same address as Cezary Ludzinski, also known as Seazy Lutz."

Big Ed jerked slightly at the mention of the name Cezary, but otherwise didn't change his expression. "Yup."

"You got a job?"

"Yup." Still looking at the door.

"You planning on going to work after this?"

"Yup."

The Lieutenant slammed both hands down on the metal table. The sound was as loud as a shotgun blast and was followed by a ferocious roar, "THEN YOU BETTER START ANSWERING MY QUESTIONS IN FULL SENTENCES!"

Big Ed leaped off his chair, his expression suddenly filled with fear. He plopped back down into the chair and literally cried, "Yessir. I'm sorry, sir!"

Behind the glass, Angel laughed aloud. He was almost certain that Big Ed had peed his pants.

In the other interview room, Sgt. Friedman stared at Seazy for several minutes in total silence.

"Why are you looking at me like that?" Seazy grew more uncomfortable by the second and started squirming and softly whining at a very high pitch. He looked left and right, over Friedman's head, under the table, glancing every few seconds at the Sergeant's eyes, fixed in an unfriendly stare at Seazy.

"Say something, will ya'? Please? Where's the other guy — the Lieutenant? I like him better. He talks to me." Seazy made himself as small as he could while whimpering under the constant gaze of Sergeant Friedman. "Whadya want from me," he whispered as a large tear rolled down his right cheek. "I came in with the cops in the patrol car when they asked. I didn't argue. Free-like. I came in. But this here--not saying nothing--it's like a torture. That's not allowed, is it? You can't just torture people for no reason, right?" He looked at the Sergeant hopefully. "Whadya want from me?"

Friedman cleared his throat, causing Seazy to jerk his head to the left and cover his eyes with his arm. "Where's Anton Wojcik?" asked the Sergeant.

Seazy let out a wail, "I don't know where he is but I sure wish I did 'cause then I could tell you but I don't know anything and I already told you guys that but maybe you weren't there when I told the Lieutenant but I don't know nothing — nothing--nothing!"

"Who is Peter Thorpe?"

Seazy looked squarely at the Sergeant. "Who? I never heard that name before."

"Ever hear of Lucas Rowden?"

"Huh? Who are these guys? Are they friends of Anton?"

"What about Timmy Ratterman?"

Seazy looked totally perplexed. "Anton never mentioned any of those guys. And I know most of Anton's friends. I never heard those names before."

"But the other day you said Anton and you weren't really that close. How do you know all his friends?"

"I…I…We're not…I mean…sometimes you just hear things, you know? Sometimes he'd talk about his friends. So, I guess I never heard those names before."

Friedman gave a wave to the mirror. "Inspector Chouteau wants to ask you some questions now."

Detective Georgina Chouteau entered and replaced Friedman in the same chair. In her husky Creole voice, she said, "Hello, Mr. Ludzinski. I need to determine whether you always tell the truth." She waved both hands in opposite directions toward Seazy's head, circling around as if his face were a crystal ball. She hummed discordant notes raising and lowering the pitch as her hands stuttered to a stop, then continued in motion as before.

Seazy sat mesmerized, mouth agape, eyes wide and unblinking, first focusing on one of her hands, then the other. His lower lip quivered, his fingers clenched tightly in each hand against his chest, not as fists but more an effort to secure his fingertips from whatever evil might escape this person who, to him, was obviously a witch.

The detective suddenly stopped moving, her hands slapped the table causing Seazy to scream. She looked straight at Seazy's chest, pointed and said, "Your heart! It says you are not telling us everything! You know things you should not know and should not hide. It will be better if you confess them. You must say what your heart knows. Now!"

His tears were now unstoppable. "I can't! I can't! Not now! Not yet! I promised myself. It would hurt me too much. Give me some time, then maybe I can say, but not now. Not yet!" He buried his face in his arms crumpled into the table.

"Where is Anton Wojcik?" said the detective.

Between sobs, Seazy said, "I wish I knew!"

"What secrets are you hiding? What is it that you cannot confess?"

Seazy shook his head. "No! No! If I say it, it won't be true. No. It's mine. My special…my….No! No one cares about me. Let me keep this one….No. No more! No more!"

Even Detective Chouteau was startled by Seazy's outbursts. Afterward, she shared with the team that, in her opinion, Seazy did have a secret, but it was not regarding the whereabouts of Anton Wojcik. Whatever was troubling Seazy, it was on a parallel to Anton's disappearance. And, as the detective put it, "It almost certainly seems to be about love--lost love."

She tried to calm him down by changing the subject. "Where is your family, Seazy?"

"Ain't got one."

"Everybody's got somebody at some point in their lives. Where's your father?"

"He's dead." After a long silence, Seazy added, "He died when I was like 10 or 11 or something. He was always busy, either working or trying to do stuff around our house. I remember him painting the outside, fussing with electricity, trying to rebuild the attic. Busy, you know? No real time for my sister and me."

The detective expressed surprise. "You have a sister?"

"Not anymore. Used to. She drowned."

"Oh, my goodness. That's too bad. How did that happen?"

Seazy buried his face in his hands. "I dunno. No one ever told me. Just after that, my mom disappeared. Dunno where she went either."

"When did all this happen, Seazy?"

"Few years ago. I dunno. I don't like to think about it." He sat upright and sighed. "We about done here? I don't think I want to talk anymore."

"Where's Anton?"

Seazy's mouth opened, his eyes closed and his face turned toward the ceiling. A high-pitched wail started softly and built in a crescendo. Tears streamed down his face. Amid the wail came the barely decipherable words, "I don't know!"

. . .

The four interrogators gathered for a debriefing and analysis of what they knew, which was not very much. Detective Chouteau sat cross-armed, looking glum. "He's very fragile. Reminds me of one of those antique glass items--so many different colors delicately brushed onto the thinnest of glass you're sure it will shatter if you breathe on it too heavily. I think I may have breathed on Seazy too heavily. I may have broken him."

Angel Lopez said, "Big Ed is just Big Dumb. He didn't understand the subtle sarcasm I hit him with and I don't think he ever paid any attention to what Seazy was into."

Sgt Friedman said, "I ran the names of everyone we've come across. Big Ed has some minor scrapes, nothing major. Same for our parking lot guy, Buddy Ward. Peter Thorpe left the Marines as a Staff Sergeant, lots of commendations. But his girlfriend, Rosie Dwyer — she's not quite as clean."

"How bad," asked Lt. Wesner. "She didn't seem to know which end of the gun to hold."

"Nothing so violent involving a gun, although there was one disorderly arrest. Mostly kiting checks, minor theft, DWI. Beat up her former husband after he got nasty physical with her. That was the disorderly. Nothing much during the past five years. Maybe Thorpe's been good for her."

"Beat up her old man? Good for her," growled Detective Chouteau. "I mean, assuming he had it coming."

Friedman looked up from his report. "Oh, he deserved it, alright. But I believe it is still a crime to knock out your husband's teeth with a baseball bat." He continued with his report. "Our homeless guy and witness, Cyril 'Butch' Herman, has a Distinguished Service Cross and Purple Heart from the Army. He was in the early deployment to Vietnam. Saved half his platoon in the early days of fighting in '64 or '65; other half of the platoon was wiped out. Butch sort of lost his way after that. I'd love to get him some help, if we can."

"Do whatever you can for him. How about those main office guys?" asked Wesner.

Friedman said, "Jonas Tripp is clean. Been with Rubicon Steel about three years; left City Power and Light to take his current job. No record or priors. Now, Timmy Ratterman--there is an interesting little fellow. A handful of delinquency charges, several sealed files, and more expunged records than might be expected for a young man, unless your granddad-who-is-a-board-member-for-Rubicon is the golfing buddy of a judge. Grandpa Ratterman, Donald F. Ratterman, is a winner, too. He has a few lawsuits against him pending, plus the I.R.S. has him on a watch-list."

Angel Lopez said, "You gotta introduce me to your contact with the Feds. That kind of information doesn't come easily."

"That brings me to our star of the day, Lucas Rowden." Benny Friedman smiled as he pulled several sheets from out of his file folder. "Lucas Rowden is 47 years old, and has led an adventurous life complete with a checkered history. Most of his Juvie Record from Arkansas is semi-sealed, but I was able to piece together a fascinating biography. Mother was a druggie who died a few days after his birth. Father was shot in a liquor store holdup when his gun jammed but the store owner's didn't. He bounced around some foster homes until a cotton farmer took him in at age 11 where he joined three other foster kids--two boys and a girl—essentially to serve as indentured servants for the farmer. Except for the girl. She was the farmer's maid and possibly his sex toy. Children's Services was glad to have four kids out of their hair, so no one seemed to check up on what was happening. The boys built their own bedrooms in the barn where they were told to stay, no matter the weather. They were expressly told to never enter the farmer's house.

"The Farmer's wife was a holy roller of some sort, and insisted that the boys take her to church every Sunday, leaving the farmer alone with the foster girl. The church preacher's daughter and Lucas were found kissing in the basement of the church one Sunday evening, which led to a series of beatings from every adult who could get their hands on Lucas. He was 15 at the time. As retribution, he took the broken handle of an ax, entered the farmer's house despite it being off limits, and beat the farmer around the head so severely that the old man was never able to speak again. Lucas grabbed the Bowie Knife off the old man's pants, rescued the foster girl--broke a few household items searching for the keys to the pickup truck, and headed toward Texas.

"Arrested in Texas and sent to Juvenile Detention until he was 18. I don't know what happened to the girl. There's about a 10 to 12-year gap where we lose track of Lucas after his Juvie release. Then he shows up in East Texas in the oil industry. Works his way up to Wildcat Foreman at an oil field where three men died mysteriously under a collapsed rig--which somehow collapsed a few days before the men went missing. Then some five years later he was the Floor boss at a riverboat casino in Kansas City. A couple big winners ended up with knife-gashes through their guts. They were found swimming face down in the Missouri River without their cash. That was just before he quit. Again, he disappears for a few years. Shows up again in Miami where he managed a boat dock for wealthy yacht owners. He had a way of procuring whatever the yacht owners might desire, legal or illegal. At one point, an apparent drug deal went bad, leaving two Haitians with their guts ripped open, found at low tide under the dock. Rowden's 10-inch Bowie Knife, which he always wore on his hip, was unavailable for examination by the police. He told Miami PD it must have been stolen."

Wesner said, "Knife attacks, you say? Both at the KC Casino and the Miami docks. What a coincidence. And Thorpe has a gut wound with a knife. How did Mr. Rowden get here to Cleveland, Benny?"

"Mystery of mysteries. Just showed up one day at Rubicon Steel and got a job as Head of Security for them. We need to request his personnel file to see who recommended his hiring."

Wesner shook his head, "No, we have to be careful at that office. Timmy could get wind of any inquiries and cover up what we need. I'll make a wild guess at who Rowden's employment godfather is, though. Ben, ask your I.R.S. contact if they are looking at any Texas oil deals by Timmy's granddad, Donald F. Ratterman. Georgie, make a call to the Kansas City police and see what they've got on those riverboat murders, I.D.s and details on the victims, and who the owners of the casino were at the time."

He smiled at Detective Lopez. "Angel, you get the best assignment of all. Catch a morning flight to Miami. See what Miami PD has on the Haitian murders. Then dress casually as if you belong there and go to the Marina. Talk to some of the regular dock hands and ask them if a Ratterman-owned yacht ever tied up there. Take some pictures of the area and the docks where the bodies were found. But be careful! At this point we don't know the good guys from the bad guys. If I'm wrong in chasing after Ratterman, well it's on me."

■ ■ ■

Even though the interviews had concluded a few hours earlier, Wesner put Seazy and Big Ed in holding cells until late afternoon to give the detectives time to conclude their debrief. Nothing of substance regarding either of the cases was learned. Eventually,

Seazy and Big Ed were released, again with a warning that neither should leave town. Secretly, both Seazy and Ed had doubts they would ever be able to leave Cleveland for anyplace else, no matter where or when. Individually, they both dreamed to escape to someplace wonderous, but real life events or frightening nightmares always seemed to block them from following the dreams. Neither would ever admit it if they did plan to leave, for fear that openly speaking of their plans would expose them to ridicule and make the escape impossible. Even so, the detectives didn't really expect Seazy or Big Ed to follow the direction to avoid travel, primarily because it didn't seem to matter one way or the other if they remained close by.

Seazy and Big Ed got a ride home together in the back of a patrol car. Ed leaned toward Seazy, pointed toward the driver and whispered, "Don't say anything. That cop will hear us." Seazy continued to look out the window with no intention of starting a conversation with Ed. A few hours earlier he was thinking about going to Canada. Now he was in the back of a squad car on a slow trip to his home. No, not his home--just his house where he had a bed. No, not his house. Someone else's house where Seazy put his clothes and personal items, kept fairly safe under someone else's roof. It didn't matter that he grew up with the mistaken belief that this house was his home. So, what? Not his place. Just the address on his driver's license. Nothing more than that. He turned further away from Big Ed. He shook his head thinking that he should have left for Canada as soon as he thought of it. Before they were summoned for the police interview.

Seazy belatedly realized he actually could leave any time he wished, because his foreman at Rubicon Steel called and said not to come to work. Given the circumstances of the investigation into his partner's disappearance, the Mill supervisors decided it was in everyone's best interest if Seazy stayed away from the Mill, far away from the cauldron. He wasn't 'suspended per se', said the foreman, and he'd receive the same hourly wage for staying away, since the Union would insist upon that. But his presence, his position on the cauldron—no one thought that was a good idea. Other workers wouldn't want to walk the rim with him. Given the circumstances, the foreman said.

The patrol car seemed to take the longest route possible on purpose, wandering up and down parallel streets like a cabbie trying to fatten up his tab. It finally stopped in front of Seazy's house. Without a word, Seazy jumped out and ran to the door, unlocked as always when Big Ed was the last to leave. He waited until the patrol car drove away, then gathered his keys and began packing up a few personal items, enough for a day or two stay away. Big Ed followed him through the house.

"What was that all about, Seazy," asked Big Ed. Receiving no answer, he continued following as they both climbed the stairs. "They're after you for more than a speeding ticket, Sleeze! What the hell have you done, Sleezy? Two cops came at me, first the Lieutenant then some big muscle-bound freak. Scared the shit out of me. What the hell is this all about?"

Seazy kept packing without responding.

"Where you going? I thought they said to stay in town?" Big Ed was frightened, his voice was warbling. And he was getting angry at Seazy's lack of response. "Talk to me, won't you? What's this all about? Why'd they ask about Anton? Don't you dare split and leave me holding the bag here." Seazy acted as if he didn't hear a word. "You give me no choice but to tell the cops everything I know. You know that, right? Right, Seazy?"

Turning to look at him, finally admitting Big Ed existed, Seazy said, "Didn't you already tell them everything you know? Big Ed, you don't know a damn thing more than your shoe size, but only if someone pulls it out of your ass." Seazy pushed past him, bounded down the stairs and ran to his car. He turned the radio up high to drown out the yells and curses from Big Ed standing on the porch. Seazy slowly pulled away from the curb and turned the corner, heading away from the city.

Following a hunch, Lt.Wesner had driven to Seazy's street, parking at the curb a few houses down the block. He had requested that the officer driving them home take a long, leisurely route, giving the Lieutenant time to catch up. After a few minutes, Seazy tumbled out of the house and threw a bag into his beat-up blue sedan. Big Ed screamed profanities through the front door as Seazy's oil-burning dented-up wreck slowly rolled away. Wesner followed a discrete distance back.

Seazy was in no hurry to get anywhere, lighting a cigarette at a stop sign and blowing a blue smoke cloud toward the afternoon shadows as he turned almost aimlessly along streets leading nowhere special. He seemed distracted, not looking into his rear-view mirror, not recognizing the following car struggling to stay unsuspiciously distant. Eventually he wandered South down the East 71st hill as it sank into the valley and connected with Canal Road. The road and the canal which lay parallel to it were remnants of the ill-fated Ohio-Erie Canal, abandoned only a few years after its original construction in the mid-19th Century, replaced by the industrious spread of the more efficient means of transportation--the railroads. To the north, the canal was dug to reach the factories and warehouses perched along the Cuyahoga River and eventually the shipping lanes of Lake Erie, where products could be distributed into what was once the Northwest Territories. In the opposite direction the canal veered Southeast snaking its way to join the Ohio River.

When it was in use, mules pulled the un-motored barges along the canal waterway. The path they followed later became Canal Road, bordering its namesake ditch. A gentle, casual two-lane, narrow enough to prevent heavy traffic or speeders, Canal Road is bordered by unhealthy land on either side. Marshy, even rumored to be dangerously measled with quicksand in spots, the poor quality of the land prevents the building of anything but the smallest of structures. After a few miles, the roadside surrenders itself to swampy parkland, some developed, but mostly not. It is the perfect route for a person seeking a casual wandering drive in the country, windows rolled down, ugly thoughts temporarily forgotten.

More than once, Wesner pulled into a gravel turnoff trying to increase his distance behind Seazy's blue, smoke-belching car. He gradually extended the tail to almost a half-mile, alternating between headlights on and off, trying to simulate two different vehicles. But, given the lazy pace, it was doubtful his prey would have recognized a tailing vehicle at all, even if it was as close as a few feet behind.

The slow-motion surveil lasted over an hour through yellow-leafed hickory trees and red-leafed maples, extending deep into farm country dozens of miles away from the city before the blue car abruptly turned back to the north at an accelerated pace. Dusk was falling, and it seemed to Wesner that Seazy quite suddenly had a destination in mind, someplace that might require a stealthy approach masked by looming darkness.

One by one, Seazy smoked his way through a pack of cigarettes, discarding the finished butts out the open window. Watching the smoke, the ashes and the flicks challenged Wesner's resolve, he having surrendered the habit less than a year earlier. The slow, two-car parade re-entered suburban sprawls and started to aim toward an older but still well-kept residential sector of the main city. Two and three-story houses pretending to be of Victorian styling squeezed next to each other lining both sides of narrow, neighborhood streets. Each house displayed a small well-manicured front yard with a bush or two, and a driveway extending to the back of the deep lot, ending at the obligatory but seldom used separate garage. Few of the residents used their front door, preferring the close-to-the-driveway side door as the main entrance. Wesner shook his head and smiled, remembering how his family had always done the same, placing heavy furniture as a block to the front door, especially during holiday gatherings. All family or guests entered through the side door, closer to the kitchen, carrying their own contribution to whatever planned feast the calendar demanded.

The blue car slowed as it approached a condensed residential intersection, then turned into a small tree-covered municipal park occupying a corner lot. Seazy drove in, past the "Park Closes at Dark" sign. Turning off his headlights, he slowly rolled to the front-most parking spot aimed directly at one of the fake Victorian three-stories across the street.

Wesner parallel parked on the side street slightly behind and to the left of Seazy, some 150 feet away. He scanned the park, anticipating a pre-arranged rendezvous for Seazy, but all he could see were the shadows of a few uneven swings, leaf-littered sliding boards and lonesome teeter-totters forlornly commiserating amidst the rustling autumn left-overs. On another night, if a bit cooler or later in the season, the spot might seem spooky. On this night it just felt sad, abandoned. The flame of a match lit Seazy's face as another cigarette was ignited. Wesner was fairly certain Seazy's cheek was moist. He tried to follow his quarry's intent gaze focused on the house directly across the street. The front windows on the first floor of the three-story spilled a welcoming soft yellow mat through the gauzy curtains and onto the closely-trimmed front lawn. To the side, more gay lighting, broken by shadows of people moving around in either a kitchen or a dining room. Seazy sat transfixed, head leaning on his left hand, his elbow perched on the open car window sill. It was obvious that Seazy would not move from that spot until his reverie was complete. In the tree-shaded glow from a streetlight, Wesner saw Seazy wipe his cheek and squeeze his eyes as his shoulders heaved up and down. It was one of the saddest sights the Lieutenant had ever witnessed.

After half-an-hour, Wesner could take it no longer. He pulled away from the curb and headed home. He wasn't sure what he had just seen, but he knew that sometimes people need their privacy to deal with whatever remorse troubles them. Wesner knew grief, what it felt like, what it looked like. He had known his own grief, keeping it buried for far too many years, avoiding far too many well-wishers who offered consolation for the unknown cause of his melancholy. He learned to hide it, to mask it, to drink it away — for a day or two. He recognized grieving when he saw it.

It was easy to see that Seazy was tormented by something, too. Watching him for the past few hours forced all of Wesner's own specters to re-emerge, and Alex Wesner didn't like it when those specters came muddling through his brain. He stopped at a late-night liquor store and bought a bottle of cheap whiskey. He was intent on drowning out the sorry spectacle he had just witnessed while simultaneously slaying the demons in his own head.

Thursday, November 4

Given the circumstances. That is what the foreman said. The circumstances being that Anton left me to take care of things and I guess I screwed it up. Actually, Anton screwed it up. Never trust someone to do exactly what you want if it is not in that person's best interest to do so. Well, what if he did fall in? Is that what people believe? If so, Anton won't care much now, will he? Maybe that's what we ought to let people continue to believe. I don't think Anton will care. Not too much.

I like spending the night camped in my car. A little snug, but you get used to it. It's an old car, so of course it smells pretty bad with the windows rolled up. But down here in the valley under the shade of these huge trees and bushes, at least it stays kinda warm. I used to ride my bike down the road into this valley, into where it dead-ends at the bottom where the trees get huge and the branches thick. I could just coast my bike all the way down. Going up — well, that was a different matter. Had to walk it up most of the way. Too steep to peddle up.

Lots of hot-rodders and gang guys knew about this valley — I guess it's more of a ravine. They'd come down here to wax and polish their cars in the shade of the big trees. At night, some hot-rodders would neck with their girls. Others, the gang guys, would buy and sell drugs. I could see a girl getting banged in the back seat of one car while an exchange of cash and grass happened in another. Cops would come down after dark to chase them all off. Didn't really stop anyone. I wonder if all those guys used to come down here when they were young and that's how they found this place.

Can't remember when we found this secret spot I'm parked in. We'd play some ball on the flat parkland up above, then run down the trails and cut through the trees until we stopped at the edge of Shit Creek. We all called it that. I think everyone knew it by that name. Comes by that name honestly — it's a filthy liquid run-off from whatever sewage spills out of the steel mill, so everyone naturally called it Shit Creek. We'd try to leap over it on a cable hung from the trees, or balance ourselves jumping from rock to rock to cross over the creek to the road. Falling into the rusty brown water was a curse of disease or death. The guys all believed we could get Polio from falling into that muck. Might have been true.

I guess it was that one time when we crossed over to the road, we found this secret hollow formed by black bedrock on one side and thick trees and bushes all around the other sides. In the center was this opening covered by leaves and pine needles, a natural alcove, almost like a cave hidden from view. Here in the center of the city less than a quarter-mile from houses and streets on one side and the steel mills on the other, we had our own secret hideout. We called it our Sanctuary. One of the guys thought calling it a Sanctuary was sacrilegious, but most of us thought it was a hoot. We loved sarcasm at that age. A half-dozen of us would find comfort and seclusion sitting around smoking stolen cigarettes and paging through porn magazines taken from an older brother's bedroom. Our Sanctuary.

If my car was any bigger, I might have had a problem fitting it into this space. It was snug, backing it in. Scraped the rocks on my left rear a bit. But once it was in, me and the car were all but invisible. I got a nice long undisturbed sleep. But now it's morning and I need coffee and a shower and something to eat.

Got to move out slowly to avoid any more scratches on my car. I can head to that truck stop on the edge of the nearby interstate highway. There are showers for long-haul truckers which I can sneak into. Plus,

I can get my first cup of coffee for the day. Since I can't go back to work at the mill, I need to figure out what to do with my time. Even more, I need to avoid any more visits with the police.

Niagara Falls is out of the question. Even if my less-than-reliable car could make the trip, I'd spend most of my time driving there and back. Not enough time to even visit the wax museum I heard about. On the Canadian side, I think they said. Can't remember who told me that. I'd like to see wax figures of famous people. Better than reading biographies of them. I want to see Marilyn Monroe in wax. I'll kiss her. I'd be afraid to kiss her in real life. I'd get slapped or something. Course, now that she's dead, I don't want to kiss her corpse. That's just weird.

Maybe they'll need me back at work tomorrow night. Maybe they will call and say its all okay now. You can come back. I prefer being punctual and reliable. If I said I will be somewhere at a given time, I will be there, maybe even five minutes early. If the mill expects me tomorrow night at 11:00 p.m., then that is where I intended to be. I give my word. My word may not be worth much to too many people, but being on time means something to me. It means I'm alive. A dead person is never on time, late for his own funeral they say. So, if I have to be at work, then there is no time for Niagara Falls, not this time. Anyway, I don't like seeing that much fresh water pour away never to return. I often wonder where it all comes from in the first place. I once thought someone left a giant faucet running and, given enough time, Lake Erie might drain totally dry.

Time for coffee. Here we go.

■ ■ ■

A weary and hung-over Lieutenant Alex Wesner arrived a half-hour later than expected. Captain Mitchell, trying not to show any concern, passed by his desk for the third time that morning and winced as he smelled the lingering odor of too much cheap whiskey. He motioned to Friedman and said, "Benny, gather your team in Interrogation #1 for a debrief with the Lieutenant, here. And bring him some coffee."

Benny said, "Okay, but Angel is on his way to Miami this morning."

"Miami? What the hell for?"

Wesner cleared his throat and croaked, "I sent him. Following a tip."

The captain glowered a stare at his old friend, then returned to his office without another word.

Sgt. Friedman turned off the microphone and recording devices before entering the interrogation room, and began the run down. "There are some sketchy details on the ownership of those Texas oil wells. Some of the ownership deeds are untraceable through a shell company headquartered in the Caymans. My guy at IRS thinks old man Ratterman is a part-owner, not sure how big a part. The IRS would love to confirm so they can collect some back taxes, but they are finding it difficult to get cooperation. By the way, the Texas State Police, the Rangers, would dearly love another discussion with Rowden if he ever finds his way back to Texas. They don't have enough reasonable suspicion to demand he be hauled in, but should he step foot again in Texas, they can hold him for 72 hours and conduct a big, old Texas-style interrogation."

Wesner rubbed his unshaved cheeks. "Huh. Shell company, Ratterman. Kinda what I suspected. Maybe when we get Rowden in for questioning, we can find a reason to send him to Texas." He looked toward Detective Chouteau. "Got anything Georgie?"

"Are you okay, Lieutenant? You look like you got hit by a truck," offered Georgie. She gathered her notes. "The Casino Boat is an actual old riverboat, refurbished and tethered up so it won't move. Some steel beams sunk into the riverbed front and rear--I guess that's forward and aft--stabilize it. The rear beam must have caught the bodies of the high rollers. They floated to the surface some five days after they disappeared. No sign of the take from their big winning streaks. Seems they each won about ten grand. Didn't have the chance to cash in their chips before they…cashed in their chips. Sorry. Bad pun."

"How'd they die," asked the Lieutenant.

"Bodies were badly bloated. Someone had stuffed a bunch of rocks down their throats as ballast, but a deep gut-slash allowed some of the rocks to leak out, which is why they started to float. Both bodies suffered the same fate. KC police don't think the two dead guys knew each other. One was some sort of broker, possibly involved in metal sales. The other was an engineer for an automobile company."

"They killed on the same day?" asked Sgt. Friedman.

Georgie shook her head, "The autopsy indicates there was at least 15 hours between, maybe more. Our Mr. Rowden quit his job as pit boss the day after the second man's disappearance. But who knows how long a time between the killings and the discovery of the floaters."

Wesner's attitude continued improving as he sucked his way through the remarkably bad coffee. "Another gut-slash, huh? Someone must really like their blades."

"I got a message from Angel," said Sgt. Friedman. "He caught a real early flight and is already talking to Miami PD. He says he'll be at the marina in an hour or two, and flying back home this evening."

Georgie crossed her arms and stared at Wesner. "You gonna tell us what happened to you last night, boss? I know we haven't worked much together, but I like to know what I may be dealing with if evil spirits start showing up."

Wesner smiled for the first time that day--maybe for the first time in several days. "Fair enough. I followed Seazy Lutz yesterday after he left the interview. He took a long, solitary drive in the country, eventually turning back at dark and ending up in the Cranwood Park area back in the city. I watched him as he stared at a house, don't know whose. I watched him cry. I saw him sob. I sensed his pain--felt it. Reminded me…well, reminded me of some of my own pain. Memories. It was too much for me, brought up some of those 'evil spirits' you're worried about, Georgie. So, I tried to drown them with some rotgut. You are witnessing the results."

"Jeez, Wheezie. You know you can always call me if things get bad," offered Benny.

"Yeah, I hear you. But it was late…and I kinda needed to be alone, know what I mean?"

Georgie moved her hands, palms open toward his face, circling as she approached. "Your aura is an odd color, reminiscent of brown mustard. It is poisoning your soul. We will conduct a ceremony, a cleansing of your spirit, when this case allows us time."

Lt. Wesner sat back, his mouth hanging open. "Uh, okay. Let's…let's hold on that idea for a while. We need to figure out our next moves. Benny, what's our plans for the day?" Even though he was talking to Sgt. Friedman, the Lieutenant didn't take his eyes off Georgina Chouteau, more convinced than ever that she was some sort of a witch. He could feel her black eyes boring into his skull.

She furrowed her brow, upset with herself for going too far. She had opened a box from her past, perhaps too soon for her new surroundings. Even so, she had spoken from the heart, realizing that the Lieutenant was suppressing something from his past—something which required special treatment. Her face reddened in anger and a touch of embarrassment for unnecessarily exposing her spiritual side before the others were prepared to accept her skills. She had not yet mastered the art of secrecy.

Sgt. Friedman was also backing his chair away from the unknown mysticism the new detective was exhibiting. He didn't want to make direct eye contact with Georgie's flashing black eyes, but he couldn't bring himself to look away completely, either. He said, "Yeah, OK, well, we've been invited, reluctantly, to view the Rubicon Hot Mill this afternoon--especially the area where Anton Wojcik was last known to be alive. They asked that we meet them at the Clark Avenue Gate at 1:30 p.m. They said they won't be pouring hot steel at the time of our visit."

"Too bad. I was hoping to see a pour first hand. Maybe on a follow up some time," said the Lieutenant. "Who all will be there for Rubicon?"

"Jonas Tripp will be our main contact. Also, the nurse who was on duty the evening of the disappearance, the foreman, and someone from their security detail. Probably not Lucas Rowden, although I did ask for him. Seems he's off investigating something in another area of the plant."

Wesner nodded. "That's okay. We'll ask some questions to make the security representative squirm, which will, of course, be reported back to Lucas Rowden. I want to make sure he is looking over his shoulder at every step. Georgie, please plan on joining us. I want your unique point of view."

Georgie was still nursing the embarrassment from her earlier comments. "My pleasure. But why do you say I have a unique point of view? Because I am a woman? Because you think I know voodoo? Because you think I talk to the dead or to the devil?"

"Calm down, detective. I'm hoping that as someone new to this town, you don't have any pre-conceived notions about what a steel mill is all about, and therefore can provide a unique point of view." The Lieutenant flashed his Pastor Smile. "As for your other attributes, if they are a benefit to the investigation, by all means please feel free to use them."

Det. Chouteau reddened even deeper as her anger morphed to complete embarrassment. Trying to regain some self-worth, she asked, "Why is there no Union Representative included in this visit? Shouldn't there be representation for the worker? They do have a Steelworkers Union in the mills, don't they?"

Bennie and Wesner looked at each other. "Damn! How did we not think of that?" said the Sergeant.

"Great catch, Detective," said Wesner, pointing at Georgie. "That is why you and your unique point of view are joining us. Benny, send Mr. Tripp a request to add a Hot Mill union rep to be present during our visit. In the meantime, I'm heading down to Tony's Barber Shop. I need a shave."

■　■　■

Detective Angel Lopez left Miami PD Headquarters without much useful information. It seems the murder of two Haitian drug smugglers who no one seemed to miss or mourn was not a high priority case for the over-stressed homicide department. Leaving Miami Police Headquarters, Angel parked the obviously rented car far away from the plush gated entrance of the Sunrise Harbour Yacht Club. He didn't want to look like an inquisitive detective. Then, he casually sauntered past the security hut toward the docks where the murders took place. Dressed in white linen pants and jacket and topped by a proper fitting Panama hat, he looked the part of a wealthy boat owner--or possibly an underworld crime boss. In Miami, the two were frequently one in the same. He scanned the veritable navy of triple-decked yachts, looking for any which claimed their home port as somewhere on Lake Erie. He puffed on a Cuban cigar while leaning against a stanchion at the edge of the main dock, casually turning toward the bobbing buoys leading out toward the Atlantic Ocean. As far as anyone could tell, he gave the appearance of an important but possibly dangerous gentleman simply taking in the sights. He passed pleasantries with two of the local dock workers tending to buoy lines tethered nearby, exchanging jokes in the Hispanic dialect common in the Caribbean. He offered a fresh cigar to each as they took a break from their work.

At first suspicious, the dock workers judged Angel to be an instant friend when the cigars were lit. The two dock hands casually excused the break from their efforts. They said none of the bigger boats would be moving for a few hours until the tide was right. Therefore, they could naturally take a short break to smoke such wonderful cigars with their new friend. Yes, they had seen the yacht of Senor Ratterman on several occasions in the past few years. No, it wasn't in port right now, but maybe in a few weeks as the weather got colder up North. Several boats from Lake Erie travelled to Miami in the Fall, just like Senor Ratterman's large vessel.

The dock hands said Senor Ratterman's yacht was very nice, very expensive, and too big for a such an unskilled man to pilot alone. He had a crew that lived aboard. It was so big that three men could bunk below and never be seen by the guests. The two dock men puffed on their cigars, and, responding to Angel's casual inquiry, said they were not on the docks the morning the two dead men were found, but they could certainly point to almost exactly where their bodies had washed up. Indeed, it was fairly close to where the Ratterman yacht was usually moored, but the workmen believed the yacht had departed the evening before the bodies were found. The other Ohio-licensed boat was still there, though, and they pointed to a large monstrosity named *The Full Nelson*. They did not know who owned this other boat, but the owner of *The Full Nelson* did seem to know Senor Ratterman.

They chuckled at the idea of being permitted to work on Senor Ratterman's yacht, or on the other Ohio-licensed vessel. Both owners were very particular about how their boat should be handled, and therefore had their own crews. It seemed that the ordinary Miami-based dock workers were not good enough for either of the two men. Some of the crewmen staffing the two boats even dressed alike, in styles that resembled military uniforms. The dock men said those crewmen were not very friendly and told the dock workers to stay far away, which the dock men were only too happy to do.

As Angel departed, the two men gave him directions to a small casita where he would find the most delicious Café Cubano. Only the local dock workers knew where the place was, but they assured Angel that he would be most welcome. Just say that Ramon and Oscar had sent him.

The Café Cubano was excellent, and the information was even more so, offered primarily because Angel seemed to be dangerous enough that withholding the truth could have deadly consequences. Angel frequently had that kind of effect on people, an effect he found somewhat baffling but very useful. He enjoyed knowing that one dark look from his eyes could serve as a type of truth serum demanding answers to his questions. He learned that some of the yachts docked in the yacht club occasionally carried more than just a crew when they traveled between the St. Lawrence Seaway and Miami Beach. Because the vessels came in such close contact with Latin America, Canada and the United States, no single authority could keep close tabs on which ones might be carrying some form of contraband, or to whom it was being delivered. The Coast Guard was busy chasing the more likely smugglers, found in gun boats or illegal submarines.

■ ■ ■

At exactly 1:30 p.m., a prompt Lieutenant Wesner, freshly shaved and feeling much better, waited at the Clark Avenue Gate with Detective Georgina Chouteau. Sgt. Benny Friedman came running up late after yet another personal phone call. The sign on the gate announced, "Hot Mill #1 – Badge Required". The mill structures were no more than 100 feet from the gate. Every structure seemed to be either painted or soot-stained a flat black color, with rusted edges adding a reddish-brown accent.

Towering black rectangles joined to even taller silo structures muscled against each other, some four or more stories tall. Lines of billowing smokestacks appeared in a row, as if borrowed from huge ocean liners. They rose as high as the cliff-sides of the surrounding valley and belched grey-black soot-filled smoke in an unending churn. Huge vent pipes added grey-white clouds of steam.

The sounds of whatever was happening inside the structures was deafening: gut-churning booms echoed in the canyon-like hollow of one structure; sirens pierced the air signaling some sort of dangerous activity within the next. The siren wails came with such frequency that they were likely ignored by most of the workers within. Dragon roars accompanied glows of red and the belches of smoke and steam. Switcher train engines rumbled around bends far too rapidly, horns blurting bassoon blasts to scatter any workers who had wandered too close to the tracks.

The acrid smell of burning coal mixed with the sickening odor of too old rancid oil. A metallic silver-black and orange dust coated everything. The detectives viewed the ominous witches brew up close for the first time. The soot and dust were daily deliveries which stuck to the lips and tongues and deep into the lungs of everyone who lived or worked in or near the valley. Layers of the stuff built up for years, for decades, and left many people debilitated, others buried. A steel worker would smell like a steel worker forever, even into the grave.

Wesner and Friedman had driven through the area two nights earlier, but it all looked even worse in the daylight. They had lived a long time in this city, and even though the sights and sounds and smell were jarring, they were not uncommon to the two veterans. For Georgina Chouteau, however, the many horrific scenarios she had experienced in New Orleans paled in comparison to the scale of this massive assault on her senses. She was jarred physically, emotionally, spiritually.

Wesner said, "Georgie, your mouth is hanging open and your eyes haven't blinked. Try to get it together. Our escort is just now arriving." She forced her jaw to close as Jonas Tripp, wearing a white hard hat, waved them toward the gate.

"Gentlemen, and, lady, too, I see. Here are your visitor badges permitting entry. Please clip them on securely where they can be seen. And here is a hard hat for each of you. All who enter any of our mills must wear a hard hat."

Sgt. Friedman said, "You have a white hat. The ones you gave us are pink. The guard at the gate has a silver hat. Is there a significance to the color?"

"Yes, indeed there is," said Mr. Tripp, prideful of his white helmet and happy to answer an innocuous question as he led the police down a black-topped path toward a large opening in the wall to the right. He was hoping there would be many more such easy questions to follow this afternoon. "Each function in the mill has a specific hard hat color, meaning each employee is identified by their function, with where they should be working, by the color of the hat they wear. White hats are for Senior Management, blue is worn by electricians. Dark green signifies an operator of one of the various mechanical devices--a roller, a coiler, a presser and so on. Yellow is for millwrights, to fix any machinery that might breakdown. Brown is worn by common laborers, those who clean up as best as they can in such a factory. Each color means something. As you noticed, our security team wears silver hard hats."

"And the pink?" asked Georgie with just a hint of sarcasm.

"The only color remaining to designate visitors. We want those unfamiliar with the dangers in the mill to stand out. So, pink."

"Where are the rest of the people we asked to meet with?" asked Wesner without cordiality.

"Um, we're heading to the Infirmary for Hot Mill #1. The nurse and foreman will meet us there. I've requested someone from the Security Department to join us as well. Apparently, the request was ill-timed for the Union Steward to join us."

Georgie said, "That is unfortunate. I'm sure you realize we will speak with him eventually. How many hot mills does Rubicon Steel operate?"

"Currently we have three, but one is undergoing significant repairs and retooling. A hot mill can only operate so long before requiring some rebuilding. That's why we have three. The big bosses want to add a fourth as we are running on maximum output right now. If one of the two functioning mills were to shut down for a period of time, there would be serious consequences."

"Like lost profits and a mess of steelworker layoffs, I suppose," said Wesner.

Tripp's head snapped toward the Lieutenant, then looked away trying to maintain cordiality. "Yes, I suppose some workers would be facing unexpected time off should a hot mill shut down. There would be implications all the way down the line, including for one or two of the cold mills." Anticipating the question, Tripp said, "We have four distinct cold mills, two to a building a quarter-mile south of here. It's actually a North-to-South operation. Raw material comes in from ore boats from the lake docking on the river to our north where the Hulett Cranes empty the ore boats. The Huletts are unique to this city's port. The ore material then feeds into the hot mills. The produced hot steel proceeds south to the cold mills where it takes its final shape. Then, onto trucks or trains at the far end of the property. From top to bottom, the mill is well over a mile long."

The group passed through another large opening at the waist of the building and approached a small, silver galvanized steel Quonset hut with a screen-printed sign over the door reading 'Infirmary #1 – Hot Mill'. The Infirmary stood out as the only building not blackened by the soot from its surroundings — making it appear like the recently added after-thought that it was.

Inside the infirmary they were introduced to the nurse and the foreman, and were told a representative of the Security Department was on the way. Benny made note that the foreman's name badge said Archie Lynch. Such information might be needed later. Neither the nurse nor foreman knew anything about the disappearance of Anton Wojcik. Even though they were both on duty the night of his disappearance, neither was at the scene when his absence was discovered. His orange-red helmet, now in the hands of the foreman, was found on the catwalk surrounding the pour cauldron. He had not clocked out after his shift the night of his disappearance. Everyone feared the worst.

"What is the significance of the orange helmet," asked Lt. Wesner. "There seems to be significance to the colors worn by everyone."

The foreman replied, "These bright orange--some say hot red--helmets are for those workers who come in contact with molten steel during their normal day's work. Anton had one of the most dangerous jobs in the mill, walking the rim of the hot cauldron and kicking glowing ashes back in."

The nurse shook her head. "I've often thought it's like walking the rim of a volcano trying to manage a lava flow."

At the insistence of the detectives, the foreman led the group from the infirmary to the cauldron cat walk even though the Security Guard had not yet appeared. They climbed the stairs and examined the narrow circular walkway. No cauldron was present in the middle, removed to ensure the safety of the investigators. Even so, a residual rise in ambient temperature was almost stifling. The foreman said, "This area stays hot for days after a pour. At this moment it's almost 40-degrees hotter than the rest of the mill." He pointed to a circular thermometer registering 108-degrees.

"What safety measures do you have in place?" asked Sgt. Friedman.

Before anyone could answer, a voice from behind bellowed, "Lynch! Archie Lynch! Just what the hell do you all think you're doing up there? No one's supposed to go up those stairs without my permission!" All eyes turned toward an overly officious, narrow-faced, angular and angry man who fancied himself a military officer. His matching dark green khaki shirt and pants were ironed and creased, his black steel-toed boots were spit-shined mirrors, his silver helmet immaculately polished. To complete the affectation, he carried a small riding crop which he whacked against the railing as if awaiting a victim for a thrashing. "Everyone, get down from there! *Mach schnell!*"

Slowly the police officers took a last look at the catwalk and descended the twenty steps to the floor. On the way down, Wesner leaned to his team members and said, "He's all yours, Benny. Do whatever you want with him."

As they gathered at the base of the stairs, Lynch the foreman said, "This here is Mr. Brodick from the Security Department. I was up there with them, Eugene. Everyone was safe."

"Major Brodick, Lynch! You will address me as Major Brodick!"

Sgt. Friedman stepped forward and said, "I'm with the Cleveland Police Department. My name is Sergeant Friedman. I don't know who you think you are, but I must assume you realize you just tried to give orders to law enforcement. We don't play that game, buster. You may think you rule this mill, but this mill is inside the city of Cleveland, so you are on my turf. Now, you will show me your identification right now or you'll spend the night in jail."

"You can't intimidate me like that!"

"Try me! Your I.D. right now." Sgt. Friedman pulled his hand-cuffs and rattled them under the nose of the self-important Eugene Brodick, who dropped his swagger stick as he fumbled for his wallet.

Examining the badge and driver's license, Benny said, "Nothing here says you earned the rank of Major. Did you just give that title to yourself? Never mind. I don't think I'll care for your answer. Did you give approval for Anton Wojcik to be up on that scaffolding the night he disappeared?"

"Why, no. I did not."

"Then how did he get up there? You said everyone needed your permission to be up there."

"I meant you. You all. None of you are employees, so I thought—"

Benny jumped on him with both feet. "You thought? Since when did someone tell you to think on your own? Your job is to provide security in this mill, correct? How did someone disappear right under your nose if you were doing your job? If he's dead then you may be guilty of non-feasance, if not outright manslaughter."

"That's not fair! I—"

"Maybe we'll let the judge sort that out. Couple weeks in jail should allow us to get all the evidence we need."

"There's no evidence to find! Nothing to show I did anything to anybody!" Brodick's voice climbed two octaves into a screech. He was digging a hole where no dirt existed as Benny continued to raise the pressure, adding to Brodick's anxiety.

Lt. Wesner picked up the swagger stick and took on his Pastor Smile. "Oh, Sergeant. Maybe we should wait to hear what Mr. Brodick has to say before we haul him in." He handed the fake-major his slightly bent swagger stick, which was quickly stashed in a rear pocket, out of sight. "Were you on duty the night of the disappearance, Major?"

Brodick bowed his head. "Yes, but I was in another area. I didn't become aware that anyone was missing until I got a call the next morning."

"Who called you?"

"Our head of security, Colonel Rowden."

"Everybody's got a military rank, huh? Why isn't the Colonel here answering our questions, then?" The Pastor Smile was quickly disappearing.

Brodick took two steps back, saying, "I dunno. You'll have to ask him." He touched the walkie-talkie on his hip, causing it to squawk. "I'll be right there," he said into it. "Please excuse me. Duty calls." And he ran off into the mill.

Georgie could barely control herself. "Why Sgt. Friedman, I think you may have frightened him!"

The foreman chuckled. "It's about time someone took that pimply-assed, no-good excuse for a human being to the wood-shed."

Wesner said, "Give us the nickel tour on what happens here when the hot steel pours out."

The foreman said, "We've got two hot mills working these days. The system is identical in both. This happens to be the one where Anton Wojcik was working when he disappeared, or left, or…." He pointed to a huge rectangular channel tilted toward the cauldron area. "The hot stuff comes out of the blast furnace on that channel, filling the cauldron. There's usually some splatter, hot chunks on the edge of the cauldron. The guys on the catwalk watch for the loose hot nuggets that miss the mark and they kick it back in with one of those ten-foot hooks," pointing to several heavy rods leaning against a sign demanding safety gear be worn. "Once the cauldron is full, an overhead crane grabs the back hook of the bucket and tilts it, pouring the cauldron contents forward, filling a row of small slab-shaped train cars on the track below." The Foreman pointed to a line of railroad tracks ten feet below the level of the cauldron. When we've got lots of orders, that might happen three or four times per shift, per cauldron, or basically several times every day. The train takes the slab cars away to cool. All of that has to happen fast, so the hot stuff doesn't cool inside the cauldron. Eventually, the slabs will be reheated enough to be shaped into whatever is ordered--pipe, re-bar, sheet steel for cars. Sheet steel is by far our biggest seller."

Jonas Tripp quickly interrupted, saying, "Let's not give away our product mix numbers, Archie. Proprietary information isn't needed here." To the Lieutenant, he said, "I believe you have all the information currently available, detective. Unless there is something else, I will request that we leave so that work may continue here. We can continue interviews at the Infirmary or elsewhere, as you may wish."

■　■　■

Returning to the squad room at Police Headquarters, the detectives concluded little of substance was learned at the mill about Anton Wojcik's disappearance, other than it would be very easy for someone to trip--or be pushed--off the catwalk and into a vat of molten steel. The foreman pointed to the spot mere feet from the stairway where Anton's bright orange helmet had been found the morning after his disappearance. He also shared that Cezary Ludzinski was excused from work on a temporary basis, until a resolution of the inquiry. The Union was preventing Rubicon from labelling it a suspension, since such a statement without evidence of wrong-doing could permanently harm a worker's reputation.

Discussing the placement of the helmet, Friedman said, "Could have been left on his way down the stairs and out the door. Sort of an 'I quit' statement."

Wesner said, "Or as a final gesture before taking a nose dive into the lava pit."

Georgie added, "Not the place you'd expect to find the hard hat if he had been pushed. The vat that fits between the edges of that catwalk must be 30-feet across. No reason to leave evidence of a murder in a very conspicuous spot. No reason to leave the hard hat at all."

Lt. Wesner was reading notes from his desk while his team continued their debrief. "Angel is on his way back. Flight lands around 6:00 p.m. The note says 'Ratterman docks here.' I assume that's the same dock where the Cuban's were gutted."

"They were Haitians," said Georgie. "Cubans are much more cautious than to be caught in an ambush, which is what the event seems to be. Cubans would have been far more likely to have left some others as victims. Haitians, on the other hand, are trusting souls. They believe their Xango Voodoo dolls will protect them from evil doers, or at least put a curse on those who attempt to do evil to them."

Wesner gave Georgie a long look while slowly backing into his chair, distancing himself from her piercing and fiery black eyes. "Okay. I stand corrected. They were Haitians. My apologies to their Voodoo dolls." He looked down at his notes then back to her. "How can you be sure they practiced Voodoo?"

"Almost all Haitians believe in Voodoo," she replied, "and many practice it even if they do not attend services or participate in any of the customary rituals. All who grow up on the island fear both priests and priestesses--especially priestesses who are far more likely to cast spells and curses. No Haitian would conduct dangerous business without a talisman on their neck…like this one." She pulled on a leather cord around her neck revealing a small, iridescent blue-purple stone, carved with figures and letters. She tucked the talisman away before anyone could determine the design.

Benny was transfixed. "Are you a native Haitian, or a Voodoo priestess?"

Georgie smiled gently, never taking her eyes away from Lt. Wesner. "There are those who say it is improper to ask such a question unless one is requesting intervention."

"Forget I asked," said the Sergeant sliding his chair further away.

Lt. Wesner shook his head to clear away whatever thoughts he might have. "Let's focus on this case. We still don't know what has become of Anton Wojcik, despite our visit to the Hot Mill. I think we gave Major Eugene Brodick enough heart-burn to ruin his sleep for the next few nights. He'll be reporting his fears to his Colonel, Lucas Rowden. That is perfect. Raise his anxiety, too. I wonder if the Colonel is arrogant enough to come in here on his own?"

"Why do you suppose they've given themselves ranks," asked Friedman. "Not many guys want to be soldiers these days."

"Intimidation seems to be their purpose," said Georgie. "Playing soldier is more fun than being one. And if no one tells you to stop, you have tacit permission to become as militarized as you want."

Lt. Wesner agreed. "The key to what you said, Georgie, is no one is telling them to stop. Senior Management obviously approves of the results, not worrying about the process used. That emboldens the security staff to get bigger and harsher at what they do. Brodick is a petty demigod because Rowden encourages him. The guard at the parking lot lives in fear of the man he calls Rowdie. His military bearing allows his Security Team to run the place like a fearsome special forces unit under whoever is pulling the strings at the top." Wesner smiled at his team. "The worst part about it is, what they are doing is not illegal, at least on the surface. They keep everything nice and tight and secure for Senior Management. I bet most of the mill workers seldom cross paths with Rowden and his team of paramilitary playmates. As long as the workers do what they're paid to do and look the other way if something appears amiss, they are left alone. If there is something illegal going on, I'd bet it will include those suspicious trailers in the back of the parking lot. Workers with a full pocket of cash in a secluded but secure spot can get into a lot of trouble."

■ ■ ■

He tasted his truck stop coffee. Terrible stuff. Nonetheless, he bought a second cup, then snuck in to steal a trucker's shower. It was daylight, so he dared not go back to Cranwood Park. He might be seen, recognized. That was both his greatest desire and his biggest fear. In his dreams, he was smothered in kisses and hugs, soft lips tasting like honey, soft tear-covered cheeks mingling with his own tears. In his nightmares, he was cursed and beaten, thrown away and forbidden to return, laughed at, ridiculed, brushed off as yesterday's dust.

But he could not just sit here at the truck-stop coffee shop. Loitering would be frowned upon, would attract unwanted attention, maybe even spook the waitresses to call the cops--they'd ask questions. He could not handle another one of those police inquiries. His spirit had no room for further interrogation. He was not welcome at the Mill. He was told to stay away. He could not return to the ravine Sanctuary. Too many kids, car polishers, and maybe even more cops down there. He had sensed his soul was cracking, his heart was being crushed the last time he entertained police questions. Another such shattering experience would be too much. It had been too much already. Seazy stirred his cooling coffee and considered his plight.

If only Anton was here. He would know what to do. He always knows what to do. He is insufferable that way. That's why I hate him. But I would love to talk to him. I rely on him more than I rely on anyone else. I need him. He is my friend. It's not like he's a know-it-all. He never makes you think you are stupid or anything. He's not like Big Ed, always trying to belittle you. I can't talk to Big Ed. I would sooner talk to the cops again. That Lieutenant was nice. He I could talk to. Maybe not about everything, but some things. He listens. I just wish I could talk to Anton, even just be with him for a while. It's weird, but I just feel more comfortable when Anton is with me. Like he's family, or something. I wish I knew where he is. But he doesn't like being with me, I think. He prefers that I stay away, I think. No one likes to be too near me, I think.

My cash is running low. I don't know where to go, but I know that, wherever it is, I need some of my hourly wages, no matter what. Maybe I should take all of it out of the bank now. No, maybe not yet. That would raise questions maybe, if the police ever asked. Do they know where I have my checking account? Do they know more than I think they do, more than I want them to?

He drained what was left of his now-tepid coffee, the drips at the bottom of the cup swirling, refusing to provide guidance to his next destination.

■ ■ ■

Angel returned to the squad room around 7:15 p.m. to brief the team on his findings. He was still wearing his white linen suit and fedora. The image he portrayed, the swagger in his step, gave everyone pause. He was still a detective, but it was easy to imagine he was from Hispanic royalty—or had become an underworld gangster, ready to control a Miami cartel. The others were still there, eager to hear from him, but he caused quite the stir.

Each detective shared the bits of the puzzle they each were pursuing throughout the afternoon. Since Thorpe was still alive, albeit comatose, only a cursory forensic search of the crime scene was conducted, unlike a full search which might follow an actual murder. No clear evidence was found pointing toward any one or two perpetrators. The only evidence was the testimony of Butch Herman. The police department was able to convince the hospital to list the knife-wounded and concussed patient as a John Doe, assuming that if someone knew the real whereabouts of Peter Thorpe, they might want to finish the execution and permanently extinguish his life. For now, he was safe, if only marginally alive.

Georgie asked, "Do any of you know where Seazy is now? We seem to have lost our concern about him lately."

Wesner said, "Our focus has shifted more to the assault on Thorpe and whether there is a connection to Anton's disappearance. Seazy doesn't seem to be involved in the Thorpe attack, and I'm not sure he knows much about where Anton might be. But you are correct, Georgie, we should not let him slip too far out of our sightlines. Ask the patrol boys to swing by his house a few times to try and spot him. If they strike out, there's a small neighborhood park in the Cranwood area where I might be able to find him after dark."

"I worry about him," said Georgie. "He is a fragile young man…boy, actually. He's just a child in many ways. While your aura is brown mustard, Lieutenant, Seazy's is almost transparent, non-existent. That is much worse."

Angel grinned, "You can smear that aura of yours on some hotdogs and call it dinner."

Georgie snapped at Angel, her deep voice turning almost guttural. "Do not make jest of the spiritual things which you pretend to disbelieve! You, of all people—despite your outward bravado and arrogant costume—should know better than to tempt the fates with your mockery. *La sorcellerie* is much closer to you than you imagine and such cynicism is not appreciated."

Angel's expression dropped in fear. "*Si, senora. Oui, madame.* I transgress. Please excuse my fault."

Wesner intervened. "Okay, let's just calm down. Everyone needs to take a few steps back. We're all on the same team here. It's been a long day, and we're all a bit on edge and worn out. Let's end this for now. Everyone, go home. Get some rest. We'll start fresh tomorrow. We'll try to get Rowden to come in voluntarily for questioning. In the meantime, if I have any updates overnight, I'll give you all a call."

Benny said, "Say! Uh, before you all leave. I want to let you all know. I'm throwing a clambake on Sunday afternoon in my new big backyard. I'd like you all to come. Feel free to bring your family along. My family and some neighbors will be there. We got lots of room."

"Wow! I haven't been to a Cleveland-style clambake in years," said Angel. What time?"

"Come around 1:00 p.m., we'll be cooking all afternoon. Browns game on the radio, cold beer, it'll be a great time. I'll give you the address."

"Thanks, Ben," said Lieutenant Wesner, smiling at the tension breaker. "I'll be there. Georgie, how about you?"

She looked suspicious. "What is a Cleveland-style clambake? We have clam bakes in Louisiana, but this sounds different somehow."

Lt. Wesner said, "Yeah, the same, but very different, I expect. You'll see. Why don't I pick you up since you don't know the directions to Benny's place. That will cut down on the parking issues, too."

"Great!" said Benny. "Sunday afternoon, everybody!"

Watching the rest of his team gather their personal items and leave for the night, Wesner called Thorpe's cabin for the daily wellness check on Rosie Dwyer. She reported that she was fine, but going quite stir-crazy. Wesner promised to deliver some of the provisions Rosie said were missing from Thorpe's cabin pantry. Rosie requested that Wesner bring the most important stuff, like coffee. And Scotch.

Friday, November 5

It's here somewhere. It has to be. It is the last thing I remember getting from my mother…or maybe my grandmother. Don't recall. A tiny bottle with a stopper. Grandma used to say it was from the Romanovs. I don't know how she got it, but I believe her. It was painted purple halfway down. Cut glass, how they painted it I don't know. Or maybe they used colored glass? Could be, I suppose. Could hold a liquid…or a powder, I guess. The stopper could hold stuff in. But it's very breakable, delicate. I need to make sure I have it, not leave it where Big Ed could smash it or something. Where can I keep it where it will be safe? My car glove compartment? Unless the car gets stolen. Of course, who would want this bucket of bolts. But still — thieves. Maybe my locker at work? I know the combination, but someone could easily break the code.

I need to keep it safe. Part of the Romanov collection. From my mother. From my grandmother, maybe. Neither one liked me. I don't know why I have It, anyway. But I can't let it break. I just can't.

. . .

The day dawned gloomy, bitterly cold and painfully wet with sharp, stinging raindrops trending toward sleet. The low sky grumbled. Ominous clouds mixed with the murky smoke from the valley, melding into a heavy ceiling, neither rainy grey nor industrial black--best described as a nasty brown. The clouds seemed held aloft by the almost invisible tops of the tallest buildings. Precipitation pelted down, each drop with its own special color--some tinted black from coal dust, others tinged an acidic orange-trending-brown, carrying particles of iron dust in each droplet. Alex Wesner watched his car windows stain from the rain, wondering ruefully if those raindrops were really the color of his aura, whatever an aura might be. Buildings, houses, cars and streets took on the color of the steel mill effluence. Where once indigenous children caught raindrops on their tongue, now forewarned youth did so only on a dare.

Lt. Wesner dried his head with a paper towel from the men's room as he lumbered toward his desk. His mood matched the weather. Despite the information gathered over the past few days, the case was going nowhere. Questions outnumbered answers with very little cooperation from people at the Rubicon Steel Mill. A note on his desk from the morning clerk provided the phone number for the Union Steward for Hot Mill #1, a man named Arthur Setter. Without even taking off his topcoat, Wesner dialed the number.

"Yeah. Whadya want?"

"I'm trying to reach Mr. Arthur Setter. Is that you?"

"Who wants to know?"

"This is Lieutenant Alex Wesner, Cleveland Police. May I speak to Mr. Setter?"

"Oh. Yeah. Speaking. That's me."

"You are Arthur Setter, Union Steward at Hot Mill #1 for the United Steel Workers at Rubicon Steel?"

"Yeah. Whadya want with me?"

"We are investigating the disappearance of one of your Union members, Anton Wojcik. You weren't available yesterday when we visited the Mill. We'd like any information you might have about Anton's disappearance."

"I don't know nothin'. Bye."

"Hold on, Mr. Setter. We'd like you to come downtown to Police Headquarters to make an official statement. We'd like that to happen soon. What time today would be convenient?" Wesner sensed the steward was anxious to avoid any discussion, and chose to ramp up the pressure. "How about 10:00 a.m.? That works fine for us."

"What? Today? Ten o'clock--uh, I need to call my Union lawyer."

"Well, that's up to you, although unless you are involved in the disappearance, I don't see why legal counsel is needed to answer some simple questions. But you're paying his bill, I guess. Headquarters is at the corner of East 21st and Payne. See you at ten. Fourth floor. Ask for Lt. Wesner."

With that, Wesner hung up, a wry smile expressing his improving mood. He spun around in his creaky brown vinyl chair to see the rest of his team assembling at their desks, eyeing him cautiously. Benny had warned Angel and Georgie that a smiling Wheezie was a dangerous Wheezie, and if he started to hum, someone was going to get hurt.

"We'll need interview room #3 at 10:00 a.m. for today's special guest, Arthur Setter, Anton's Union Rep. Let's all four be there and put the fear of God into him." Wesner took off his overcoat and strode into the captain's office to brief him on the status of the case. He correctly suspected Captain Mitchell would be interested in anything Mr. Setter might say.

Benny turned to the others, saying, "I think Mr. Setter may have pissed Wheezie off!"

■　■　■

At 10:00 a.m., Arthur Setter, dripping from the icy rain and dressed in his work clothes and steel-toed shoes, got off the elevator on the 4th floor of police headquarters, warily peering left and right. He was a large man, overweight enough to waddle more than walk. His reddish-blond hair was thinning and greying at the temples. Accompanying him was a large, white-haired man in an expensive three-piece blue-pinstriped suit. He carried a leather brief case and an attitude. They were ushered into a room labelled #3.

The three-piece suit said, "Which one of you is Lt. Wesner?"

"I am Lt. Alex Wesner, Cleveland Police. Who are you?"

"I am C.W. Rathbone, Esquire, representing Rubicon Steel and, temporarily, Mr. Arthur Setter. We object to being given last second instructions to appear here with no probable cause for such an indignity. Mr. Setter had to request time off from his job to accede to your directive to appear here. If he is not under arrest or suspicion, I must protest on his behalf."

Wesner never rose, simply smiled, motioned to two chairs and said, "Have a seat Mr. Rathbone, Mr. Setter. We appreciate your cooperation in volunteering to come in today to help us with an important case: the disappearance of Anton Wojcik." As they took the two open seats, the Lieutenant introduced the other three detectives seated around the large table, notepads open. Accepting the lawyer's business card, Wesner said, "Shall I assume you represent the United Steel Workers, Mr. Rathbone?"

"Ah, no. No, in this instance I solely represent Mr. Setter."

"Oh. I see. Does Mr. Setter believe he requires personal legal counsel?"

"Well, the Union attorney was unavailable on such short notice. The immediacy of the requested visit implied some possible suspicion on your part. Therefore, it was deemed appropriate that I attend the interview along with Mr. Setter."

Directing a question toward Arthur Setter, Wesner asked, "Is Mr. Rathbone your regular attorney, do you have him on a retainer?"

"What? No. Ah, I mean…."

Rathbone replied, "Since the regular Union attorney was not available, it was requested that I accompany Mr. Setter. I represent Rubicon Steel, so I was asked to step in. Frankly, this is the first time Mr. Setter and I have met."

"What is the company afraid of," asked Georgie.

"I beg your pardon?" said Rathbone.

Benny added to the thought. "Seems pretty heavy-handed for Rubicon Steel to call in a big, corporate attorney to help a Union Rep answer some simple questions about a person he represents, don't you think?"

"A man's life may have been lost under mysterious circumstances. Rubicon Steel takes the lives of all employees very seriously and wishes to resolve the mystery surrounding the man's disappearance as soon as possible. If we can assist in any way, we are prepared to do so."

"Nice speech," said Angel. "You practice that a long time?"

Interrupting the bluster that was building from Rathbone, Lt. Wesner said, "Mr. Setter, what do you know about the disappearance of Anton Wojcik?"

"Like I said on the phone, I don't know nothin'."

"If Mr. Wojcik is current in his Union dues, shouldn't you be more concerned about his well-being?"

"Yeah, I mean we're all real concerned about what maybe happened, but as I was sayin', I don't know nothin' directly 'cept what I been told."

Benny asked, "Who informed you about Mr. Wojcik's disappearance?"

Looking to the attorney who offered no help, Setter said, "Uh, let's see. First, the foreman I think, then the nurse said somethin'."

"Did you investigate what had transpired?"

"Naw, that's for Security to do. They check up on everything and let me know stuff I should know. They gave me the inside dope, too."

Wesner asked, "Who in Security briefed you?"

"Uh, I'm not sure. I think Brodick told me what he knew."

Benny said, "Do you know Lucas Rowden?"

"The Colonel? Sure! I--"

"This line of questioning does not seem relevant to the missing worker," Rathbone interrupted. "Let's remain focused, please."

Wesner gave the attorney a questioning look. "If we were in a courtroom, counselor, you could certainly object all you want. Similarly, if this were a deposition, I would expect such defensive comments. But this is simply a preliminary investigation, looking for any friendly and innocent assistance we can get from the company, the fellow workers, and the Union Steward of the missing man. Your interference--frankly, your presence here today--makes me think there are some questions not being answered, some facts being avoided, some truths being covered-up. My mind tends to work that way, understand?"

The rest of the interview proved equally fruitless. Setter truly knew nothing of consequence. He claimed to not recognize the names Seazy Lutz or Cezary Ludzinski, and only provided a cursory overview of the Union's unhelpful position regarding a worker who never managed to clock out of work. On their way out of the interview room, Attorney Rathbone surprised Lt. Wesner by shaking his hand and palming a note to him. It read: 'Phone conversation soon. – C.W.R.'

The detective team remained in Interview Room #3 as Wesner guided the Union Steward and lawyer to the elevator. He read the note to the team upon his return. "Seems Mr. Rathbone is eager to continue the discussion without Art Setter at his side. Sounds a bit strange, don't you think?"

Benny said, "If Rathbone really is Setter's attorney, he can't tell us anything of any value without breaking client privilege, right?"

Angel nodded. "That's true, but maybe he wants to talk about something else."

"I suspect he's not really Setter's attorney. At least, not officially," offered Georgie. "He actually said they had just met for the first time. I think he was here to protect the interests of Rubicon Steel, not to support the Union guy. What possible motive would the company have to provide their legal counsel for the support of the adversarial Union? No, he was here to make sure the Union guy didn't throw the corporation under the bus."

"Or into the lava soup," said Benny. "I think you're right, Georgie. And he succeeded in keeping Setter's mouth shut. I wonder if we should meet with Art again in a more casual way. No interview room, no attorney."

"And I believe I will contact Mr. Rathbone, since he kindly invited me to do so, once he has a chance to return to his office," said Wesner, twirling the business card in his fingers. He got up, intent upon updating Captain Mitchell about the session with Setter. He turned and gave instructions. "Benny, see if you can locate the mysterious Colonel Rowden. If you find him, go ask him to come in for a visit. Maybe use your boyish charms to convince him to accompany you. Angel, try to find out who the real Union attorney is, and if he was available this morning or not. Georgie – I've got a strange one for you. There's a bar on the western rim of the valley overlooking the steel mills. It's called the Steal Inn. Head down to the Hall of Records. See if you can locate ownership papers on that place. But do not attempt to go into that bar. It's unfriendly to anyone who doesn't wear a steelworker hard hat, and I don't want to spook them with too many police visits."

■ ■ ■

C. W. Rathbone's receptionist put Lt. Wesner on hold as she scrambled to her boss explaining a police officer was on the phone requesting to speak to him. In the interim, Wesner turned on the phone recording device, assuming the lawyer would do the same.

Rathbone picked up his phone. "Hello, Lieutenant. I was hoping you would accept my offer to talk privately."

"I took from your note you didn't want Mr. Setter involved in our further discussions. By the way, I must inform you that I am recording this call and it may be used as evidence should any wrong-doing be discovered." Wesner tickled the belly of his now golden-colored glass horse ornament.

Understood, Lieutenant. I, too, am recording this call as-- shall we say--insurance should any wrong-doing be discovered."

"Very well. You requested this call. I assume you have something you wish to make us aware of. By 'us' I refer to the law enforcement bureaus at work in the Greater Cleveland area."

"Bureaus, Lieutenant? Am I to take it that there are more agencies investigating this worker's disappearance than just the Cleveland Police?"

"At the present time, the detectives you met are the primary officers on this case. But when new evidence shows up or secondary events manifest themselves out of one singular situation, there is no telling how many different law enforcement agencies may take an interest. So, with that being explained, what's on your mind?"

The attorney cleared his throat and paused to gather his thoughts before continuing. "As I noted in the police interrogation room, my law firm and I represent Rubicon Steel, not the Union Steward, Mr. Setter. As I stated at the time, he and I met only this morning for the first time. It was at the request from the Board of Directors that I attended the inquiry meeting to protect the interests of the corporation. Whether or not this 'Red' fellow is involved in illegal activity is beyond my knowledge and beyond my responsibility for representation."

"Who's 'Red'?

"Oh. Yes, you don't know him by that name. It turns out Mr. Setter's nickname is Red. His red hair, his florid complexion, his

Irish heritage. 'Red Setter'--apparently a natural nickname. In any event, I was asked to attend this morning to learn how much Mr. Setter knows, to learn what he would say to you. In that manner, the corporation could discover if he, or any of his associates, might actually be a liability."

"And is he? Is he a liability?"

"It doesn't appear so. He seems as mystified as the rest of us."

"So, you are mystified, too?"

"Why, yes! No one at the corporate office seems to know specific details about the disappearance of Mr. Wod...uh, Wajio...."

"It's pronounced 'Woy'-chick'. His name is Anton Wojcik. Better learn how to spell it, too. Might come in handy. Why did you stop 'Red' from talking about the Head of Security, Lucas Rowden? Seems like no one wants to mention his name around the police."

Rathbone sighed and sniffled like a man fighting autumn allergies as he formulated a response. "There is a fine distinction between workers who are members of the Union and those designated as corporate employees at Rubicon Steel. None of the corporate employees are represented by the Union. That includes almost all those who work in the headquarters building. Further, the Security Staff are all considered corporate employees. Therefore, the Union does not represent them in any actions. So, whether or not Mr. Setter knows or has spoken to Mr. Rowden, he may not give any testimony regarding any supposed communications with him. He might inadvertently suggest some activity of which he is not privy, or wrongfully imply any untoward actions by Mr. Rowden or any member of the Security Staff."

Wesner guffawed in disbelief. "Wow! That is one heavy load of bullshit, C.W. It's going to be hard to get that turd airborne if we end up in a courtroom. By the way, how can I get in touch with Mr. Rowden? He seems to be avoiding us. Another bad omen should we end up before a judge."

"I see no reason that any of this needs to be a matter which might enter into litigation. You are simply searching for a missing person. I'm trying to be helpful by providing context for individuals you are interrogating."

"Interrogating! You make it sound like we're conducting an inquisition of repeat offenders. That's a dark perspective, Rathbone. I'm curious. Specifically, who asked you to accompany Mr. Setter today?"

Rathbone mumbled, "The request came from among the Board of Directors."

Wesner sensed a nerve had been pinched. "The entire Board? Were they in session this morning? Are they all so worried about our investigation that they asked you to attend?"

"No. Not the entire Board. And, no, there is not a general concern by board members, simply a desire to head off any public relations issues."

"So, it was the Chairman of the Board who requested that you become involved, huh? What's his name? Don't make me look it up in the public records."

"Umm, it was not the Chairman who suggested I attend. It was one of the other members who called."

Wesner paused, letting Rathbone's own blunder sink in. He imagined sweat beads forming on the lawyer's upper lip as he curled away from the phone. Eventually the Lieutenant said, "Of course, you realize I will want to know his name. And I will want to know exactly when he called you. You know better than to hold back information at this point, correct?"

"And here is where I must claim attorney / client privilege. All I can say is that, to the best of my knowledge, none of my clients are guilty of anything regarding the disappearance of Mr. Wojcik, nor do they have any information regarding his disappearance--beyond the idle speculation which seems to have run rampant over the last several days."

"I'll tell you what. You don't have to admit anything. Just save me the time it takes to research public records by making a list of all the Board Members so I can do my own process of elimination. Send the list to my attention at police headquarters this afternoon. And get word to Rowden that he needs to get his butt in here to answer my questions. In the meantime, you mentioned 'idle speculation' regarding the disappearance of Anton Wojcik. What's the favorite theory going around the Board Room?"

Rathbone sniffled again while calculating that sharing a widely held rumor would implicate no one. "Many people are speculating that Mr. Wojcik met his demise through an evil deed committed by his work partner. They reach that conclusion because, unfortunately, it has happened before. We, that is Rubicon Steel, tries to make every effort to pair friendly workers on the cauldron, but--and this is my own speculation--there are times when even the best friends can become the worst enemies."

"Interesting, Mr. Rathbone. Sounds like you are speaking from personal experience. What could make a best friend become a worst enemy?"

"In my experience there are only two things, Lieutenant, only two things: money or love."

■　■　■

It was midday. Everyone was off on their separate assignments and the Hall of Records employees left Georgie sitting in the waiting room. The city auditor's office said they were checking their records for deeds and liens on the Steal Inn, although such a search might take another two hours given the usual lunch breaks. Her boredom was unbearable. She figured a drive-by was in order, just to see the actual building she was investigating. She drove the unmarked police car on the most direct route to the bar, along a heavily travelled road crossing the industrial valley, a road which was a decade past its scheduled destruction.

The arrow-straight, two-lane, pot-holed road led from the Eastside of the valley to the Westside, dropping down like a roller coaster ramp on one side and up the other at the same steep angle. Over a mile long, the road was often referred to as a bridge since the steep ramps were held up by rickety girder supports and a bridge section of the road did span the river at some point in the mid-section. The crossing from east to west rather demanded a long, sturdy bridge, but, given the length of the span and the steepness of the valley, an actual long-span bridge would be both impractical and dangerous — both to build and to cross. The city fathers struggled to determine a remedy. In the meantime, the road remained a precarious challenge for travelers.

It was wide for a two-lane, built to accommodate large trucks, although both the road and its girdered supports shook and seemed to wobble when two semis passed each other. In the center where the pavement reached its lowest point, an actual steel frame structure crossed the polluted river swirling some 30 feet below. The road sank so low into the valley that the crossing seemed like a descent into and through a hell's cavern of menacing mill structures and spewing smoke stacks, built tight to the edge of the road's guardrails. Rising high on either side of the pavement, the blackened buildings hissed and belched their disapproval at gawkers. The Friday morning shower became a cold pelting rain which instantly turned to steam as it struck the stained dark walls of the mill structures, failing the effort to cleanse them. The darkened sheet steel appeared close enough for passengers to imagine they could touch the hot metal sides. Shivers ran down Georgie's back. It was almost as bad as the House of Horrors at the old abandoned amusement park in New

Orleans where she had been taken against her will several years earlier.

Letting out a sigh of relief as she reached the uphill western side, she spotted the unlit sign for the Steal Inn almost at the top of the hill. From the road, it looked like an old, large three-story clap board house. What had once been the front door was covered by plywood, painted with an arrow saying 'parking in rear'. The windows all appeared to be painted black. No one could see what was going on inside. Maybe no one would want to. She drove past, unable to slow down as tail-gating traffic behind was eager to continue the final few feet up the hill. Turning around at a side street, she decided to head back and pull into the Steal Inn parking lot so she could see whatever served as the entrance door in the rear.

The lot was only partially full, but even that meant a reasonably large crowd was inside. As she stopped to turn around in the narrow lot, a man came to her driver's side door.

"Hey, sweetheart! You comin' in for a drink? I'll buy!"

She shook her head and put the car in reverse, looking over her shoulder.

He pulled open the driver door. "I axed you a question! Least you could do is answer p'litely!"

Two men approached the rear of the car and pounded on the trunk. "Watcha got here, Mikey?" said one of them.

"Seems like this little lady ain't got no manners. I was just inviting her in for a drink."

"Why, that's right kindly of you, I'd say," said the one sliding up the passenger side of the car.

A tall, muscular man appeared at the main entrance door of the bar facing the parking lot. "What're you fools doing!" he shouted, suddenly doubling his pace. His dark green khaki shirt and pants were crisply ironed, the pants legs tucked into high-topped, steel-toed, brightly polished boots. "Don't you recognize an unmarked police car when you see it?"

Whoever this man was did recognize police-issued vehicles, outfitted with black-wall tires, spotlights next to the side view mirrors, and large antennas curling from the rear as clear giveaways of law enforcement transportation. The car Georgie drove didn't have the long antenna, but the rest fit. The three men stepped away. Georgie slammed the driver-side door and gunned the engine screeching out of the parking lot.

She was still shaking when she turned into the parking lot at the Hall of Records. No longer frightened by the encounter, she was just angry at herself. Lt. Wesner had warned her not to go into the Steal Inn. He did not mention that the danger could extend into the parking lot. Nevertheless, she should have known better. The one thing she could not afford to do is warn the occupants of the Steal Inn that they were being watched. She had screwed up. She parked the car in an 'Officials Only' spot at the Hall of Records and pounded on the rim of the steering wheel. She got out of the car and, leaning against the hood, pulled out a cigarette. She had a pack stashed deep in her bag for use in dire circumstances. This was a dire one, she reasoned. Her hands shook involuntarily as she struck match after match hoping to ignite the cigarette tip. Finally, one hit its mark. She inhaled deeply.

Should she tell Lt. Wesner of the encounter, or pretend it didn't happen? Either way, she could be in trouble with the boss. If Wesner knew what she had done, entering the parking lot after he expressly told her to stay away, he might ask her off the case. She'd probably end up reassigned to guard the lions cage at the zoo for the next six months.

On the other hand, if she said nothing and the men at the Steal Inn simply laughed it off as just another of their attempts at sexual harassment, no one would be the wiser. The only way this could go terribly wrong is if the men at the Steal Inn were now on high alert because an unmarked police car was spotted. If that were the case, if they were somehow involved in the attempted murder of Peter Thorpe or the disappearance of Anton Wojcik, then the situation might be very dangerous.

But if they were not involved in the Thorpe or Wojcik matters, if they were simply jerky apes, then the encounter in the parking lot of the Steal Inn could be ignored. No one would be the wiser. She considered the three men who accosted her car. None of them looked like the murderous type. Would they have raped her? Maybe. Maybe not. Individually, none of the three could have survived the beating she would have administered. Even as a group, there would have been three very bruised individuals, like the men from the House of Horrors in New Orleans. Had she pulled her service revolver—well, she was a crack shot.

Women in any work force, not only in the police force, face a double kind of discrimination. Clients, customers or criminals all view the woman as inferior, unable to hold their own physically or mentally. Men view them as mostly incompetent versus their male counter-parts. And their beauty—or lack thereof—adds or subtracts from the evaluation. The judgement is doubled by their work partners and superiors who mirror those same opinions and make those opinions known in personnel evaluations.

As one of the few women detectives on the Cleveland Police Force in the early 1970s, Det. Georgina Chouteau was carrying the weight of opinions fostered over several generations. Misogynistic attitudes persisted, sometimes heavily, sometimes only in small ways, and sometimes without the men even knowing what they were saying. How she handled this latest situation would determine how long she could remain on this case.

In her experience, men gain courage when in a group. And as a group, they also lose common sense along with morals and ethics. It might have gotten ugly had the uniformed fellow not come out of the bar. What about him? Who was he, and why did he seem to have control over the three apes? He wore the same uniform as Eugene Brodick, the security guard at the mill, although the man she saw was much more muscular, and the uniform fit much better, as if it was professionally tailored. Could he have been the elusive Lucas Rowden? She focused, recalling his physical appearance. As she mentally etched his face, she realized the only way she could tell Wesner what he looked like is if she explained about the entire incident. She wasn't going to do that. She hated the smell of the zoo.

■　■　■

Alvie's Deli was on the corner just a few blocks away from headquarters. It was Wesner's favorite place to grab a late lunch or an early dinner--always a Reuben Sandwich. He returned to the office, toothpick working against some deeply lodged tough corned beef. Reaching his desk, the lieutenant found his detective team hovering, all eager to report simultaneously on what they had learned during the last few hours. Wesner held up his hands to halt the cacophony. "Whoa, whoa, whoa! Let me take of my jacket and grab a note pad. We got an open interview room somewhere? Let's head down the hall."

Benny reported that Lucas Rowden was nowhere to be found. A uniform car was sent to retrieve him at his home address, only to find the apartment unoccupied. The building Super let the uniforms in. To everyone's surprise, the apartment was almost spartan. A card table served as a kitchen table; one easy chair and a portable TV defined the living room; a single bed and small dresser with only enough clothes for a day or two comprised the master bedroom, the spare bedroom remained empty; the bathroom held an old dry tooth brush with no paste. An empty six pack was in the garbage bag, but no food graced the refrigerator. Earlier that day, Rowden reported to work at 7:00 a.m., but abruptly left a few hours later. No vehicle was licensed in his name, so an APB using a car identification was impossible. None of the Security Department Jeeps were reported to be missing. It seemed that Rowden was in the wind.

Angel had located the Attorney for the Steelworkers Union, a fellow named Abe Gagliardo. He claimed he had not been contacted by Arthur Setter before the morning interview, although he would have attended the meeting without hesitation had he been asked. Mr. Gagliardo seemed to share a less than glowing opinion of 'Red' Setter, adding a few uncomplimentary epithets in his description.

Georgina Chouteau said she learned that the Steal Inn was owned by Pitz-Rat Limited, a St. Louis-based holding company that itself was owned by Luc-Nel Entertainment, which appeared to be a Houston-based shell corporation. The Auditor's Records Department was still searching for the individual ownership of both Pitz-Rat Limited and Luc-Nel Entertainment, although frequent filings for the company seemed to suggest the corporation originated in the Cayman Islands. Of all the reports, Wesner thought the one by Detective Chouteau was the most intriguing, although her delivery of the information on the Steal Inn lacked enthusiasm or excitement. Wesner made note of it, determined to follow up with her later.

"Good stuff! Let me tell you about my call with the Attorney, C. W. Rathbone. I believe he shares in the unflattering opinion of Arthur Setter, just like Angel's Union attorney guy. Rathbone was here only to protect the already sketchy reputation of Rubicon Steel, and to determine how much Setter knows or might say. He's also keenly interested in how much we might know. It seems that Rowden and the entire Security Team are considered corporate employees, not Union Workers. As such, you can imagine the distrust and enmity that must exist between the two groups: security and the working stiffs. Using their own helmet-coloring identification system, the white hardhats run the place, the various colorized hardhats do all the hard and dangerous work, and the silver hardhats make sure no one steps out of line.

Their sole responsibility is to Senior Management. The Union, for all intents and purposes, is a paper tiger taking direction from the silver hardhats. It's a hell of a system."

Wesner turned to Sgt. Friedman. "Benny, what do you think we should do to find Mr. Rowden? He's got his fingers deep into something, and I think those fingers are blood-stained. From all appearances, he knows we'd like to meet him, which is why he's trying to be scarce. Where do you think we should look?"

Benny thought for a minute. "You want to play it straight or bend some rules? We can just go bust into those trailers in the Mill parking lot."

Wesner considered the options. "Better go by-the-book. Might end up in court and we don't want technicalities letting bad guys off the hook. Any other ideas, anybody?"

After a few moments of silence, Georgie said, "Why don't we send in some troops to clean out The Steal Inn? If Rowden is not living in his apartment, he's got to be somewhere, likely close to the Mill. The Steal Inn looks like it was an old house. Probably some livable rooms on the second floor." Georgie caught Wesner's hard stare out of the corner of her eye at her admission. She looked toward Angel and said, "I did a drive-by of the place while waiting for the Records Department to come up with the ownership information." She looked down at the floor.

Wesner continued to stare at Det. Chouteau, not ready to fully believe her story, fairly convinced that she omitted some pertinent information. "We would need Probable Cause to invade a business with one of our heavy teams--unless, of course, you can give us some sort of Probable Cause." He glared at Georgie who refused to give him reciprocating eye contact.

Angel sensed his partner was in trouble and offered an enhancement to the idea. "If the Steal Inn is a plausible target, let's see if the State Liquor Board has any complaints about the place which they might want to pursue. We can go in as back-up to the State boys, and toss the place all we want while blaming the Highway Patrol for the damage."

Benny chuckled. "You ever see those guys go in? They call it their investigative wing. Hah! A dozen or more in military helmets, combat boots, armor, riot gear, heavy weapons…they don't fool around. They tossed a carryout on my beat once. Within 15 minutes, not one bottle in the place was unbroken, all the documents from the back room boxed and taken away, three workers in cuffs, chains around their waist and ankles, perp marched to a waiting wagon, trying not to shit their pants."

Wesner finally let Georgie escape his withering gaze, exchanging it for a stare at the ceiling. He almost smiled as he considered the idea. "You know, that would work on a lot of levels. Whether Rowden is inside the place or not, The Steal Inn is not an innocent little corner bar. Any documents we find may provide a name for whoever is behind the scenes calling the shots."

"You don't think Rowden is the brains behind this?" asked Benny.

"No. Rowden is the muscle. He's the enforcer, hired to his job so he can be close to the action. He has the tacit permission to carry weaponry and use it as he sees fit as long as he doesn't break the law. He provides protection for the mastermind. We just don't know who that person is, or what he may be the mastermind of."

"And the mastermind doesn't know whether Rowden has broken any laws, or is planning to. The mastermind has some built in deniability," said Benny.

"We haven't issued any reports on the 'John Doe' in the hospital, so there's no reason for anyone to be suspicious. Only Rowden knows what he's done, and he's probably running scared because there's been no report of a dead body under the bridge, and he saw our car arriving as he departed. He must realize his latest knifing didn't have the lasting effect he intended.

Even so, the mastermind probably doesn't care if laws are broken as long as he can stay clean himself." Wesner started humming and slapped his hands on the table having reached a decision.

"Angel, you know some of the guys at State Liquor Control, don't you? Give them a call and see if they'd like to have some fun at the Steal Inn. And then maybe we can find something in there, some ownership records, maybe even Rowden himself. And, whatever we find may give us an excuse to knock on the doors of those trailers." Wesner held up his hands. "One more thing. I trust you all, but it seems to me that Rowden—and maybe some other big-wigs—seem to know what we're doing before we do it. Let's be careful who we tell about our plans. Just in case there's a leak somewhere, let's keep the Steal Inn plan on a need-to-know basis."

■ ■ ■

"Just what do you think you're doing, Wheezie," questioned Capt. Mitchell. "This is our case. You can't just turn it over to the State Highway Patrol!"

"I totally agree, Ted. I'm not giving them anything on the attempted murder of Thorpe, nor anything about our cauldron jumper. I just need them to bust us into the Steal Inn, the place that may be Lucas Rowden's hide-out. Plus, we may get some helpful information on who's calling all the shots, who's giving Rowden his marching orders. His past record doesn't give me the sense that he's the brains behind any of this, and he doesn't seem to have a distinct motive, other than to cover for someone else. And that someone else is giving him direction, or at least permission, to be the Colonel.

"Liquor Control has had a series of complaints about the Steal Inn--everything from potential gambling in the back rooms to assault of a few patrons. They just need a reasonable excuse to go in, like a suggestion from us, the Cleveland Police. Also, we've got a file on a guy who was beat to a pulp and left for dead some hundred feet down the hill from the bar. He was so scared he wouldn't talk, even when the wire on his broken jaw was removed. Something ain't right about that place."

"You've been in there, right? What's your gut say?"

"Barmaid is an older, tough-looking woman. She's got a well-used baseball bat under the counter, and a sawed-off shotgun right near the cash register. Ceiling tiles show signs that the shotgun's been used in the bar recently. I'm betting the baseball bat has some human hairs stuck in the wood. The regular patrons clam up when a stranger happens in. Not a friendly place, all in all."

"Any of your other team members been inside?"

Wesner grimaced as he paused. "Don't think so. I told them all to stay away so we don't spook them with too many cop visits."

Capt. Mitchell picked up on the hesitation. "You think someone didn't listen so good?"

Wesner shook his head. "Georgie's acting a little squirrelly about the place. Says she did a drive by, just to see where it was. I'm not sure. Something more, maybe."

"You better find out what it is before you all go marching in there with the State Highway Patrol. We don't want anyone getting hurt. Okay, Wheezie?" After a too long pause, the Captain said, "What else is on your mind? You've got that look about you."

"Not sure of this either, Ted. I have no facts. It just seems that everyone we want to talk to is a half-step ahead of us. Like they know what we're after before we know it ourselves."

Captain Mitchell glowered. "I've been having that same gut feeling, but thought maybe I was over-reacting. You have to first look at your own team and clear each of them before we look elsewhere. One by one, examine their actions. Who might be spilling info, to who are they giving it, and why? This whole thing is about to get very real, and we need everyone on our side." He picked up the phone. "Tell Angel that I'll make the arrangements with the Liquor Control Board and the Highway Patrol. The proper way to do this is to contact the Lt. Colonel in charge of Field Operations. We can't be trying to back-door this thing with the old 'I-know-a-guy' routine. It may take a few days to set it up properly, but there won't be any second-guessing when we're done. In the meantime, find out what's bothering Georgie, and find out if she is the mole or if it's someone else."

■ ■ ■

It is late at night, too late to be out alone on a Friday night. If I'm seen walking around it will look suspicious. I already look suspicious sitting alone in a car on this deserted stretch. The pay phone up the way is under a street lamp. Too visible. But a deal is a deal. Maybe. He said to call with any information, anything that would directly affect him or the business. What makes me think I have news that would interest him? Do I have anything to say to him, really? Anything concrete?

If I place the call, tell him what I know, things might end up happening differently, a change to what has been planned. And that could lead to trouble for me. That's dangerous. But to not call—what then? If he found that I was holding back…. Would he turn on me? Would anyone even believe him? Does he have anything on me? Anything that could hurt me? I don't think he could rat on me, not without risking his own exposure. That's my guess. But maybe I wouldn't be his target. Maybe he'd go after someone I cared for. Make me hurt that way. That sounds more like his style.

So, if I do place the call, what then? Who would be in jeopardy? Me, or someone else? Could someone get killed if I told what I know? But what do I know? Everything, or only part of the plan? What if it is all a set-up? None of it is really going to happen. They just want the informant—me—to show myself. Pretty sneaky. That would be a classic Lieutenant Wesner move, I think. Some people are already suspicious, I think. There are fingers pointing—at someone, everyone, anyone. Could they suspect me?

Here's what I'll do. I will just go dial the number. Let it ring five times, no, maybe just four. Yeah, four. Maybe he won't answer. Then I'll be free of guilt, either way. I've kept my part of the bargain, but you didn't keep up on your end. I did as I was instructed. You didn't answer. Sorry it didn't work out. That way, I haven't turned on my partners at Headquarters. No one's blood will be on my hands. Everybody just keep your head down and it will go away, right? Just…don't pick up before the fourth ring.

At the phone booth, head covered to avoid recognition, dialing the number, ready to hang up at the fourth ring. There is the first ring. The second. Three times. It was picked up. "…What can you tell me?" the usual response.

"I…." The caller hangs up. The call is disconnected.

SATURDAY, NOVEMBER 6

I hope I can go to sleep. My internal clock is really off kilter. Nearly fell asleep on the catwalk between pours a week or so ago. Wouldn't that have been something? Me taking a header into the lava soup. Hah! They'd never find me then. Best way to go, I guess. Nothing left for anyone to worry about. I wonder if I'd feel anything. A little heat, then…. Who knows. The only ones who can say for sure are those who've already fallen in. But they're not talking very much, are they. Hah!

I wonder how many have taken the dive. There are stories about one or two in the past — the ones people remember. But there must have been some before — before anyone still working there can remember. The Mill is almost a hundred years old, or something like that, I suppose. Had to be some Lava Divers in the past. Some probably did it on purpose. Lava Divers…that's what Anton called them. But I don't think he knew how many there were either.

Should I keep sleeping during the day, staying awake all night? Nothing on TV in the wee hours. Nothing to do if I can't go back to work. But if I change my sleep pattern I'll really be screwed up when they call and say I can go back to work. I'll get a crossword puzzle book maybe. That will keep me busy during the night. Wish I could go to sleep. Maybe something unusual will happen tonight. Maybe then I can enjoy a deep sleep tomorrow morning.

■ ■ ■

The weekend, but not a day of rest for a group leader like Lt. Alex Wesner. He was at his desk by 7:00 a.m., deep into an analysis of what facts he knew, finishing the report for the Highway Patrol and the State Liquor Board to approve a hands-on investigation of the Steal Inn. To get the required search warrant, he would need to make it sound both plausible and heinous--not easy since he had no real facts. Likewise, a report on the physical property and whether there were likely danger points would help the State Highway Patrol develop an attack strategy. He had a gnawing feeling that a search of the Steal Inn would not be a gentlemanly affair, but would be more like a wrestling takedown.

The case itself was a bit of a mess. He felt like he was playing chess with the various characters involved in this melodrama. He had to figure out who took down his white knight, Thorpe, and why. Further, he was trying to see if one game of chess fit on top of another, searching for an elusive--possibly incinerated--missing person. A person or a pawn? He wondered whether two separate games were being played, or if this was a single, three-dimensional match against a multitude of unknown opponents. On top of all of that, there could be a mole among his group of detectives, or perhaps nearby the group. Another detective who was a bit too nosy, perhaps; the desk Sergeant who knew almost all of their movements; or one of his own—Benny, Georgie, Angel. Could he even eliminate his old friend, Captain Mitchell? Maddening!

Beyond those concerns, what was it about those trailers in the parking lot that rankled his nerves? Plus, the verbose but enigmatic Seazy Lutz, or Cezary Ludzinski, was now playing a game of hide-and-seek. Unwilling to answer questions in a straightforward or believable way, he now had become unavailable, not seen at his residence for a few days. What Seazy actually knew was a mystery. Where he had gone also unknown. To put out an APB would require Wesner to have a legitimate reason, not simply a request to know his whereabouts. So regular precinct patrols around Seazy's house was about all he could ask for. Or Wesner could wait for him to show up at the park opposite the fake Victorian.

A call to the hospital confirmed that 'John Doe', aka Peter Thorpe, was still in a coma, but his vitals were improving since the knife wounds were sutured and holding. Wesner remained hopeful that Thorpe would regain consciousness soon to identify his assailants. He made a mental note to drive out to the cabin and check in on Thorpe's girlfriend, Rosie Dwyer. It would do her good to see other humans. Maybe he should take her to the hospital for a visit to Thorpe. Might help both of them.

An hour or more later, Capt. Mitchell shuffled toward his office, a briefcase full of paperwork under his arm. He paused facing Wesner's desk. "Got your whole team here, I see. Tough task master."

"I've got the report for you to send to Columbus. Hopefully, my people are all having a nice morning at home."

"Not from what I see," said Mitchell, motioning to the desks behind Wesner.

Wesner turned around to see Detectives Friedman, Lopez and Chouteau digging through the files, trying to organize their own perspectives of the case. "Hmm. Looks like I owe some people a nice breakfast." His chair creaked as he swiveled toward them. "What're you all doing here?"

Friedman said, "Same as you, Wheezie, just trying to make sense of all of this. My brother-in-law is picking up the clambake supplies, so I've got the morning free to sort through my notes."

"I missed the cauldron visit Thursday, flying back from Miami," said Lopez. "Georgie is sharing her notes with me. I traded her my write up on Miami. She seems to have some strong opinions on what may have happened there."

Detective Georgina Chouteau looked up. "Definitely an evil presence took those men. The medical report indicates the murderer was experienced at gutting his quarry. What do we know of Lucas Rowden's distant past? We should ask the doctors for an evaluation of Mr. Thorpe's injuries."

The lieutenant smiled at his team's willingness to put in extra hours on the case, and their thoroughness exploring details. "I'm thinking of taking Rosie Dwyer up to see Thorpe. The sound of her voice may bring him out of his coma. Plus, she's got to be going nuts out there in the woods by herself. While I'm there, I'll quiz the doctor on the nature of the wounds." He turned to Sgt. Friedman. "Benny, would it be alright with you if we welcomed Ms. Dwyer to the clambake tomorrow? A more casual, friendly gathering might have a positive effect on her attitude, and might get more information out of her."

"Sure, that's fine. There will be plenty of food. Angel and Georgie haven't had a chance to talk to her yet. Probably a good idea to get their perspective on her as well."

Georgie said, "Perhaps she can better explain to me this strange clambake practice of yours. Maybe I can try to befriend her a bit at the event."

Almost under his breath, Angel said, "Good luck to her if she accepts that friendship."

"I've warned you, Mr. Muscles!" Georgie was on her feet closing on her partner with a dark, malicious look in her eye.

Wesner stood up. "You guys hungry? Bacon and eggs breakfast on me at the diner."

Georgie said, "I suppose it's too much to hope they have beignets."

"Just for that, you need to come with me out to Thorpe's cabin after breakfast. Grab your stuff. You can make friends with Rosie on the ride to the hospital."

. . .

The breakfast was casual and unrushed. Wesner's toothpick jabbed at some bacon stuck between his teeth as he led Georgie to an unmarked police car a block from the breakfast diner. "It'll take us about 45 minutes to get there--maybe a little less on a Saturday. Have you spent any time exploring the Eastern suburbs since you got here?"

Georgie gave him a strange look as she shut the car door. "Learning the city itself has been challenging enough, let alone venturing out beyond the city limits. Why are there so many oddly angled streets?"

Wesner nodded knowingly. "I hear you. This city can be a bit of a challenge. The valley where the steel mills are--the river that created the valley--it forms a gouge in the geography of the city, like a hatchet cleaving a piece of green wood, all irregular like. Despite the best attempts of the city planners to develop straight North-South numbered streets and right-angle East-West Avenues, the geography of that river valley and the irregular coastline of Lake Erie forced a hodge-podge of primary roads fanning out from the city center in all directions. I'll bet there are more acute angle intersections in Cleveland than any other city in America."

Georgie nodded. "Even though New Orleans is built on land formed by a severe bend in the Mississippi River, the developer managed to maintain square-road sanity. How long does it take for someone to become acquainted with these Cleveland streets? I've been here just over three months, and I still get lost with some regularity."

Wesner grinned, saying, "I've lived her just over 50 years and I'm still discovering short cuts I never knew existed. To make matters worse, as a road passes from the city proper to a suburb or crosses a township line, the name of the road changes. There's one road I know has four different names, even though it's as straight as an arrow."

The conversation lagged as they headed toward the east, gradually climbing the gently sloping land into suburbs designated as "The Heights". Far enough away and on higher ground to avoid the black and orange soot impurities which fall from the industrial smokestacks, The Heights is comprised of several well-planned neighborhoods and municipalities where wealthier families raise children in an environment of purer air. The fanned-out, too-tight city streets leading from the city center give way to suburban boulevards with park land separating the eastbound lanes from the westbound. Both sides of the boulevards showcase manor homes, some resembling mansions, sedately set back on two-acre-plus lots and tucked under massive oaks and sycamores. Maple trees are too plebian for these privileged patrician landscapes.

Georgie asked, "You've been in this area for over 50 years, you said. Does that mean all your life?"

"Most of it," replied Wesner. "My family moved here when I was about 3-years old from someplace in Indiana. Dad died when I was still young. He was a cop, too. Bank robbery went bad. Shoot-out. He got hit. Mom took to working until I entered the Police Academy. Then she dropped dead, too. Heart attack. I've been at this for just over 30 years."

"So, you're about 55 years old or so?"

"Personal question, don't you think? But yeah, just now 54. What about you, if you'll permit an equally personal question."

"I'm 36 years old. Unmarried. Lived in a number of places but New Orleans is what I call my home. Lived there the longest."

"Family there?"

Georgie paused before answering. "I don't think so. I grew up in an orphanage near Baton Rouge. I was told my parents abandoned me, but I later learned that the authorities removed me from my home because my parents were the high priest and priestess of the local Creole church. For my own protection, the documents said. Later, as I grew older, I searched for my folks. Records were sketchy, but I believe they likely died in a mysterious fire in the Vaudou Chapel, the center of their worship. Authorities were reluctant to call it arson. At 18, the orphanage gave me $100 and a 'good luck' card along with my one suitcase of personal items. I moved around a bit. Finally found a home with the NOLA Police Department. So, to answer your question, no, I don't think there is any family in the region--not any longer."

Wesner's jaw tightened. "Tough way to grow up. Why'd you come to Cleveland?"

Georgie looked out the passenger side window holding her response, considering how to answer, whether to answer at all. Wesner sensed he had touched a nerve, and let the question and the conversation drop. The further east he drove, the more pleasant the scene. "Cleveland is an old city," said Wesner, "goes back to the late 1700s. Industry helped it grow bigger quickly over the decades, but it also made the town as dirty and rusty as it is today. Still, there is some beauty out here in the country. Numerous small towns lie just a stone's throw from the city center. They all look like they were dropped in here from New England. Pretty town squares with gazebos in the center, white clapboard churches, the whole bit. So, it's not such a bad place."

Georgie looked toward the Lieutenant. "I do not think the city is bad at all. There is beauty everywhere if you look for it. The skyline is magnificent in a true 'downtown' fashion. The ethnic neighborhoods offer so many varied restaurants. Even the steel mills—they are both fearsome and beautiful. They glow such bewitching orange colors in the dark of the night. I find the city fascinating."

"Does Cleveland compare favorably to New Orleans?"

She sighed, "Each city is unique. No two can be, nor should be, compared one to another. What one has the other does not. You will find people that love New Orleans, and others who hate it. Same is true for Cleveland. The charm of each city finds its champions. If a person finds no charm, they move on to somewhere else."

"Did New Orleans lose its charm for you?"

Again, Georgie grew silent and looked out the window. Eventually she said, "There are more reasons for changing your residence than a city losing charm. Occasionally, the charm is not a sufficient reason to remain. Perhaps a day will come when I go back. I still do love the city."

Wesner had turned off the main road onto a narrow, two-lane country road. He slowed and found an unpaved, gravel lane on the right about a half-mile in. He continued to watch for anyone following him. He had done so since leaving the police parking lot. "This was not easy to see in the dark when I first came out here. But now, I think it wise to be sure we are not followed."

A quarter-mile further and the gravel road curved in an 'S', with scrub trees bordering both sides. In the middle of the 'S', the cruiser turned onto a dirt drive, blocked by a rusty steel gate half-off its hinges and half camouflaged by the overgrowth. Wesner pulled to a stop on the dirt drive and got out to move the gate. He motioned Georgie to pull the car through so he could close the gate afterward.

"She's going to be jumpy, so let's drive in slowly. She has a gun, so we've got to be a bit more careful. This is the same car I brought her in, which should calm her some if she recognizes it. I told her to expect us and that I'd beep the horn twice, then twice again as a signal it was me." Georgie stayed in the driver's seat and followed the winding driveway, two dirt ruts cut in the weeds. When she spotted the cabin nestled deep in the trees, she gave the two-beep signals as Wesner described. A motion at the curtain suggested Rosie Dwyer was watching.

Stepping out of the car, Wesner shouted, "Rosie! It's me, Lieutenant Wesner! One of my fellow detectives is driving. Can we come in?" Detective Chouteau exited so Rosie could clearly see who was approaching.

The door opened a crack. "Why is she here? Is something wrong with Petey?"

"No, no. Pete is getting better. We'd like to take you to see him. Detective Chouteau is working the case with me. You haven't really met yet, so I thought you two could talk on the way to the hospital."

"I'm not on display like in a zoo, you know. Don't be bringing strangers here to see the crazy lady in the woods."

"C'mon, Rosie! We mean you no harm. Put the gun down. I know you're holding it."

Georgie turned to the Lieutenant. "Wheezie, let me go speak to her." She held her hands open at shoulder height and walked toward the cabin door. The Lieutenant made note that it marked the first time that Detective Chouteau had addressed him with his nickname, 'Wheezie', and he liked the affectionate way she said it.

He couldn't hear what they were saying, but it didn't take long for Georgie to lower her hands and lean against the door jamb as the two women chatted. A few minutes later, Georgie returned to the car. "She's getting her purse. She's excited to be going to the hospital. Why haven't you kept her up to date on Thorpe's condition?"

"Excuse me? I call her every day and check on her and let her know if there's been any changes."

"Clearly insufficient. She needs friendly communication, and lots of it. You weren't providing what she needs."

Wesner went to the driver's seat mumbling, "Seems I'm never providing what women need."

"I'm sorry, I didn't quite catch what you were saying," Georgie said, trying to mask her grin.

Wesner started the car. "You two sit in the back and get friendly. I'll try to shut up and play chauffeur."

The Lieutenant took the Expressway to the hospital figuring that a rapid route was best. For tracking possible tails, the slow, stop-and-go surface roads were better. But there were no tails on the way out, and it was quite a distance from Thorpe's eastside cabin to Metro General Hospital on the near westside of the river valley. He wasn't sure the two women in the backseat would be able to communicate, so he reasoned a quick trip was in order. He couldn't have been more wrong. Georgie quickly learned how Thorpe and Rosie Dwyer met, and that Rosie's first husband was a first-class bum, albeit a bum without real front teeth anymore. And it became obvious that Wesner's original opinion that Thorpe was a good guy proved completely accurate. He had rescued Rosie when she was most vulnerable with no preset conditions, set her up in a safe apartment building owned by a friend, and checked up on her periodically. Eventually, and gently, their mutual affection melted into love. They have been living together in Thorpe's house for about 18 months awaiting her official divorce decree.

Of course, Georgie had to share some of her own personal details in the give-and-take between the women. Something bad had happened in New Orleans — bad enough to cause Georgie to leave the town she loved and start her life over. The orphanage information came out again, matching what Wesner had heard earlier.

Along the way he learned that both women liked jazz. Not necessarily the New Orleans / Dixieland style, more in the Miles Davis / Stan Getz realm. Wesner smiled at that, since that also matched his tastes. He took a deep breath and felt a soft warmness in his chest, a feeling he hadn't felt in a long time. He shook it off and concentrated on his driving.

Arriving at the hospital, Wesner took a wide loop around the block twice, then a smaller circle around the parking lot and garage. Rosie paid no attention to what he was doing, but Georgie knew only too well. She reached over to the front dash and pulled the police radio to her. The dispatcher connected them to the guard on the 7th floor, stationed outside Thorpe's room. He gave them the all-clear from inside. Wesner pulled the car into an "Official Parking Only" slot and quickly exited, scanning for anything suspicious. Seeing nothing, he motioned an all clear to the backseat.

Rosie was suddenly alarmed. "Was that necessary? What are you looking for?"

Georgie said, "We've got a guard on Pete's room. Whoever tried to kill him may feel the need to try again. We're just being careful."

"Oh, my god! I didn't think he'd still be in that kind of danger! I was focused on his regaining consciousness."

"Why do you think we asked you to stay at the cabin? We can't take a chance they won't be after you as an additional threat or a bargaining chit," said Lt. Wesner.

"Who are they, Lieutenant Wesner? Who's after my Petey?"

He ushered them into the 'Emergency Personnel Only' back door, constantly checking all around. "We have a hunch, but we're lacking evidence right now. And the primary suspect is nowhere to be found."

A private elevator whooshed them to the 7th floor. The officer guarding the door rose as they approached. "The medical staff is just now finishing another check on him. They sound encouraged," the patrolman said.

"Did you check that those folks are actually who they say they are?" asked Wesner.

"You bet, Lieutenant. As you instructed, no one gets in that I haven't checked. That goes for the two ladies with you, too. Can I see identification, please?"

Wesner smiled. "Good man," motioning Detective Chouteau and Rosie Dwyer to produce their I.D.s.

As the medical staff concluded their exam, Rosie rushed in, hugging and kissing the prone Peter Thorpe. Georgie went to her side holding her shoulders. Wesner stepped outside the door with the lead doctor and primary nurse. "What's his condition?"

The doctor pocketed his stethoscope and smiled. "His vitals are strong and gaining. I suspect he will come out of the coma at any time." Motioning to the loving attention he was receiving, he added, "That will help. Soon after he comes to, I'd like to get him to his home for recuperation. That will be more beneficial than anything we can do for him here."

Wesner said, "I may need a favor, then. Let's go somewhere private to talk."

. . .

On the drive back to the cabin, Rosie jabbered excitedly about how she was planning to take care of Petey during his recovery. Neither of her police companions had a chance to get a word in as she listed and added to her affectionate plans. Finally, Wesner broke through. "Hey, Rosie! It's going to be another few days before Pete can be moved. In the meantime, one of our guys is throwing a clambake at his place tomorrow. It'd do you good to get out. You like clambakes? How about we pick you up tomorrow just after noon. Fresh air, good food, friendly people...whadya say?"

"Oh? Yeah, I like clambakes. Who's throwing it?"

"You remember Sgt. Friedman? Benny? You met him the first night we visited you at Pete's house."

She frowned. "Yeah. He was kinda mean. He thought I was gonna run out on Petey."

"He was just doing his job, Rosie. Remember, you were holding a gun on us."

"Yeah, well…. Is Georgina going to be there?"

Georgie leaned toward her. "Yes, I'll be there, too. I won't let Benny bite you."

Rosie giggled. "Okay! Sounds like fun. God, I'd love to get out of that cabin for a while. It's nice, but being alone gets spooky."

Wesner had been studying the rear-view mirror as they approached the gravel road. He suddenly sped up, quickening his pace down the narrow two-lane. About a mile up, he turned down a paved driveway leading to an estate. A small sports car zipped past, careening down the two-lane.

"Hey! You missed the turn back there, didn't 'ya? Happens to me all the time," said Rosie.

Wesner watched to see if the sports car would turn around. It didn't. "Yes, I sure did miss it. Let's try again."

Arriving at the cabin, the two detectives walked through the place as though they were house hunters searching for a new home. In actuality, they were making sure the cabin was secure and that Rosie would be safe.

Heading back to the city, Georgie said, "The sports car bothered you, didn't it?"

Wesner said, "Yep. It was following me for about three miles, turning down the two-lane just like we did. Maybe just coincidence, but I don't like coincidences."

"I'm glad you didn't alert Rosie. She's already pretty jumpy."

"I know. I'm glad she's coming to the clambake. And she kind of locked you into it, too! I had it figured that you'd try to excuse your way out."

"You are learning my methods. I'm not sure I like that. You are correct. I was developing an angle to spend the day alone, not shucking clams."

"Good food, good friends. You need it as bad as Rosie does."

Georgie looked toward the western sky. "Already approaching sunset. Speaking of good food, I'm starved. Nothing since breakfast. Get me to my car so I can get something to eat."

"What's on your menu tonight?"

Georgie had a sudden thought, absent for many years. Just as quickly, she shrugged it off. "Oh, I think I'll just pick up a pizza, or maybe something Asian."

"You live on the Westside, right? Have you ever tried Mama Madonna's Pizza? Ahh, it's the best! Haven't had a pie from there in years. My mouth's watering just thinking about it."

"Yes, Westside. I'm renting an apartment in Old Brooklyn--that's what everyone seems to call it, although it doesn't resemble Brooklyn, New York. Haven't tried Mama Madonna's, although I think I know where it is. Pretty good, huh?"

"I mean to tell you, they've got one of those old brick ovens, must be 100 years old. Their crust is somehow very special. Home-made sauce, top quality pepperoni--so delicious. I highly recommend it."

Georgie grew silent for a few minutes, then abruptly turned to the Lieutenant. "Would it be improper for us to share that pizza? At my apartment?"

Wesner felt his stomach tingle. In his brain he knew he should decline, that sharing a meal in her apartment, given the jumbled thoughts and feelings coursing through him, was likely inappropriate. But in his heart, he contrived a series of acceptable excuses. "I suppose we could use the time to talk over the case, go over everything we've learned. See if we've missed any details. And in the meantime, enjoy a great pizza...Okay!" Pulling into the Police Headquarters parking lot, they each headed to their personal vehicles. "Write down your address on my notepad. I'll pick up the pizza and join you there shortly."

■ ■ ■

A sharp North wind blew fresh, cold Canadian air across Lake Erie. The healthy breeze became a serious blow as it funneled into the industrial valley. What had been a pleasant autumn temperature dropped rapidly to pre-freeze-warning levels. Seazy shivered his way toward Hot Mill #1, not dressed for the rude cold blasts. Once inside he would be fine, too warm actually. Earlier he received a call from his foreman. They were short on crew. Needed his help. Come in, don't worry about the suspension.

His shift time was still a few hours away, but he had nowhere else to go. He knew of a secluded spot where he could escape whenever life became too difficult. Tucked away in a corner alcove, hidden from the view of any passersby, a fire hose was loosely coiled up. Few workers knew it was there, and those who did would never search it out. In the event of a fire in the hot mill, everyone would just run away. One fire hose, even a dozen fire hoses, would not be useful if hot steel began pouring out. The hose had some pliable give, just enough cushioning to make a passable lounging couch. Not overly comfortable, but not horrible either. Seazy waited until all possible witnesses were busy elsewhere. He then quickly snuck into his hiding spot and settled in for a few hours of privacy until his shift began.

Seazy didn't realize that his foreman had a work station, a partially covered office, on a platform a floor above and overlooking the cauldron and the entire area. The foreman shook his head, watching Seazy sneak into the alcove just like he had done a few times before during the past several months. He was fairly certain that bringing Seazy back to work was a mistake while the Anton investigation was still ongoing. But Management insisted. He'd received a call from Timmy in Human Resources to put him back on the payroll. So Seazy was back. The foreman recognized that Seazy had issues. The exact nature of the issues he did not know and was not about to pry and find out. He was a factory foreman, not a psychologist, which the foreman believed was exactly who Seazy needed to talk to. As bosses go, he was a good man, empathetic of the issues of the men he directed. He recognized a troubled soul among his roster of workers when he saw one, and Seazy was a troubled soul. He wrote a reminder note to have Human Resources remove Seazy from the cauldron, the most dangerous place in the mill. He winced as he jotted the note, realizing that by filing such a report, Human Resources would not simply change Seazy's job. Rather, the report would give H.R. the excuse to sever Seazy's employment at Rubicon Steel.

Seazy sighed as he relaxed his body into the coils of hose. "I need to leave town. There's nothing but trouble left for me here. It won't be long before everyone knows what I've done...what I haven't done. Everyone will know my deepest secrets. No, not just my deepest secrets...also my darkest secrets. I am dark. I am evil. I know it. I can't stand thinking that everyone else would know it, too. Where could I go to escape? I need to go somewhere where the fire won't burn me. Does such a place exist?

"When I die, will I burn in hell? Is all that even true, that stuff we learned about hell in church? Is there such a place as hell? There was a discussion in one of my college classes...how did the theory go...a place is a temporal concept. Without time, there is no such thing as place. All very meta — meta...something. So, if place doesn't exist after death, just like time wouldn't exist after death, does that mean hell doesn't exist? It's all so confusing. My head hurts. If that's the case, what will happen when I die? Maybe I should try to find out. Maybe if I die in a cauldron of hot steel flames, then I won't have to spend eternity burning in hell, if there is a hell. A cauldron, like what witches use to make their soup, or potions, or whatever. If I burned up now, I wouldn't have to in the afterlife.

"Maybe Lucifer needs a bag man. I can be his assistant. No fire that way. He knows I'm a bad person, so maybe he'll take pity on me and give me a job as one of his faithful servants. Are there jobs in hell? Can someone be considered faithful in a place full of rotten souls? But here we go again, there's no such thing as place in the afterlife.

"Oh, but what if Lucifer prefers to ice down those who die in flames. Freeze them to death. But they're already dead so…my head is really starting to hurt. Can't concentrate on this stuff too long. But, yeah, that's another way to go. Freeze yourself. They say there's no pain in freezing to death. Your body just shuts down and you go to sleep. A really long sleep. Like forever. Would Lucifer admire someone who did that, so the warmth of hell would actually feel good. Maybe that's the way to get in his good graces.

"Hah! I bet that's the first time anyone imagined Lucifer having good graces. According to the priests and rabbis, there is nothing good about the devil, and he has no grace. Wait…is Lucifer a he? Could the devil be a she? That might be why I'm in the kind of situation I'm in. No, it's gotta be a man. No woman could be so evil to drive me to do what I've done. Or not done. Lucifer is a he. He knows how to twist my nose, my fingers, my mind.

"So, which is it? Do I stay here and face the music? Do I run away? Do I face the cauldron? Do I go freeze to death? Where do I go to find the answer? Who can I tell these thoughts to? My church priest? No, he told me to stay the hell away from his church. Pretty mean of him to do that. Why can't I--oh, yeah, he did catch me stealing from the Poor Box. But I was poor at the time, right? Well, where's the forgiveness? If not a priest, then who? Where's Anton when you need him. When I need him. He would know what to do. He would give me good advice. Maybe. Until he found out…. No, not Anton. Then who? Maybe that detective. He seemed to understand me as much as anyone. But he can't tell me to run away. He would say 'tell the truth', as if I knew what truth was. What is Truth? What is the philosophic reality of Truth? Does Truth even matter anymore?"

He laid back into the hose, sinking into a comfortable crease, closed his eyes and fell asleep. He had not slept so soundly in weeks.

■　■　■

Wesner found himself avoiding the truth. He twisted his logic to convince himself that there was nothing wrong with sharing a pizza with one of his subordinates, and certainly not with this particular subordinate. He had started the day wanting to learn more about Georgina Chouteau as a person, as a law officer, as a detective. He needed to know how good a cop she was. He needed to know what made her tick, what positive attributes made her a credit to his team, to the police force. Beyond that, there was something about her description of her drive-by of the Steal Inn that made Wesner think there was more not being said. So, sharing a pizza--this was a way to find out who she was and if she could be trusted in the troubling days ahead. That was what he told himself. But in the back of his mind, he now wondered if he was the one who could be trusted. It had been a long time since he spent an evening alone with a lady.

The buzzer opened the building's front door. A half-flight up, Georgie stood by the opened apartment door. Already changed out of her work clothes, she stood barefoot in a blousy, shapeless, full-length long-sleeved multi-colored casual robe. The transformation was so startling, Wesner had to look twice to make sure it was Georgie. He had never seen her jet-black hair dangling down. It was always rolled up in a tight bun or tucked under a hat or scarf. Tonight, it hung freely over her shoulders and half-way down her back.

"You coming up? I'm starving!"

He ascended the stairs, struck speechless, handing her the pizza box. She swirled into the apartment, he tailing like a needy puppy dog. He was trying to determine how many different vibrant colors were in the cloth of the robe: bright red, screaming orange, slices of lemon yellow, boldest of blues and purples, both forest and lime green, slashes of white and black all mixed in what appeared to be no distinct pattern at all — a jigsaw of casually arranged shards of fragile broken glass transformed into silk.

He stood transfixed in the middle of her living room, his mouth slightly open. The room was definitely decorated as if dropped into the building from a New Orleans tea room…or an expensive brothel…or a voodoo chapel. Candles burned in several places giving off the soft scent of bee's wax. Subdued lamplight barely escaped the heavily painted but fragile-looking glass lamp shades, each trimmed at the bottom with brilliant, reflective glass beads, blood red, sunlight yellow, amethyst purple, emerald green. The shades appeared to be fashioned from exquisitely thin glass, breakable if breathed on too heavily.

"Beer okay?"

"Huh?"

"Do you want a beer with your pizza, Wheezie?"

"Oh. Beer. Yeah. Beer would be great."

"Come sit at the table. You seem to be distracted by my appearance this evening."

He sat at the small round table that served as a dining area. "Well, it is quite a change from the way I left you about 45 minutes ago. Your sarong, or whatever you call it, is very colorful."

"And it is comfortable after wearing a gun belt and badge all day. I hope you don't mind my being barefoot. My feet like their freedom just like the rest of me."

Wesner fought the mental image of what other parts of her body were enjoying freedom. "Hey, it's your home. Be as comfortable as you wish." He wasn't sure if that also sounded wrong, just as wrong as the mental image he was fighting.

"What kind of toppings did you get?"

"I wasn't sure what your favorites might be, so I got pepperoni, Italian sausage, green peppers and mushrooms. I figured you could scrape off anything that you don't like."

"Mmm. Sounds like a perfect pie. Dig in." She handed him a plate and fork if he needed them. He did not.

During bites, Wesner tried to be business like. "So, what do you make of Rosie?"

"She's a good kid. Had a rough life, haven't we all. She's still trying to trust people. Seeing Peter Thorpe today really brought her out. She was almost bubbly at the thought he might be re-leased soon."

"Yeah. About that. The doc said he might be released in a little more than 48 hours. Monday or Tuesday, let's say. He still can't care for himself. He'll need someone to nurse him for a while. Do you think Rosie can do it?"

Georgina thought for a minute. "She was talking as if she might have had some nurse training somewhere in her past. I think if we give her the necessary materials--whatever a nurse should have in these circumstances--I think she can handle it."

"Do you think we can get him to the cabin without arousing too much interest?"

She looked at him out of the corner of her eye. "What are you thinking of doing?"

He was regaining his composure as he detailed his plan. Suddenly it was Georgie who had a look on her face of incredulity.

They devoured most of the pizza and started a second beer, moving their discussion to the couch. Wesner went over again what he thought might be a workable plan to protect Peter Thorpe, explaining Georgie's role, asking for and receiving refinements.

She nodded and said, "Well, it appears that is what we will have to do. When do you think the Liquor Control raid will happen?"

"I got a message from Capt. Mitchell. He says the Highway Patrol is very eager to move on it. The raid will probably go down this coming Tuesday or Wednesday, just a few days from now. Quicker than most of us expected. That's why getting Thorpe somewhere safe needs to happen first and quickly."

Georgie paused, as she examined Wesner's eyes. "This may be a dangerous operation, all phases of it. I really should cleanse your aura before either of us go running into harm's way."

"What have you got in mind?" asked Wesner with both skepticism and a hint of libidinous hope mixed with fear. He was enjoying Georgie's company too much and realized that what he most desired was against the department's policy of fraternization or relations with a subordinate. For the sake of his future, his pension, he had to resist.

"What I am proposing is a ritualistic cleansing of your aura, of your chakras. Each of us has seven chakras which must be in balance for our lives to be in balance. As I have observed you for the last several days, it is apparent that you have done as well as you are able to fight the imbalance which pervades you spirit. But your life is a struggle because you are constantly seeking to clear your aura without knowing how to do so. You require a personal and spiritual forgiveness of whatever sins you think you have committed in the past. You will soon understand that you have not actually sinned. You just think you have. And that perception can be more dangerous than having actually committed foul deeds."

"I don't know about this," said Wesner shaking his head while his chest both tingled and squirmed.

"I promise you, nothing will harm you, and nothing untoward will happen, even if you wish it to." She smiled knowingly as Wesner's face gave away his disappointment.

She went to the kitchen and prepared a cup of what seemed to be strong tea. She gathered candles and arrayed them on the floor, roughly outlining where Wesner would position himself. "Here. Drink this. It is a strong brew and may not favor your tastes. But it is essential for what will follow. This will be a simple procedure for you, the recipient. Not so simple for me, the priestess. But when done, you will be cleansed of all bad karma. Strong spirits will come to protect you."

Drinking the potion or tea in three quick gulps, the awful taste made him gasp. "How do we do this," he coughed his words.

"Please sit on the floor. Soon, I will ask you to lie flat amongst the candles, eyes closed. Your eyes must remain closed throughout. You must take off your shirt so I have direct access to your heart. I will place various objects — candles, oils, talisman figures--on your chest at various times. There will be chanting, water for cleansing, and some music I will play in the background. All part of the purification ritual. Have you ever received a reiki treatment?"

"No, not that I recall."

"Well, this will be somewhat similar, but using different talismans, different incantations. Some people who go through the ritual see images in their mind, or think they see or hear spirits. All very normal, and possibly true. Most of all, you must remain calm, say nothing, and not be frightened. Are you okay with this? May I proceed?"

"With one request."

"What is that?"

"First, you must tell me what really happened when you made the drive-by of the Steal Inn. Your story doesn't seem to have a conclusion that makes sense. You are holding something back. I cannot have you participate in the plan we've outlined without knowing full well what happened there and where your head is at, and if any of our people will be at risk."

Georgie slid next to him on the floor. She retrieved the empty cup from the tea. Grabbing Wesner's hand, she pulled him toward her. Unbuttoning his shirt, she told him exactly what had transpired at the Steal Inn, and how it reminded her of the awful memory of the abandoned amusement park in New Orleans. At length, she said, "I hate the smell of the lion's cage."

"What's that supposed to mean?"

"You will now take me off the case and send me to guard the lion's cage at the zoo. That is what I fear."

The two were only inches apart, close enough to smell the others scent. His head was spinning. "You have become too important to this case to remove you at this time. No lion's cage. But do not keep anything else from me going forward."

She put her hand on his forehead and held it there. "This is where your third eye chakra is hiding. Always keep it clear. Yes. In the future, I will tell you everything, whether you may wish to hear it or not. Starting now." She pulled away from him and motioned to the circle of candles. "At this moment, we are both very close to one another, physically, emotionally. We are both aroused--sexually. We are feeling a heat between our souls. But to cleanse your aura, we must be as kindred spirits, not united spirits. Perhaps in the future we can revisit our feelings, our longings. Not now, not this evening." She spread her hands toward the opening of the candles. "This ceremony is difficult enough without the addition of sexual union. Please position yourself within the candle outline."

Wesner's mouth hung open. He was too embarrassed to ask how she knew he wanted her. He was too alarmed to ask about her desires toward him. He removed his shirt as instructed and lay amid the candles. Georgie repositioned some to be neither too close nor too far away from his body. "Do not get any amorous ideas. I must remove my gown to prevent it exploding in fire. And I must wear certain ceremonial vestments. It is best that you close your eyes for the remainder of the cleansing. You must focus on a clear and bright aura."

Try as he might, he could not resist sneaking a peak at the rustling and movements occurring around him. Georgie had removed the airy multi-colored robe and stood with her back to him, clothed only in a tight red and black corset. A very long and loose necklace made of what appeared to be human bones hung around her neck front and back, mixing with her long, jet-black hair. Positioning a headdress and mask, she turned toward him.

"I told you to close your eyes! You must forget what you now see!"

He shut his eyes hard, but would never be able to erase the image. Her face, except for her mouth, was covered with an all too realistic skull mask, feathers rising from the top as a type of crown. Golden snake bracelets clung to both arms. Intentionally or not, the corset was incredibly sensuous.

As she dropped to her knees next to the fire-encircled man, a distant drumbeat and chanting began. Wesner couldn't tell if it was a recording or something going on in his head. A heavy, metal object was put on his chest. He felt the presence of a hot flame reaching into the metal object. Acrid smoke rose, followed by the addition of sweet incense, the odors being purposely blown toward his face. Something else was mixed in, something unidentifiable, but he felt his head swimming. Soft chants, whispers, more like hisses actually, flooded over him. He saw things on the back of his eyelids: scenes—were they from the past or the future—people he knew but didn't recognize, actions. Feathers touched his chest, the chanting volume increased as did the distant music—drums and flutes and unidentifiable instruments—forming melodies both soothing and frightening. An object was positioned over his heart, moved and repositioned, other objects replacing them. Chanting grew more intense. Time was suspended. He was totally immobile, unable to flex a muscle even if he wanted to. He felt the warmth of her body close to his. Felt the touch of flesh on flesh. He was convinced that the corset was gone, even as he kept his eyes tightly closed. An image, a man, a shaman, hovered over his face to the right side. The shaman smiled and nodded. Warm water dripped on his chest, in the hollow beneath his heart. Warm water, the temperature of one's body. So slight was the drip as to be almost imaginary. Was it water or tears, he could not be sure. Oil. The smell of a fragrant oil. A sharp instrument with a point was blending the oil with the water in the hollow of his chest just below his heart. The shaman bent low to his right ear and whispered a question. Wesner replied, "My real name is Alexi Wisniewski." Again, the shaman bent low, whispering in his right ear. At the same moment, the Priestess bent low to his left ear and whispered. They both said the same thing, but Wesner could not decipher it. He wanted to hear more, he needed to know what they said, but just as suddenly as they had spoken, they were gone. Moments passed, or possibly minutes, maybe even hours.

Silence. Not a sound. No chanting. No images in his head. No scent of incense or sacred oil. He took a chance and opened his eyes.

"Welcome back," smiled Georgie. She sat at his side, dressed again in her gown. There were no candles anywhere. No ritualistic items, no music, no chanting. "How do you feel?"

Wesner tried to rise on one elbow with great difficulty. "What happened? How long have I been out?"

"Careful. Do not try to rise too suddenly. You have been through a very deep cleansing. There was much to clean, and you will find that all of what you have been suppressing will now be very clear, able to be faced. Your aura is now very clear. Your chakras all properly positioned. You will have the urge to explain to everyone what you have been holding inside for far too long. Resist that urge, at least until you have fully considered everything yourself. Then you can determine which truths are meant to be known by others, and which are meant to be held in your heart." Georgie handed him a facial tissue. "Here. Wipe your tears. You have been crying for quite some time."

Wesner felt his face, soaking from salty tears. "I'm sorry," he said. "What time is it?"

"It's about 1:30 in the morning."

"Good god," he struggled to rise. "I've been here too long. Please forgive my…whatever this was."

"Sit for a minute. Button your shirt. Regain your breathing, your balance. A ritual as deep and in depth as what you just experienced requires a lengthy recovery. Do not push yourself too far or too fast. I have made a pot of strong coffee. I will pour you a cup. It will help."

"Okay. Thank you," said Wesner between deep breaths. "Tell me. Was someone else here?"

Georgie returned with a cup of black coffee, a wise smile creasing her face. "Drink it black now. Better to not put any cream in your system for a while." She sat in a nearby chair. "No, there were no physical beings here beyond you and me."

"I could have sworn...wait. 'No physical beings' you said. What does that mean? Were there other types of beings here?"

Georgie laughed. "What other type of beings are there, Alex? Ghosts? Angels? Shaman spirits?"

Wesner sipped his coffee and shook his head. He rose awkwardly, able to thump onto the couch. "But someone was near me. He whispered in my ear." He touched his right ear, then his left. "And so did you! What did you whisper? I couldn't understand."

Her face gentle but blank, Georgie said, "I don't know what you think happened. It was all in your own head, not in mine. If voices spoke to you, they spoke to your subconscious, to your soul. Eventually, the meaning of the whispers, perhaps even the words themselves, will be made clear." She rose and helped him to his feet. "But now, dear Lieutenant, you seem to be well enough to drive yourself home. Tomorrow we will attend Benny's picnic, or whatever it is to be called. I believe you will pick me up an hour or so before noon, as then we can retrieve Rosie. *N'est-ce pas?*"

"Right. Right, I should be going. Thank you. I mean...thank you...I think. And yes, I'll be around to pick you up here well before noon. Good timing. Right. Uh...." He paused at the door, turning to look at her. "I have many questions about tonight. I'm not sure I'll ever get an opportunity to ask those questions or have them answered. But please do understand. As I am able, as it is permissible, I will eventually seek those answers." He stared deep into her black eyes and somehow felt he had just received one of the answers.

SUNDAY, NOVEMBER 7

Wesner awoke to bright sunlight searing through a gap in his bedroom curtains, blinding his still closed eyes. He cursed at the intrusion while shaking off the remnants of whatever dream bounced around in his brain.

"Did I dream all of that, or did some of it really happen? There was pizza. There was a flowing, brightly colored robe. There was fire. No, actually candles. Yes, there were candles. There was chanting, right? Yes, and feathers and some sort of mask. There was a man--no, a vision of a man--but he spoke to me. Actually, just whispered. What did he say? I didn't understand. Was it all a dream? A nightmare? What did I do? Nothing, I think. I wanted to, but I don't think I did anything to Georgie. But she did say she was aroused, too, didn't she? What did she mean by that? Was she in some sort of voodoo outfit? God, I think it was very sexy, but I can't recall. If she wasn't aroused, I sure was. But did I just dream all of it? She gave me something to drink. What was it?"

Wesner got off his bed, realizing he still had on all his clothes from the night before, recognizing that he had fallen straight into a deep sleep upon his return home. His shirt was somehow buttoned wrong, but everything else was intact. He had slept sounder and longer than he had in months, maybe years. He felt fresh, buoyant, almost giddy. He smiled into his bathroom mirror, something he had not done in ages. He shaved and showered with youthful vigor. He swept open the curtains and welcomed in the sunlight. He felt light on his feet, light in his head, light in his soul.

A strange day, almost like Spring. Warm, southerly breezes rustled the thinned-out leaves, bright sunshine blazed brilliantly, not a cloud in the sky. A true Indian Summer kind of day, such as come too infrequently and are gone too soon. Wesner suddenly wished he had a convertible, even though he had always hated the idea of convertibles. Just after 11:00 a.m., he arrived at Georgie's apartment to find her sitting on the front step dressed in blue jeans and a light sweater. She jumped up even before the car came to a stop.

"A nice day for a clambake, or whatever you call these things," said Georgie, hopping into the front seat. She, too, had a skip in her step.

"Yes, it is a beautiful day. Clambake or not, just a fantastic day for this late in the year." He returned Georgie's smile as he headed east toward the cabin where Rosie was waiting. He was in such a pleasant mood and joyfully distracted that he hadn't been paying attention to following traffic. If he had, he'd have seen the tan-colored Jeep pulling away from the curb a half-block behind him--the same Jeep that had followed him from his house minutes earlier.

Wesner couldn't help himself. He needed to ask Georgie for a clarification. "About last night."

Georgie was quick to answer. "I enjoyed the pizza. Where did you say you bought it?"

"Not that. I mean the--what was it you called it--a ritual?"

"I don't know what you're talking about."

"You said some things."

"I said I enjoyed the pizza."

"No. You know what I mean. You've got to talk to me about what you were feeling, what we were feeling, what I'm still feeling."

Georgie looked at the skyline of the city as Wesner entered the freeway traffic. "It is said that a man who discovers a way to make great pizza should keep the secret of the pizza to himself until he writes down the recipe and fully understands what ingredients make the pizza so delicious. Until then, any words he uses to describe the pizza will come out wrong, and the man will be disappointed whenever he tries to make the pizza again." She looked at Wesner whose mouth hung open. "I do believe your aura is much brighter. Possibly a light blue, but crystal clear. If so, that is wonderful. We knew it needed cleansing."

Wesner closed his mouth and drove on in silence. Was he being told to forget what had happened last night? Was he being told to be a professional cop, to not let his emotions get the best of him? He knew that was the correct thing to do. He knew that is what the rule book said to do. But it was not what he wanted to do, not what he wanted to think.

Or did he just imagine the whole thing? Did none of what he was remembering even happen? Perhaps it was all a dream, a nightmarish dream, an erotic imagining like he had as a child. But if that were so, for this one time he wanted to act like a kid again. Maybe he always was just a kid, a punk, a pretend tough guy from the old neighborhood, but someone who cried himself to sleep with romantic fantasies. So, what was going on? Maybe someone had finally dope-slapped him really hard, hard enough that he was somehow wandering into and out of a fairyland. And the fairy princess was right by his side, but he was only the coachman driving the enchanted pumpkin.

Wesner tried to focus on the traffic. Something caught his eye in the rear-view mirror. Was that the same vehicle he'd seen a few miles back when they got on the freeway? He purposely slowed his pace. The tan vehicle slowed, too. He sped up his pace slightly. The tan car stayed about a quarter-mile back no matter the speed. Now on the eastside of the city, Wesner crossed several lanes to the left, then veered right abruptly, taking an exit far too early to be a shortcut to the cabin. The tan car followed the odd lane changes, and was now quite clearly identifiable as a Jeep.

Georgie said, "Interesting maneuver. We got someone following?"

"Looks like a tan Jeep has decided he likes our license plate. I assume you don't have your service weapon. I've got a .38 in the glove compartment. Get it out. My .45 is under my seat. I'll grab it if we need it. I'm going to try to make this guy go away."

Wesner headed down a quiet urban parkway that wove through curves and bridges around streams, ponds and statuary. Speeds in excess of 35 mph were difficult to manage on the narrow two-lane, above 45 mph almost impossible. Wesner's smaller car could handle the curves better than the Jeep, a more rugged, higher-profile vehicle. He gained several yards of distance over the Jeep.

The normal temperature in November would chill outings to the park, but today's balmy weather had brought out many families--kids on the playgrounds, touch football games in the open spaces. An elusive car chase in such tight quarters would be highly dangerous for the families at their impromptu picnics.

Wesner dug deep in his memory bank. There was a hard left curve into a short tunnel ahead. The parkway turned sharply to the right out of the tunnel. But even tighter to the right was a short off-cut that quickly entered a tree line. Many years ago, Wesner had taken his girlfriend there to neck. She later became his wife--for a short time. He told himself he'd never revisit the tree line again. Strange how the mind congers odd thoughts at odd times. He suddenly realized the loss of his wife was the initial event when his aura began changing to dirty colors.

"Hang on. I'm going to make some sharp turns. If he follows, we may need to defend ourselves."

"Got it," said Georgie, checking the .38 for ammunition.

Bright sunlight switched to deep darkness in the left-sweeping tunnel followed by blinding brightness at the other end reflecting off the large arrow sign directing traffic to the right. Wesner braked hard and fish-tailed onto the poorly paved off-cut, then braked hard to a stop beneath the covering trees. He grabbed his .45 from under the seat and vaulted out the driver's side door onto the ground. Georgie was already in position, aiming the .38 over the trunk toward the tunnel.

Squealing brakes were followed by the thump of the Jeep's right rear careening into the side abutment of the tunnel's exit arch. Pieces of metal and a tail light flew around as the Jeep tore off into the distance, still trying to find his prey.

Minutes passed in alert silence as the two officers waited to see if their pursuer would double back. "You bring your girlfriends here often?" asked Georgie.

Wesner smiled wryly. "Only once. It was okay for a short time, actually kind of great. Then turned dark, sort of a brown-mustard color."

Georgie gasped at the admission. "Sorry. Didn't mean to…."

"It's okay. Forget it. Our follower seems to be gone. Let's get out of here and go get Rosie. That's who the Jeep-guy wants, I believe. He probably thinks she saw him knife Thorpe and can therefore I.D. him. This guy hates loose ends. There are a few others who may be in danger, too."

"You mean besides us," deadpanned Georgie.

"Exactly."

Rather than retracing the route back the way they came, Wesner took the first road to the left off the parkway. "He'll either keep going straight or reverse his route to search for us. We'll take this small street through the neighborhood. I don't think he'll be searching back through here."

Georgie turned to look through the rear window. Seeing no sign of the Jeep, she scanned the houses, buildings and driveways, alert for signs of danger or possible escape routes if needed. "My, what a lovely neighborhood you found," she said sarcastically. Several buildings or houses were boarded up, plywood replacing what had been doors or glass windows. A few were burned out shells, residences no more. Here and there an open lot of turned earth and weeds marked where some sort of structure once stood.

Wesner nodded. "This area used to be one of the nicer parts of the city. Good place to raise a family. But times change. Shit happens. Property owners stop caring. The good news is this is no place for a guy driving a banged-up Jeep to be nosing around."

A group of five young wannabe thugs slouched around one of the few corner markets still showing signs of commerce, despite the iron bars over the windows preventing after hours entry. "Perhaps we shouldn't be nosing around here either," said Georgie, as the five started pointing and shouting at them as they drove slowly by.

"Main road up ahead. Then a short cut toward the cabin," offered Wesner.

Once they got to the four-lane, both detectives felt better about the safety of their surroundings. Georgie was thinking ahead. "Given what just happened, I don't think the cabin is such a safe place anymore, especially not for Rosie alone. It's only a matter of time before Rowden or one of his silver-helmet boys figures out where it is."

"Agreed. We'll have to find a safer place for her tonight until she joins Thorpe tomorrow in rehab. And, I'm sorry to say it, but you need to leave your apartment for a few days, too. The Jeep guy followed us from there. He knows where you live, and probably who you are. Let's see what we can arrange with our folks at the clambake."

Rosie was less than thrilled about abandoning the cabin and relinquishing her weapon, but she warmed to the idea that she'd be with Peter Thorpe as early as the middle of the week. In only a few minutes she was packed and sitting in the rear seat of the car with Georgie. Wesner hung up the cabin phone after quickly setting wheels in motion for safe lodging for both Rosie and Georgie for the night.

"By the time we get to the clambake, we should have safe lodging arranged for both of you," said Wesner.

Taken aback, Rosie gasped. "Oh! Why do we both need safe lodging? I thought I was leaving the cabin to be closer to Petey. Does Georgie need protection, too?"

Georgie responded for Wesner's tactless blunder. "Rosie, the truth is that someone tried to follow us to your cabin. We lost him, but he seems to know where my apartment is. Otherwise, we could have both stayed there for the night. But that's now out of the question. So, the Lieutenant is having the team make other plans for us both."

"Is Petey in danger, too?"

"The guard on his room is still there. He's safe. And a day or two after tomorrow you will both be safe together. Not to worry. What concerns me right now is whether I'll find anything worth eating at this picnic clambake, or whatever it may actually be."

Rosie laughed. "Petey tried to explain it once to me. But you just have to experience it, I guess. One of Pete's friends works for a seafood supplier here in Cleveland. He said during the late fall, the market for clams used to be non-existent. So, this supplier devised a fall-of-the-year clam boil mixed with other specialties. They provide all the equipment for home-made cookouts. The idea caught on. Now, the biggest market in the country for clams in October and November is Northeast Ohio. Go figure."

Unconvinced, Georgie said, "Another new experience, I suppose."

Wesner spent most of his time at the clambake on private phone calls in the study of Benny Friedman's new home. While admiring the new residence, he finalized the details for a safe house where both Rosie and Georgie could spend the night. Several uniform officers were sent to retrieve Georgie's badge and weapon from her apartment. Between calls, Wesner scanned the room. It still needed painting, but the quality of construction was evident. He wondered who Benny had chosen to be the contractor. He was obviously a top-notch builder. Near the peak of the arched roof, an eight-sided stained-glass window faced the sun, the shafts of colored light slowly circling the room. The reflected design was intricate, somehow whispering in faint shades of yellow and green and blue as it delicately slid from wall to wall.

The Lieutenant refocused on the coming days. He was confident that the plans were solid and that very few people were aware of all the unusual arrangements he had put in place. But even the most solid of strategies could be at the mercy of the vagaries of chance. Wesner wondered where the first wobble would occur. He did not have to wait long to find out.

Captain Mitchell entered Benny's new study. "Quite the new digs, huh?"

Wesner said, "Yeah. Not sure it looks like the kind of place Benny will enjoy as much as his wife. I've been looking for you. Where have you been?"

"In my squad car. I just got a message that the State Patrol boys are jumping at the bit. They got one of the Supreme Court Judges out of bed last night to sign off on a search warrant. They are assembling a team and expect to be here tomorrow for a Tuesday take down of the Steal Inn."

"Holy sweet mother…. Then we need to move up all our plans on this end, too."

The Captain held up his hand as he spun around in a circle surveying the corners of the ceiling and peering out the door. "Let's take this discussion outside where we can talk more freely. Then you can tell me where you've set up Rosie and Georgie."

MONDAY, NOVEMBER 8

The short Indian Summer did not last past the clambake. Northwest winds blew hard into Monday morning, ushering a twenty-degree temperature drop and mists of rain trending toward sleet. A stray snow flake or two blew in harshly, trying to add the pretense of some sort of early winter romantic hug to the day, but the flakes only furthered the misery for those wandering about unprepared in too-light jackets. The morning newspaper carried a small note on page two, a follow up to a story from a few days earlier. It said that a John Doe knifing victim was out of his coma at Metro General Hospital and was being transferred to a nursing facility a few blocks away where it was hoped he would fully recover and his amnesia would disappear. The hope was that he would then be able to tell police what had occurred.

At 10:00 a.m., Wesner waited at the emergency loading area of Metro General Hospital, providing a one-man escort as the gurney was lifted into the waiting ambulance, the victim's head still heavily wrapped. Curly-haired Rosie hopped into the ambulance to accompany Thorpe on the journey to the nursing home. Benny was told to drive a patrol car in slow circles around the hospital—lights flashing but no siren. The goal was to dissuade any eager assassins from closing in on the ambulance carrying Thorpe and Rosie to their safety. As the ambulance departed, Benny picked up the very cold and unpleasantly taciturn Lt. Wesner.

A quarter-mile away, up a steep hill and hidden from sight by unkempt bushes and trees, a man sat in a black Jeep focusing binoculars on the hospital's emergency loading area below. The black auto paint was shiny, still wet in spots, an obviously amateurish job. The painter even sprayed over a damaged rear-right quarter panel. The Jeep driver scanned the area for any signs of extra security. He was pleased to see that only the two detectives seemed to care about Thorpe and his girlfriend. So much the better, he thought. He turned the ignition key and followed the slow-rolling ambulance at a reasonable distance. The driver watched the man who seemed to be the chief detective enter a patrol car and head in the opposite direction, back downtown, exiting the emergency loading area just as another ambulance approached. A small group of well-wishers, mostly nurses and doctors, were cheering for a patient in a balloon-decked wheelchair, his thick blonde wig whisked by the wind, almost revealing the bandaged head beneath.

The man in the Jeep focused on the ambulance he was following, the one carrying his prey. He thought about taking care of matters immediately, but reasoned that it would be easier to eliminate those he viewed as witnesses later, after everyone achieved a decent level of comfort and security became lax. He followed the ambulance toward a broad avenue, once the main street of a fashionable showplace neighborhood replete with turn-of-the-century three-story houses, most of which were no longer used as private homes. One of the old homes was converted into a nursing facility. He watched the unloading of Thorpe and his girlfriend at the massive front doors of an old castle-like 1890s-era structure. One old chubby security guard, chewing on an apple, held the doors open in a mostly unhelpful manner. If there were any additional guards inside, they were not evident. This might turn out to be the easiest of them all, he thought. He whispered to himself, "I'm glad I didn't waste time trying to get him in the hospital. That would have been tricky. This is much better. Much better! Tomorrow. Sure, tomorrow. No sense waiting any longer. Once he is dispatched, I can make my other moves."

■ ■ ■

Wesner focused his attention on the industrial valley below as the patrol car crossed the Guardian Bridge with its muscular art deco pillars buttressing both the western and eastern entrances. Benny thought Wesner's silence was a sure sign that the Lieutenant needed to think about the situation and scenarios rather than communicating. Nonetheless, Benny believed the Lieutenant liked a light banter to break up his linear thought, forcing him to change perspectives.

"Big change in the weather from yesterday, Wheezie," said the Sergeant. "Nice warm day for that clambake."

"Yeah. Pretty day."

"Did I tell you that my brother-in-law is a partner in the fish market that did the cooking? All I had to do was buy the food. Equipment, the staff to run it--all on my brother-in-law. He does these events *gratis*, to work in his trainees, learning on the job."

"Great. He's a good man. Wonderful clambake," whispered Wesner, looking at the approaching skyline although none of it was registering.

"Maria, my wife, said--well, she was just wondering--she asked what was going on between you and Georgie. I told her 'nothing was going on', but she said you kept looking at her like you wanted to say something important to her."

"Uh-huh."

"And she said when you weren't looking, Georgie kept her eye on you, too."

Wesner was suddenly drawn in, looking hard at Benny, silently for several seconds, then wincing as he looked down at his hands, fingers meshed as if in prayer. Finally, he said, "Yeah. Tell her nothing is going on."

Unconvinced, Benny said, "Sure. That's what I said. Nothing." After a few minutes of total silence, Benny continued. "You know you can tell me anything and I'll keep it to myself. Not even tell Maria. That's what partners are for. And we been together for a long time, so...."

Wesner again stared out the window. The cruiser crossed into the downtown area. Billowing smoke from the steel mill stacks in the valley below rolled up the sides of the buildings, meeting the charcoal clouds starting to spit sleet. Above was a solid leaden layer, a lid keeping all sunlight a distant rumor. "Benny, if I can figure out what to say, or how I can say it, you'll be the first person I come to." Turning toward the Sergeant, Wesner smiled wanly. "Or maybe the second."

■ ■ ■

The Highway Patrol and State Liquor Enforcement officers were wasting no time. They were extremely eager to try out their newly formed Joint Task Force. The leaders of the group left Columbus in the mid-morning and were ready to set the stage rapidly. Captain Mitchell organized a 1:00 p.m. meeting between the Commandant of the Ohio Highway Patrol, ATF Division and the key Police Department personnel to be involved in the search of the Steal Inn.

The Commandant was a large, burly, no-nonsense trooper. He gained his rank by following his personal axiom that proper planning eliminates mistakes, and zero mistakes means no lost lives, especially his own life or the lives of his troops. And no lost lives in high profile cases means career advancement. He and his second-in-command led the briefing in the third-floor presentation room. His Chief of Operations had photographs and maps of the immediate area around the Steal Inn. Only a half-dozen Cleveland police--each Division Commanders--were invited to attend.

"Gentlemen, I am Colonel Rick Peldner, Commandant of the Alcohol, Tobacco and Firearms Division of the Ohio State Highway Patrol. Many people—even many in law enforcement—do not understand that this Division exists. Frankly, ATF is the heart, the very backbone, of the State Highway Patrol. Without it, we are simply chasers of speeding cars. No, my Division is one that brings teeth to the corps. We bring honor to our State.

"Now, it is my understanding that a tavern on the near westside of Cleveland is a favorite location for workers from the steel mills in the valley, and that this same institution, known as the Steal Inn, is likely a center for several types of illegal activity. We have a duly signed search and seizure warrant, issued late last night by an Ohio State Supreme Court Judge, to arrest any evil doers, and to acquire any and all evidence of wrong-doing. Our goal is to arrest anyone who attempts to prohibit our investigation, to detain any persons who have any outstanding warrants or are considered persons of interest, to collect all evidence regarding any illegal activity within the bar or elsewhere as the evidence may suggest, and to arrive with sufficient force and surprise to prevent counter-force activity from within. Should we encounter any counter-force activity, we are permitted to protect ourselves as necessary. While crimes against the City of Cleveland Charter are the jurisdiction of the Cleveland Police Department, violation of the State Code on Liquor Control or racketeering on a large-scale will fall to my ATF Division. We have had complaints in the recent past about this tavern at this location, and now again from the detectives of the Cleveland Police Department, indicating that several laws may have been broken, to wit: watering down alcoholic content for profit; possible bookmaking and / or gambling; murder for hire; assault;

assault with intent to do bodily harm; conspiracy to defraud; and possible prostitution."

Benny passed a questioning glance quietly mouthing 'prostitution' toward Wesner seated next to him. Wesner shrugged. "Sounded good, so I threw that in. We'll see what evidence pops up, maybe about those trailers."

The Commandant continued. "We will proceed in assault-style against the establishment with an armed team of Highway Patrol ATF Officers in riot gear with vests in place. I recommend that any Cleveland Police Officers involved in the assault be so protected as well. It is our understanding from Captain Mitchell, here present, that members of the tavern management who we expect to encounter have the likelihood of being armed. We want no injuries to any of our troopers or your officers. I believe in preparing for all possible scenarios. Prepare for the worst, be surprised when things go well. You will note that the only Cleveland Police personnel present here today are those within the command structure. That is purposeful. It is our practice, and our sincere hope, that limiting local knowledge of our planned activity until minutes prior to 'go-time' will prevent information leak. Now, let me introduce Captain Taylor, our Chief of Operations, who will provide maps and photos of the site, and the logistical and tactical details of the assault."

Lieutenant Wesner felt his stomach churn each time the word 'assault' was uttered. He recalled the tough older woman behind the bar with the sawed-off shotgun. And the blacked-out upper door where military-dressed steel mill security hung out. The more he pictured the layout of the bar, the more he suspected this would not be a peaceful raid. Captain Taylor showed a large-scale map of the streets around the Steal Inn, and photos where city police units would be stationed to block surrounding streets, preventing incoming or escaping vehicles. The next slide was a crude layout drawing of the inside bar area, as sketched by Lieutenant Wesner. The following slides were photos of darkened exterior windows and shuttered doors where escape might be attempted. Troopers would be positioned at each such location, ready to deter exit, and prepared to enter instead if needed. All troopers and police command officers would have communication devices set for a specific channel. The channel would be announced only a half-hour prior to the initiation of the assault. Four troopers would burst in through the primary entrance, followed by a support phalanx of city police. Wesner planned to be in that phalanx.

Capt. Taylor said, "The staging area will be the parking lot of St. Theodosius Russian Orthodox Church, positioned on a wide but seldom traveled residential street a few blocks North of the Steal Inn. Units will convene there at 12:30 p.m. on Tuesday, with the assault scheduled to begin at 1:30 p.m. Given that time frame, no school children will be nearby if and when any gunfire erupts. Police units will be dispatched to all nearby schools or large businesses putting them in a lock-down during the assaulting raid." Wesner's stomach churned again.

At the conclusion of the briefing, and after all questions had been answered, Wesner and Benny followed Captain Mitchell into his office at his invitation. "Nothing is ever easy with you two, you know what I mean?"

"God, I didn't expect a commando raid when we suggested the Liquor Control Board get involved," said Wesner, falling into one of the chairs facing Mitchell's desk.

Mitchell rubbed his balding head. "Well, hell, Wheezie! What did you expect? These 'Rambos' train all year long for something like this. When given the opportunity, they go 'all-in-all-day'. Make sure every one of our folks there have those new bullet-proof vests and helmets. These 'heros' are likely to shoot up the place just for grins. Even ricochets can kill you."

Wesner said, "I've not heard any evidence that those vest things even work."

"Better than going in with nothing but a prayer book."

Benny was visibly nervous. "What units do you want us to lead in?"

"You are not leading anybody," said the Captain, shaking his finger at the Sergeant. "You will stay on the outside with the prisoner bus, recording identification information on anyone who may be arrested. Your buddy, here, will follow the direction of our riot police leader, Lieutenant Urso, who has experience in these tactics and who will provide that ten-man phalanx requested by Commander Peldner. You, Sgt. Friedman, are not to enter that building. Understood?"

"That's a bit harsh, there, Teddy," said Wesner. "Why the tough tone to Benny? He's a smart guy, and he knows how to take care of himself."

Capt. Mitchell turned to Wesner. "If you were paying more attention yesterday at the clambake instead of being so pre-occupied about who-knows-what, you'd have heard that Maria is pregnant with Benny's third child. Congratulations are in order, but I'm not going to put him in harm's way on purpose. You, on the other hand, we don't care so much about."

Wesner turned to the Sergeant and let out a whoop. "Damn, Benny! I wish you'd have said something! Congrats, buddy. I'm happy for you."

"I tried taking you aside a few times yesterday, but, uh, as the Captain says, you were a bit pre-occupied."

Wesner grimaced. "I had some things on my mind. Please give Maria my best wishes."

Capt. Mitchell said, "Yeah. Well, Wheezie, just make sure you've got your head on straight for tomorrow. No mess-ups, no cluttered heads. I don't think this will go down easily, no matter how much pre-planning the State boys take us though. Peldner is out to make a name for himself, maybe use this for a run at politics."

Wesner nodded, then changed the subject. "We've got Thorpe and Rosie Dwyer in a protected situation. With any luck

Thorpe's full memory will be back in just a few days. I've got an APB out on the tan Jeep that was following us yesterday, and some patrol cars are swinging by various locations where Rowden might be. We will find Lucas Rowden. After the Steal Inn raid is completed, if he's not captured, I think we should get a warrant to search the Rubicon Steel Records Department."

"Holy crap, Wheezie! Why don't we just pull down the pants of the entire Board of Directors! Do you know the kind of heat we'd get from the mayor on down if we tried doing that?" Capt. Mitchell pounded both fists down on his desk, the echoes of which reverberated all the way to the elevators. "The big-wigs at Rubicon will call in every political chit they've got out there. They will make sure no one gets a look under their skirts. By the time we get into their files, any incriminating information will be long gone. You want Rowden? If he's not in the Steal Inn, you better hope your other plan works."

Benny gave a questioning look from the Captain to Wesner and back again. He wasn't aware of any 'other plan'.

Tuesday, November 9

Yesterday's cold rain had blown off rapidly into Pennsylvania and continued toward the East Coast, replaced by a frigid brisk cold front painting frost on everything. The stiff winds were denuding trees of their few remaining leaves. The bright sunshine belied the likely winter blast forecast for late afternoon. At 8:00 a.m., a shiny black Jeep, windshield totally clear of frost as only a night in a heated garage can deliver, pulled into the Steal Inn parking lot at a fast pace. The driver took a long look at the electric company service truck set up on the sidewalk a few feet off the driveway entrance. Two workers were examining the wooden pole suspending a maze of wires leading in all directions. They appeared to be confused, alternately referring to a chart on a clipboard and pointing up to the various lines. The Jeep driver shook his head at the incompetence displayed by utility workers who should know their jobs. Disgusted, he entered the bar. Hidden from his view were the three State Patrol troopers inside the closed rear door of the truck. They were ready, dressed in riot gear.

One of the electric company workers spoke into a walkie-talkie reporting the black Jeep's arrival. On the receiving end of the message, and receiving all communications, were

Commandant Peldner and Captain Taylor. They were responsible for the central control of the operation, situated in a State Patrol car a few blocks away in the parking lot of St. Theodosius Russian Orthodox Church. Lieutenant Wesner was permitted to sit in the back seat where he could listen to radio reports and watch preparations from that position. The Commandant had only granted such permission with great reluctance. This was to be his dance, and he didn't want a local officer trying to take any of his thunder away.

"That's probably Lucas Rowden in that Jeep," offered Wesner.

The Commandant replied over his shoulder without making any eye contact. "Your speculations may be correct, Lieutenant, but they are not relevant until we can verify identification. Please remain silent until we require your input."

Wesner's blood was up and he was about to reply explosively when Captain Taylor asked, "Do you have any reason to believe that this Rowden-fellow is likely to be dangerous?"

"As a matter of fact, yes. He is a primary suspect in at least six murders and one additional attempted murder. Those are what we are aware of. There may be more."

"Sounds like a real gunslinger," Taylor said, with a wry smile suggesting he would enjoy a lethal encounter.

"He seems to favor gutting his victims. He likes his knives. Not sure what it says about someone who prefers to look his victims in the eye as their life oozes away."

"Enough! We need to keep listening to this channel for status updates from the utility truck," said the Commandant. The City Power and Light Company was more than a little averse to surrendering the keys for one of their fully outfitted service trucks to the State Highway Patrol. Commandant Peldner had to lean on his superiors to intercede so that the truck could be used as an advance spy unit, put in place in what might end up being the line of fire. Not everyone was as gung-ho on the assault concept as was Peldner, and he knew that he had to make every part of the operation a success to enhance his reputation.

The walkie-talkie squawked again and again, reporting a flurry of activity as the morning progressed. The masquerading electric company workers noted that several cars had casually made their way up the hill from the mills and entered the parking lot. The filthy and sweat-stained clothes identified men who had just finished the third trick, the overnight shift. Other vehicles, likely from workers whose shift would begin mid-afternoon, slowly drifted in from the other direction. Every man who entered wore steel-toed shoes. Now and then, one or two men in fresh ironed dark green khaki uniforms exited a Jeep and sauntered inside.

Around 11:00 a.m., an unmarked school bus pulled into the church parking lot. Wesner exited the patrol car and headed toward the unmarked bus, empty except for its driver and Sergeant Friedman. Benny got out of the bus, crooking his head to view the eight onion-domed spires of St. Theodosius Russian Orthodox Church. Ranging from small ones on the edges of the building to a very large central dome, the distinctive shapes bulged into the pre-winter sky.

"Why'd they paint those domes blue, Wheezie? Not that they look bad or anything, but it just seems like they'd prefer them to be a brighter color."

Wesner looked up at the unique church domes, common on European Orthodox churches. They stood out against the puffy white clouds rushing southeastly after being blown off Lake Erie by the stiffening wind. "It's not paint on the domes, Benny. Those onion shapes are made of copper. When new, it must have been an impressive sight to see so many bright, shiny copper domes dominating the sky above the church. But copper oxidizes, and the acid-rain from the mills has an effect, too. Just like the Statue of Liberty now has a blue-green patina, same thing here with these domes."

"Wow. Still impressive though, huh? So, this is our bus for all of the prisoners we round up. I've got a box full of hand and ankle restraints for our guests as might be needed. The bus driver is a patrol officer assigned to the Collinwood area. We made sure he has no connection to this precinct so there is no connection to the people in The Steal Inn. He'll take down names and pertinent data for detainees on his clipboard."

Wesner looked over his shoulder. "You and the bus are a bit early. Commandant Peldner will probably get sideways at you for jumping his schedule by more than an hour. You've got about 30 seconds to come up with a reasonable excuse."

Benny laughed. "Hey! It's a school bus in a school parking lot. What could be more innocent? I just wanted to be here early so I could watch everything getting set up." He paused for a minute, then said, "Do you think I'm too old?"

"Too old for what, Ben?"

"For another kid. It's probably Maria's last chance to have one, but she's a lot younger than me. Will I still be able to play ball with him, or her? Teach the kid how to fish, how to box, you know."

"Jeez, Benny. You're not old at all. You and Maria are great parents, and you will be again. I don't understand what she sees in you, but you're not too old to raise a kid. Hell, the way you act I'd say you are half teenager yourself!"

As expected, the Commandant wasted no time in marching toward the bus. But unexpectedly, he was not angry at the schedule violation. "Ready for prisoners, Sergeant?"

"Yes, sir. Hope you don't mind too much, but I wanted to be here early to see your team make their final preparations. Thought I could learn some tips. We'll bring our local officers to the target in this bus, if that works for you."

"Of course, of course. It will be another hour or so before we gather everyone, but feel welcome to join us in the command car to hear reports. We'll be switching frequencies just before the team rallies here." The Commandant wheeled and returned to his command car.

"Why, Benny, you dog you. What'd you do, offer to polish his army boots yesterday? How come you get smiles and encouragement while I get told to shut up and sit still?"

"You're just naturally abrasive, Wheezie. You're not a people-person like me. So, what do we know so far?"

"The bar is filling up with guys who just finished their tricks, and some getting ready to go into work this afternoon. All looking for a little alcohol to make life worthwhile. Some of the security staff is in there, presumably in the upstairs office. And one of the descriptions sounds like it might be our guy, Rowden. He's now driving a recently painted black Jeep with body damage on the same side as where the tan Jeep that was chasing me ran into the bridge abutment on Sunday. Call me a gullible optimist, but I think it may be the same vehicle with a fresh paint job."

Benny shoved his hands into his jacket pockets, trying to sound enthusiastic. "Damn, I'd love to get him in the round up from that bar."

"There's that teenager attitude I was talking about. Just make sure everyone we take out of the place gets a complete pat down. Most of them will likely be plain old steel workers about to lose a day's pay because they're being questioned. Even so, some will be packing some sort of weapon for their own protection. Or to shoot rats. Or both. And if you do come across Rowden, special care must be taken. The guy is dangerous and will have a knife hidden somewhere. I don't want anyone getting carved up out of negligence."

"Where will you be?"

"I'm going in with the phalanx requested by the Commandant. Something tells me this is going to be noisy and violent. I hope I'm wrong, but there are too many folks eager to pull triggers. There's an angry bar maid who seems to love her shotgun, there's the mill security force which might be led by a murderous psychopath, and there's the Commandant eager to put his troopers through a live-round exercise. I don't see how it won't be ugly."

"Too late to call it off, I suppose," mused Benny. "Once we called in the State boys there was no turning back, I guess."

"Not a chance. Just look at what they've already got in place. I suspect there's some armor on its way and probably due to arrive shortly. Peldner wouldn't pass up the opportunity to bring in a tank or two. No, there's no calling it off. When there is commitment to a battle, the plans and the personnel assembled make retreat all but impossible."

Benny looked around. "Hey, we've got a few minutes. I'm going over to that carryout on the corner. There's a pay phone there, I bet. I gotta call my brother-in-law to see about picking up the tents from Sunday. Be right back."

At noon, a squad of State Highway Patrolmen in military style vests and with high-velocity weapons strapped to their back appeared as if out of nowhere and quickly surrounded the school bus. Captain Taylor hailed them and organized them in the shade of the tree-line on the edge of the lot, out of the view of passers-by. Fifty yards away, children flooded out of the school and into the fenced-off playground. They gave little attention to the men in the parking lot.

A half-hour later, just over a dozen Cleveland Policemen, most carrying duffle bags with protective armor and long guns over their shoulders, made their way toward the bus, unaware of the purpose for the exercise but assuming it was simply another drill meant to waste time. Their leader, Lieutenant Urso, loaded them onto the bus where he revealed the target and the mission. Suddenly wide-eyed, a few of the men acknowledged they had passed by the Steal Inn but none had ever been inside. All of them hustled into their armor, now recognizing the seriousness of the plan. They were going into an unfamiliar location as the second wave. They would be rushing in standing up while the first wave of four Highway Patrolmen took prone or protected positions. If there was unfriendly fire, the ten going in, now identified as the phalanx, would be easy targets. Lieutenant Wesner grabbed his gear and joined the ten men.

As the assault time approached, reports from the utility truck quieted and the advance troops readied themselves for action. Commandant Peldner announced the radio frequency change. The assault team busied themselves recalibrating their communication devices and turn up the volume so instructions could be heard in what would likely be a loud environment. Wesner's stomach churned again. "I wish we had someone on the inside, Benny. This feels wrong. You know what I mean?"

Benny nodded and whispered, "Too many heavily armed hotheads going blind into a dead-end. Yeah. I'll radio the Captain to send in some ambulances. They'll be needed." A growling noise on the street caused everyone to turn toward two armored personnel carriers, the chauffeured vehicles for the State Highway Patrol lead elements. Wesner's prediction of "some armor" was coming true. Operational departure was mere minutes away.

Inside the Steal Inn, a tall muscular authority figure peered out of the office door down toward the bar area. His dark green khaki uniform, identical to all the other security guard uniforms except for the two gold bars on each of the collar tips, was severely pressed into permanent creases. He rubbed his close-cropped crewcut as he determined that all was well in the bar. He smiled ominously. Now was the perfect time to finish the job on Thorpe. He would go to the nursing facility and sever his throat quickly, and that of Thorpe's girlfriend if she got in the way. The chubby, mostly worthless guard at the nursing home was probably deep into his lunch and would offer little resistance. A gut slice for him. A few minutes of quiet action and no one would be left to identify him. He tapped the sheaf attached to his belt, confirming his 10-inch Bowie knife was at the ready. He quickly headed to the parking lot. He left the bar just prior to an incoming phone call, asking to speak to Rowden. Someone was trying to reach him with a warning.

Commandant Peldner watched his men vault into the personnel carriers. Satisfied, he gave the 'Go' message to all units to engage. The assault, approaching from two directions, would arrive at the Steal Inn lot in exactly three-and-a-half minutes, as measured on the Commandant's stopwatch the day before. The utility truck would back into the drive way entrance to serve as a blockade preventing movement into or out of the Steal Inn. Four Cleveland police cars began to emerge at key intersections surrounding the bar, blocking all traffic from passing in any direction. One last vehicle exited the closest intersection just prior to the blockade — a black Jeep. The driver of the Jeep was startled to see so much police activity in the early afternoon, but he instinctively knew that he needed to be far away from the Steal Inn as quickly as possible. He pushed a button under the Jeep's dashboard sending a red-light signal to the barmaid.

Three troopers exited the driveway blocking truck, armed and in armament. They rapidly positioned themselves as pre-arranged, at unused windows and doors, potential exit sites, surrounding the building. The other men stayed with the truck, blocking the exit while permitting entrance only for the rest of the official vehicles needed for the assault. The State Patrol personnel carriers and Cleveland Police school bus sped into the lot, spilling the silver-helmeted assault team and black-helmeted phalanx even before the vehicles came to a complete stop. Within seconds the Troopers double-stepped forward, smashing through the entrance door, cracking it off its hinges.

Afterward there was general agreement that the Troopers properly identified themselves and did acknowledge they had a search warrant. Most concurred that someone shouted,

"Highway Patrol! Nobody move! Police!" But as to the exact sequence of events, there were no consistent conclusions.

Four State Troopers split two to the left and two to the right, the inner men on one knee, the outer men prone. All four with assault weapons raised and aimed. The phalanx entered as quickly as ten men can squeeze through a single door. It was the third man through who took the shotgun blast to the face, the blood-splatter reaching Wesner who was among the next to squeeze in. The four lead troopers all returned fire immediately. The old barmaid was thrown backward crashing into the displayed but now shattered liquor bottles, the sawed-off shotgun flying upwards, still smoking. An angry scowl on her face became her death mask as blood exploded from several well-aimed replies to her opening salvo.

Most of the patrons froze in place or dove for the floor. But two were armed when they arrived, and inopportunely chose that moment to draw their weapons. Not waiting to judge intent, the troopers blew several holes in one man's stomach, as evidenced by the eruption of blood from his mouth. The other took two shots to the neck from both right and left angles, all but severing his head from his body. Three security guards in the upstairs office crashed out the door onto the landing. Two raised their hands in surrender, while the third, Eugene Brodick, ran back inside seeking an exit to the outside through a blacked-out window.

It was all over in just a few seconds, although the horror would be remembered by some forever. Ambulances arrived to remove the injured. Two of the phalanx members closest to the unfortunate shotgun victim had superficial pellet wounds. Shaken and wide-eyed, they were treated at the scene and whisked away to the hospital as a precaution. The body of the dead officer was taken away, but those of the barmaid and two patrons remained for forensic analysis--and the necessary grizzly photographs.

The troopers knew their roles well. They proceeded to explore the entire structure on full alert for danger, through each first-floor room, most of them empty, into several small makeshift bedrooms on the second floor, many recently used. Opening the attic, they found Brodick, the third security guard who had tried to escape, so frightened that the crotch of his pants was soaking wet. Through their search the troopers discovered several file cabinets hidden inside fake walls. The cabinets were full of documents, evidence that would be quickly scrutinized in the coming hours.

Wesner slowly took it all in. The steel workers and guards marched out single file, hands on top of their heads through a corridor of police, each patrolman patting down any likely places where a weapon might be hidden. Wesner took a final look at the bodies. Two men in steel-toed boots lay lifeless on the floor. Whether they drew their weapons out of fear, or instinct, or to avoid being investigated for something they had done--no one would ever know for certain. Pinned against the mirrored back wall as if sitting on the ledge where the liquor bottles had been, the old barmaid scowled with an open mouth. Her eyes remaining wide open, filled with dead hate and a small bit of wonder at her fate. She reminded Wesner of the oversized animatronic figure of the creepy laughing fat lady at the entrance to the Fun House at Euclid Beach Amusement Park. He shuddered at a last look, then joined his team at the side of the school bus, hoping but not expecting that Lucas Rowden was among those rounded up. He had heard the report of a black Jeep exiting just before the assault began. The strong assumption was that Rowden was the driver.

Commandant Peldner marched into the center of the action with a second team of troopers whose primary goal was discovery and analysis. They carried large evidence boxes for gathering anything incriminating, and the two men assigned as photographers would provide visual proof of the successful raid. The

Commandant, expecting a grand success, enlisted a reporter from the Columbus Dispatch newspaper who was granted story exclusivity in exchange for a complimentary write up about the Commandant. The City Coroner van arrived, large enough to carry away all three victims once the forensics had been completed.

"Anybody special in the group yet, Benny?" Wesner eyed the frightened faces of the men currently filling the bus and soon to be interrogated.

"We have our old friend Eugene Brodick. Remember him from the mill when we were checking out the cauldron? He's seated about halfway back in the bus. Looks like he pissed his pants."

"No one admitting to the name Lucas Rowden, I'm guessing?"

Benny shook his head. "Maybe when we interrogate these goofs we'll find someone ready to talk about him."

"Oh, they'll talk, all right. If not, we'll just threaten to send them to the troopers for target practice."

Benny threw up his hands. "Yeah, about that! What the hell! No sooner did they bust through the door and I hear gunfire. One of our guys is flung back out the door with no face, followed by short bursts of automatic weapons. Jeez, it sounded like an Old West gunfight! How did that happen?"

Wesner looked back to the door of the bar. "I was afraid that barmaid would get trigger happy. She did. Pretty quickly upon our entrance. I think she may have been expecting trouble and was ready to defend the place, being that the shotgun was already in her hands as we entered. She just wasn't anticipating such a heavy response."

"We gonna talk to her?"

"Not much left to talk to, Benny. They'll need to scrape her off the wall." Turning back to the bus, Wesner said, "Let's get these fellas loaded quickly. Get names, addresses, pertinent contact info. Also, ask them what part of the mill they work in. We'll take the security guards downtown for further questioning, but most of the others--unless they appear uncooperative or suspicious--tell them we'll be in touch and not to leave town."

The last of the bar patrons offered their identification at the bus door in exchange for a pair of handcuffs and the direction to take a seat. Each of them complained bitterly and confessed ignorance to whatever wrongfulness the bar had done. Some of them were probably truthful about that.

"Where you headed, Wheezie?" asked Sgt. Friedman.

"I should brief the Captain about what went down here. I suspect the State Patrol report will be very sanitized, removing the gory details. The report might even be ghost written by their Columbus reporter friend."

■ ■ ■

Four blocks away, the black Jeep was idling behind a shuttered business. The driver was trying to make sense of what had just occurred. As he cleared the intersection seconds before it was blocked by a police car with lights flashing, he hit the "emergency" button on the dashboard, a message meant for the barmaid to be ready for danger. Whether or not the message was received or properly interpreted was no longer his primary concern. He recognized that he had to get out of the area and away from the Jeep. Rather than following his original plan to take care of the loose ends at the nursing facility, he circled around to the South, intent on quickly reaching the Cold Mill parking lot where Buddy Ward would be arriving shortly to watch over the employee cars and the trailers.

"There was no warning from my benefactor," he mumbled to himself. "Was he unaware of the raid? It looked like the Cleveland Police were involved, and that is where he gets his information. Why didn't he know?" Circling well to the south allowed an approach to the mills from the opposite side, from the east, but doing so took time. He suspected the police would get to the trailers soon, but he had to risk the extra time so he could hide the black Jeep.

Meanwhile, he considered the ramifications of what had just occurred. He had spent the night in the benefactor's carriage house garage in a gated community bordering Lake Erie, touching up the too quick paint job on the Jeep. Yet, no warning was provided or even hinted at. If his benefactor did not know about what appeared to be a well-organized raid, then both he and the benefactor were in grave jeopardy. On the other hand, if the man did have foreknowledge and purposely chose to say nothing—well, that was another matter altogether. Such betrayal required retribution. Maybe the man's son should suffer the loss of a finger. Then again, leaving town quickly might be wise, as neither he nor the benefactor would want an interrogation by the police.

"There may be another reason why I was not warned. It may be possible that the little bastard wants someone to kill me. Maybe he's even put out a hit on me. That's how I would handle it, after all. Either way, finishing off Thorpe and leaving town quickly remains my best plan. Retribution can come later as opportunity permits."

He cautiously pulled into the entrance road to the Cold Mill #4 parking lot and parked the Jeep at the back of the lot, between two pickup trucks that look like they had not moved in several months. There was no activity at the trailers. Over the last half hour, the cold and partly cloudy blue sky had become crowded with purple-grey roiling storm clouds blowing in fast at the front edge of an Alberta Clipper, the usher for the forecasted first heavy snowfall of the season. Rowden slid into the guard booth, wedging the old rickety chair into the far corner so he could watch for approaching traffic without being a direct target of some wicked, slicing sleet propelled at a punishing pace. Eventually, Buddy Ward parked his car next to the guard booth and shuffled his way in, a half-eaten candy bar sticking out of his mouth.

"Oh! Jeez, Colonel! You scared me half to death! Didn't expect anyone to be in here."

"Sorry about that, Buddy. I've been waiting for you. Got something I need you to do."

"Sure, Colonel. Whatever you say. You're the boss."

"First, I need to ask you. Remember back when one of the security guards, a fellow named Peter Thorpe, was asking about a secure place to meet, maybe down by the river?"

Buddy nodded. "Yeah, sure. That's the guy I was telling you about. You saw us talking and you asked what it was all about. I told you he was planning a secret meeting with someone, remember?"

"Oh. Yes. Now I recall. Sure. And you told him about that place under the bridge, didn't you?"

"I sure did. Never been there myself, but I heard it was secluded. I also heard that some ugly stuff used to happen there. Gangland hits--know what I mean?"

"Hmm. Ugly stuff, indeed. Listen, I'd like to go see that place, just to check it out. Seems our Mr. Thorpe may have been attacked and injured there," said Lucas Rowden, trying to show as much empathy as his psyche would permit.

Buddy Ward jumped backwards. "Injured? How? Was it bad? Was it whoever he was meeting? Had to be. The only people who knew where he was going were me and you and whoever he was meeting with. How bad was he hurt?"

"I believe he will survive the injuries, but whoever did attack him intended it to be lethal. So, you see, I think it is imperative that we examine the location so I can file a proper report to Senior Management."

"Well, hell, yeah! Let's go! You gotta get a complete report to those white-hat guys. We don't want no one gettin' in trouble, least of all you and me. Where's your Jeep?"

"My Jeep's been acting up--not hitting all cylinders, I think. Let's take your car. It's right here and it seems to be still warm inside. Too cold to be outside stuck somewhere in a broken-down Jeep."

"Ohh. Ahh, Ok. It's just…there are empty food wrappers all over the inside. It'll take me some time to clean it out. Sorry."

The Colonel headed for the car, wrapping his shirt tighter against the gusts howling down the river valley. "Let's see it. Can't be as bad as…oh."

"Yeah. I'm kinda embarrassed. Didn't think I'd be chauffeuring you around today," as if the car would have been cleaned out on some other day. Buddy tried vainly to sweep bags and greasy French fry bits and wrappers out of the front seat, obviously the remains from several weeks' lunches or dinners.

The Colonel said, "Tell you what. Hand me the keys. I'll drive. You can clean out your side while you give me directions." They jumped into the warm but messy non-descript several-years-old Ford.

Buddy thought he knew how to get to the railroad trestle but kept suggesting wrong turns ending at dead-ends. At one point, he pointed to an alley that dead-ended into Collision Bend, a notoriously difficult to navigate part of the river. Colonel Rowden resisted the urge to ignore Buddy and take the short-cuts he knew very well, but not wishing to make Buddy suspicious, he obeyed every wrong direction. Eventually, Rowden steered Buddy's garbage can of a car to the graveled lot under the bridge. They carefully stepped through the ankle-twisting larger slag piles until they were directly under the trestle bridge where the snow and wind did not reach them.

"Can't believe how still and quiet it is down here," said Buddy. "Blocked views. No one can see us under here. It's like a hidden spot in the middle of a huge city. No wonder that guy got hurt down here." Just then a train horn sounded above, and the silence was broken by the rumble of a freight train on the trestle overhead.

Rowden motioned Buddy to the edge of the slag between two large cement pillars, overlooking the oily brown water of the river 10 feet below. As Buddy carefully looked over the edge, Rowden pulled his knife and reached around to Buddy's stomach, jamming the full ten inches deep into Buddy's left abdomen, then twisting and ripping a smile-curve across to Buddy's right side. The painful scream was drowned out by the pounding of heavy freight cars on uneven tracks above. Rowden backed away as Buddy instinctively turned around to face him, both hands trying unsuccessfully to prevent his intestines from dripping out onto the slag. Rowden smiled. "Now, it seems that no one but me knows where Thorpe was going." He picked up a five-pound slag rock and threw it at Buddy's chest. That was all that was needed to send both Buddy and the rock into the fast-flowing muck of a river below. The cold water enveloped Buddy quickly. His soon-to-be-dead body swallowed toxic sludge while trying to take a last breath. His muscles were no longer able to follow commands from his mind. When found floating the next day a mile or so off-shore, the Coast Guard said his facial expression was one of terrified surprise.

Rowden quickly returned to Buddy Ward's pea green four-door sedan and drove away as a murder of crows descended from the trestle rafters, noisily fighting off a half-dozen rats already attacking the intestinal remains on the slag. When the train had run its course and proceeded on toward the west leaving a serene quiet in its wake, the discarded tires against the slope of the trestle jostled, and Cyril "Butch" Herman cautiously poked his head out and took another sip from his pint bottle. "Fella just can't get some peace and quiet around here. Damn if I'm not gonna hafta find a new place to enjoy a cocktail."

. . .

Lieutenant Wesner pulled into the police garage, headlights on and fully engaged windshield wipers squeaking. The constant and rapid weather changes coming off Lake Erie amazed him, despite the certain predictions of foul or frigid days. Balmy one day, freezing ice storms the next. A morning of bright blue followed by an afternoon of dark skies and a potential white-out snow storm. "They'll be yanking them out of the trees on the turnpike," he mumbled to no one else.

Exiting the elevator on the fourth floor, Wesner met Captain Mitchell looking out the window at the snow-blocked view of an almost invisible skyline. "Glad you're here, Wheezie. I'm getting reports of a cluster fuck out there. What the hell happened?"

"Whatever you've been told probably didn't do it justice. Worse. Much worse." Lt. Wesner waved toward the Captain's office for a debriefing.

"One of our boys went down?" asked Mitchell.

Wesner nodded as he plopped into a chair. "Yeah. Shotgun blast to the face. Not pretty. Gonna be a closed casket. The Commandant had his boys ready for a firefight and they went busting in with that attitude. Could have, should have gone in soft and just rounded up witnesses and evidence. But the four lead troopers went in like goddamn commandos--heavy weapons primed, armor, riot helmets.... All of it totally unnecessary."

"Who fired first?" Mitchell was anticipating the worst.

"I think it was the old barmaid with her sawed-off shotgun. The gunfire started before I even got in the door. But it sounded like the shotgun was the first. Couple patrons then pulled handguns, which was just the target practice the storm troopers wanted."

"You've got some blood on your shirt collar. You sure you're alright?"

Wesner looked down but couldn't see beneath his ear. "I was behind our guy that took the hit. It's probably his blood. Or maybe from one of the guys who took some of the buckshot spray. The blood's not from me. But maybe it should be."

"What the hell is that supposed to mean?"

"I should have worked this case differently. State Highway Patrol on a liquor raid was unnecessary, and that's what caused all the carnage. And knowing that one of my people is feeding information…. Shit, we gotta pull the snitch in, right? Down one person on my team. Maybe I'm getting too old, too lazy."

"Knock off the whining! We collectively discussed the problems and came to the same conclusion. We needed to get into the Steal Inn's records but had no legal reason for a search warrant. The Liquor Control boys gave us that legitimacy. As for the other stuff, if the barmaid fired first, I suspect she had the shotgun in her hands when you came through the door. Which means she was forewarned. That's not on you or the Commandant, it's on our snitch. We just need to play it out a little longer, like we planned. Keep an eye on the one we suspect. We need to make sure we're right and not ruining someone's career without firm evidence. There's no way you could have seen this coming."

The Captain's jaw was set. "Now, there are boxes of records from the raid headed down to the evidence room on the second floor. Shake off your self-pity and get your ass down there and dig through it. I don't want to hear any of that 'too-old-too-lazy' talk again!"

Wesner gave a strange look toward the ceiling above the Captain's head. It was not an angry look, not contrite either, more like he was considering an answer to a perplexing question that suddenly was written on an invisible blackboard where no blackboard existed. "Right. Evidence room. On my way." He got up and headed to the elevator leaving his old friend, Capt.

Mitchell, looking toward the ceiling to gauge if he could see something, too.

. . .

Lucas Rowden parked the pea green sedan next to a dumpster in the alley behind a Goodwill Store in a run-down area of the near westside, less than a mile or so from the railroad trestle. He was on a quick search for some different but cheap clothes in his size. Color did not matter, as long as they were not dark green khaki. He found some ill-fitting pants, a stretched-out flannel shirt and a medium-weight black jacket, not warm enough for the snowy weather outside, but enough cover until he could get to his own stash of travelling clothes. Next to the dumpster behind the Goodwill Store he changed out of his Security uniform, unworried that any witnesses would pay attention. Odd behavior, such as a man undressing in the alley, was not unusual in this dying decrepit district of the city. The only thing he could not replace was his size 12 shoes, so the steel-toed boots had to remain.

He added to his disguise by putting on a dirty old baseball cap found in the back seat of the car, likely not used for playing a sport by the overweight and out of shape Buddy Ward. Brushing snow from his shoulders, he carefully scanned around to make sure no one was watching too intently as he threw the security uniform into the dumpster. He pulled out of the back alley and headed west, away from the mills, away from downtown, and away from the railway trestle of his recent attacks. He ignored the slag-dust-covered bum shuffling across the street draining the remains of a pint of liquor. The bum was headed into the military veteran's welfare home across the street from the Goodwill store. The bum flipped the empty pint bottle into a trash can at the entrance door. He hummed a familiar tune, changing the words to match the letters and numbers of the license plate of the pea green car, recognizing it as the same car he recently saw at the bridge trestle. He supposed that the nice police lieutenant would appreciate having that plate number, maybe in a trade for a cocktail. As soon as he entered the house, he wrote down the plate number and driver description so that he wouldn't forget, just in case he somehow got his hands on another pint.

In the nearby Western suburbs, Lucas Rowden eased down a narrow road into a rarely used municipal park running alongside a small river notable for its large rocks. No other cars were around and it was doubtful any would be during what had become almost a full-blown blizzard. Rowden was determined to leave town, but not until he had tied up the final loose end--killing the only person he believed could identify him for the attack, Peter Thorpe. All other misdeeds were at the request of the person who gave him direction, the person known as his Benefactor. The Benefactor had more to lose if Rowden were caught and would therefore be forced to cover for any activities which would be discovered. "No, all I have to do is take out Thorpe and I'm home free. Maybe I'll exchange this dumpy car for one of the nice ones in the Benefactor's carriage house. He has several to choose from. Then I'll be clear of this town. The Benefactor will be pleased and will fund my disappearance, whether he knows it or not. Then, of course, he will contemplate blaming everything on me, so I'll need to remind him what I'm capable of. His son might have to learn to live without the pinky of his left hand. But then, his children can enjoy a long life--my gift to the Benefactor." He growled a wicked laugh.

Windshield wipers squeaked under the weight of snow wedges piling on the sides of the windshield glass. Wet snow, large flakes, not yet ready to cover the slightly warmer streets, at least not for the next hour or so. The snowstorm made the skies darker than expected, even at the late afternoon hour. Rowden nodded, thinking his attack on Thorpe would be more successful after darkness had fully fallen. There would be less light for him to avoid, while everyone in the facility would be settling down for a snow-filled evening, seeking as much cover and warmth as possible. When done, he would head to the storage locker in the carriage house, change out of the Goodwill clothes--which may or may not have some of Thorpe's blood splattered on them. Then he could gather his gear and be gone in one of the nicer cars from the garage. Buddy's nondescript bucket of bolts had to suffice for just a short time. The benefactor could worry about removing Buddy's old Ford from his multi-bay garage.

Still an hour before sundown, but with the heavy snowfall and low dark clouds, most of the traffic switched on their head-lights. Rowden emerged from the park road and fumbled to find the headlight switch on Buddy Ward's dashboard. He crept into the line of traffic, already slowed by the accumulating snow. About a half-hour to get there, he thought, maybe a bit more with this weather. By then, it would be dark enough to park be-hind the old nursing facility without being noticed. Further, no one will be outside in this near-blizzard, so no one will hinder his entry.

The traffic crawled forward at an impatient pace. An abrupt and elongated stop permitted a fire truck to return to its engine house, backing in off the main street. Rowden irritation grew into a smile. "A fire! What a wonderful way to cover one's tracks," he whispered. The nursing facility where Thorpe was recovering was an old converted mansion. It had probably been over 100 years since it was originally constructed. Old wood. Very old wood. Old wood burns fast. Slow traffic with the snow-storm, slow response by the fire department. Rowden had no experience with arson, but how difficult could it be? Whatever the result, no matter how successful the fire, it would add at least a day--maybe longer--before anyone would recognize that the victims had been knifed before they were burned.

How to proceed? Gasoline would be the easiest accelerant, he supposed. He pulled off at a gas station, purchased a five-gallon metal gas can, and told the attendant to fill it with the cheapest mix.

"Snow blowers need high test."

"What?" said Rowden.

"You're going to use this in a snow blower, right? Most of 'em require high octane gas."

"Okay, fill it with high test, then." He was getting exasperated with the delays. He believed that his plan, although nascent and lacking thoroughness, was ready to be put it into action. By quickly completing this final act he could manage an effective escape while road travel was still possible in what was becoming an early winter storm. The sky was dark, only a sliver of a purple sunset remained in the Western sky, barely visible under the heavy lowering clouds. Street lights glowed soft yellow, early ornamental snow globes failing at their attempt to set a romantic mood. Instead, the slanting blasts of a lake-effect mini-blizzard shocked the city. Rowden recalled snow globes on the fireplace mantel in the farm house of the foster home, visible on those rare occasions he was able to sneak in. He was warned to never touch the snow globes. Even so, perhaps in spite of that order, on the way out the door of the farm house that final time, he whacked a large one with the axe handle and smashed the fragile glass globe on the granite fireplace hearth. Glass and liquid splattered in a final act of defiance, freeing for all time the encapsulated miniature figures with their fake smiles.

The snow was almost two-inches deep by the time Rowden slowly rolled into the alley behind the nursing home. Even with the headlights turned off, visibility was easy. The white snow acted like a reflector of all light, whether from inside or the street. He fingered his knife as he stepped out of the car, quietly closing the door just enough to turn off the vehicle's interior light. He scanned the alley, and every window in the building. Three stories tall, but the top floor was dark--probably an unused attic. Second floor looked like it had private rooms, probably outfitted for patients. More lights on there. First floor was maybe administration. Only a few desk lamps on in those windows. No sign of the security guard. "Probably stuffing his face again. Maybe I won't have to kill him for being in the way. Leave him alive so he'll have to explain how the patient he was guarding got knifed while he stuffed his face."

Rowden stepped tentatively toward the side door near the rear. He left the gas can nearby for retrieval after the planned knife work. He dearly loved the feeling of the sharp blade slicing flesh, and the occasional snapping of bones. The snow-covered slate sidewalk beneath the door was so slippery he nearly lost his balance. Amazingly, the door handle turned easily as he pulled the oversized steel door outward. It was wide enough to permit a gurney to roll in easily. Rowden smiled and shook his head at the lax security. Inside, he was in what seemed to be the kitchen. Distant bells and buzzers, the kind of noises heard in a hospital for monitoring patient vital signs, rang in rooms far away. He stood quite still for several minutes, waiting to see if anyone would appear. A TV announced weather reports in the front of the first floor, likely the original living room. A few muffled nurse-like voices commented on the snow.

Across the hallway and next to an ancient-looking elevator, a rear staircase promised to lead to the second level, the probable recovery rooms. Rowden tiptoed toward the stairs, leaving snowy drippings on the tile floor behind him. Another loud buzzer. Maybe someone went into cardiac arrest. He paused on the landing where the stairs turned. No one came running. At the top of the stairs an old, dark-oak door was on swinging hinges. He breathed a sigh of relief that the hinges didn't squeak.

It was easy to spot the correct room. A large placard with "Thorpe, P" was taped to the door jamb. Modified from a bedroom to its current use as a recovery room, a large window had been cut in the wall to enable staff to look in at the patient without disturbing him. The door itself was full length glass, and stood slightly ajar. Thorpe was lying in bed still comatose, his head heavily bandaged like a turban. His face seemed discolored. In a stuffed chair facing the foot of the bed, Thorpe's curly-haired girlfriend sat head down, a magazine splayed across her lap. She, too, was asleep.

Rowden figured he would take out Thorpe first with a quick neck slash. No more gutting. While he personally enjoyed watching someone's pain-filled dying gasps, stomach cuts weren't all that quick. No, a jugular cut was needed here. Then, for good measure, he'd slit the girlfriend's throat whether she woke up or not. No sense leaving possible witnesses. He pulled his knife and entered the room quickly. His knife hand rose in the air as an evil grin bared his teeth.

"Hold it right there, Rowden! Police!" He spun to see the supposedly sleeping girlfriend toss off a curly wig and level a .45 Magnum at his midsection.

Rowden roared in anger and moved toward the police woman. "You're dead this way, too!"

He spun back to see another policeman fling the turban of bandages away while pointing another weapon at him from the bed. Rowden leaned toward the door preparing to flee, but realized these two had to die before he left. He wheeled toward the bed, let out a roar bordering on a scream, and lunged toward the bed. Four bullets pierced him, two each front and back. One of Georgie's slugs shattered Rowden's spine and severed his spinal cord. The two by Angel tore huge holes in his aorta forcing bloody geysers to appear while his heart managed a few final beats. Downward energy sent the knife plunging deep into the mattress of the bed, barely missing Angel's leg as he scrambled out of the way. Rowden lay dying on the floor, a look of surprise and sadness on his face as his eyes glazed over focusing on nothing.

The chubby security policeman, gun drawn, was at the doorway seconds after the gun shots rang out. "You heard the buzzer, right?"

"You did good, Danny. We were prepared," said Georgie.

Pointing toward the body on the floor, Angel said, "There are so many bells and buzzers with the medical equipment that our visitor here never caught on to the signal you sent."

Danny holstered his weapon as he headed down the stairs. "I gave the night nurse your Lieutenant's number to call just now. The cavalry should be on the way. I'll go give them the all clear so they don't come in guns blazing."

Angel shook his head. "Wheezie's gonna be upset he can't question Mr. Rowden."

"It's alright. I doubt if this asshole would have said much more than he is saying right now," whispered Georgie.

Wednesday, November 10

Captain Mitchell was not in a good mood. He called a meeting with the detective team in his own private conference room, just to the side of his main office. The four detectives were shoulder to shoulder around a small round table. Captain Mitchell took up the largest space with files and new electronic gadgets, some of which were unfamiliar to the group.

"That was quite the shit-show out there yesterday, boys and girls. Commander Peldner is trying hard to put out the fire that is currently scorching his butt down in Columbus. His little military action cost us a good Cleveland cop. It may end up costing Peldner his Commandant rank. When their State-led Internal Affairs people come to each of you—and they will—I suggest you tell the unvarnished truth. No need to try and sugar coat anything or try to defend the Commandant's plan. Ahh, and then on top of that debacle, last night we lost the one guy we've been waiting to interrogate. That's just swell. I'm not weeping tears for Rowden, but I just wish you two remembered we wanted a half-chance to find out what he knew."

"They didn't have a lot of options, Cap," said Wesner, defending his team.

"You weren't even there, Wheezie! The way you set up that room, there was not a high probability of Rowden walking out in one piece."

Benny leaned toward Wesner. "I don't get why you kept me in the dark about that. I could have maybe helped Angel and Georgie somehow."

The Captain snapped, "Doesn't look like they needed anyone's help, now, does it, Benny?"

Shaking off his anger by blowing out several deep breaths, Captain Mitchell consulted a file folder while continuing the after-action review with the four detectives on the primary team. "In the meantime, there's been some interesting stuff dug up by the Highway Patrol Investigators from the confiscated files found in the Steal Inn. They're been working hard, digging through everything that was found. They spent all night long down in the evidence chamber while you four were sleeping soundly."

Wesner wanted to defend his team again as hard workers, but a frosty stare from the Captain told him to keep his mouth shut. Mitchell continued. "Seems the bar is owned by a shell corporation headquartered in Barbados."

"I'm not sure where that is, but it sounds warm," said Angel. "I'll volunteer to go check it out."

"Awfully nice of you to offer your assistance, Detective, but unnecessary given the rest of the report. Seems there have been a number of inquiries about that shell corporation by the Federal authorities. They isolated the primary financial investor--fellow by the name of Nelson Pitzger. Let me tell you what they found out about Mr. Pitzger."

Angel clapped his hands together. "The other boat!"

Georgie gave him a look. "What other boat?"

"Down in Miami at that marina. The yacht next to where Ratterman yacht is docked and the next slip over from where the murders took place—the boat was named 'The Full Nelson'.

Kind of a wrestling term. But I'd be willing to bet this Nelson Pitzger guy owns that thing."

Captain Mitchell nodded. "I have to admit that sounds like a good bet, detective. Nelson Pitzger is an investment tycoon, a hedge fund guy, who leverages stock manipulation to make companies do his bidding, whether they want to or not. He makes a lot of money for himself and his few partners while sometimes ruining the companies he tries to control. He obviously makes some enemies along the way, but doesn't much care as long as he makes a profit. If a company goes under, he'll sell his share before the bottom collapses. In the old days, we called such guys dirty names."

Mitchell turned to the next page. "The documents from the Steal Inn lead us to believe that Mr. Pitzger introduced his favorite muscle, the dearly departed Lucas Rowden, to one of his contacts on the Rubicon Steel Board of Directors. That person is Mr. Donald F. Ratterman. Records indicate they first communicated a few years ago when their two boats casually docked next to each other in Miami. Receipts show that Mr. Pitzger paid the harbor master for that less than accidental docking arrangement."

Wesner said, "Not to interrupt, Captain, but this guy Donald F. Ratterman is Timmy Ratterman's grandfather. That implicates quite a few folks in this scheme."

Georgie added, "Remember what the records said about the Steal Inn? It is owned by Pitz-Rat Limited. Pitzger and Ratterman?"

"When can we pick up this Nelson Pitzger?" asked Lieutenant Wesner.

"He'll be lawyered up pretty good if we go in with only circumstantial evidence. But allow me to finish, which may provide some ribbon you can use to tie this case up with a bow," chuckled the Captain. He turned a page on the report in front of him. "There was a purchase order and receipt in the Barbados file approving the acquisition and modification of three large, slightly used house trailers. Seems some of the fellas involved had an idea to make some loose cash to pay off their special employees without digging into their own wallets. According to a ledger sheet, the scheme involved some serious drug sales, gambling and prostitution occurring in those trailers, with some of the activities spilling into the Steal Inn. And who do you suppose is the manager over the hookers and the casino dealers? Here's a hint--think of someone who might have some previous casino experience, but currently has a few holes in his resume, so to speak."

Benny suddenly stood up. "Oh, crap! I was supposed to call a guy about picking up the clambake tents. Mind if I jump out for a quick phone call?"

The Captain looked surprised. "There's a phone right there. Call him from here."

"Ahhh…I don't want to interrupt. Keep going, I'll catch up when I get back."

"Then use the phone on my desk. I don't want to wait too long," said the Captain. As Benny left the room, Wesner and Capt. Mitchell shared a knowing glance and a nod of the head. Mitchell flipped a switch on the equipment in front of him. Angel and Georgie glanced at each other wondering if they had missed a clue.

Benny didn't know how to refuse the Captain, so he did as he was told, dialing the private number from the Captain's desk phone. Checking to ensure the conference room door was securely closed, Benny whispered, "Your name has come up….Not sure….Some big guy is down permanently. Do you know him….I don't think I can….I'll try. No promises. Getting too close." He hung up and returned to the meeting.

The Captain said, "Good. That was quick. Thanks, Benny. He referred back to the file. "Where was I? Oh, yeah. Here we go. It seems the drugs came via a pipeline back to Haiti, which is likely how the murders at the Miami yacht harbor get hooked in. The yachts were the primary means of transportation back north. Seems like they each made the trip a couple times a year through the St. Lawrence Seaway. Something must have gone wrong with one of the deliveries which led to the two Haitian floaters, effectively shutting down the pipeline for a while during the murder investigation. That seems to be when Rowden ended up as Security Chief--or is it Colonel--at the Steel plant."

"It's a bit too neat. And small potatoes," said Wesner. "Sure, there's money in drugs and prostitution. But not the kind of gazillions to make you put your whole fancy life at risk. Plus, you have to assume the big gangs would not appreciate amateurs muscling in on their drug, prostitution and gambling monopoly. It makes me wonder if Pitz-Rat Limited was also a squeaky clean supplier for the local drug lords, too. Why would a member of the Board of Directors and what I must assume is a big money guy--this Pitzger fellow--why would those two get involved with what has to be a relatively penny-ante scheme with drugs and prostitutes and a guy who uses his knife like the chef at a Japanese Steakhouse unless they were further protected by the local mob? What's in it for them?" He sat back, smiled toward the Captain and started to hum. The three detectives on his team were startled, knowing that a humming Lt. Wesner was a dangerous Lt. Wesner.

The Captain closed his folder with a slap. "Those are very good questions, Lieutenant. And I have to ask myself why some people seem to know all of our next moves, even before we make them. You all see these strange looking machines on the table here? I got them as a gift — okay, maybe a loan — from Lt. Friedman's FBI contact. Seems the FBI is concerned we may have a mole on our team, and they have a pretty good idea who it is. From what you told me, Wheezie, you do, too. The Feds provided this fancy, sophisticated stuff to help us find the mole. Let's listen to this recording to see if we learn anything." He hit a few switches and touched the 'Play' button. Everyone clearly heard Benny's voice: "Your name has come up…." The tape continued with both sides of the conversation clearly audible. Benny froze in his seat, then tried to rise. Angel put both his hands on Benny's shoulders, holding him in place. Georgie reached over and removed Benny's service weapon from its holster.

"Any other weapons, Benny? Ankle gun?" asked Wesner. Benny shook his head no. "Then give us your badge. You are suspended as of this moment. We will deal with further ramifications over the next few weeks. For your protection and to ensure the investigation continues without your interference, we've arranged for you to be sequestered. No phone calls. I'll tell Marie you are on an extended assignment."

Benny hung his head. "I…. How…." He looked at Wesner. "I'm sorry, Wheezie. It got away from me. Thought it would be no big deal…."

"Too many odd phone calls, Benjamin. Too much rich spending—bracelet, big house, new car for Marie. Just go. The desk Sergeant is waiting for you outside the Captain's office."

After Benny left the room, The Captain addressed the amazed faces of the other detectives. "Okay, folks. I know that was tough to swallow, but we needed to see it through to the end. Without Benny feeding additional information to Pitzger, we may now have the advantage. We are still missing something, something big enough to make it worthwhile for Pitzger and Ratterman--and who-knows-who-else up the food chain who may be involved--to make a huge risk employing Rowden and other thugs, and to turn a police officer into an informant."

Wesner said, "We need to refocus on the job ahead of us. This seems to be a relatively minor league operation, too small to require several murders as cover for their screw-ups. Maybe Rowden got too physical all on his own. Or, it could be that he was tougher than the guys who hired him, and they ended up stuck. What Benny just said to Pitzger—'the big guy is down'—

may have been a reference to Rowden, but I'm not sure Pitzger caught on."

"What should we do now?" asked Angel.

The Captain continued. "We must now assume that Pitzger has been aware of almost all of our investigative activity. Benny has been feeding him information for quite some time, according to the Feds. Wheezie, I want you to take this motley crew of yours down to the trailers tomorrow and empty them out. I got you a warrant from Judge Titas giving you permission to tear them apart as you see fit. Find something useful, but try not to get anyone else hurt."

Wesner said, "That's tomorrow. Tonight, I want all of you to join me at Pat Joyce's Tavern for a couple drinks. We need to have a few to…I dunno…call it to mourn a little."

Georgie said, "Yes. I know I need a drink or two. I'd love to know how you figured out what Benny was doing. You and he were…."

"Yeah. 'Were'. I sometimes get too close to those I work with. Too close…." Wesner stared into Georgie's dark eyes.

Angel said, "I'm in for those drinks. Say, I wonder. Now that Rowden is dead, hopefully the murders will stop--unless they've got another hitman in the group."

"One little wrap-up on the Rowden murders," said Captain Mitchell. "Our friendly whiskey loving ex-Army Sergeant, Butch Herman, called in a tip. Seems he and a friendly pint took a stroll down under his favorite bridge yesterday, just before the snow squall hit. Butch says he saw some guy gut-slice a chubby fellow, then push him into the river. He got his license number. Car was owned by someone named Arthur Ward. That same car was found behind the wellness house. A gas can found just outside the back door leads us to believe Rowden was planning a barbeque after he killed Thorpe. He likely stole the car from his latest victim, Arthur B. Ward. This morning, the Coast Guard fished up someone named Arthur B. Ward just as the body with most of his guts missing was floating on a course heading toward Kelley's Island. Mr. Herman, our whiskey-loving eye witness, said both the guy who ended up floating and the assailant were wearing dark green khaki-like pants and shirts. He said the guy with the knife was much bigger than the one butchered. I'm guessing the victim was Mr. Buddy Ward, the parking lot guard. And, given the car connection, Ward was likely Rowden's final kill before Angel and Georgie used him for target practice."

The Captain stood to leave. "Tonight, we go to Pat Joyce's, as Wheezie has recommended. We all need a stiff drink. Tomorrow, we've got to find whatever we can in those trailers that made it worthwhile for Ratterman and Pitzger to risk it all to keep this little intrigue running. Georgie and Angel, I'll try to fast-track your Internal Affairs investigations to get you off desk-duty as soon as possible. I gotta believe they'll rule your shootings justified, although four at close range front and back might seem a bit over the top. In the meantime, your guns and badges will remain locked up. I'll get a few more uniformed officers to provide additional manpower for Wheezie as he hits the trailers."

Thursday, November 11

Internal Affairs reached an unusually quick decision, ruling that both Angel and Georgie had acted appropriately, albeit harshly. It was judged that neither officer could see the other's situation or intent to fire on the murderous Lucas Rowden, who himself blocked the line of sight between the detectives. That both fired their weapons simultaneously was considered sufficient casual evidence that neither had intended an execution. Their badges and fire arms were returned and the two were reinstated off desk duty. At 10:00 a.m., they joined Lt. Wesner and several uniformed officers in the Cold Mill #1 parking lot, just outside the three trailers.

Most of the heavy snow from the past few days had melted off, the result of slightly moderating temperatures and several hours of persistent sleet masquerading as rain. On this particular morning, only leaden skies remained, wedded to an icy wind. Five police cars, two of them unmarked, a small ersatz criminal transport bus, and an ambulance Wesner hoped would be unnecessary formed a semi-circle around the main trailer entrance. High-beam headlights and red and blue and yellow emergency flashers provided an odd celebratory gaiety to the scene. The nine police and two medical officers stood outside the vehicles, chatting casually and unthreateningly as if discussing the nasty weather. Some were doing just that.

Wesner made it clear to the team that this was not going to be a repeat of the Steal Inn fiasco. They would politely knock on the door and request admission, using the court-ordered search warrant as final leverage. Any person inside will be asked to show identification. However, Wesner made it clear that none were to be arrested unless their uncooperative actions or criminal activity made hand-cuffs necessary. Based on incriminating information gathered from the Steal Inn safes, the team expected to find a stash of drugs including cocaine, hidden gambling tables and other devices, and several small bedrooms—available for a steelworker to sleeping off a 'double trick', or for a prostitute to turn her own type of trick, or both simultaneously.

"You know, Lieutenant, these trailers are much bigger than I thought," said Angel. "At first glance they looked older and small."

"You're right, Angel. These are 'double wides', but this earthen berm was built up in front to sort of hide their height. Other than getting rained on from day to day, I doubt anyone ever bothered to wash them down. From a distance they look pretty old and gritty—steel dust, I guess—but up close, they show off as relatively new."

Angel motioned over his shoulder. "Buddy's shack looks like it's been empty since his disappearance. There was even a girlie magazine left open under his chair."

Wesner looked back at the shack, over a hundred yards away. "I don't think they'll bother replacing Buddy with a new guard. His job was to watch over these trailers, not the workers cars, although I don't think he ever knew what his real job was. And after today, the trailers—if they survive at all--will only be for worker sleep-overs." He turned back toward the door of the left-most trailer and addressed the team. "Everybody ready? You all understand what we are doing? We are executing a search warrant and seizing evidence of illegal activity. Keep your weapons holstered unless someone inside takes a stance. Let's keep everyone in one piece today. Remain in groups of two or three throughout the search. Officers Minton and Lancaster, you two will be stationed at the front door. No one is to exit until we've cleared the entire set of three trailers. They're connected somehow ass-to-nose."

He caught the gaze of each of the officers in the huddle to ensure they were attentive. Then he ordered, "No slip-ups! Let's go!"

Wesner took the lead and pounded on the door. "Cleveland Police! We have a search warrant to enter these premises. Open the door!"

A few seconds later, just as Wesner was preparing to pound on the door again, the handle turned slowly and the door creaked open toward the inside. An old, frail man peered around the corner of the door. "Let me see that warrant you claim to have."

Wesner flashed the document directly under the old man's nose, and said, "Open the door and do not hinder our entry, or you will be arrested."

Stepping back, the old man swung the door wide. "You don't have to get rough! I'm just doing my job, protecting this place from outsiders. Come on in. Try not to bust everything up too bad. They'll take it out of my hide."

"Angel, lead the teams through and assign starting places. Georgie, team up with one of the patrolmen and do the frisking of any women you find. I'm guessing there may be a couple. Watch out for anyone who wants to object violently. I'll join you all after I interview this fellow who seems to be the maître d'." The teams proceeded cautiously but rapidly deeper into the trailers. "Okay, old timer, sit down at this table and answer some questions. What's your name and why are you here?"

"Name's Joe Pasco. I'm the fulltime caretaker of this place."

"Fulltime? What, do you live in this trailer complex?"

"Got a room in the middle trailer. Little kitchenette, bath-room. Nice set up."

"Who was the nice guy that set you up in here?"

"Big money fella who controls the Board of Directors. Took pity on me, I guess, after the accident. Said if I kept quiet about it, he'd make sure I was set up for life. Even gave me one of his old cars so I could go buy stuff I need. Put me on the payroll, too."

"What kind of accident was this, Joe? Don't worry, I won't blow the whistle on your deal here. I just need to know if it matches the investigation we are on."

Joe squirmed. "I dunno if I should be tellin' much about it. But, hell, you got a search warrant so ain't nothin' sacred, I'm guessing. 'Twas a crane accident. I was a Millwright at the time. Hoist cable snapped at about 20-feet up. The hoist was holding one of them big rollers used to flatten the steel into thin sheet. Two guys got caught under the roller when it fell. I was luckier. Cable hit my face here and took out an eye. This here one is glass. Whiplash tore off three fingers of my left hand here." He raised the nub still attached to his left wrist. Only a thumb and forefin-ger remained. "So, I couldn't be no Millwright no more. Some guys said I should sue. But, hell, I just wanted to work. That's when I get invited to dinner at this big place out in Bratenahl where the host proposes a deal and says, 'This will be better for everyone and you will get a job for life.' So, here I am."

Wesner blinked a few times as he pictured the accident in his mind. "What happened to the two fellas under the roller?"

Joe shook his head. "Them rollers weigh about 10-tons each. Boys were flattened. Ugly scene. Instant death, though, so no sufferin'. Did leave quite a mess. Amazing how much fluid comes out of a squished body."

"How did the Mill handle their families?"

"Don't rightly know, for a fact. Weren't but a few of us on the crew that night what witnessed the accident. Seems one of the boys just got here from Europe. Spoke broken English and a lot of Polish. No family here to speak of, I was told. I'm guessin' those back in Poland never knew what became of him. The other fella might just have been on the run from somethin'. I heard his next-o-kin papers were mostly lies. There's a lot like that workin' the Mill. So, I was the only one needin' help, you see? I was the only one who was--what would you call it--a liability. Yep. So, here I am."

Georgina came forward from deep in the trailers leading two women dressed more for a cocktail lounge than for a factory. "Lieutenant Wesner, may I introduce Angie and Faye. I assume those are not their actual names. And here are their raincoats, worn when they come and go from here. I recall Sgt. Friedman mentioned something about people in raincoats. I have frisked them for weapons. Neither lady has an explanation for their presence here."

"Thank you, Detective Chouteau. Perhaps Joe, here, can provide their job title."

Joe chuckled. "Ain't no real job title, I reckon. They…."

Either Angie or Faye interrupted. "Shaddap, Joe! The Colonel will get us a good lawyer. Don't need you making this more difficult."

Lt. Wesner said, "Have a seat, ladies. If you mean Colonel Rowden, I'm sorry to inform you that he has become indisposed…permanently. If you have your IDs with you, please provide them. If you do not have them, you will be accompanied downtown to an unpleasant waiting room while we process your fingerprints." He turned to Joe, who sat back whistling softly at learning the fate of Colonel Rowden.

"The Colonel is the guy who took me out to meet that fella in Bratenahl. Seems they know each other pretty well. Or maybe used to know each other, I guess."

"Joe, this is going to be a lot quicker if you can tell us what goes on in this train of trailers. As a cooperative witness, we can put in a good word for you when the illegal activity gets prosecuted."

Again, an interruption from the women. "Joe! Keep your mouth shut! Don't tell them nothing!"

To one of the patrolmen at the front door, Wesner said, "Uh, Officer Lancaster! Would you please handcuff these two young ladies and escort them to the waiting police wagon. Chain the handcuffs to the seats so they don't accidentally wander off and get lost."

As the exploration of the trailers continued, only a few more occupants were discovered: three steel workers who were asleep, having just finished a double trick from Wednesday night, and two dealers asleep on the couches in the casino area. Joe would later point out that the two were only a few of the dealers employed at the trailers, and their dealing was not simply in cards or dice, but also in illegal pharmaceuticals.

It may have seemed like Joe Pasco was the perfect patsy for Lucas Rowden and the mysterious Bratenahl benefactor, but Joe was nobody's fool. He kept perfect records, even though untrained in such matters. It was that very lack of training that made him cautious of his own questionable ability to manage the activity in the trailers. Not wanting to forget some expenditure or the amount of collections he was responsible for, or the comings and goings of the various sleazy regulars, he kept meticulous records with a system only he could explain. And explain it he did.

While he could not identify the man who lived in the Bratenahl mini-castle (his term for the estate), nor exactly where it was located (a half-bottle of liquor was consumed during the meeting to fog his memory), he did provide a fairly accurate description of the man, one which matched a PR photo of Mr. Nelson Pitzger. It seems Mr. Pitzger was the organizing agent for this little enterprise, and Rowden was the bag man. The set-up reminded Joe Pasco of what he witnessed during his youth. Back then, he earned money sweeping floors in a bar late at night. It was at the corner of the street where he grew up in a section of the city with the over-glorified name of Newburgh Heights. The large back rooms of the bar had been converted into a gambling and prostitution playground for the well-heeled. Affluent big spenders would rub shoulders with local mobsters, politicians, wealthy businessmen and hitmen alike. Now, some 50 years later, Joe was again tending the same kind of place, but this one was set up for the steelworkers. And this time he made notes--lots and lots of carefully detailed notes.

TUESDAY, NOVEMBER 16

God, it's cold. But I think I like the cold more than the heat of the cauldron. Or the flames of big fires. I thought we'd have more time before the heavy snow hit. But not this year. There was that heavy squall last week but it melted pretty quick. This new snow fall, it looks like it's here to stay. It's always pretty, the first big snowfall. Everything coated a frosty white. Tree branches look twice as big with a big white shawl like my grandma used to wear. Huh. Haven't thought of her in years.

Big, thick snowflakes look as big as silver dollars. Pretty. Romantic. Oh, if only I could show them to her. Not grandma, but her. She likes new fallen snow, loves to be the first to walk down an unshoveled sidewalk. I remember she said that. Once…when she was talking to someone else. Try not to think that way. But how can I not think of her when I see such pretty snow. Maybe I can get her a shawl, like grandma's.

I need more clothes — maybe a week's supply. Then I won't have to go back and talk to that slob, Big Ed, or listen to his whining. I think I can get in after he leaves for work. Take anything of value to me. Not that much there, I guess. I can't imagine what might be of value to me or anyone else. No reason to keep anything that reminds me of the hurt — the big, awful hurt that comes every time I walk in the door. The door--that needs to go, to disappear. It reminds me too much. Reminds me of time gone by.

That old house is always cold these days, not warm like when I was growing up. I'll pack some sweaters. Not too many. Too much bulky stuff will be hard to carry. Won't need much stuff where I'm going. Can't carry much with you on your way to hell. But until I get there.... Yeah, that old house is too cold these days. Wasn't always that way. Now it needs new insulation. Needs a fireplace. Yeah. A fireplace. Nice and warm. That house needs a fire. A big fire.

■ ■ ■

It took a few days to link the evidence from the Steal Inn with the trailer notes from Joe Pasco, but when the pieces fit together, it pointed straight at the less-than-reputable hedge fund capitalist named Nelson Pitzger. Despite his appearance on a federal watch list for several years, the FBI had been unable to come up with any criminal linkage. Sometimes the only way to see the big picture is to examine the little pieces of the puzzle at the local level.

A gloating Captain Mitchell was not about to be denied the pleasure of witnessing the arrest. Once in Cleveland Police custody, Mitchell would graciously hand Pitzger over to the Federal boys, promising himself he wouldn't smirk—too much. He joined the other three detectives as they made themselves comfortable in the over-plush camel-colored chairs forming a curved nook in the reception area of NP Financial, LLC. The office screamed of opulence.

The light brown fabric wall covering absorbed almost all the normal office sounds: ringing phones, file cabinets slamming shut, chattering employees. Even the gentle tapping of a distant typewriter was a muffled match for a cat's dance on a window sill. The appointment had been made for 9:30 a.m., but Nelson Pitzger was making the Cleveland Police officers wait, one of his favorite methods for distracting opponents into fits of anger or confusion. Pitzger chose to keep others off-kilter, unable to use any of their prepared speeches or organized thoughts to their own benefit. To Nelson Pitzger, everyone was an opponent.

He believed that no one was so important that they couldn't be kept waiting. Then, as he was ready, he permits them to enter and interrupt his 'very busy schedule'. In so doing, he limits a visitor to half the appointment time promised. Miserably short-ened presentations forced weak people to stumble their way through. Any glimpse of a decent idea could be stolen or handed off to one of his silent partners. Any visitor strong enough to withstand his withering indifference or off-topic questions might actually be a person with whom business could be con-ducted — or was someone who was a sufficient threat to be considered a candidate for purposeful elimination, one way or another.

Bored with the delay, Lieutenant Wesner strolled around the waiting room until he found a picture window with a clear view of the industrial valley below. Choked with steel mills, oil refin-eries and several supporting factories or businesses jammed together, every available space in the river valley was paved or worse. No flora or fauna were permitted a place to exist. Each business contributed to the thickening of the air and the wrench-ing of the odors. Even so, Wesner loved the view. To him, it was a symbol of America, a symbol of achievement. He believed that if none of this existed, we would all still be riding horses and buggies around town. Without all the devastation he saw in the valley, no modernization of America would have occurred, could have occurred.

He was never sure if his opinion merely represented a ration-alization. Did people have illnesses and horrid deaths because of what the valley produced? Probably. But more people lived longer and better lives because of the progress steel and oil fos-tered. Should those living near to all the soot and smell move their family far away? Undoubtedly. Conversely, the salary generated by their industrial jobs allowed them to do just that, to buy a better home far away from the smoke and the soot and the acid rain. One was impossible without the other. Wesner knew many a family who had paid the price yet reaped the benefits of that unholy trade-off. Achieve a better life and die a horrible death. That was the bargain. Was it a bargain with the devil?

In the next room, Nelson Pitzger sat mulling possibilities. He was not entirely sure why detectives from the Cleveland Police were requesting an interview today. His normally reliable informant had become curiously silent over the past several days. Worrisome. The last he heard was that his name had been mentioned in the inquiry, but the promised follow up call with details never occurred. There were several possibilities, none pleasant. Given recent events, he assumed the police visit was due to his financial investment in a bar called the Steal Inn, which, according to the recurring stories in the morning Plain Dealer, had been the site of a large-scale raid a week ago resulting in deadly violence. He was fairly certain no other involvement could be proven. There were no reports of Lucas Rowden being captured, although he had been silent lately, too. Nonetheless, to insure he would not fall into any mis-steps or mis-statements, Pitzger summoned his personal attorney, C. W. Rathbone, to join in the meeting. Mr. Rathbone had just arrived in Nelson's private and secluded elevator twenty minutes earlier.

Pitzger slowly rotated the camera in the reception lobby, scanning the four poker-faced detectives, the images visible on a television screen on his wall. "Well, C.W., what do you make of this?"

"I spoke to that lead detective several days ago. He was working on the case of a missing steel mill worker who may have fallen victim to foul play. I did not know he was also working on the raid of the Steal Inn. Perhaps the two cases are related. As you suggested when we spoke this morning, the interest from the police may be regarding your unfortunate investment in that bar, the purpose of which, for the life of me, I still fail to understand. You will be lucky to get any return on your investment out of what is now nothing but a pile of junk lumber after that raid. Honestly, what were you thinking, Nelson?"

"I know, I know. An old acquaintance of an even older friend needed some start-up funds, so I concocted a deal for him. In retrospect, it might have been better to provide a bag of small unmarked twenties and wave him away. At least then my name wouldn't be associated as it is now."

"That might have been even worse. Certainly, whoever received such a 'bag of cash' would quickly offer you up in any subsequent investigation. The State Liquor Control Board would have had a field day with such an illegal gift to a licensed liquor establishment. They would report your, shall we call it, 'donation' to the nearest elected officials who would gleefully dangle you from a hangman's noose as a representation of their aggressive anti-corruption agenda. Or, they would have demanded a significant campaign donation--their own under the table 'bag of cash'--to make the accusations go away. In either instance, you would be in more trouble than you are now. At least now you have plausible deniability since you aren't actually the owner of the bar. Isn't that so?"

"Hmm. I'm not sure what the documents might say."

"What do you mean you're not sure. What documents? You surely are not named on the building deed, nor the Liquor License, correct?"

"Hmm. Don't rightly recall."

"You are beginning to scare me, Nelson. As your attorney I need to know the truth. I can't represent you if you are holding something back. Even if it is borderline illegal, I need to know how to defend you."

"And if it's more than borderline?"

Rathbone's jaw dropped open. He was speechless for several seconds before replying. "Ahem. Attorney/client privilege will prevent me from divulging anything incriminating."

Nelson Pitzger smiled wickedly. "I think I'd prefer to follow the adage, 'What you don't know can't hurt you.' You just be prepared to keep these detectives focused on the missing steel worker and not on anything involving me." He punched his telephone intercom. "Marcia, please see the detectives into my office." He clicked the remote to shut off the video feed from the lobby.

As they filtered in through the double doors, Pitzger said, "My goodness! What a large contingent! Gentlemen and lady, please make yourself comfortable on the couches and chairs. May I introduce my attorney, C. W. Rathbone." The detectives shook hands with the attorney before sinking into the soft brown leather chairs and couches forming a semi-circle before a massive walnut desk, itself positioned on a raised platform. The resulting impression was of a regal Pitzger deigning to allow lowly minions to bow before him.

Lt. Wesner had calculated that Pitzger would not be alone, but was nonetheless surprised to see that the legal representation was none other than C.W. Rathbone. His presence answered the question of who had assigned him to represent the Union Steward, Arthur 'Red' Setter. He nodded toward the attorney. "Mr. Rathbone and I have met before. I was not aware his list of clients included you, too, Mr. Pitzger." The detectives' business cards were shared with the two men.

"He comes highly recommended," said Pitzger, again smiling wickedly at his attorney. "May I ask what brings you and your army of detectives to my office?" Pitzger sat down behind his impressively huge desk.

Wesner began in a sitting position, but as he made his presentation, he eventually rose and paced between the soft couches where his fellow detectives sat. "We appreciate you seeing us this morning, Mr. Pitzger. We understand that you may not know why we are here, exactly--unless, of course, you have a way to peek into our files or receive information from within Police Headquarters." Wesner paused to see if Pitzger would blink at that accusation. He did not.

Wesner continued, "Perhaps you will bear with me as I tell you a short story which may explain the reason for our visit."

"Lieutenant, uh, Wesner, is it?" said Pitzger sorting through the business cards. "I hope you will not take too much time with your fiction, as I am quite busy today."

"Ah, but it's not a fictional story, sir. If only that were the case, I could then concentrate on what I plan to do in my retirement. No, this is all too true. You no doubt know about the raid conducted at the Steal Inn by the Liquor Control Board last week. The event has been reported in all the newspapers. During that raid, many documents were discovered hidden in file cabinets behind false wallboards in the attic eaves. You know, the State Patrol doesn't just catch speeders, despite their reputation in that area. They also have an entire division of very smart agents who are skilled at finding and deciphering even the most cryptic or arcane type of documents. That's where this story begins."

Mr. Rathbone stood up. "See here, Lieutenant. None of this is of any concern to my client. Why are you here?"

"Oh. But it does concern Mr. Pitzger." Turning toward the man behind the desk, Wesner continued, "Doesn't it, Mr. Pitzger?"

Pitzger's face expressed the sourness roiling in his stomach. He sat very still, unwilling or unable to move.

"Here's where we get to the story," continued Wesner. "It's all about steel, right Nelson? Or, perhaps better stated, about the profits from steel. And what some people will do to make a bigger profit than might be expected. Not a profit for the mill itself, or to any of the workers in the mill, but into the pockets of certain investment bankers. Like yourself, right, Mr. Pitzger?

"You see, Counselor, your client has made a habit of arranging the sale of inferior products to companies at discount rates. Oh, the companies may not have actually known about the inferiority of the product. After all, a car made with gauge 3 thickness steel doesn't look or feel that different from one made with gauge 6 thickness steel--at least not until it is in a collision with another car. And if a consumer dies due to the switch? Well, that's no one's fault but the bad driver, right?"

Wesner stopped pacing and stood facing the stone-faced capitalist. "It's difficult for an investment banker or a hedge fund manager to arrange for that kind of deal, between two companies for which he is not a representative. But given the right kind of contacts at the right places, such a deal can be worked out. As long as the profit is large enough to ensure that all the partners--or shall I say, collaborators--are handsomely rewarded. Still, such a venture requires the skillful manipulation of stock purchases, and sometimes a bit of muscle. And it helps if the muscle is experienced, right Mr. Pitzger?"

Turning toward the attorney, Wesner continued. "Past experience. That's especially true for the man who sets the plan in motion. You see, cheapened steel wasn't Pitzger's first such effort. There were the wells in Texas that kept producing low grade black ooze, unfit for most oil companies, unless the test samples were doctored to show the oil was top grade and worth more per barrel. If using the stuff caused an engine to choke or blow up due to inferior fuel--well, that was the engine's fault, not manufactured with enough variability. And only a couple of the bigger ones actually blew up causing the death of anyone. In any event, that's what insurance is for, right?

"Not too many buyers were interested in verifying the ratings, whether it was oil or steel. After all, they were getting the product at a reduced price, saving their companies millions of dollars, ensuring high Christmas bonuses for themselves and their bosses. Along the way, they jump to the head of the line for promotions. Records we discovered show that Nelson Pitzger brokered the deals, serving as the middle man, skimming profits off both ends, from the producers and the buyers. Millions slipped into his hands each time a deal was consummated. And no one was the wiser, or even looked too hard into the deal."

He returned to addressing Pitzger directly. "No one wanted to look too hard at the deal because everyone was making money. But there are a few ethical people still around, right Nelson? Those two fellows who discovered the fraud. You commended them, and gave them a free night at the Riverboat Casino in Kansas City for being so observant and honest. Asking for all their evidence so you could compile a report and blow the whistle on the evil-doers. They never filed their reports to the companies they worked for, did they? Because you received their reports before they went to their supervisors, and you destroyed the reports immediately after their untimely deaths at the Riverboat Casino.

"Now, the grunt workers who produced the product—oil or steel—they sometimes caught on. If someone looked too closely at the suspicious order for the sheet steel several mills too thin, or for the specially mixed oil to be sent for improper inspection, they received a visit from a unique agent of yours. Most of the do-gooders could be bought off. Sometimes with cash, or drugs, or sex. If they were too honorable for any of that, there was always that muscle, Lucas Rowden, who could be counted on to convince the fellow that maintaining their silence was the healthiest thing they could do."

Nelson Pitzger scowled and said, "As I predicted, your story is quite obviously fiction. There is no proof of any of what you are saying. As for this Rowden-fellow, I have no idea who that even is."

Wesner hummed and smiled. "Does 'Luc-Nel Entertainment' sound familiar? 'Luc' for Lucas, 'Nel' for Nelson. How arrogant could you be? You see, Lucas Rowden has been located. We have him. And we are convinced he would prefer to cooperate rather than face severe punishment. His corroboration of the documents found in the attic eaves will send you to prison for life--assuming Mr. Rathbone here can keep you out of your own special seat in Old Sparky, Ohio's electric chair. It still works, doesn't it?"

Detectives Lopez and Chouteau stole a glance at each other, trying to keep their poker-faced expression from revealing that, at that moment, Rowden was not giving up information. He was laying on an anonymous slab in the morgue. The only truth was when Wesner said 'we have him'.

The attorney said, "You have over-played your hand, Lieutenant. Such meager evidence for what appears to be industrial misfeasance, whether intentional or accidental, must be considered at worst a misdemeanor, not a crime worthy of a death sentence."

"On that you may be right, barrister, if that were the only reason for our visit today. You see, the charges are not just corruption. They include murder for hire and conspiracy to commit murder. Mr. Rowden has spelled it all out for us." Again, a shared glance between Angel and Georgie. Wesner continued, "There are six, no, seven murders which we know were commissioned by Nelson Pitzger and perpetrated by Lucas Rowden in a failed attempt to keep all his dealings--oil scams, drug purchases, steel profiteering--silent and hidden. Mr. Rowden was very adept at his job. But there is one count of attempted murder. A security guard at Rubicon Steel survived an attempt that went awry. That guard has recovered and is telling us what he discovered that put his life in jeopardy. Most interesting."

Wesner motioned to Captain Mitchell, who stood and pulled a pair of handcuffs from his belt. The Captain said, "Mr. Nelson Pitzger, we are here to place you under arrest for murder-for-hire, attempted murder, conspiracy to commit murder, conspiracy to commit fraud (I think the Federal boys will want in on that one), racketeering, and--oh, likely several other crimes like drug smuggling and promoting prostitution. And then there is the matter of corrupting a law officer, exchanging thousands of dollars to a police officer so he would provide potentially incriminating information. All of this will become publicly known very soon when we hold our afternoon press conference. I understand the Mayor plans to hang you in public—figuratively, I think. Please come forward."

Pitzger rose from his chair, turned away, and stood inches from the floor-to-ceiling window, staring at the valley below. Rubicon Steel belched a roar and flared orange as a cauldron prepared to pour its molten lava. Pitzger said, "You know, this valley, those factories—the steel mills, oil refineries, trucking and railroad companies--they all owe their existence to men like me. Men like Carnegie, Rockefeller, all the big barons of industry, we built this country. We made this land the success that it is today. Not the politicians, not the government, not the millions of little people who owe their livelihood to the mills or the wells or the mines. No, it was us. Men of vision who make money for everyone. Without us, there would be no big cities, no progress, no advancement. Oh, sure. Now some people say we destroyed the beauty of the land, or the flow of this river. They say we cut corners and cost people their lives. Killed some fish. But really, who cares? A few meaningless little people are out of the way, no longer an impediment to our progress.

I should not be held to account for what occurs in the name of progress and increasing wealth. Yes, I profit. As it should be.

I've taken the risks, used my acumen to set it all in motion. I should get an award, not a pair of handcuffs. I do not wish to be paraded in front of the filthy citizenry, made to reside next to true criminals, just because I arranged for a different way to measure success. It's all in the count, you see. Who makes the most money — that's who wins in the end.

"I hope you don't forget to round up those Rattermans in the next few days. He and his grandson are in this up to their necks, the stupid weasel. My mistake. Should never have linked up with such an idiotic man. Buying a yacht just so he could dock it next to mine…. He never understood the value of wealth. The true value of wealth is exoneration. The richer you are, the more you can get away with. I believe I should be permitted to do…almost anything I wish.

"My children will understand. They do understand now, even though they prefer not to admit it. They live in a fine home in Bratenahl. They have their own expensive sports cars. They have all the clothes and money they want. They should learn not to complain or criticize my methods, the ungrateful little…. All their mother's doing, I suspect. Well, if a few corners were cut, so what? We shouldn't have to live by the same laws as common folk. We actually run this country, not the politicians, certainly not the common man. Oh, they'd like to think so, but no. They have no say-so, no power. We make our country a success, we give the steel workers the chance to own their own nice homes, to have vacations. Sure, a few of them die in accidents. The corporation tries to make a show, say things are as safe as possible for the workers. All a PR stunt, I say. It's a tough existence, a dangerous job. For which the workers are amply compensated, I must say. Damned Worker's Unions caused much of the trouble, all the way back 60, 70 years ago.

"We must be permitted to make as much money as we possibly can in whatever way we want. That's where real progress happens, when profits out-weigh the concerns of a few modest little dents in metal products, a few extra deaths. Crying women are the cause, by god. Keep them from making a scene and we can get away with…." He paused and folded his arms in front of his chest, still facing the window, gazing at the steel mills below.

"What I did is nothing in comparison to Rockefeller. Or Carnegie for that matter. What was it they did? Oh, yes! They hired armed thugs to shoot dozens of their own workers. So, with me, a few malcontents got knifed. So what? There will be a day…mark my words…there will be a day when even the poor workers will prefer a strong man to lead them out of the pit of darkness rather than some elected weak-willed politician. Yes, the common man will one day beg for a strong leader who doesn't bother with the laws…who doesn't worry about offending the lower half of the population. They will want an authoritarian, a demigod, so they can enjoy life and not worry about choosing right from wrong, not worry about selecting someone in a vote who half the people dislike. They will want a king, an industrialist, a money-man like me!"

C.W. Rathbone jumped up. "Nelson, please stop talking right now! This is not helping. Lieutenant, I…."

"Oh, shut up, C.W. You are just worried that my wife won't inherit my wealth and that would cut you out of a handsome commission." Pitzger continued, still facing the glass wall of the office. "He is really something with that knife, I'm told. Never saw him do it. Love to watch some day. He likes to gut people, I'm told. That would be something to see. He was going to throw someone into the cauldron once, just to watch the effect. Got to experiment, he said. He was to invite me to watch. Wonder if he ever did it."

A roar from the valley, almost silenced by the thick glass, signaled the beginning of a cauldron pour. "It's actually quite beautiful when the hot, gold steel pours out into the rail cars. Perhaps the only preciously beautiful sight in the whole valley. It's a sign of progress, a sign of wealth, a sign of … prosperity!"

He spun around, a handgun pointed under his chin. Shouts of "GUN" from all the detectives. Before they could rise and draw their own weapons, a harsh blast rang out, slightly muffled by Pitzger's brains which were now splattered on the window and were backlit by the glow of the cauldron pouring hot steel.

Thursday, November 18

Despite the suspension of Benny Friedman, Alex Wesner was starting to feel pretty good about his team's accomplishments. A few arrests, a conviction-by-suicide, a round-up of conspirators including both of the Rattermans--a case that was more difficult than first anticipated was coming to a conclusion. Even the wounded Peter Thorpe was starting to recover, out of the coma that, at first, had the doctors fearing the worst. Wesner still had to resolve the disappearance of Anton Wojcik, but it was more and more likely that he was in the hot steel soup. Yes, a little more time, a few final details, and this one would be over. Then he'd have some time to consider…who knows what.

Benny would have to pay a price for his misdeeds. A few months suspension, loss of his Sergeant badge, back on the street beat. After all, it could have ended worse. Yes, he had shared investigation information with a citizen, but not someone who was considered to be involved at the stime. As Benny put it, a rich guy who had ties to the Rubicon Board of Directors wanted to protect his investments. He paid Benny handsomely for any information about investigations of Rubicon Steel. That's how Benny could afford the new house and car and jewelry for his ever-impatient, never satisfied wife. All borderline illegal, to be sure, but not worth an indictment that would crush the career of an otherwise good cop. That's what Wesner told the impromptu Board of Inquiry meeting yesterday. He shook his head to put all that aside. He still had to put the finishing touches on this case. If he lost his focus now, the tiny details that separate a good job from a bad one would slip by. Not the kind of stain he wanted on his legacy.

Legacy. What the hell does that even mean? He'd seen other cops leave--quit, retire, or die on the job. Everyone rallies around, says nice things, pays their respects, jokes that they'll stay in touch. But that never happens. Oh, for a few weeks someone calls, then once a month, maybe. A round of golf, a few beers. But that was about it.

If the cop was a good cop, the force would hold their heads high and say what great things he had done. They'd say it once at the going away party. Maybe give him a plaque to display in his man cave. There was never a statue, never a golden bust on display. You never knew when some past arrest would be re-investigated to find some mis-step that turned a good cop into one with a dark cloud hanging over his entire existence.

If he was a bad cop, a not-quite-illegal-but-no-boy-scout type, they'd might slap him on the back and say thanks for your service. Thanks for getting up each day and coming to work. There's the door, don't let it hit you in the ass. The sooner you are gone, the sooner your desk can be fumigated, the sooner your badge can be melted down. Bad cops were the scourge of the force, causing everyone to suffer. Guilt by association, even though you never wanted to associate with him before or after.

If he was a really bad cop, they'd ask the other officers, those who may have worked with him, to testify against him. Sometimes it was just an inquiry by the chief, sometimes it was in a courtroom. Either way, the Union was sitting by the bad cop's side, and whatever friends he might still have on the force would make note of those who ratted him out. Everyone knows that a rat is the worst, and bad cops, especially bad cops, knew how to deal with rats. They are only too happy to give future false testimony against you or fudge some evidence to ruin your career. Payback for rats.

Talk about your no-win situations. You want to walk away feeling good about what you've done for the past 25 or 30 years. You want others to think you are irreplaceable. But no matter how proud you are of your accomplishments, no matter how much you think no one else will do as good a job as you, your desk is emptied and someone else will sit there tomorrow. Whatever you did is buried in the records department. No one will gather it all and write your memoir. In fact, you hope no one ever goes down there to pull your records. Why? Because that means you are under an inquiry, and your retirement funds might be put in escrow. Like Benny's.

Wesner stretched and sipped his awful, police station coffee. "I gotta stop thinking like that. We're not there yet. Close, but not yet. Still got loose ends on this case. We're missing a steel worker and we're not sure about his buddy."

Wesner knew he needed to get the team focused on finding Anton Wojcik, if he is actually findable. And Seazy…. What the hell has become of Seazy? With everything else going on, the team lost track of him over the past few days. Innocent, guilty, or just one of the walking unconscious like so many others his age, Wesner still needed to know where Seazy was and what he may have done. Without tying that up, the entire case could not be wrapped.

The desk Sergeant strolled up to Wesner's desk. "Wheezie, got this message from one of the cars you asked to run by that address on the southside. They said the house is now in ashes."

"What? Is that the place where Seazy Lutz lived?"

"Don't know who lived there. Here's the address. Fire Department report says 'suspicious cause'. Place is still smoldering, so they can't get in to check for victims."

Wesner shook his head. "Fires everywhere," he mumbled. He had a bad feeling that the news today might get worse. He was right.

Wesner picked up his ringing phone. "Lieutenant Wesner."

"Uh, Lieutenant, this is Archie Lynch. We met several days ago at Hot Mill #1, remember?"

"Oh, sure, Mr. Lynch. You're the foreman over the cauldron. You were telling us what you knew about the disappearance of Anton Wojcik. What can I do for you? Do you have more information?"

"Well, yes, I suppose I do. Listen. I shouldn't be talking to you. I could get in a lot of trouble. But I know who you and the other officers are looking for, and who he hung out with."

"Okay. Sounds like you can't really talk right now. Should we meet somewhere?"

"No, no. I'm at a phone booth over at Cold Mill #4. I don't think anyone is watching me. It's just…well, I don't think anyone in Security or Headquarters will tell you this, and I think it's something you should know. You see, I'm supposed to watch the teams that walk the rim of the cauldron. Gauge whether anyone acts…I dunno…off in some way. Know what I mean? File a report if someone shouldn't be working there anymore. I did that a few days ago. Bosses didn't have time to react yet, I guess."

Wesner waited expectantly as the foreman told his story. Wesner's face went from smiling anticipation to shock to a grim frown. His chin drooped to his chest. He covered his forehead with his off hand. A look of painful remorse is what Georgina Chouteau saw a she passed by. She waved to Angel at his desk, pointing to Wesner's back as he slumped in his chair.

"Okay. I see…. Yes, thank you Mr. Lynch…. No, I won't let on that you called. I understand that things remain kind of touchy over there…. Sure…. Feel free to call me any time. Goodbye."

Wesner slowly lowered the phone onto its cradle. He sat quite still, not wanting to make eye contact with anyone. Standing at his office door, the Captain grabbed Georgie's arm preventing her from approaching the Lieutenant. He motioned to Angel and her to huddle in his office.

"Folks, I've seen him like this before. We need to give him space. Something about that phone call upset him, upset him real bad. He just lost his partner, Benny. And now something else has come up. When he's ready, and if he thinks he should share it, he'll tell us what it was all about. Until then, let's just stay clear."

"But I think I can help him," said Georgie.

"At the right time, I will gladly encourage you to do so. But not at this moment. Let's just get back to our desks and continue what we were doing." Their attention was shifted to two people heading toward Lieutenant Wesner's desk.

The desk sergeant approached Wesner again, this time with a young man behind him. "Lieutenant Wesner. I'm sorry to keep bothering you today, but I think you'll want to talk to this young fella. He says you've been looking for him."

Wesner forced himself to look up and tilted his chair, causing it to squeak. "Oh yeah? Who might you be?"

The young man said, "My name is Anton Wojcik. I am told that you have been looking for me. Why?"

For a second, Wesner was speechless. Then, as the other detectives began to gather around, he said, "You are Anton Wojcik? Do you have some identification I can see that proves that?"

As the Lieutenant examined both the front and back of the Driver's License, he motioned to Angel. "See if one of the interrogation rooms is available. Let's all sit in on this one."

Captain Mitchell directed Angel to select the room that was more of a conference area and less like one where criminals were put through a tough grilling. This room even had two windows facing North, offering a not unpleasant view of wind-swept and chilling Lake Erie, white caps and all. On his way to the conference room, Wesner pulled the Captain aside to tell him about the house fire and the phone call he had just received.

Angel directed Anton to take a seat at the middle of the conference table with his back to the windows. Even though the room did not feature a one-way mirror, Georgina turned on the video and sound recorder assuming that whatever was said would be important enough to be reviewed over and over again. The chair directly opposite Anton was reserved for Lt. Wesner, who arrived a few minutes later with a very interested Captain Mitchell at his side.

Wesner, sitting directly across from Anton, began the interview. "Anton, let me start by saying it is good to see you. We want to put your mind at ease. At this time, we have no reason to believe you have done anything illegal, despite this rather intense gathering of officers." Wesner spent a few minutes introducing everyone in the room.

"Anton, just over two weeks ago, we were called by Rubicon Steel to investigate what seemed to be, at the very least, a missing person's report, and, at its possible worst, a homicide. In between was everything from amnesia to accidental death--and anything else you can imagine. The person we were told was missing was you."

"But I have not been missing. I have not been harmed. I am here. How can I be missing?"

"That's what we'd like to find out. Where have you been?"

Anton screwed up his face, considering how to answer, how much to say and how to say it. "Slightly more than one year ago, I was offered a scholarship to a very prestigious university a few states away. But accepting the scholarship was difficult. It seemed like a pipe-dream. You see, leading up to that wonderful offer, my personal life was--maybe I should say still is--rather complicated with family issues and...some other matters I thought were very important. That being the case, I was uncertain whether I could accept and take advantage of the opportunity. Even though it was a lucrative scholarship, including room and board and many other special considerations, I knew I would need some pocket money just to survive. Actually, I would need more than just a little pocket money, I'd need quite a lot of what I refer to as survival money. I would need funds to travel back and forth, and food and who knows what else. I even considered the option of just moving closer to the school and not bothering to return back here to my hometown between semesters. But that, too, would be expensive, and, as I mentioned, my family could be of no help. Plus, there were other people I did not want to leave behind." Anton's voice softened and trailed off at the mentioned of those he did not want to leave behind.

"So, back a year ago, I contacted the university and asked for an extension of the scholarship offer which would permit me to work full-time for a while and earn enough to survive during my studies for at least a year, possibly even two. I reasoned that if I could earn a substantial nest egg, then find some sort of work while taking courses at the University, I might be able to make my money last even longer, possibly all the way to graduation. At least, that is what I was thinking. The University reluctantly agreed to delay my enrollment.

"As luck would have it, I got a job at Rubicon Steel. They were offering jobs to college students, mostly through the summer, but sometimes at other times of year, too. I took some courses at the local state college which qualified me for the steel mill's student employment program. The courses I was taking also would transfer to the big university, so that was a double win. Rubicon Steel allowed me stay on even past the summer, so I was able to make some very good money, putting most in the bank toward my future needs." He stopped to consider his next comments.

Wesner prompted him. "That was very fortuitous. I'm guessing no one told the draft board you were no longer enrolled in our local college."

Anton smiled knowingly. "Sometimes government bureaucracy works in your favor. There are times when documents can move through the system very fast, but mostly, they move very slowly. No one wants to make a mistake, especially involving documents that will pass through a draft board where a mistake can cost someone his life. It's the same with college paperwork and documents. It can take a school a full quarter, sometimes two quarters, to figure out that you are no longer enrolled. Sometimes a student's advisor or professor can intercede, delaying scrutiny. In the meantime, if luck is on your side, six to nine months can go by for you to arrange your life on your terms."

Georgina couldn't help herself. "You must give me lessons. I don't think I've ever lived my life on my terms."

Anton again smiled, this time with a look of intense understanding directed at Det. Chouteau. The fingertips of both hands met together in an inverted 'V' in front of his face. "I'm sure you are living life on your terms, whether you wish to admit it or not. You see, if you have already wished to live your life on whatever you consider your terms, you have made a choice that will dictate all that you do. The terms you have chosen are what you are living by."

Wesner said, "What does all this have to do with your disappearance from Rubicon Steel? Your absence is why we were called into this case."

"That's what I don't understand. It was all supposed to be taken care of. I left work to meet with the University Admissions Officer to re-accept my scholarship. I thought I'd only be gone a few days. My cover was arranged. He told me he'd take care of it. Sure, it took longer than I thought, more like two weeks, but there should have been no reason for alarm. After all that had happened, no one would miss me. No one at Rubicon knew I was pursuing the scholarship other than—a friend. They just knew I needed some time off. I figured they'd see it as a vacation or something. It was all supposed to be arranged."

Wesner asked, "Who was supposed to be arranging things, and exactly how were these arrangements supposed to happen?" Wesner thought he knew the 'who' part, but needed the missing pieces filled in.

Anton looked around the room, trying to assess the reason so many police detectives were listening to his narrative. Something had gone wrong, maybe terribly wrong, for so many law officers to be interested in his college application. He quickly reasoned that he had to protect his friend who may have become implicated beyond the simple rule-breaking efforts agreed to several weeks back.

Anton looked down at the back of his hands, running his fingers in circles on the grey metal table top. "I do not think any of that is important," he said slowly. "A close friend may have done some favors for me. Nothing illegal, I can assure you, but you may consider them unethical."

Georgina asked, "Would that friend be Seazy Lutz?"

Anton tried to gauge how much the detective knew. "Perhaps. What if it was Seazy?"

Angel Lopez fired in a question from the opposite end of the table. "Are you aware his legal name is Cezary Ludzinski?"

His confidence suddenly shaken by the ping-pong questioning, Anton stuttered, "Wha…wha…so…he goes by Seazy, even though his name--say, what's this all about, anyway? I came here because my landlord said you were looking for me. Now I get this inquisition from all of you. Do I need an attorney? Am I in some sort of trouble?"

Lt. Wesner jumped in. "When you first sat down, I told you we don't think you've done anything illegal. However, if you believe there are illegal acts that may be exposed by answering any of our questions, then by all means you may call your attorney. On the other hand, if you choose to be less evasive and more forthcoming, none of us will consider what you say to be personally damaging."

Anton nodded. "Okay, okay. I'll be straight up, but can we leave other people's names out of this? If any of the things I did are wrong, I'm the one who did them."

Wesner said, "I'll tell you what. Let me continue the story, and you tell me where I'm wrong. Okay? Here's how I see it. You needed to leave town right as your night shift ended at 7:00 a.m. a few weeks ago. You were on a tight schedule because you had an appointment with the university and you couldn't afford to be late or cause them to doubt your interest. As you say, the school is a few states away. I'm going to guess that it might be near Chicago, for example, or maybe New York State. Someplace that is about a six-or-more-hour drive. You had to change out of your work clothes, maybe take a shower. So, time was tight. Let's say your appointment was early afternoon. Someone--I'm guessing it was your friend, Seazy Lutz--agreed to clock you out and put your orange helmet in the locker. How am I doing so far?" Anton sat very still.

"What do you suppose would happen if Seazy decided not to clock you out for some reason? Not to punch your card on the time clock? What do you suppose would happen if he left your work helmet sitting on the catwalk instead of putting it in the locker? And what if Seazy left work and headed home without telling anyone anything? What would everyone think happened to you? What would they do next? And, what if Seazy refused to answer any questions about what he knew?"

Anton's expression was one of total shock. "He would not do that! He's a straight-arrow kind of guy. He's boring that way. He always follows the rules. That is why I could depend on him."

Captain Mitchell leaned toward the center of the table. "Well, Anton, it seems that what Lt. Wesner has outlined is exactly what Seazy did, or perhaps, didn't do. We got a call from

Rubicon Steel's Human Resources Department concerned that some sort of foul play may have occurred. You were missing from a dangerous job, hadn't clocked out, Seazy wasn't talking, and everyone feared the worst."

"You mean he didn't clock me out? He said he would! Why would he not do that?"

"Aside from it being against company rules, you mean," questioned Lt. Wesner.

"Well, yeah. I mean, I've done it for him on occasion. And he's done it for me in the past. Not a lot, but when we each had something important to do after work, when we were in a rush to be somewhere, we'd stick up for each other."

"So, Anton, would you say you were close friends?"

"Yeah, I guess so. I mean, we did some things together after work or on the weekends--movies, bowling, hitting some bars. It's not like we were always together, but we got along well. That's why we're a good team on the cauldron. We've got each other's back."

"Do you think Seazy would say you two are good friends?"

Anton frowned at the question. "I don't see why not. Like I say, we could count on each other."

"Seazy said he didn't know where you were for the past two weeks."

Anton sat back in his chair and let out a whoosh of air. "Huh! But he did. He did know where I was. I told him what I was planning to do. We talked it over. He thought it was the right move, especially after everything else had gone so...so badly. Actually, it was kind of his idea. I can't imagine why he might have said he didn't know what I was doing."

Wesner picked up the thread. "You said 'everything else had gone so badly'. What went so badly, Anton? What was it that made going off to college several states away the right move for you?"

Anton got a wistful look on his face. It was at first a gentle fondness, melting toward sadness, subtly evolving to anger, and now simply forlorn. "It's all very personal. Private. I guess I'm too emotional sometimes. Seazy says so. My emotions got the best of me. I might have done something foolish if it wasn't for Seazy. He straightened me out. For such a goof-ball, he sometimes makes a lot of sense."

Wesner's face was suddenly soft and smiling. The Pastor Smile had returned. "The most painful kind of love is that which is unrequited."

Anton jumped in his chair. "But she DID love me! It was real! I know it. It just…I don't think I will ever understand."

The other detectives in the room were in the dark about where this was going. Only Lt. Wesner had an idea of how the pieces of what he was hearing fit together. Pastor Wesner pressed on. "But somewhere along the line, that love you shared with the girl turned sour, isn't that so? And somehow Seazy was involved, right?"

"Seazy's a good friend. He let me know what was happening. He spelled it out clearly, even though it was painful to hear. What I thought would be my future, our future, was apparently only my dream, not hers. Goddamn Navy. So, after a few days of feeling sorry for myself and a few too many drunken nights, Seazy set me straight. I followed his advice. I decided to accept the scholarship and move on with my life." He sat up straight. "And now I'm sitting in a Police Station with no idea what's going on."

Det. Chouteau was starting to understand what Wesner seemed to already know. She asked, "Who was the young lady who broke your heart?"

"It doesn't matter," Anton quickly replied. "She has moved on. I must move on. Her name is not important and is best forgotten. I think it best to just call her 'Mary Stone'. That's what Seazy used to call her."

Capt. Mitchell asked, "Why did you say 'Goddamn Navy'? What does the Navy have to do with any of this?"

"She should have told me she was once engaged to a sailor. Why did he have to come back?"

Lt. Wesner chose to move to a different topic. "Does the name Peter Thorpe mean anything to you?"

"Never heard of him."

"How about Lucas Rowden?"

Anton shook his head. "Never heard of him, either. Who are they?"

Angel chipped in, "Is Timmy Ratterman a friend of yours?"

"I have no idea who that is," said Anton, his face contorting into a question mark.

"You ever been to the Steal Inn at the top of the valley on the westside?" asked Georgina Chouteau.

"Yeah, a few times. But that place is kinda weird, mostly just the old-time steel workers go there. Young guys like me don't feel welcome there." He looked around the room. "What's with the twenty questions?"

Captain Mitchell wanted specific information. "Where is Seazy Lutz, also known as Cezary Ludzinski, at this moment?"

"I honestly don't know. I stopped by his place yesterday morning, woke up Big Ed. He says Seazy left with a small bag of clothes or personal stuff several days ago and he hasn't seen him since. He said he and Seazy were here for interviews about me, and that I needed to talk to you guys. Which is why I decided to come down here. I didn't necessarily believe it when my land-lord told me the same thing about the cops being after me. Seems he got knocked sideways by someone reporting his treatment of his sister. About time, too. Anyway, he's not the most trustwor-thy person. So, I tried to find Seazy. But no dice. Then, Big Ed said you guys were after me. I figured he was over-dramatizing the situation. He usually does. But whatever the deal was, it seems you wanted to talk to me. So, now I'm here."

"Do you know if Seazy went to work last night," asked Wesner.

"What day is it? Yeah, he probably was on last night's trick. They generally assigned him the Wednesday shift through Sunday, third trick, because they know he won't complain. He always gets the shittiest tricks because they know he doesn't have anywhere else to be or anyone to be with. Did you check with the mill? They can tell you if he worked last night."

Wesner looked down at his note pad where he had been idly doodling in a saw-tooth pattern with a red pen. But now, the doodle looked like a series of red-hot flames. "Sure. We'll check with the mill."

■　■　■

It was late in the day. Time for everyone to think about heading home.

"Alex." Georgina interrupted Wesner from the report he was working on. "I need to speak with you."

Surprised to hear his first name uttered softly and not 'Wheezie' or 'Lieutenant', he said, "Okay. I'm all ears."

"I'm leaving. Tonight. I just turned in my badge and gun to the Captain."

"What?!?" Alex Wesner leaped to his feet. "Why? What makes you…. Is it about what happened that one night? My aura thing? We can talk our way through whatever is troubling you. That should be no reason for you to leave."

Georgina smiled gently. "No, not that. Well, not just that. This is wrong for me. Here. Right now. I thought a change of scenery would be exactly what I needed, coming to the North, to Cleveland. But I think I was simply running away from those things I need to face head on. I need to return to New Orleans and settle things down there. To face my demons. Until I do that, I cannot be good for anyone."

"Why don't you stay through the holidays? Through Thanksgiving, maybe. Or just take a leave of absence? You can return in a few weeks, a month or so, and still be on the force. This is a big town, full of interesting people. You fit right in." He smiled. "You make it more interesting. You make it more interesting for me."

"Maybe, maybe when I've buried my demons, maybe then I can return to...revisit my friends in new and different ways. I must clear my own Chakras. Right now, they are blocked."

"So, you just decide to up and leave, huh? Where does that leave me?" He sat down hard, realizing he had blurted his feelings out into the open. "I mean...not just me but the team...all of us, the rest of us? The case is almost wrapped, but not all the way. You've been an important member of our team. You have a unique perspective." He looked down at his desk. "Exactly what am I supposed to think? Should I assume I'm only another passing spirit? How am I supposed to react? Just wave goodbye, say have a good life, buy a bottle of booze and try to forget everything that has happened?"

She bowed her head and looked down, unable to look into his eyes. "Leaving may seem to you to be the easy way out for me, but it is not. Not easy. Not a way out. It is something I must do for me. I'm sorry if I have hurt you. I hope that, someday, all of this may make sense to you--and to me. And maybe, when that day comes, our spirits can reunite." She turned and walked into the open elevator and disappeared, leaving Alex Wesner sitting dumb-founded at his desk. The amber-colored horse had fallen off the gold hanger.

Standing in the dark corner of his office, Captain Mitchell watched the cold exchange between Georgina Chouteau and Alex Wesner. His heart ached for the pain he knew his old friend was feeling.

▪ ▪ ▪

An eventful day, a painful day, was slowly coming to an end. Wesner's entire insides ached. It was not just his heart that ached, it was his entire being. But he had one more task that had to be done. No one else knew all the pieces. No one else could imagine the pain. No one else could do what he was about to do.

Dusk was arriving earlier and earlier as each day crept closer to the inevitable Northern Ohio winter freeze. Wesner drove to the little park where he had watched Seazy grieve. It was sad, remembering what he saw. Witnessing that mournful scene made Wesner feel dirty, like an old man too engrossed to stop staring at someone being beaten senseless with a club and yet unable to come to the person's defense. If you don't look away, if you don't make it stop, then you are as guilty as the person doing the beating. It is like you are also holding the club. Even now, now that Seazy wasn't present, there was a certain shame that came with returning to the place.

He stood where Seazy's car had once parked and looked straight ahead at the three-story fake Victorian that had captured Seazy's gaze. The same warm lamps glowed against the same gauze curtains. The same soft yellow light from the kitchen--it had to be the kitchen, he supposed--cast rectangles on the driveway. Wesner returned to his car and drove about a quarter of the way into that very driveway. An older woman in a frumpy dress covered by an apron came to the side door in response to his knock.

"Excuse me, ma'am. I am Lieutenant Alex Wesner from the Cleveland Police Department. Here is my card. I'm looking for someone who I believe may live here. Unfortunately, I don't have her name. The only name provided was 'Mary Stone' and we believe that is likely an error. Do you know if a young lady lives here, by chance?"

Shock and concern covered the woman's face. "Oh, my! I hope no one is in trouble!"

"No, ma'am. Sorry to shock you that way. The person I'm looking for is not in any trouble. She just may have information that will make a case I'm working on make sense. Sorry to have concerned you." He turned to go back to his car.

"Wait, officer! I mean, Lieutenant. Yes, my niece, Jessica, she lives here, along with her mother--my sister. My niece is a young lady, although I don't know if she is who you are looking for. I can vouch for her honesty and virtue."

"Oh. Okay. Like I said, the young lady I'm looking for is not in any trouble at all. She may have the information I need without even knowing it. Is your niece available for me to talk to?"

"Why, yes. Please do come into the kitchen. I'll call for her." She motioned to a vinyl covered chrome-legged chair surrounding an old kitchen table, its laminated marble-patterned top on chrome legs, glisteningly clean. "Please sit down." To a young boy eating a cookie at the table she said, "Tommy, go get Jessica. Tell her a policeman wants to ask her some questions."

Tommy's eyes grew as big as the cookies as he ran off to get his sister. Tommy had never seen a policeman in his house before.

Cautiously, Jessica peeked into the kitchen, startled to actually see a man in a business suit sipping on a cup of coffee offered by her aunt. He rose to greet her. The Pastor voice said, "Hello. My name is Lieutenant Alex Wesner from the Cleveland Police. I'm working on a case that is almost over, but has a few loose ends. I'm looking for someone who can tie up one of those loose ends, and I think that person may be a young lady. She's not in any trouble. She may have information that doesn't seem important to her, but would be to me. That's why I've asked to see you. Are you Jessica?"

Trembling, she said, "Yes, I'm Jessica. Jessica Bartunek."

"Would you mind sitting down for a short interview? If you are the young lady I'm looking for, some of what I say may shock you." Jessica looked fearfully at her aunt, who nodded as Jessica sat down. Her aunt gathered up Tommy and went into the living room.

Lt. Wesner began, "Does the name 'Mary Stone' mean anything to you?"

Jessica screwed up her face. "Wasn't she the daughter on the 'Donna Reed Show'?"

Wesner smiled. "Why does everyone know that except me? Jessica, do you know someone named Cezary Ludzinski? He also goes by the name Seazy Lutz."

"Yes, I know Cezary. What's he done?"

"And, do you happen to know someone named Anton Wojcik?"

"Oh, my God! Yes! Is he alright?"

Lt. Wesner nodded. This was going to be the hard part. "Mr. Wojcik has been away for several days, and we were concerned for his welfare. It turns out he is fine, but has told us a strange tale involving an unnamed girl. We think that girl might be you. Did you have a romantic attachment to Mr. Wojcik?"

Jessica began to sob. Her aunt appeared at the doorway with a box of tissues. Wesner motioned for her to sit next to Jessica as a comfort.

"I love him," she wailed softly. "I still do. But Seazy told me I had to let him go so he wouldn't give up his dreams. Seazy said he wouldn't go to college on that scholarship if I didn't let him go. Anton was supposed to get a scholarship to some really prestigious college a long way from here, but he was going to give it up because of me. Seazy said he wanted to marry me. He was going to propose! Seazy said that instead of going to college, Anton would continue to work in the Steel Mills to support us, and that eventually he'd get drafted into the army—either way he'd get killed. He said Anton wasn't careful enough, either in the mill or probably in the Army. He said Anton would try to make friends with a Viet Cong fighter and get his head blown off. He said he was careless at the mill, too. Any number of times, Seazy had to save him from getting too close to the edge, too close to the hot steel. If we got married, he would either be shot in Viet Nam or die in a Mill accident. Either way, he'd die from hot steel. That's what Seazy told me. The only way Anton would be safe and successful is if I let him go." The sobbing got stronger and her aunt pulled her tightly to her side.

The aunt knew the next part. "He came here one evening, maybe a month ago, Anton did. We knew he was coming, because Seazy was here first, and told us that Anton was going to propose to Jessica that very night. He suggested that Jessica meet Anton at the door but not let him in. He suggested we tell him she was getting engaged to the sailor she had dated before Anton, and that the sailor was in the living room at that moment, home on leave. That's exactly what Jessica did. She said all that to Anton, trying to protect him and send him off to college. It seemed like a convoluted story to me, but it worked. Anton was shocked. Speechless. I watched him walk away, his head down, his eyes watery. He was broken." She looked at her still sobbing niece. "So was Jessica. She ran into the living room where Seazy was sitting on the couch. He held her tight and kissed her cheeks gently, caressing her hair until she eventually fell asleep. I wanted to think he was being a helpful big brother to Jessica, but I don't know. I don't know."

Jessica looked up, "What do you mean, Aunty? What do you mean you don't know?"

The aunt's face grew stern as she looked out the window. "Seazy is a weak boy. He tries to live according to all the proper rules, but he is weak. And he has no one who cares for him, no one who loves him. I don't think he lies on purpose, but sometimes…. Sometimes you can't believe everything he says." She looked at her niece. "Seazy has no one who he can love. He looks for people to love him, someone who he can love in return. When he finds that person who he wants to love, he grasps onto them. Hard. So hard he won't let go. So hard he might say anything, whatever he thinks he needs to say to keep that person close."

Lt. Wesner said, "You think Seazy told Jessica to dump Anton so he could have Jessica for himself?"

The aunt nodded. "Yes. That's exactly what I think. It was in the back of my mind the night it happened, and the suspicion grew since then. He's a sad boy. What's surprising is that he hasn't come around since then to visit Jessica."

Jessica spoke up. "I told him to not come around for a while, that seeing him reminded me of Anton. I just couldn't take it. Besides, I thought his pawing my hair that night was a bit creepy." For the first time, Jessica and her aunt allowed themselves to giggle a bit.

"Well, that matches up with the other information we've gathered, so I think that about sums it up. Thank you for sharing that information." He paused before continuing. He decided not to mention the evening stalking done by Seazy from the park across the street. It was now irrelevant and unlikely to be repeated. All it would do is give the ladies an uneasy feeling whenever they looked across the street. No sense adding that to what was to follow.

"There is one last thing, and this may be shocking, although in an odd way, possibly a relief for you. Seazy will not be bothering you any further. You may be aware that he and Anton worked on the molten steel cauldron at the mill. They were a team. With Anton being away, the mill assigned another man to be Seazy's partner, as there always has to be two men on the cauldron rim. It's dangerous work."

Jessica said, "I remember them talking about it when we were all together. Sounds like a freaky place."

"Yes, it is. And, if you find that life is no longer worth living, it's a grim place to end it quickly."

The two women gasped.

"I received a phone call from Seazy's foreman. This morning, at the end of Seazy's shift, his new partner found Seazy's helmet on the scaffold surrounding the molten steel cauldron. There was a note inside that read '147 pounds'."

The aunt covered her mouth. Jessica asked, "What does that mean?"

Wesner said, "There are occasionally accidents that occur in a place as dangerous as a steel mill. There have been past incidents involving the molten steel. You see, that stuff is as hot as a volcano, over 2000-degrees. Anything that falls in is instantly incinerated, including the body of any unlucky worker who falls in. The steel mill company wants to provide the next of kin with the body of the deceased individual, but with the molten steel, well, that's impossible. So, they determine the weight of the lost person and cut an appropriately sized block of steel to match the weight. That way the next of kin have something to bury, even though it is merely symbolic. The note was telling everyone that Seazy weighed 147 pounds."

The aunt made the sign of the cross and uttered a blessing in Polish. Jessica looked from one to the other. "Seazy is dead?"

"All the evidence indicates he committed suicide by leaping into the cauldron. There are no known next of kin. Do either of you know any?" They shook their heads. "There is an outside chance someone at Rubicon Steel may contact you about the disposal of his remains, that block of steel weighing 147 pounds. Some of his paperwork may have listed your family as contact persons."

Jessica said, "Oh, Lord! How terrible! What should we do?"

Wesner held open his hands. "I don't know how to advise you. I cannot imagine what the proper thing to do might be. I just thought it best to warn you." He rose from the table.

"Lieutenant, do you think I should call Anton? Go to visit him? Reach out to him?" Jessica was hoping someone would tell her what to do about her lost love.

Wesner tapped the table next to his now empty coffee cup. "Most folks will tell you that I'm the last person you should ask about affairs of the heart. You see, I have a lousy track record. But my two-cents advice--and it's probably only worth two cents--I'd say follow your heart, no matter what may happen. Otherwise, you will reach my age and always wonder 'what if I had only done what my heart told me to do'."

The aunt rose smiling, and grasped Wesner's hand. "Something tells me you need to follow your own advice, Lieutenant."

Wesner smiled in return and said, "Thank you for clearing up my loose ends, and thank you for the coffee. I hope I haven't ruined your evening too terribly."

Monday, November 22

Alex Wesner got off the elevator and took a deep breath. The smell of the old wood floor and the stale coffee of the 4th Floor were neither sweet nor pleasant, but on this day, Wesner wanted to take it all in. A final remembrance. He stopped and looked down at his desk and smiled. There was little on the desk that he would miss. Pulling out his handkerchief, he gently wrapped the glass ornament horse, a fragile survivor of his career, and slipped it into his jacket pocket. He smiled at the gold ornament stand, but laid it on its side, and left it on the desk. One final form, the recommendation for leniency for Sgt. Benny Friedman required his signature. He signed it without even sitting down, then continued to the door of Captain Theodore Mitchell. Instead of just barging in as was his custom, he politely knocked on the partially open door.

"Whadya want?" barked Captain Mitchell, his face buried in a stack of reports.

"Permission to enter, sir?"

Mitchell looked up. "What the hell!" One look at the beaming face of his old friend told him everything he needed to know. "Get in here, you sonofa…. What makes you think you can just waltz in here and…."

"Yeah, I know. I love you, too." He pulled out his badge and removed the weapon holster from his belt, laying both on the captain's desk. "I've got enough time in for full retirement, right?"

"We've been over this before. You've got more than enough time in to receive your full pension. Plus, you've got about six weeks of saved up vacation time you can take before you do anything too damned foolish."

Wesner sat down and waved his hand dismissively. "I've been doing foolish things all my life. What's one more."

Capt. Mitchell got up and closed his office door. Returning to his desk he pulled a bottle of bourbon and two glasses out of his bottom desk drawer. He poured two stiff ones. "Mind if I ask what you have planned?"

Alex Wesner leaned back, tipped his glass and drained it. He put it back where it begged to be refilled. "Teddy, did you know I used to have a mustard-brown aura?"

"Where'd you get that idea? I mean, that you actually have an aura? The only thing about you that could possibly be mustard-brown is your underwear."

"Say what you will," said the grinning former Lieutenant, "but I think my aura has been cleared. It's no longer an ugly color. It's crystalline blue and silver and, depending upon the angle of the sun, it shines like a polished diamond throwing off a rainbow of colors."

"Are you drunk?"

"No, Ted. Not drunk. Not on booze, anyway. For the first time in a long time, I have a clear view of the road ahead."

"So, are you planning to visit whoever it was who cleared your aura and made you see unicorns floating in the sky?"

Wesner grew pensive and stared at his hands. "There are times when two people meet and everything seems just right. It can be the start of something big and long lasting, or it can be a brief pause in your daily life. Too often, the encounter is fleeting.

It doesn't last. Oh, maybe it lasts for an hour, a day, a month, several years. But before too long it becomes only a memory. You know what I mean? The fates can be cruel, Teddy. Just when you think you may have struck gold dust, the wind blows and the dust is gone. All you have to show for it is a few grains, stuck in the corners of the life lines in your hands."

The Captain poured another round of bourbon. "Since when did you become a poet?"

Pointing at the Captain's chest, Wesner said, "If you stop and listen to your heart, you, too, can be a poet."

"Wheezie, you can follow her, can't you? When she left, I got the impression she would welcome your company."

"No," he sighed. "I don't think I should. I don't think she wants me to, at least not yet. She's got her own aura to clear, you know? She needs time and space to deal with her own demons, and I don't think me going to look for her will help her chase the demons away. The worst thing someone can do is act like an unwanted stalker. That's not me, Teddy. I can't do that. Not proper etiquette, if you know what I mean."

"Then, why retire now? What will you do? Why not stay on here for a few more years? I'll keep you on only the easiest cases."

"Oh. Mercy cases, huh? Keep the old guy happy, send him out chasing lost cats or old ladies getting locked out of their car. No thanks!"

Capt. Mitchell shook his head. "That's not what I meant and you know it. I just don't want you wandering around with nothing to do but feel sorry for yourself. Not healthy, you know?"

Wesner drained his second bourbon. "I appreciate your concern. I'm actually thinking of hanging out my own shingle. 'Private Detective Alex Wesner'. Has a nice ring to it, don't you think? I'll be able to track down bad guys anywhere I want, any time I want, and not just in our fair city."

Mitchell picked up Wesner's badge and gun, thought for a moment, then placed them in the bottom drawer of his desk. "I'm not accepting your resignation at this time. I'm putting you on paid leave for an undefined time period. You come back and see me in a month--maybe two. Get through the winter. Go South for some warmth, maybe. Get your head straight. Then we'll talk again. If you're still adamant, I'll file the papers for you and help you get your P.I. license--which I think is a lousy idea, by the way."

"I knew this wouldn't be easy," said Wesner. "Okay, have it your way. Just know, I'm not going to New Orleans."

Mitchell drained his own bourbon. "What if she calls looking for you?"

"Tell her I'm not here. If she really wants to find me, she knows how to be a good detective."

"You're a damn fool, you know that? She's the best thing that could happen to you!"

"Oh, that may be true. At least it's nice to think it may be true. But in reality, I know I'm the worst thing that could happen to her right now. She needs someone without baggage, and I have far too many bags piled high in my trunk. Maybe someday we will reconnect. I'd like to think we would both be happy if that could happen. Or, maybe someday I'll come across someone who answers to the name Mary Stone. The philosophers say there are fires that burn everywhere and the best kind are the fires that inspire our imagination. I'd like to think there is some-one out there who can light a very hot fire in my heart and in my soul."

Epilogue

August, 1972

It is early in the evening of a late summer day in Northwest Ontario. Two old Canadian lodge owners sit on the deck adjoining the dining hall, the largest building at a fishing camp on the eastern edge of Golden Eagle Lake. The lodge and its deck are on a low hill overlooking a quiet bay lined by boat docks and the beautiful, quiet lake beyond. Looking to the west beyond the docks, the old men enjoy a heavenly view of the calm and crystalline water, only gently disturbed by zephyrs. A rock reef, the temporary rest stop for a flight of pelicans, breaks the calm surface soaking in the last rays of the setting sun. Large and small islands supporting awkward stands of pine trees dot the distance in no distinguishable pattern, but providing sufficient perspective for an artist's easel. As the evening approaches, gulls settle into a final position for the night, their frantic chatter replaced by the calming hoot of a loon.

"Been a while since I could get over here and pay you a visit, Jacob. How's everything been at this camp of yours?"

"Pretty good, Noah. We've been running almost 85% occupancy since ice-out. Lots of American fishermen have filled us up, and the walleye have cooperated to keep everyone happy. How about your place?"

"Pretty close to the same. Got a half-dozen new boats this past Spring. Need some new motors to go with them. Maybe next year. I saw a pile of old wood on my way in. You tear something down?"

"Oh! You saw that, huh? Yeah, I gotta get that old wood hauled away. Maybe burn it up in the fire pits. Yessir, we finally tore down cabin Number 2. That was the oldest building still on the property. Porcupines tore up the underside. Had to eradicate them, too. New cabin going in, more than half built. Gonna have a fireplace and even insulation, just in case we get any late Fall hunters up here."

"Well, hell, Jacob. You're getting too old to stay up here in the winter. Don't you usually head down to the States for the winter?"

Jacob chuckled. "Oh, sure. I'll be heading south toward the end of October. One of the guides wants to tend to the place and handle any hunters crazy enough to come up." Turning toward the dining hall, he shouted, "Micah! Bring us out two fresh Molson's, hey?"

Noah pointed down at a rail thin boat boy hustling from dock to dock, resetting the boats after filling their gas tanks. The boat boy ran between the docks, as if on an urgent schedule to get each gas tank filled before anyone might want one to explore the night-bite. Noah said, "Where'd you get someone so energetic like that? The boys at my place can't be made to go faster than a mule's shuffle."

Jacob shook his head. "Ain't he something? He's always like that. Running and rushing like his tail is on fire. Almost was, I suspect. Apparently, he volunteered to fight that forest fire up North in the Spring. He stumbled out of the forest when it was over, covered in soot and pretty banged up. Mounties found him and brought him here for a shower and food. He asked for a job. I couldn't say 'no'."

Noah watched the boat boy run to the next boat, maneuvering it to the gas pump at the end of the boat house. "Looks like he knows what he's doing. How much you paying him?"

"That's just it. Nothing!"

"What? How'd that come to be?"

"C.Z.--that's what he asked us to call him--C.Z. just wanted a place to stay and some food. He found that old 14-foot Lund in the shed and soldered the leaks; got that old 20-horse Evinrude running; recovered a rod and reel some goof-ball threw in the lake. He asked if he could use them. I told him, 'Hell, you can have 'em to keep if you want'. They were just taking up room in the work shed anyway. He uses the boat and motor to get back and forth from a lean-to he built on one of the islands out there. That's where he sleeps."

Noah looked out beyond the bay as the setting sun kissed the still water without making a hiss. "Those islands are all Tribal Land. The chiefs won't be happy if they find him camping out there."

"I told him so," said Jacob. "But he said he won't leave a big footprint, whatever that means."

Noah sipped on the beer that was placed in front of him. "Works that hard for no money?" He scratched his chin. "And just initials for a name, huh? Sounds like he's running away from something. Where'd he come from before the fire?"

Jacob shook his head again. "No idea where his home is. He won't talk about anything before the fire. I'm guessing he's about 22, 23 years old. Pretty young. Oh, he accepts tips from some of the guests for filleting their fish. And he'll go with me to town to stock up on supplies. But he's very quiet about his past. I once asked where home is. He pointed to the islands out in the lake."

Noah said, "Well, once you close up for the winter, you'll see which way he'll head."

Jacob sipped his beer and looked off toward the distance. The lake ripples reflected yellow and orange and red from the setting sun igniting the pines with a fiery illumination, a glow to be savored. "He says he plans to winter on the island out there in his lean-to. Just asks me to give him 50 pounds of potatoes to make it through. Gave me a small glass vial — part of it is painted glass, kinda pretty — in exchange. Said it might be valuable. From Russia or something. Didn't need to give me anything. He can just have the potatoes. But I told him if he wasn't wrapped up tight with some heat he'd freeze to death out there. It gets to minus-30 Celsius come January."

"My god, Jacob. You can't let him do that! That's crazy."

Jacob's jaw set firmly as he nodded. "I know. But there are some men who need to choose their own destiny for whatever reason. He says stuff—I think it's meant to be philosophical--he says he can handle cold, that he's been treated coldly all his life and he understands 'cold'—deep inside. Know what I mean, Noah? He says it's fire that scares him. He says fires burn every-where, even in his heart and soul. It's a fire that needs to be extinguished. That's the way he put it. He'd sooner face ice and snow than any more fires, the kind that burn the soul, burn right through to the very bottom of his soul, he says. I don't know. Maybe the forest fire scared him. Maybe something else before that. But he stays away from the fire pits in the evening, and coming inside the lodge seems to make his skin crawl. If he chooses to stay in his lean-to, there's not much any of us can do to make him change his mind."

Noah sucked on his beer and took a long time to respond. "My granddad once shot a man by mistake. Hunting accident. They were off hunting a bear that had gone loco. Attacked a fam-ily in a camper, damn near killed a small child. So, a bunch of guys went in looking for it. Not sure if it was a rogue black bear or a brown or grizzly that had wandered too far toward civiliza-tion. Granddad said he was sure he had a big brown bear in his sights. But it wasn't. Happened on a night when it was pitch dark, the night of a new moon. Never forgave himself.

After that, he said he feared the night of a new moon more than any other. One evening, he laid out all his important docu-ments so the family could find them, then took off in his boat. It was a bright, full moon the night he took off. You could see the lake and the islands like it was daylight. The only thing he took with him was his old revolver. We never saw him again. I re-member standing on the dock listening to his old motor get fainter and fainter the further away it got until I couldn't hear it no more. Not sure whether he was a brave man or a coward. I'd like to think he was brave, but I still have a hard time reconciling how he left us and how he ended my days with my granddad." Noah took another deep swig of his beer. "I think your boat boy is preparing to fulfill his own death wish, just like my granddad did. He figured if the forest fire didn't kill him, he'd have to find another way."

Jacob looked at his friend and said, "I reckon you're right. I'd rather not admit it, but I reckon you're right. And I think I've got to just stand back on the dock and let it happen."

The two men both pulled their caps down tight over their thinning white hair blocking the bright final rays of the setting sun. In silence, they watched the boat boy sweep the wooden docks clean of pine needles and fallen pine cones, running from one dock to the next ahead of the setting sun. As he reached the end of the docks he was no longer in their view. They heard the sound of the old Evinrude kicking to life and reluctantly engaging its forward gear. The old men listened intently as the sound of the engine grew fainter as it ran off to the distant islands to the west. They listened and listened until the motor sound was heard no more, replaced by the soft, mournful calls of the loons.

THE END

ABOUT THE AUTHOR

Photo by Tess Smith Photography

Native Clevelander Robert Allen Stowe delivers a gritty realistic canvas of the industrial Cleveland Flats of the 1970s, and captures the gut-wrenching fear that pervaded many souls during that era. A former musician, teacher and business executive, Stowe experienced both the bright lights and the dark underbelly of his native city. He served his time working in the steel mills, leading to the accurate portrayal of the ruins they spawned.

A veteran writer, Robert Stowe paints scenes and characters with a style that allows the reader to join the story throughout the book. The realism is breathtaking, the views outstanding. There is never a question about the authenticity of the words.

ROBERT ALLEN STOWE

THE THIRD PITCH

Note from Robert Allen Stowe

Word-of-mouth is crucial for any author to succeed. If you enjoyed *The Fires of Rubicon*, please leave a review online—anywhere you are able. Even if it's just a sentence or two. It would make all the difference and would be very much appreciated.

Thanks!
Robert Allen Stowe

We hope you enjoyed reading this title from:

www.blackrosewriting.com

Subscribe to our mailing list – *The Rosevine* – and receive **FREE** books, daily deals, and stay current with news about upcoming releases and our hottest authors.
Scan the QR code below to sign up.

Already a subscriber? Please accept a sincere thank you for being a fan of Black Rose Writing authors.

View other Black Rose Writing titles at www.blackrosewriting.com/books and use promo code **PRINT** to receive a **20% discount** when purchasing.